Rana Dasgupta was born in Cambridge. Having lived in France, Malaysia and the US, he moved to Delhi in 2001. *Tokyo Cancelled* is his first novel.

Visit www.AuthorTracker.co.uk for exclusive information on your favourite HarperCollins authors.

www.ranadasgupta.com

From the reviews of *Tokyo Cancelled*:

'Fabulous . . . a kind of *Canterbury Tales* for a sedentary, globally savvy era, executed with elegance and charm'   *Observer*

Only the most gifted writers, like Gabriel García Márquez and Jonathan Safran-Foer, can hold the surreal and the real in satisfying equilibrium. This elite now welcomes Rana Dasgupta to its ranks. He makes magic realism his own, and his debut novel is superb . . . Spellbinding . . . Composed in crisp but poetic prose which already has the hallmarks of a signature style. Dasgupta's gift for inventing stories is quite remarkable: you feel he could go on forever and never get boring . . . A treat'
    Time Out

Rich, strange, pulsing with colour, the stories leave iridescent trails that criss-cross the globe like a flight map'   *Guardian*

In classic magic realist mode, the stories both recreate the texture of real places (Delhi, Paris, London, Buenos Aires, Lagos) and suggest that a unifying mythic structure underlies those surfaces. Dasgupta has steeped himself in folk and fairytale tradition (as well as Borges and J.G. Ballard) and inventively adapts many stock characters and devices, such as changelings and dolls, that come to life and refuse to do their creator's bidding'
    Telegraph

RANA DASGUPTA

Tokyo Cancelled

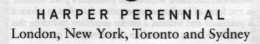

HARPER PERENNIAL
London, New York, Toronto and Sydney

Harper Perennial
An imprint of HarperCollins*Publishers*
77–85 Fulham Palace Road
Hammersmith
London W6 8JB

www.harperperennial.co.uk

This edition published by Harper Perennial 2006
1

First published in Great Britain in 2005 by Fourth Estate

ISBN-13 978-0-00-718213-8
ISBN-10 0-00-718213-9

Set in Minion by Palimpsest Book Production Limited, Polmont, Stirlingshire
Printed and bound in Great Britain by Clays Ltd, St Ives plc

For my parents

ACKNOWLEDGEMENTS

The city of Delhi. The fecund ground where this book unexpectedly took root.

Steef Heus (1953–2002), whose humanity during the last months of his life helped to teach many of us what it meant. *The Changeling*, which was written at that time, is for him.

All the people in all the places who have discussed this book with me, and read along with its writing – without whom it would have been a much duller thing.

Philip Gwyn Jones, Nicholas Pearson and Elisabeth Schmitz, each of whom made an invaluable contribution with their imaginative editing.

Toby Eady. For so many unreciprocable gifts.

Jeebesh Bagchi, for being a hearing aid.

Monica Narula. This book's colloquist and companion. Its critic, its accomplice. Its fish in the sky.

ARRIVALS

THERE WAS CHAOS.
Will someone please explain why we are here? – What are we going to eat? Who has thought of that? – Who is in charge here? Let me speak to him!

A 747 had disgorged its 323 passengers into the middle of a vacant, snow-brushed tarmac expanse, left them to trudge across it through the cold and the floodlit glare to a terminus whose neon name was only illuminated in patches and anyway was in a language most of them could not read; had abandoned them, in short, in the Middle of Nowhere, in a place that was Free of Duty but also, much more importantly, devoid of any obvious egress, like a back corridor between two worlds, two somewheres, where people only alighted when something was seriously kaput with the normal eschatological machinery.

Do you realize I have a vital meeting tomorrow morning? I haven't got time to be here!

Sir: we have already explained it to you several times. This snowstorm breaks all of Tokyo's records. The city is blanketed, completely inaccessible. Do you understand? Absolutely no possibility of landing there. Everywhere in this hemisphere planes are lurching as we speak,

1

U-turning, overnighting where they can. We cannot argue with the weather. These things happen.

Three hundred and twenty-three people clamoured for a hearing for their unique Woes. My husband is waiting for me at the airport. I'm only going to get one honeymoon. I have to be back in New York on Friday: my vacation is Over. Over. This cannot be happening. Heads in hands, bloodshot eyes towards heaven.

A queue formed, of sorts, at the one open desk where a man tried to hold off the snaking, spitting vitriol long enough to find a solution. We understand Madam it's very late yes the little one looks quite unhappy please bear with us. .

People checked for passports, money. Do Americans need a visa to be here? – What are the hotels like? Where can we sleep? –

What is the problem here?

The man stood on his chair. Hands raised to beat down the voices, you had to give it to him he wasn't going to let himself get intimidated, Can you please listen?

I don't know if any of you has read the newspapers recently but if you have you will know you've just landed up in the wrong place at the wrong time – latecomers to the world fair, no room at the inn. *Everyone* is in town right now and there isn't a hotel room in the entire city. Well what were you expecting? Every world leader is here and ten thousand journalists and forty thousand demonstrators. Don't you people watch the news? We've had water cannon and barbed wire and rubber bullets and all kinds of other frolics. In our streets! What I Am Trying To Say ladies and gentlemen is that the city is full to overflowing, getting proper accommodation is going to be a problem for you and there's no point getting hysterical about it. We should be able to get you on a flight in the morning – the worst possible scenario is that you have to spend a few hours here and that, I am confident enough, is not going to kill you – but don't worry, calm down! we are going to do our best to make sure it doesn't happen.

The crowd detested him already and as he abused them in this manner a wave of foul language gushed from their several mouths, shivered and swelled and crashed over him full of lonely feelings and terrible thoughts. He was undeterred:

I would like you all to know that my wife is a travel agent and I have already informed her you are here and that you'd all like a place to stay for the night. She's at home as we speak calling round all the hotels for you and trying to sort you out. We'll do it first-come, first-served and we'll try to get you in bed as soon as possible.

The place felt like an emergency ward. Captions on the departure board rustled frantically – TOKYO CANCELLED TOKYO CANCELLED TOKYO CANCELLED – and the packed baggage carousel squeaked like an anxious heartbeat monitor under the weight of hundreds of suitcases it had not been expecting.

You don't understand. I need to get out of here right now. I was never supposed to be here. I'm presenting at a conference in eight hours.

No – excuse me all of you – excuse me! – sorry sir you'd better make your phone calls now. I don't think it's likely you'll be anywhere but here in eight hours. Can you all try and remain calm please! Thank you!

Somebody made the discovery that mobile phones worked. Even here! The tumult diminuendoed into urgent private consultations and intimate reassurances: No I may not be there tonight, they're telling us tomorrow now, Of course I'm safe no this place stinks but the people look OK. Yes tomorrow I promise I think you ought to warn Bob that he may be doing the presentation – yes get him out of bed for God's sake! – the file is on my computer. My Documents. I love you too. Sir would you mind if I made a really quick call from your phone? It's just that it's really important.

OK good news ladies and gentlemen! We have ten double rooms in a hotel downtown. Yes Madam I think that's a good idea there's no point your little one staying up please go this way. Three star. Nine more people please! Sorry that's the best we can do for now. We will call you all in the morning. By 8 a.m.

People filed out into the cold, foreign night, got into a minivan, were gone. 'At least he looks as if he's in control' spread between people,

3

maybe it's best to just wait like he says. Wry smiles passed between strangers sharing their Why does it always happen to me!

If the company had sent me here I'd be in the Hilton . . .

It only happened when it was absolutely crucial that everything go smoothly, on the one day: that constant small-minded cattiness of the cosmos, the incompetence of people with insufficient awareness of the importance of Things who are unfortunately indispensable in the system, you have no choice but to depend on so many people who don't know and don't care.

We've just found a hotel out of town that can take eighty of you! This way! Quickly. Thank you. Fifty. You're together? Seventy. Seventy-eight. Thank you. No I'm sorry Sir they told us strictly no more you'll have to wait for the next place.

The crowd diminished slowly, the noise separated out from its hubbub into discrete conversations and exclamations. Ruminations. People were Taking Stock. Tokyo tomorrow night that means I miss the connection the next one is Thursday which means I have to spend a couple of days there God I've always wanted to see Tokyo! The snow-storm was like a wall across a highway that brought cruise control to a whiplash standstill: but as you thought about it there were ways around it, through it even, and the other possibilities started to seem more, well, *felt*. Fists and tempers were still shaken at the blatant injustice of it all, but around the airport hall the mutant seed of *force majeure* was already sprouting up through the edifices of cherished Plans, cracking the walls and floors until they crumbled in a cloud of dust which, as it cleared, revealed something new. Well anyway what can you do? – I think the insurance covered this. – We've just got to see what time we get out of here in the morning.

Buses and taxis bustled outside, headlights clipping the snow, and the man on the desk, phone cocked between shoulder and ear, hands busy on the keyboard, produced regular triumphant announcements: guesthouses and bed-and-breakfasts and undocumented hotels that the global visitors had missed. It was late: lights went off in the Duty Free stores and the snack bar closed. Someone summarily extinguished CNN's airport news service, and grandiose light boxes

4

advertising American Express and *The Economist* flickered, and became dull. Middle-aged women with headscarves and mops started to trace epic shiny corridors from one end of the floor to the other, shaking themselves free of detritus – plastic cups, newspapers, baggage tags – each time they turned around. An assortment of almost unnoticeable people – who *were* those people? – settled down in various shadowy corners to sleep on vinyl chairs.

Thirteen people were left, muted by fatigue, able only to stand and try to follow the curlicue meanderings of the phone conversation that contained their future. Full too? OK. And no dice with the Sunshine Hotel. Yes, I remember. What other options do we have? Really. Yes I know what time it is. No I think you're right. You're sure there's nothing else? OK. Thank you so much. Thank you. I'll see you later. He put down the phone slowly, tenderly.

Ladies and gentlemen I apologize for the time you've had to wait here, you've been very patient. Now I'm afraid that there doesn't seem to be a single place left for you people to stay. We really have tried everywhere but as I said to you earlier it's not a good time to be looking right now. I haven't got anything left to suggest. I'd invite you all to spend the night at my place but unfortunately my wife and I have only a one-room apartment and I'm not sure that you'd be very comfortable there. So I think that – I'm really sorry about this – you're going to just have to do the best you can right here. Now the good news is – I've just got the schedule confirmed – your flight is leaving at 09.55. The snowstorm has already subsided in Tokyo. Check-in time is 7.30. So it's really just a few hours. I'm really sorry.

It wasn't his fault. No point making a fuss. This place was depressing and dead but what could you do? He'd tried his best. Just a few hours, as he said. He picked up his jacket and left. Good night. Good night. Night.

The baggage carousels were still and silent, and in the half-light there stood security people with guns and military uniforms. The great windows of the building revealed nothing but blackened copies of the hall where they stood, with a huddle of thirteen in each one. They felt an inexplicable need to stay close, as if during the reconstitution of

5

themselves around this new Situation a sort of kinship had emerged. They moved towards the chairs like atoms in a molecule, no closer but also no further away than their relationship dictated.

They sat. Wearied smiles were exchanged. An American woman spoke. I'm going to see what the little girls' room has to offer. Another woman joined her. Everyone faced each other on rows of chairs, three sides of a square. – I was supposed to be on my way to Sydney by now. My brother's wedding. Maybe I'll still make it. – Everyone had a story.

(One man watched in fascination as, in the distance, an astounding, prehistoric kind of thing, a land mollusc, a half-evolved arthropod, all claws and wing cases, limped slowly from one side of the hall to the other. An insect, surely, but from here it looked the size of a rat. No one else seemed to notice.)

The two women returned with water bottles and packets of snack food. The guards got us these. It's something, anyway. Toilets are OK if anyone was wondering.

You know this is the first night I have spent away from my wife in fifteen years of marriage. Can you imagine? (A Japanese man with his tie loosened.) Every night for fifteen years I have slept next to her. It feels strange to think of her lying alone on one side of the bed right now. Lop-sided. If she only knew I am spending the night with so many new friends – and so many pretty ladies! – boy what would she think! Oh-boy-oh-boy-oh-boy! The first night I ever spend away and here I am staying up through the whole night! This is wild.

I haven't done this for years.

There was little to say, but an undeniable warmth. People passed round peanuts. A large middle-aged man with remarkable crevasses across his face accepted the last cigarette of the backpacker girl next to him and they smoked slowly, occasionally dropping ash into the empty Marlboro box she cupped in her hand. No one spoke. The guards dozed with rifles sticking up between their legs.

You know friends I don't think we know each other well enough to sit in silence. Have to go through a lot before you can do that. But we shouldn't ignore each other. Don't you agree? Let me make a humble suggestion – maybe you don't agree – but I was thinking just wondering to myself: Does anyone know any stories?

When I was a student we used to tell stories in the evenings. No money for anything else! I'd love to hear some stories again. It calms you down, you think of other worlds. And before long we'll all be ready to check in for our flight. What do you say?

I don't know any stories. I'm not very good at that kind of thing.

But everyone felt it was good there was talking.

Look sir you're not going to tell me that! Everyone knows stories! I just told you I slept in the same bed as my wife every night for the last fifteen years in the same bedroom of the same flat in the same suburb of Tokyo – and look at all you different people! You just have to tell me how you travel to work every morning in the place where you live and for me it's a fable! it's a legend! Sorry I am tired and a little stressed and this is not how I usually talk but I think when you are together like this then stories are what is required.

Someone spoke: I have a story I can tell.

Simple, just like that.

THE TAILOR

The First Story

Not so long ago, in one of those small, carefree lands that used to be so common but which now, alas, are hardly to be found, there was a prince whose name was Ibrahim.

One summer, the usual round of private parties and prostitutes became too tedious for Ibrahim and he decided to go on a voyage around the provinces of the kingdom, 'to see how those villagers spend all their damned time'. So he packed clothes and American one-dollar bills (for letting fly from the windows of his jeep) and set off with his young courtier friends in a jostling pack of father-paid cars, whooping and racing.

Despite themselves, the young men fell silent when the ramshackle streets of the outskirts of the city finally gave way to open country-side. The smooth, proud highways built under the reign of Ibrahim's grandfather began to loop up into the hills and, as the morning mists cleared, the city boys looked out on spectacular scenes of mountains and forests. For several hours they drove.

By early afternoon they had travelled a great distance without a single halt, and as they approached a small town Ibrahim pulled off the road and stopped. The scene was all polo shirts and designer jeans amid the slamming of car doors, the stretching of limbs, the pissing behind bushes – and the townsfolk quickly assembled to find out who these visitors were. 'Certainly they are film stars come to make videos like on MTV,' they said to each other as the band of young men strode onto the main square of the town, sun glaring from oversized belt buckles and Italian sunglasses. Goats and chickens whined and clucked their retreats, as if to clear the set.

On the minds of the young men was food; and very soon orders had been placed, chairs brought from front rooms and the local inn, and they were sitting sipping coconut juice in the shade of a wall. Around the square, the whole town stood and watched. Children stared, shop owners came out onto the streets to see what was going on – and a number of youths who were no younger or older than these visitors stood wondering who the heroes could be, and committing to memory every gesture, accoutrement, and comb-stroke.

The food was brought and Ibrahim and his companions began to eat vigorously. The boldest of the villagers stepped forward and addressed them,

'Please, kind Sirs, tell us: Who are you?'

None of the courtiers knew what to say. Which was more sophisticated: to tell the truth, or to remain silent?

Ibrahim himself spoke.

'We have come from far away, and we are very grateful for your kindnesses.'

What a fine answer that was! The local people felt their civic pride swell, and the prince's companions thought once again to themselves, 'That is why I am me and he is a prince.' As women brought more and more food, the sun's rays seemed to glow more yellow with the harmony that could exist between these two groups who seemed to have so little in common.

The meal was over; and with much wiping of hands and mouths the party left their plates and large piles of dollars behind and began to explore the narrow streets of the town, followed by a crowd of excited townsfolk.

They saw small houses with children playing and women sweeping, stalls piled high with fruit and vegetables, and shops of shoemakers, butchers, and carpenters. Finally, at the end of an alleyway, they came to a little store hung out front with robes and dresses: the tailor.

'Let's see what this fellow has to offer,' said Ibrahim. A bell rang as they opened the door, and they pushed past it into a gloomy room overflowing with clothes. The tailor rushed forward to greet them.

'Come in, come in gentlemen, plenty of room, please!' He hastily pushed things out of the way to make space for them to stand. 'What can I do for you?'

'What is your name, tailor?' asked Ibrahim.

'Mustafa, at your service, Sir.'

'You live here alone?'

'Yes.'

'And what do you make?'

'I make anything and everything that can be worn. The people here are poor, so mostly it is simple work. Cotton dresses for the ladies. Shirts for the men. But I can see you are grand visitors. I will show you something special.'

He went to the back of his store and took out a large packet wrapped in brown paper. The young men drew around as he reverentially laid it out on the workbench and untied the string. He slowly unwrapped it, and there, inside, glowing with pent-up light, was the most magnificent silk robe any of them had ever seen. Cut in the traditional style, it was intricately patterned, delicately pleated, and slashed on the sleeves and flared skirts to reveal exquisite gold brocade beneath. The web of stitches that covered the whole robe, holding it in its perfect shape, was entirely invisible, and all the sections fitted together without a single break in the pattern.

The men stared, taken aback at this unexpected splendour.

'This is a fine piece of work, tailor. There are too few people in our country who have respect for these old traditions,' said Ibrahim.

'Thank you, Sir. This is the achievement of my lifetime. It has taken me years to save the money to make this. It was my own little dream.'

Ibrahim gently felt the textures of the shimmering robe.

'Tailor, I would like you to make me a robe even more magnificent than this.'

Ibrahim's companions were amazed. Was he in earnest? They had never seen this seriousness in him.

More amazed still was the tailor himself.

'I am deeply honoured, Sir, at your request. But may I ask first – please do not misunderstand me – who you are and whether you are sure you can afford what you ask for. These materials come from far away and are now very rare. I will need to travel to meet with merchants. They will have to send out orders far and wide. It will take six months, and –'

'Do not worry. I am Ibrahim, eldest son of King Saïd. I will see that your expenses are covered and you yourself are handsomely paid for your pains. Please embroider the robe with the royal stag and crescent moon, and deliver it to the royal palace when it is finished.'

The tailor was moved.

'Your Highness, I will do what you ask. You will not be disappointed. I will make the most splendid robe you have ever seen, and I will bring it myself to your palace.'

'I thank you, tailor. I have every confidence in you.'

And with that, they left.

For several weeks the tailor did not sleep as he made the arrangements for the new robe. First of all he needed a bank loan to cover the enormous costs of the materials he was to buy. Luckily, news of the fabulous order had immediately spread across the town and the quiet tailor had acquired a new fame. Within a few days he had managed to find funds and take on an assistant to help with the work. He set off immediately on a tour of the surrounding towns to look at the finest fabrics, and when nothing was satisfactory he sent the incredulous merchants away to find better. Normally a thrifty and reclusive man, the tailor suddenly became bold and extravagant in the accomplishment of this fantastic project. He bought books of old artworks to ensure he had understood every nuance of the traditional styles. The usually silent alleyway outside his shop became crowded with the vans and cars of merchants bringing samples and deliveries. The racks inside were packed away to make space for the accumulating piles of luxurious silks and brocades.

He meditated on the antique familiarity of the royal crest until it came to life in his head as a magnificent design: while the stars circled at the edges and a grand city twinkled in the distance, the whole chain of animal life arranged itself among the trees to gaze upon the stag who stood alone in a clearing, silvery in the silken light of the crescent moon.

For days at a time the tailor would not move from his workbench as he drew and cut, pinned and sewed. New lamps were brought in to allow him to carry out the intricate work at night, and with astonishing rapidity the flimsy panels of silk assembled themselves into a robe as had not been seen since the days of the old court. After four months the job was finished, and the robe was carefully laid out in the workshop, complete with its own shirt, pantaloons, and matching slippers. The tailor rented a small van, loaded up his precious cargo, and set out for the capital city.

The skies were full of the radiant expectation of morning when the tailor made his approach to the royal palace. In the busy streets trestle tables were juddered and clacked into readiness, and a procession of vans spilled forth the goods that would festoon their surfaces: sparkling brassware, colourful fabrics, beeping alarm clocks, and novelties for tourists. People were everywhere. Men smoked and talked by the side of the road, waiting to see how the day would progress, village women found patches of ground to arrange displays of woven bedspreads and wicker baskets, and boys hawked newspapers full of morning conversation.

As he drove through the unfamiliar streets the tailor felt elated by the crowds. 'What wonders can be achieved here!' he thought to himself. 'Everywhere there are great buildings housing unheard-of forms of human pursuit, new things being made and bought and sold, and people from all over the world, each with their own chosen destination. Even the poor know they are treading on a grander stage: they

13

look far into the future and walk with purpose. What clothes might I have made had I spent my life here!'

The road leading to the royal residence was generous and pristine, with lines of trees and fountains converging in the distance on the domed palace that already quivered in the heat of the morning. The tailor stared at the big cars with diplomatic license plates, marvelled at the number of people that worked just to keep this street beautiful and clean. He arrived at the palace.

At the entrance, two guards signalled to him to stop. Their uniforms were tight-fitting, made of fabrics the tailor had never seen, and packed with a fascinating array of weapons and communications devices.

'What is your purpose?'

The tailor explained.

'Do you have any paperwork? A purchase order from the palace?'

'No.' The tailor hesitated. 'It wasn't like that, you see –'

'Every delivery must have a signed purchase order from the appropriate department. Go away and obtain the necessary documentation.'

The tailor explained his story again. 'Please inform Prince Ibrahim that I am here. He is expecting me. My name is Mustafa the tailor. He has ordered a silk robe from me.'

'Please leave at once and do not come peddling to the king's palace.'

'Will you speak to the prince? He will remember me . . .'

But the guards would listen no more. The tailor had no option but to get back in his van and drive away.

He camped in the van and came every day to the palace to wait outside the gates. The guards proving intransigent, he scanned the windows for signs of the prince's presence, looked in every arriving car for any of the faces that had come to his shop that day, tried to imagine how he would get a message into the palace. All to no avail.

Where could he go? He owed more money than he had seen in his whole life, and it was unlikely that anyone except the prince would buy such an extravagant, outmoded robe. All he could do was to wait until someone vindicated his story.

He ate less every day in order to save his last remaining coins, and he became dirty and unkempt. By day he sat and tracked every coming and going with eyes that grew hollow with waiting. By night he had nightmares in which the prince and his band of laughing noblemen walked right by him as he lay oblivious with sleep.

The van became an expense he could not support. He drove into the desert to hide the robe, which he wrapped carefully in paper, placed in an old trunk, and buried in a spot by some trees. And he sent the vehicle back.

He became a fixture by the palace gates. The guards knew him and tolerated his presence as a deluded, but harmless, fool. Passers-by threw him coins, and some stopped to listen to his story of when the royal prince had once come to visit him and how he would one day come again. He became used to every indignity of his life happening in the full view of tourists and officials.

At night when the streets were free he wandered the skein of the city. His face shadowed by a blanket, he trudged under spasmodic street lights, and gazed into shadowy shop windows where mannequins stood like ghosts in their urban chic. Everything seemed to be one enormous backstage, long abandoned by players and lights, where dusty costumes and angular stage sets lay scattered amid a dim and eerie silence. There danced in his head the memory of a search, a saviour, but it too was like the plot of a play whose applause had long ago become silence.

Years passed. He knew not how many.

One night, as he walked past a cheap restaurant where taxi drivers and other workers of the night sat under a fluorescent glow shot through with the black orbits of flies, he saw that there were some unaccustomed guests eating there. A crowd of men sat eating and drinking and laughing with beautiful women, all of them in clothes not from this part of town. And with a shock that roused him from years of wearied semi-consciousness, he realized that one of them was Prince Ibrahim.

'Your Highness!' cried the tailor, rushing into the restaurant and flinging himself to the floor. Everyone looked up at the bedraggled newcomer, and bodyguards immediately seized him to throw him out.

But the prince interjected, looking round at his friends and laughing, 'Wait! Let us see what this fellow wants!'

Everyone fell silent and looked at the tailor as he stood in the centre of the room, fluorescent lights catching the wispy hair on the top of his head.

'Your Highness, many years ago you came to my tailor's shop in a small town far from here and ordered a silk robe with your royal insignia of the stag and crescent moon. I spent four months making the finest robe for you, but when I came to your palace no one believed my story or allowed me to make my delivery. I wrote you letters and waited for you day and night, but all to no avail. I have spent all the years since then living in the gutter and waiting for the day I would find you again. And now I appeal to your mercy: please help me.'

Everyone looked at Ibrahim. 'Is he speaking the truth?' one of the men asked.

The prince looked irately at the tailor, saying nothing. Another man spoke up.

'I was with you that day, Prince. The tailor's story is true. Do you not remember?'

The prince did not look at him. Slowly he said: 'Of course I remember.'

He continued to stare at the insignificant figure in the centre of the room. 'But this is not the man. He is an impostor. The tailor I saw that day never brought what I ordered. Get this cheat out of here.'

And the bodyguards threw the tailor into the street.

But the prince's companion, whose name was Suleiman, felt sorry for him. As the party of men and women heated up behind steamed-up windows and its separate elements began to coalesce, he sneaked out to catch up with him.

'Sir! Stop!' The tailor turned round, and Suleiman ran up to meet him.

'Allow me to present myself. My name is Suleiman, and I was present when the prince came to your shop several years ago. I feel partially responsible that you are in this situation. Tell me your story.'

Standing in the dark of the street, the tailor told him everything.

Suleiman was much moved. Overhead, the night sky glistened with stars like sequins.

'Listen Mustafa, I would like to buy this robe from you myself. I know it will be an exquisite object, and I feel unhappy at the idea that you will continue to suffer as you are now. Take my car, fetch the robe, bring it to my house, and I will pay you for it.'

In the splendid steel surrounds of a black Mercedes the tailor flew along the smooth tarmac of the national highway as it cut into the rippling desert and its lanes reduced from six to four, to two. He watched the prudently designed cars of the national automobile company flash past each other in 180-degree rectitude, and, fighting off the drowsiness of the heat and the hypnotic landscape in order to concentrate on the road, he looked out for the lone group of trees under which he had deposited the trunk.

When at last the Mercedes came to rest at the spot, he was surprised to see that there was a crowd of people there. It looked as if some sort of major construction was going on. Muddy jeeps were parked around the area, and under the blinding glare of the sun a team of men painstakingly measured out the land with poles and ropes while local people stood around and watched. Terror wrung the tailor's organs as he approached one of the spectators to ask what was happening.

'You don't know? A great discovery has been made here! A poor villager found a trunk containing a magnificent silk robe right in this spot. He took it to the city where an antique specialist identified it as royal ceremonial wear from the eighteenth century. He sold it to a French museum, who paid seven million dollars! Now everyone is looking for the rest of the treasure!'

What could the tailor say? Which of these people who laboured all around him in pursuit of some ancient hoard would believe his unlikely story? All he could do was to climb slowly back into the Mercedes and return to the city.

Eventually the car returned to the leafy streets it knew well, all iron railings and columns, and the tailor found himself climbing the stone steps to the mighty front door of Suleiman's residence. He was greeted by his would-be patron's wife, who welcomed him warmly, sat him down and surrounded him with a plush arrangement of mint tea and sweetmeats. Finally Suleiman himself entered.

'You return empty-handed, tailor! How could this be?'

The tailor told him what he had found. Suleiman, looked at him with some uncertainty.

'How do I know that there ever was a robe?'

The tailor had no answer.

The three of them sat in a tense silence that was flecked only with the occasional sound of cup on saucer. Finally the tailor got up to leave. Suleiman took him aside.

'My good fellow. You do seem honest enough, but given the circumstances, I don't know if I can really help you. Here's some money for your board and food. I hope your lot improves.'

Once a year in that land there was a festival whose name roughly translates as the 'Day of Renewal'. This was an ancient custom, a day of merrymaking and of peace between all citizens. Gifts were given to children, prisoners were set free, and there were public feasts. All the royal residences were opened up to the general public, who could enjoy food and music in the gardens. Everyone was happy on that day: there was handshaking in the streets between strangers, flags fluttered gaily from every rooftop, and the sky became thick with kites. Of late, foreign corporations wishing to show their commitment to the nation had become particularly extravagant in their support for this festival. Pepsi gave out free drink in all public places, Ford selected 'a worthy poor family' to receive the gift of its latest model, and Citibank surprised its ATM customers with cash prizes given out at random throughout the day. And, in the afternoon, the king would hear the cases of those who were in need of redress.

The tailor came to the palace early, but there was already a row of aggrieved citizens waiting. As each one arrived, a kindly attendant noted down the details of the case. Then a bailiff called them, one by one. At length, it was the tailor's turn.

At the far end of the vast marble room, the king sat on a throne surmounted by a canopy of silk and jewels. Down either side sat rows of learned men. To the right of the king was Prince Ibrahim. His blue pinstriped suit contrasted elegantly with his sandstone face, on which a shapely beard was etched like the shadow of butterfly wings.

'Approach, tailor,' said the king patiently. 'Tell us your matter.'

Pairs of bespectacled eyes followed the tailor as he walked across the echoing expanse towards the throne in the new shoes he had bought for the occasion. He stood for a moment trying to collect himself. And then, once again, he told his story.

As the king listened, he became grave.

King Saïd believed that the simple goodness and wisdom of village people was the best guarantee of the future prosperity and moral standing of the country. The possibility that his own son might have taken it upon himself to tread down this small-town tailor was therefore distressing. The prince's lack of constancy was a continual source of disquiet for the king, and the tailor's narrative unfortunately possessed some degree of verisimilitude. On the other hand, he received many claims of injustice every day and most turned out, on inspection, to be false.

As the tailor finished, he spoke thus:

'This is a case of some difficulty, tailor. There is much here that it is impossible for me to verify. What say you, my son?'

'As you know, my Lord and Father, I have the greatest sympathy with the needy of our land. But his story is preposterous.'

'Is it possible that you could have failed to recall the events of which the tailor speaks?'

'Of course not.'

King Saïd pondered.

'Tailor, our decision in this case will hinge on your moral character. It will not be possible today for us to verify the details of what happened so long ago, the fate of the clothes you say were made, or your financial situation. I am therefore going to ask you to demonstrate your moral worth by telling us a story. According to our traditions.'

Utter silence descended on the room, and all watched the tailor, expectantly.

'Your Highness, I have now been in this capital city for some time. And I recently met another tailor who told me the following tale.

'There once came to his shop a wealthy man who was about to be married. This man ordered a luxurious set of wedding clothes. The tailor was honoured and overjoyed and went out to celebrate with his family.

'It so happened that the bridegroom had a lover, a married woman from the city. Each visit she made to him he vowed would be the last. But he never seemed to be able to broach the subject of their rupture before their clothes and their words had dissolved between them and they were left only with their lovemaking.

'Ignorant of this, the tailor began to order the finest fabrics for the wedding clothes. But as he set to work on the new garments, the cloth simply melted away as he cut it. Again and again he chalked out designs – but each time the same thing happened, until all of the valuable cloth had disappeared.

'When the bridegroom came to collect the clothes he was furious to discover they were not ready, and demanded an explanation.

'"I think the explanation lies with you," replied the tailor. "Since your wedding clothes refused to be made, I can only suppose you are not ready to wear them. Tell me this: what colour are the eyes of your bride-to-be?"

'The bridegroom thought hard, but the image of his lover stood resolutely between him and the eyes of his betrothed, and he was unable to answer.

'"Next time you come to me for clothes," said the tailor, "make sure you are prepared to wear them."

'With that, the young man left the tailor, called off his marriage, and left the city.'

The tale hung in the air for a while, and dispersed.

'What do you say, scholars, to the tailor's story?' asked the king.

'Sire, it is a fine story, constructed according to our traditions, and possessing all the thirteen levels of meaning prized in the greatest of our writings.'

'My son, what do you think?'

'There is no doubt,' replied the prince, 'that this fellow is accomplished in the realm of fantasy.'

The king looked pained.

'I myself feel that the tailor has proved himself to be a man of the greatest integrity and probity. Such a man will never seek to advance himself through untruth. Tailor, I can see there has been a series of culpable misunderstandings as a result of which you have suffered greatly. Tell me what you would like from us.'

'Sire, I am sunk so low that all I can ask for is money.'

'Consider it done. We shall settle all your debts. Please go with this man, my accountant Salim. He will tell you what papers you need to provide and will give you all the necessary forms to fill in. We are heartily sorry for the difficulties you have had to encounter. Go back to your village and resume your life.' Mustafa the tailor was anxious to leave the city, whose streets had by now become poisoned with his memories. But he did not wish to return to his village. It seemed too small to contain the thoughts he now had in his head.

He took up residence in a distant seaside town where he made a living sewing clothes and uniforms for sailors. In the afternoons, when his work was done, he would sit by the shore looking into the distance, and tell stories to the masts of boats that passed each other on the horizon.

Faces were in shadow. The ceiling lights were far above their heads, and not all of them still worked. You could not really tell what people were thinking. Perhaps the game was slightly outlandish, perhaps it was not for everyone. Some would surely fall asleep – or pretend to do so. There would be a loner who would stroll off, unnoticed, to the gloomy recesses of the arrivals hall only to discover there a listless and yet thoroughly absorbing interest in the health warnings posted on the wall, the rows of leaflets outlining visa requirements, tobacco and alcohol allowances, and the lists of objects prohibited in hand luggage. Surely! – for in everyone's head there were still so many Issues of purely private concern that twitched distractingly, that flickered behind the glass of vacant stares.

She spoke with authority:

Next!

She was broad and tall, she sat back in her seat with some abandon, hands on the back of her head, elbows wide. The kind of person who liked groups, not afraid to rally people she had only just met. There was an ease about her: she had already taken off her high heels. There were smiles all around but she did not give up.

Who will be next?

THE MEMORY EDITOR

The Second Story

I N THE CITY of London there was once a wealthy stockbroker who had three sons. Even when they were all still young, everyone could see that while the first two sons were able and hardworking, the youngest, Thomas, had his head in the clouds.

Thomas liked nothing better than to bury himself in history books and read of how the world was before. He thrilled at the struggles of Romanovs and Socialists and put his face close to black-and-white photographs of firebrand Lenin and little haemophiliac Alexei, trying to envisage the lives that hid behind the scratched surfaces and foreign-seeming faces. He read of places that were now summer holiday destinations where millions were killed just a few decades ago, and wondered at how death had in that short time become so exotic. He could never quite become accustomed to the idea that people were growing old long ago when the world was so much younger; so he knew he had not truly understood the scale of time.

One day Thomas sat in his customary reading seat in the Islington Public Library, not two minutes from the monumental black front door of his father's Georgian townhouse that sat in a serene row of precisely similar houses on Canonbury Square. He read of the slow rot in the

Ottoman Empire, of schemes hatched in Berlin, London, and St Petersburg to divide the imperial carrion, and of Bulgarian and Romanian revolutionaries studying poetry and explosives in Paris. The library was still save for a few occasional page-turners and the strenuous silence of the librarian who wheeled a cart of books and re-shelved them under *Crime* and *Local Interest*. Thomas thought of Thrace and Thessaly.

An old woman entered the library and sat down next to him. She lowered herself slowly into her seat and began to lay out things: a rain-coat (on the back of her chair), a handbag, an umbrella in a nylon sleeve, a stick, a set of keys, a Tupperware lunchbox. The ritual was so deliberate that Thomas could not shut it out of his head, and he wished she had not chosen that particular place.

He tried to concentrate on sensational insurgencies and brutal massacres but now she had unwrapped the tin foil from her egg sand-wiches and the smell was banishing the past. NO EATING said the big bright sign with the green logo of the Borough of Islington: Thomas looked hopefully around for someone who might enforce the rule, but suddenly there was no one else there. The old woman began to mash her bread noisily with toothless gums and he stole at her what was calculated to be an intimidating glance. He saw that she was blind.

'I can see' – she hesitated, as if playing with his thoughts – 'you don't like me being here.' She spoke loudly, oblivious to the silence of the library. Thomas felt ashamed. She was fragile and tiny.

'No it's not that. It's just –'

'You don't think I should eat egg sandwiches in a library. Luckily there's no one here to catch me!' She shot him a conspiratorial grin. 'And anyway, a blind woman is not likely to drop her mayonnaise on the pages of a book, is she?' Her eyes were like marble.

'You are reading about the past. Making mental notes of dates and names, fitting together all the little things you know about a place and a time. Trying to remember what happened long ago. But here's a question. Can you remember what *will* happen? In the future?'

She seemed to expect an answer.

'Clearly not,' Thomas ventured. 'Remembering is by definition about the past.'

'Why so? Is to remember not simply to make present in the mind that which happens at another time? Past or future?'

'But no one can *make present* that which hasn't happened yet.'

'How do you know the future hasn't happened yet?'

'That's the definition of the future!' Thomas's voice betrayed frustration. 'The past has happened. It is recorded. We all remember what happened yesterday. The future has not happened. It is not recorded anywhere and we cannot know it.'

'Isn't that tautology? *Remembering is the recollection of the past. The past is that which can be recollected.* Well let me tell you that I am unusual among people in being able to remember what has not happened yet. And the distinction between past and future seems less important than you might imagine.'

Thomas stared at her. He assumed madness.

'For you, the present is easy to discern because it is simply where memory stops. Memories hurtle out of the past and come to a halt in the now. The present is the rockface at the end of the tunnel where you gouge away at the future.'

There was still no one else in the library. They talked naturally, loudly.

'I, on the other hand, was born with all my memories, rather as a woman is born with all her eggs. I often forget where the present is because it is not, as it is for you, the gateway to the future. My future is already here.'

'So tell me, if I am to believe you, what I am going to do tonight, when I leave this library.'

'You make a common mistake. I didn't say that I know everything that will ever happen. I said only that I already possess all my memories. (And they run out in so short a time! I have lived through nearly all of them, and now there remain just a few crumbs in the bottom of the bag.) Still, I do have more memories of you.

27

You will spend your life in the realm of the past
You will fail entirely to keep up with the times
But your wealth will make your father seem poor
A mountain of jewels dug from mysterious mines.'

Thomas thought over the words.

'What does all that mean? Can you explain?'

The old woman gave a flabby chuckle.

'Surely you can't expect me to tell you more than that? Isn't it already encouraging enough?'

She put the lid on her lunch box.

'Anyway. It is time for me to take my leave.' Her possessions found their way back into her bag and she stood up, slowly and uncertainly. 'But I have just remembered what will happen to you tonight. My mind is more blurred than it once was. You are going to have an encounter with Death. Don't worry – you will survive.' She smiled at him – almost affectionately – and departed.

Thomas could not return to his books. He sat for a long time reciting the woman's words to himself and wondering about his future. He left the library in a daydream and wandered home. Full of his thoughts he rang at the wrong bell. A hooded figure answered the door, black robes billowing around its knees and only shadows where its face should have been. The figure carried a scythe. Made of plastic. Thomas remembered it was Halloween.

Not long afterwards, Thomas's father received a big promotion. He worked for a small but thriving investment firm in the City that had made a name for itself in private financial services. He had joined the firm twelve years ago from Goldman Sachs and had from the outset consistently delivered better returns to his clients than any of his peers. Tall and attractive, with an entirely unselfconscious sense of humour, he also had a talent for entertaining the high net-worth individuals that were the firm's clients. Now the board had asked him to take the place of the retiring managing director. He had agreed unhesitatingly.

In celebration of this advancement, Thomas's father took the entire family to the Oxo Tower for dinner. They drove down from Islington in the car, crossing over Blackfriars Bridge from where the floodlights on St Paul's Cathedral made it look like a magnificent dead effigy of itself. The restaurant was a floating cocoon of leather and stainless steel with lighting like caresses, and their table looked down over the row of corporate palaces that lined the other side of the Thames. Thomas thought his father looked somehow more imposing even than before. His mother had put on a new sequined dress and talked about the differences in the dream lives of modern and ancient Man as described in the book she was reading about Australian Aborigines. Champagne was poured. They all clinked glasses.

'So here's to the new boss,' proclaimed Thomas's father.

'I'm so proud of you, darling,' said his wife, kissing him on the cheek.

'I can tell you boys: investing is a great business. A great discipline. It forces you to become exceptional. Most people are just interested with what's going on now. Getting a little more, perhaps. But basically turning the wheels. When you're in investment you have to be completely sceptical about the present, aware that there is *nothing* that cannot change, *no* future scenario that can be discounted. You exist on a different plane, predicting the future, making your living by working out how other people will be making their living tomorrow. And not only that, but *making* that future materialize by investing in it. There's no sphere of knowledge that's not relevant to this job. It might be water, it might be toys; it could be guns or new kinds of gene. The whole universe is there.'

His wife looked lovingly at him through mascara-thick lashes. Sculpted starters were brought that sat in the middle of expansive plates and seemed inadequate to the three brothers.

'So tell me, boys – you're all becoming men now – what is it you'd like to do with your lives? What is your ambition?'

The eldest spoke first.

'Father, I have been thinking about this a lot recently. I think after I've finished at the LSE I'd like to get a couple of years' experience in one of the big management consulting firms. I think that would give me a broad exposure to a lot of different industries. Then I can do an

MBA – maybe in the US. At that point I'd be in a really good position to know what direction to move in. But what I'd really like to do – I say this now without much experience – is to run my own business.'

'Sounds good, son. Make sure you don't get too programmatic about things. Sometimes the biggest opportunities come at really inconvenient times. If you've planned your life out for the next twenty years you may not be able to make yourself available for them. Next!'

The second son spoke.

'Father, I want to work for one of the big banks. The money industry is never going to be out of fashion. I can't see the point of working in some shoe-string business for just enough to live on. The only respectable option to me seems to be to work damn hard and earn serious money – and retire when you're forty.'

'Well I'm forty-nine and I haven't retired yet! Remember that it's not enough simply to desire money very much. You have to be good at earning it. But I'm sure you will be. So finally to young Tom. What about you?'

Thomas looked around at his whole family, his eyes glinting with champagne.

'I will surpass you all,' he said. 'I will make you all look like paupers.'

The paterfamilias smile vanished.

'Oh really, Thomas. And how are you going to do that?'

'You will see. One day you will see my mountain of jewels.'

His father's voice became unpleasant.

'Thomas, I'm just about sick of your stupid talk and your irresponsible, lazy behaviour. How dare you talk to me like that when you haven't got the first idea of the world – especially on a night like this!'

His mother continued.

'Your father and I never stop condoning what you do, tolerating your insolence and absent-mindedness. But sometimes I think we go too far. Do you realize who your father is? He is not just some average man who can be talked to like that. I don't know how a member of your father's and my family came to act like you. Think like you.'

Thomas's brothers looked under the table. Waiters glided around in practised obliviousness. 'Sometimes the future is not just an extension of the past according to rules we all know,' said Thomas. 'Look at revolutions, the collapse of empires. I think that something will happen to all of you that you have not even thought about. And you will not have devoted one minute of your lives to preparing yourselves for it. I don't even know what it will be. But I know it will happen.'

The silence that followed was the silence of Thomas's father's rage. When he spoke it was with a self-restraint that burned white.

'Thomas, when we go back home tonight I want you to pack your things and get out of our house. I will not have some mutant element in our home. Our family will not be abused by someone who is ungrateful, someone who likes thinking about the destruction of his brothers and parents. You will get out. Do you understand?'

Thomas nodded slowly, amazed and aghast that things had gone this far.

His father left the table and did not come back for half an hour. No one spoke as they drove home.

The family went to bed with raw feelings and empty stomachs. Thomas's mother whispered to him that they would discuss all this in the morning. But Thomas could not bear the idea of waiting for such a discussion. He lay still until he could hear no movement and then silently got up, packed some clothes by torchlight into a school sports bag, and crept downstairs. He took two antique silver picture frames he had once helped his father choose for his mother's birthday in a gallery on Ladbroke Grove, a gold pocket watch that was on display in the drawing room, and his father's state-of-the-art SLR camera that had lain untouched in its wrappings for the last year. He disabled the burglar alarm, undid the locks on the heavy oak front door, eased it open, and stepped out.

The moon was so bright that the streets seemed to be bathed in an eerie kind of underexposed daylight that was even more pellucid for the absolute quiet. Insomniac houses and Range Rovers blinked at each other with red security eyes. Thomas wandered aimlessly, up to the point where gentility broke and the streets opened up around King's

Cross station. He bought a bag of greasy chips in an all-night kebab shop and sat in his coat on a bar stool at a narrow strip of tabletop looking out through his own reflection at the sparse traffic of taxis and night shelter regulars. He studied a much-faded poster of Istanbul hanging on the wall next to him, the skies above the Hagia Sofia unnaturally turquoise and the cars on the streets forty years old.

He left and wandered aimlessly around the station. It was late November, and morning came before the sun. Timetables took hold again as commuters arrived in waves and departed in buses and taxis. Eventually it grew light, and the shops opened.

Thomas went to a pawn shop. He removed the photographs from the frames and placed his items on the counter. The shop owner offered him £2,000. At the last minute he decided to keep the camera, and took £1,750.

Next to the pawn shop was an advertisement for a room for rent. Thomas called the number from a phone box; a woman came downstairs in her slippers and showed him up to a single room overlooking the station. He paid her £600 for the deposit and first month's rent and closed the door behind her. He sat on the bed and looked at his photographs. One was of the wedding of his mother's parents, both of whom had died before Thomas was born. The other was a studio portrait of the same couple with a baby – his mother – in a long white christening robe. Between the two photographs the man had developed a long scar on his right cheek that Thomas had never noticed when he had looked at them before.

For several days Thomas walked everywhere in the city taking photographs of his own. He went to the sparkling grove of banking towers that sat on the former dockyards among the eastern coils of the Thames and took pictures that were rather desolate. He took photographs of pre-Christmas sales in Covent Garden. He photographed Trafalgar Square at 4 a.m.

He called his mother to say 'Hello'. She was frantic with fear and pleaded with him to come home. He said he would at some point.

One day he was sitting having lunch in a cheap sandwich shop in

Hackney. A woman sitting at the table next to him asked, 'Are you a photographer?' He looked at her. She gestured towards the camera.

'Not really. I take pictures for fun.'

'What do you take pictures of?'

She wore lithe urban gear that looked as if it had been born in a wind tunnel.

'I don't really know.' He had not talked to anyone for several days and felt awkward. He thought for a moment. 'I am trying to live entirely in the realm of the past. Trying to take pictures of what there was before.' He looked at her to see if she was listening. 'But I don't seem to be able to find it. Sometimes it's not there anymore. And sometimes when it is there, I can't see it.'

She looked at him inquisitively.

'How old are you?'

'Eighteen.'

'Do you need a job?'

'Actually I do. I have no money.'

'Can you keep secrets?'

'I don't know anyone to tell secrets to.'

'Come with me.'

She led him to an old, dilapidated brick building with a big front door of reinforced glass that buzzed open to her combination. They stepped into a tiny, filthy lift and she pressed '6'. They were standing very close to each other.

'I'm Jo, by the way.' She held out her hand. He shook it.

'I'm Thomas. Pleased to meet you.'

The lift stopped inexplicably at the fourth floor. The doors opened to a bright display of Chinese dragons and calendars. Chinese men and women worked at sewing machines to the sound of zappy FM radio. The doors closed again.

On the sixth floor they stepped out into a vestibule with steel walls and a thick steel door. There were no signs to indicate what might lie inside.

'Turn away please,' said Jo.

He turned back to face the closing lift door as she entered another combination. He heard the sound of keys and a lock shifted weightily.

'OK. Come on.'

He turned round and followed her inside. Computer lights blinked in the darkness for a moment; Jo pulled a big handle on the wall and, with a thud that echoed far away, rows of fluorescent lights flickered on irregularly down the length of a huge, empty expanse. The floor was concrete, speckled near the edges with recent whitewash whose smell still hung in the air. The large, uneven windows that lined one wall had recently been covered with thick steel grills. Near the door stood three desks with computers on them and a table with a printer and a coffee maker.

'Have a seat, Thomas. Coffee?'

'Yes please.'

She poured two mugs.

'We are setting up probably the most extraordinary business you will ever encounter. I'd like your help and I think you'll find it exciting. Your interests will qualify you very well for the task and I'll pay you enough that you'll be satisfied. I will need from you a great amount of effort and imagination – and, of course, your utter secrecy. OK?'

He nodded.

'Right. About twelve years ago there was a round of secret meetings between the British and American intelligence agencies. They convened a panel of visionary military experts, sociologists, psychologists, and businesspeople to look at new roles that the agencies could play in the future – particularly commercial roles. It was felt that organizations like the CIA were spending vast amounts of money on technology and personnel and that it should be possible to make some return on that investment – in addition to their main security function.

'The most radical idea to come out of this concerned the vast intelligence databases possessed by the CIA, FBI, MI5, MI6 and a number of other police and military organizations and private companies. As you know, most of this information is collected so that security forces have some idea of who is doing what and antisocial or terrorist activities can be thwarted. One of the social psychologists suggested, however, that there might be a very different use for it. He pointed out that average memory horizons – that is, the amount of time that a person can clearly remember – had been shrinking for some time: people were forgetting the past more and more quickly. He predicted that memory horizons would shrink close to zero in about twelve years – i.e. now.

'I won't go over all the research and speculation about what kind of impact this mass amnesia would have on the individual, society, and the economy. But one thing became clear: the loss of personal memories would be experienced as a vague and debilitating anxiety that many people would spend money to alleviate. Our databases of conversations, events, photographs, letters, et cetera, could be repackaged and sold back to those individuals to replace their own memories. This would possibly be a huge market opportunity for us. It would also serve a valuable social and economic function in helping to reduce the impact of a problem that was likely to cost hundreds of millions of dollars in psychiatric treatment and several billions in lost labour.'

Jo took a sip of coffee. 'Is this making sense?'

'I think so. Yes.'

'We started with a small group of people and started to record everything they did. We looked at what systems we had available and invented new ones. We put cameras absolutely everywhere. We developed technologies that recognized an individual's voice, face, handwriting and everything so that the minimum human intervention was required to link one person's memories to each other in a single narrative. Gradually these systems were expanded to cover more and more people. We finally reached 100 per cent coverage of the populations of the US and UK around nine years ago, and we have been working with partners in other countries to gather similar data there too. This is the largest collection of data ever to exist. We will be able to give our future customers CD-ROMs with photographs of them getting on a plane to go on holiday, recordings of phone conversations with their mother, videos of them playing with their son in a park or sitting at their desk at work . . . It will really be a phenomenal product.

'Now we're ready for all that work to pay off. We have the stuff to sell. We're working with an advertising agency on a campaign to launch it in the next few months. We just need to work out a few final details. That's where you come in.

'You see there is one issue we didn't think about very carefully when we started this project. Some memories, of course, are not pleasant. We are making all kinds of disclaimers about the memories we are selling, but we would still like to minimize the risk of severe psychological trauma caused by the rediscovery of painful memories that had been lost. There's no point selling bad memories when we know what kind of an impact they will have on individuals' ability to perform well in the home and the workplace. So we want to take them out.

'This is going to be a massive job that calls for someone with your unusual empathy with the past. What we need you to do is to go through the memories manually and produce a large sample of the kind we're talking about – the most traumatic memories. We will analyse that sample and find all the parameters that have a perfect correlation with memories of this sort. Then we can simply run a search on all our databases for memories matching those parameters and delete them. But we need to go through a lot of memories to get there. The statisticians tell us we need a sample of not less than twelve thousand traumatic memories in order for the system to be perfect.'

Jo stopped talking. Thomas said nothing. The idea was so far-reaching that he did not have an adequate response.

'Do you have any questions?'

He searched within himself for the most urgent of his doubts.

'Assuming that everything you've said is true – from the shrinking memory horizons to this massive database of memories – and it still seems rather incredible – I can see why people might want to come to you to retrieve some of the memories they have lost. That makes sense. But isn't it only fair to them to give them everything? Who are you to edit their memories for them? They are a product of the bad as well as the good, after all.'

'Thomas: we are not making any promises of completeness. We are providing a unique service and it's totally up to us how we want to design it. It has been decided that we are not prepared to sell just any memory for fear of the risk to us or our customers. That's that. Any other questions?'

He could find only platitudes.

'What is the company called?'

'Up to now we've been working with a codename for the project: Memory Mine. That name will no doubt fade out as the advertising agency comes up with a new identity for us.'

A mountain of jewels dug from mysterious mines went off in Thomas's head. Was this what the old woman had been talking about? Was this where the prediction was supposed to take him?

'So are you going to do it?'

'I think so. At least – Yes.'

Thomas began work the next day. Each morning he would arrive at the office in Hackney and he and Jo would sit in silence at their computers at one end of this huge empty space. He would wear headphones to listen to recorded phone calls and video; the room was entirely still.

'We have short-listed around a hundred thousand memories that you can work from. They've been selected on the basis of a number of parameters – facial grimacing, high decibel level, obscene language – that are likely to be correlated with traumatic memories. It's a good place to start. Within these you are looking for the very worst: memories of extreme pain or shock, memories of unpleasant or criminal behaviour. Apply the logic of common sense: would someone want to remember this? Think of yourself like a film censor: if the family can't sit together and watch it, it's out.'

Some were obvious. A woman watches her husband being run down by a car that mounts the pavement at high speed and drives him through the door of a second-hand record store; two boys stick a machete into the mouth of an old man while they empty his pockets and take his watch – a sign in the video image says Portsmouth City Council; four men go to the house of an illegal Mexican immigrant in Milwaukee, Wisconsin to collect a loan – when he can't pay they shoot him in the knees; the police inform a mother by telephone that her daughter has been violently raped while taking a cigarette break from her job as a supermarket cashier and has almost died from loss of blood.

In other cases, Thomas was not so sure. He found a sequence in which a man in a business suit met up with a young girl – fourteen or fifteen – in a car park by night. He seemed anxious, but she pulled him to her and they began to kiss against a concrete pillar. Her fingers made furrows in his hair; he tried to stop her as she undid his trousers but she seized him still harder. 'Fuck me!' she said as she lifted her skirt to reveal her full nudity. They made love greedily. Thomas watched to the end.

'I don't know what to do with this,' he announced to Jo, his voice breaking the silence in the room. She remained absorbed in her computer screen for a few seconds before getting up to look at his. He started the scene again and watched with some embarrassment as Jo leaned fixedly over his shoulder, scentless.

'What are you thinking?' she said. 'This girl is blatantly under age! Get rid of it!'

'But don't you think – I just thought – it might be a very important memory for her. I mean – she looks as if she really loves this man.'

'Thomas. This is a criminal act! We don't get mixed up in this kind of thing. Delete it.'

Thomas became fascinated by his power to watch lives unfold. For two days he followed the experiences of a young aristocrat named William who worked for *The Times* as an obituary writer. He would go to spend lengthy afternoons with ageing baronets and senile Nobel Prize winners, interviewing them about their past, and filing the review of their life in anticipation of its imminent end. Memory Mine had purchased the rights to much of *The Times*' archive so that Thomas could listen to the actual recordings of these conversations. He witnessed the young man's respectful grace as he sipped tea with old men and women, the feeble voices with which memories of past greatness were hesitantly recounted, the antiseptic interiors of old people's homes, the soothing effect of the distant past on a young man who was not very comfortably contemporary. He listened to William in phone calls and read his emails, followed the course of a love affair that ended painfully. Thomas explored every document, every conversation, every relationship, and became absorbed completely in the largeness of so many lives and so much time.

He worked till late and spent his evenings thinking about the memories he had examined during the day. His own past merged with those of so many others; he began to have startling dreams. He dreamed that he was looking for his room but could not remember where it was. He had lost his arms and legs and could only wriggle on his stomach. He squirmed on the ground, unable to lift his head to see where he was going. He realized he was wriggling on glass – thin glass that bowed and cracked with his movement, and through which he could see only an endless nothingness. He sweated with the terror of falling through, could already see his limbless body spinning like a raw steak through the darkness. And then he reached a green tarpaulin that covered the glass and he could stand again and walk. He entered a corridor of many doors. Every door looked the same: which was his? He tried to open doors at random but all were locked. As he was becoming mad with apprehension, one door loomed in front of him, more significant than the rest. He turned the handle and entered. Lying in his bed was a man with a bandaged arm. Thomas realized he was dreaming not his own dream but that of the man in his bed. The dream of a man whose memories he had been scanning that day: a construction worker who had walked across a roof covered in a tarpaulin, stepped unknowingly on a skylight, and plunged through the glass to fall three storeys and lose a hand.

One day Thomas asked Jo a question that had been preoccupying him for some time.

'Are we going to lose our memories too?'

Jo was eating a sandwich at her desk. She looked at him and smiled.

'I don't think *you* are. That's why I chose you. The past is tangible for you in a way that is quite exceptional. You seem to have an effortless grasp of it. I don't just mean dates and facts. It's as if memories seek you out and stick to you intuitively.'

'So what about you?'

'This was of course one of the things we were all most concerned about. How could we run this project if we all forgot everything? So we tried to understand exactly why this was happening to see if we could avoid it in ourselves. The fact is that no one really knows. Some say it's to do with the widespread availability of electronic recording formats that are much more effective than human memory, which have gradually removed the need for human beings to remember. Others find the causes in the future-fixation of consumer culture. People cite causes as diverse as the education system, the death of religion, diet, and the structure of the family. There's not just one theory.

'But they put together a lifestyle programme for all of us to try and ensure we would escape the worst of the effects. No television, weekly counselling sessions. We all have to keep a journal. We are all assessed every three months to monitor any memory decline. Et cetera.'

A strange image was fluttering in Thomas's head while Jo was talking. All the memories of the world were stranded and terrified, like animals fleeing a forest fire. With nowhere to go, they huddled in groups and wept, and the noise of their weeping was a cacophony of the centuries that filled the skies but could not be heard. And the earth became saturated with their tears, which welled up and dissolved them all, and they seeped away into nothingness.

Not long after, the office had a visitor.

. 'Good morning Jo. How are you?' The man wore an impressive three-piece suit and his bright greeting sounded mass-produced.

'I'm well, thank you. Larry – meet Thomas. Thomas – Larry runs Memory Mine in the US. He's our boss.' She shot a playful smile that Thomas had not seen before.

Larry gave a handshake that felt like a personality test. 'Good to meet you, Thomas. Jo – can we talk?'

They moved over to the window and talked quietly. Thomas could hear them perfectly but pretended to work.

'How's this one doing?'

'Well. A bit slow.'

'Look, Jo – the whole thing is waiting for him now. Everything is in place. We just need that sample of twelve thousand grade D memories so we can clean up the whole database and launch. How many has he done?'

'I think about six hundred.'

'Six hundred! At this rate it will take him a couple of years. Let's get someone else.'

'No, let's keep him. I think he's the best person for this. We'll just speak to him about the urgency and get him to work faster.'

'Are you sure? We don't have much time.'

'Yes, I'll talk to him.'

From then on Thomas did not have time to explore the lives of people like the obituary writer or the construction worker. He rushed through as fast as he could, working later and later in the office to keep up with his deadlines. He found so many memories of terrible things: deaths, betrayals, injustices, accidents, rape, ruthlessness, ruin, disappointments, lies, wars. He saw mothers losing their infants, suicides of loved ones, devastating financial losses, children beaten and brutalized by parents, countless violent and senseless murders. Every minute was a new horror, a new nightmare that forced its way inside him and unfurled unexpected lobes of dank emotions that grew in among his organs. At night he left the office bloated and dazed with hundreds of new memories that leapt in alarm at their new confines, beating against the sides of his mind, flying madly like winged cockroaches in a cupboard. He could not separate himself from the memories: they lodged in him and burst open like over-ripe fruit, their poison sprayed from them and seeped through his tissues. He wanted to vomit with the sickness of the thoughts, to purge himself. But there was no escape: the memories seethed and grew in his mind during the day and erupted into startling, terrifying dreams at night. Thomas arrived at work each day pale and wide-eyed, ready to sit again and absorb more of this acid from the past.

At last, after one month, it was over. Larry came to the office and sat at Thomas's machine. Twelve thousand memories exactly sat in his folder.

'Jo – are you confident this is 100 per cent accurate?'

'Sure. We've checked it very carefully. I'm confident.'

'OK. Now we should be able to calculate the parameters.' He logged in to the administration section of the system and activated some functions. 'There. And now we can run a search on the entire database and locate all grade D memories.' He hit *Run query*. Numbers started mounting on the screen.

He unbuttoned his jacket. 'So: many thanks to you, Thomas. You got there in the end. What now?'

'Er – no plans really.'

'I see.'

'Maybe we can find something,' said Jo.

Larry looked at her. 'Your budget is already blown. I hardly think you're in a position to make suggestions like that. Please get real.'

The search ended. '2,799,256,014 results found.'

'Christ – that's nearly ten per cent of our database,' said Larry. 'That's a lot of trauma. And this is just in the US and UK where life is pretty good. Imagine how many we'll get in all those places where life sucks. My God. Let's just check some of these before we delete them.'

He opened the first memory. A daughter found her tycoon mother dead in a running car full of carbon monoxide after a major feature in the *Daily Telegraph* detailing her illegal business ventures. The second was a man being beaten by the police in prison and threatened with razor blades.

'OK, this looks good. This is the kind of stuff we really do not need. Good job, Thomas. So I'm going ahead and deleting these.'

Jo and Thomas looked at him and said nothing. He pressed *Delete all*. '2,799,256,014 records deleted.'

'Excellent. Now let's start selling the hell out of this thing.'

That night Thomas had a vivid dream. He dreamt he was back at his parents' house in Islington. The house was empty. Sun poured in through the windows and he sat in his bedroom reading books rich with tales and characters from history. Suddenly he looked up; and through the window he saw a beautiful thing floating slowly down to the ground. It was magical and rare and he felt a deep desire to own it. He ran down the stairs and out into the garden, and there it was floating above him: a delicate thing, spiralling exquisitely and glinting in the sun. He stood under it and reached out his hands. Spinning like a slow-motion sycamore seed, it fell softly and weightlessly into his palms. It looked as if it was of silver, beaten till it was a few atoms thick and sculpted into the most intricate form: a kind of never-ending staircase that wound round on itself into a snail shell of coils within coils. He looked at it in rapture. How could such a beautiful object have fallen from the sky! He was full of joy at this thing that had chosen him and fallen so tamely into his hand.

And then he understood that the thing was a memory. It was a wonderful memory: of music first heard by a young woman – a big concert hall – a piano that produced sounds so astonishing that the woman was lifted up on their flight. And Thomas was exhilarated: he laughed out loud with the memory of those passages that seemed like they would burst the limits of loveliness.

But as the memory entered him and took root in his heart he realized there were many more falling from the sky. He looked up and saw there were memories of all kinds and colours dropping not only around him but as far as he could see. He went out into the street, where memories had already begun to cover the ground. Each gust of wind would send them skating across the tarmac to collect in the gutters. They fell everywhere: some wispy, some like multicoloured feathers, some fashioned out of a substance that collapsed and became like tar when it hit the ground.

All day and night the memories fell. They floated on puddles like a layer of multicoloured leaves, and stuck in trees, giving them new and unnatural hues of cyan and mustard yellow and metallic grey. They accumulated in clumps on the roofs and window sills and porticoes of Georgian houses, softening right angles and making a kind of pageant of the street.

The next morning the skies were low and dense and the memories fell harder than ever. The roads had become impassable and people had to clear paths to their front doors.

He left the house and wandered until he reached King's Cross Station. The memories fell on his head and shoulders. Everywhere they lay flattened and dead on the ground, as if there had been a massacre of insects.

Sometimes Thomas saw people picking up the mysterious new objects to examine them; but the experience always seemed to induce some kind of nausea, and they flung them hastily away. After a few such experiences everyone tried not to notice what was happening. They swept the memories away, they drove their cars more and more slowly through the accumulation, they were inconvenienced everywhere they went – but they asked no questions. The more the memories fell, the more blank their faces looked. Their eyes became hollow, their skin yellow and desiccated. They seemed to move differently, shiftily, darting from spot to spot.

For days Thomas wandered around London, sleeping on car roofs and other raised surfaces while the downpour continued. He watched people leave their houses and become wild. They began to build camps on high ground and on flat roofs. They squatted naked around fires on the steps to the buildings around Trafalgar Square while the entire piazza was filled, only the column protruding from a writhing, harlequinesque sea of baubles and crystals.

Weeks passed. For five whole days only memories of war fell from the skies. No daylight could penetrate the clouds of terrifying leaden forms that rained down on London, and only streaks of fire gave any illumination. It was now rare to see any people at all. They hid, clung like babies to anything that seemed familiar.

Thomas's wanderings led him to the Thames. Rains had carried streams of memories down into the river until they filled the riverbed entirely, rising above the water to enormous mounds of multicoloured sludge. Its course was completely blocked; the water flooded out, rising above the bridges and submerging the quays. Tourist boats lay wrecked on the terraces outside the Festival Hall and everywhere was the stench of rotting fish. Dogs chewed at carcasses at the edge of the water; flocks of gulls perched on the huge misshapen islands that looked like waste from a sweet factory.

As he looked out over the river he realized that all these millions of memories had begun to whisper to him. He heard voices from every place and time talking in every language about terrible and wonderful and everyday things. He had the impression that all the memories had been cast out, that they burned with the ferocity of a dying parasite searching for a host. They stalked him, would not leave him alone, seemed to be speaking right up against his ear, called him by name. He tried to flee, but more and more of them billowed up, following him in a quivering line. Memories flowed out of everywhere until the trail was like a canopy over the city. And then, with a shriek from the depths of time, they rose up in one vast motion, descended on him, and buried themselves in his soul. It was like a gigantic explosion converging on its centre in a film run backwards. At that point, he passed out.

The predictions of Memory Mine executives turned out to be correct. There came a point in time when people lost their memories on a mass scale. They were unable to remember even the most basic outlines of the past – their own or anyone else's – and could therefore not engage in normal human interactions. They began to be withdrawn and suspicious, and the public spaces of the city became empty and eerie. This phenomenon was accompanied by – or caused – a major economic recession; and the two blights swept entire continents hand in hand.

Memory Mine was well prepared. Under its new name, MyPast™, its advertisements suddenly flooded the media and the city. An elderly couple hugged each other affectionately as they played their MyPast™ CD-ROM and remembered more youthful times. A grumpy businessman played the CD at work, saw himself as a young man laughing in a group at college, and was driven to make phone calls to friends he had not seen in years – bringing the smile back to his face. Despite the economic slowdown, the product was an instant hit. People sensed great relief at seeing evidence of their own past, and though for many this 'quick fix' actually worsened their psychiatric condition, nothing could prevent people rushing to buy editions for everyone in their household in order to try and re-experience the familial bond that was supposed to link them.

While most people were suffering from total amnesia, Thomas seemed to bear the burden of an excess of memory. He appeared haunted, and wandered the streets slowly and gingerly, as if afraid of upsetting an intricate balance in his head. His mind was crammed full like the hold of a cargo ship, containers packed in to every inch of space, every one roasting in the airless heat below deck, and heavy with a million whispers that each tried to rise above all the others. He could take in no more thought or experience of any kind and avoided all human contact.

He was aware, of course, of what was happening to the people around him. He tried to call his parents on a couple of occasions to see if they were all right – but there was no answer. He could not face the flood of memories that might be released if he went home, so he did not.

He ended up one day back at the office in Hackney. He had nothing to do there, but it was a place to go that had a connection, however strange, to this thing that had overtaken everyone and it exerted a pull over him.

It was very different now. The huge empty space of the office had been entirely filled with lines of desks, where incessantly ringing phones were answered by clean young people with their efficient 'Good morning, MyPast™, how can I help you?' People ordered memories for themselves and their friends and families; they were located immediately on the database and burned straight onto CDs; the printer spat out attractive labels and pockets with pictures of happy families and a personalized message. The CDs were stacked in big plastic bins and dispatched twice a day.

Thomas sat in a corner, preoccupied and detached. He went there every day, and Jo did not try to stop him. She may have felt slightly responsible for his state of mind. People got used to him being there. Sometimes he lay down and spent the night under a desk. The murmurings in his head kept him haggard and silent.

Those forgetful times, while they remained, were terrible, even if few could remember them afterwards. But they did not last.

One day Thomas awoke and felt that his mind was lighter. It was as if a thick splinter that had been lying buried in his brain for months was now removed. The voices diminished. He could look outwards again at the world without feeling that the incoming information would make him explode.

The memories were departing.

Very slowly, the city started to be populated again. People's faces regained their depth, and they started to talk to each other. They could remember more and more.

Frantic phone calls raced between the MyPast™ offices in London and Washington. They had assumed that their graphs of diminishing memory horizons only moved in one direction and had never accounted for this sudden upswing. Very soon sales had dropped alomost to zero; the workforce was sacked en masse. The office in Hackney became almost deserted again. Even Jo did not bother to turn up. Thomas spent days there without seeing anyone.

One evening the phone rang. Thomas picked it up.

'Is this MyPast™?'

'Yes.'

'I need memories. Everyone else's memories seem to be returning. But my mind is still empty. I can't do anything. Can't work, can't sleep. I need my memories.'

Thomas realized with a shock that it was his father on the phone.

'I think I can help you, sir.'

'How long does it take?'

'I can send them out to you tomorrow. You should get them on Monday morning.'

'Where are you? Can I come over myself and pick them up?'

'You could. We are in Hackney.'

'OK. What's the address?'

Thomas told him.

'I'll be there in a few minutes.'

Thomas logged in to the MyPast™ database. He entered his father's name and searched. There were nearly a thousand memories. He saved

47

them onto a CD and printed out a label. He decided to go down to the street to wait.

His father came with his two brothers. Thomas watched them approach from a distance. They all looked strangely diminished. His father had lost his poise and sophistication and walked wild-eyed and hunted, and his brothers scuttled close to him for safety. They drew close without any sign of recognition.

'MyPast™?' asked his father aggressively.

'Yes,' replied Thomas.

'Where are they? My memories?'

Thomas led them inside and they crammed into the tiny lift. His father breathed heavily and he twitched with impatience, but somehow it felt good to Thomas to touch him again. They arrived at the sixth floor. Brightly coloured MyPast™ signs announced their arrival.

'I need this quickly. Right now. Where is it?'

Thomas picked up the CD from the desk. 'Here it is. You can see it has your name on it here and today's date. I'll need to ask you for a cheque for £999.'

'Don't waste my time. Just show it to me.'

Thomas grew nervous.

'Perhaps it would be best if you took it home. There's a lot of stuff here and that way you can share it with – with your wife and sit in comfort. In your own home. In fact I'm just locking the office up.'

'I'm losing my mind here. I haven't got time for your – just put this damn thing on for me. I won't pay you a penny till you show me.'

'I'll tell you what – just take it. I don't need the money. I can see you're in need. Take it as a gift.'

'I need it now.'

Thomas saw a menacing look in his father's eye that brought back old fears. He took the CD from his hand and fed it into the computer. It started up on its own, a 20-second promotional jingle that talked in a comforting voice about MyPast™. Then it gave a menu of memories. Thomas selected one. It showed his father addressing a banking summit organized by the Confederation of British Industry three or four years before. He was confident and funny and people responded loudly, applauded.

'Is that me?' asked Thomas' father, incredulous. 'Is that me?'

'Yes, it is.'

'Is that who I was?' The speech ended to camera flashes and applause. The video faded. The boys looked on mutely.

'Show me more. More.'

'Really, sir, I must close the office now.'

'Don't give me that bullshit. Get out of my way.'

Thomas's father seized the mouse from him and pushed him out of the seat. He stared impatiently at the screen and selected another memory.

He saw himself sipping wine with his wife in the bar at the Barbican in the interval of some concert. They were both dressed up. Thomas's mother spoke passionately about something that could not be heard.

'That's my wife. How strong she used to be. How attractive. I wonder where she is now.'

'What do you mean, *Where is she now?*' asked Thomas, alarmed.

'I don't know. I can't remember where she is.'

He clicked on something else. The whole family was on holiday in Florida, several years ago. Thomas was still a young child. The three boys were sunburnt and carried fishing nets. Their mother wore a wrap-around skirt and expensive sunglasses.

'Look – there are three boys. Who's the other one?' He watched them playing in the sand, building mounds taller than they were.

He carried on clicking avidly. The family was wandering round the Natural History Museum – just a year or so before. Thomas was clearly visible.

'Isn't that you?' asked his father looking round at Thomas. 'Isn't that you there – in the museum at the same time as us? What a bloody coincidence. Do we know each other?'

'Not really *know*. No.'

Another scene opened up. Thomas froze with fear. It was a recording of their evening in the Oxo Tower. The lights of the Thames spread out behind them; the waiters served champagne, and Thomas's father talked about investment to his family.

'What the bloody hell is going on?' he said. He turned to Thomas, his face hungry and furious. 'Can you please explain what the hell is going on? Is this some kind of disgusting joke that you people play? You put yourselves into our memories? You sit yourself down at dinner with us, at our most intimate moments? You insert yourselves into our thoughts, our families, our past? Is that what happens? Just as I was coming to believe in my past I see you sitting there grinning out of it like some monster – and realize all of it is fake. What the hell is your game?'

The video continued quietly. Thomas saw out the corner of his eye the moment at which his father had told him to leave the house.

'Sir, please understand. This is no falsehood. I am your son. My name is Thomas. These are my brothers. I am part of your family.'

Thomas's father looked at him, looked deep into his pupils. He seemed to see something that he had been looking for, and the emptiness of his eyes was filled with a question. But something washed over the surface again and Thomas could peer in no more.

'You bastard!' His father hit him so hard around the head that he fell to the ground, dazed and astonished. 'Think you can betray people like this and get away with it?' He kicked him in the groin. 'You bastard!' He became wild, kicking him again and again in the groin and stomach.

His brothers joined in, kicking his head and face and back with all their strength. 'You bastard!' they chanted viciously, imitating their father. Thomas blacked out, became bloody and limp – but they did not stop beating him until they were too exhausted to continue.

Reality returned only half-way. He saw himself lying in an emergency ward. Jo had brought him there when she had discovered him lying in a kidney-shaped arc of congealed blood in the morning. He could not make things out, but his mind felt lighter. He realized that nearly all the memories had left him and soon he would be alone again.

He had the impression that he knew the person in the next bed. It was an old woman he had seen before. Gradually he remembered. She had given him a prophecy long ago. So long. She looked very sick.

'Hello.' His voice reached out to her, but she did not seem to be aware. 'It's Thomas. Do you remember me?'

She turned painfully towards him, her eyes like albumen. 'Of course I remember you.'

'What happened to you?'

'It's not easy being blind and old. I fell. Fell down the stairs. Broken my pelvis. I don't feel well. I'm at the end.'

'Everything happened as you said. My father became poor and I became rich. But it wasn't how I imagined.'

'It rarely is.'

The various sounds of the hospital seemed to become ordered and intended, like a fugue. Thomas listened for a moment.

'As soon as she said "Memory Mine" I remembered what you said. I knew this was it! It was a good job. There was a nice woman. Her name was Jo.' Thomas felt weightless, the memories breaking away like spores and floating back to where they came from.

'A packhorse was needed. To get the memories through this ravine. This time. You happened to be the one. It could have been someone else. But it wasn't. I'm sure you've worked that out.'

'Yes. I think I understand things now. Things seem so much clearer.'

The old lady did not seem to be listening any more. Doctors whirled urgently around him, nurses came running, but he was content inside his mind. All that now remained was his own past; and it was good.

THE BILLIONAIRE'S
SLEEP
The Third Story

I N THE CITY of Delhi there once lived a man who had never been able to sleep.

In appearance he had everything he wanted – more, in fact, than one person could ever want, for he was the owner of a vast industrial group and one of India's richest men. Rajiv Malhotra lived in an elegant colonial mansion on Prithviraj Road with a garden full of gulmohar trees and parakeets; he was attended by servants and cooks and chauffeurs; he ran households in Jakarta, New York, and London; and he was married to a beautiful former film star. But it was as if fate, in bestowing so many blessings, had sought to ensure he would not be ignorant of suffering, and sleep was something he could not achieve.

'To sleep is as to breathe!' he would think to himself as he sat alone in the back of his tinted Mercedes on his way to work every morning. 'Just look at all the people who have nothing, but to whom sleep's treasures come every day, like a lifelong, unbidden friend. People sleep on the highways and in the train station, they sleep as people step over them and dogs bark around them – young boys, old women – all are able to sleep. But I, who have so much, have not this thing that the poorest beggar is able to enjoy.'

He led a double life. By day he would lead the life of people: working, eating, attending social functions, chatting to family and friends. Of course fatigue gnawed at him like a cancer: his organs felt as if they were of lead and ready to drag him down into a void, his eyes were like boulders in his head. But there was light and there were people, and he felt a part of the world. He worked endlessly, slowly transforming his father's steel company into a global industrial empire that made him feel involved, significant.

But his nights were another life altogether. A life of black solitude when everyone around him demonstrated a loyalty more primal – happily, eagerly, gratefully, and so simply! – leaving him behind for the arms of sleep, abandoning him to wish away the hours of night, to experience time as something he had somehow to *get through*, and thus to become submerged in pointlessness.

While his wife slept upstairs he would wander through their many rooms, like a ghost condemned to revisit a castle every night for eternity, slinking tediously through the same corridors centuries after the life he once knew has given way to silence and dereliction. He would rifle the house aimlessly for new soporifics – books to draw him out of his boredom and panic enough that sleep might steal up on him unnoticed; videos or TV shows for him to surrender his mind to for a while. He wandered in the deep shadows of the garden smoking unaccustomed cigarettes, read the day's news again, finished off bowls of peanuts that had been put out hours ago for evening guests; finally, he went drowsily to bed to lie next to his wife only to find in his horizontality some kind of strange excitant that would send his exhausted mind scampering aimlessly around labyrinths of irrelevant problems to which he needed no solution. At length, the windows would lighten, the azan would sound from distant mosques, and he would start to change from yesterday's clothes into today's, simultaneously relieved to be no longer alone and tortured that his strange impotence had been confirmed once more.

Of course he had consulted doctors. He had tried sleeping pills, relaxants, anti-anxiety drugs, meditation and hypnosis. He had diligently read the publications of the Sleep Disorder Society of America and the scientific publications of all the leading somnologists. He had tried every kind of therapeutic bed, pillow, earplug, and eyemask. He had followed the suggestions of friends to play Mozart or classical ragas very softly in his room, had even given a chance to the *Sounds of Nature* CD collection someone had sent him, lying in bed to the surround sound of cicadas in the rainforest or underwater whale recitatives, and trying to detect signs of somnolence inside himself. None appeared. No therapy, from folk to pharmacological, had managed to prise open for him the gates of the kingdom of slumber, and after some years he stopped looking for help. He did not sleep, and that was that.

It was doctors who confirmed to him, however, what he had himself long suspected: that a lifetime without sleep was almost certainly responsible for the fact that, after ten years of marriage, he and his wife had never conceived a child.

When Rajiv Malhotra had married the Bollywood superstar Mira Sardari, the newspapers had been apoplectic with idolizing, goggling glee. The romance had every element of legend: the society man of the 70s who was jilted by the beautiful – and older – mother and waited twenty years to marry the daughter; the helicopter accident that orphaned the teenage Mira and made her the child of India herself, with doting parents in all the leading families; the secret wedding in a Himalayan resort while Mira was at the height of her fame and in the middle of her classic *Exile* (no one was there, but everyone was an eyewitness); the ending of her film career 'so I can devote myself to helping those less fortunate than myself'; his sophistication and massive commerical power. But children, which they both saw as the fulfilment of their lives, did not come. Doctors advised the couple that Rajiv's sleepless body, incapable of rejuvenating itself, would never produce seed. His private thoughts, that had dwelt single-mindedly on iron and tin for so long, became more and more obsessed by flesh and blood. There was a quietness between him and his wife. And after a while, the editors of newspapers, obsessed with dynasties even more than with money, themselves turned quiet.

One night Rajiv decided to go to one of his factories to inspect how business was being conducted. He was that kind of businessman: he liked to see every detail for himself.

As he arrived it was already nearly midnight, and the discreet lighting along the pathway to the main entrance left most of the vast building floating unseen in the darkness. This was the site of one of his newest ventures: a telecom centre where honey-toned Indian operators with swiftly acquired American accents gave free 1–800 telephone succour to the throngs of needy consumers of the United States.

He swiped a security card at the entrance and day struck; the lights inside burned in the night like a sunny afternoon. Rajiv scanned the rows of cubicles critically, saw a Coke can on the floor that immediately irritated him, watched for any malfunctions in the efficiency of the place. Every worker had to average thirty calls an hour. Nine-hour shifts, one 45-minute break, two 15-minute breaks. Efficiency was everything.

He walked down the length of the hall unseen by the headphoned workers at their screens, and climbed the staircase to the mezzanine where the floor manager sat in a glass booth.

The manager jumped as if he had seen a television image come to life.

'We are honoured, sir – extremely honoured – sir –'

'How is everything?'

'Extremely well. Thank you. Thank you very much.'

'I've come to spend a bit of time listening to the calls. Want to see how everything is working.'

'Of course, sir.'

The manager took off his headphones and switched the output to the speaker.

From above, the cubicles looked like a magnified insect battery, a nest uncovered by mistake, a glimpse of geometrically precise rows of pods, lines of tiny vespine heads, shining with black Sony ovals, trembling with larval energy on T-shirted thoraces.

'Is this the number for customer complaints?' A crystalline American accent asserted itself over the speaker.

'Yes it is, madam. What can I do for you this morning?'

At that inconvenient moment, Rajiv's mobile phone rang.

'Hello?' he said, in one quick syllable.

'Hi, it's me.'

'Hello, Mira. I'm at work. What are you doing? It's late.'

'Last week I was on one of your flights from San José to Boston. There was a stop-over in St Louis. The flight out of San José was delayed by one and a half hours and I missed the Boston connection.'

'I'm having a massage. At home. There's something important I want to discuss with you.'

'Not now.'

'When then? Do I have to make an appointment? You *never* have time. There's something very important to both of us that I want to tell you about and at ten past midnight on a Tuesday night I feel I have a right to expect that you'll be available. And since you're not actually in the house –'

'You people didn't have another flight to Boston till the next morning. So I had to buy another ticket on American to get there on time.'

'OK quickly. I don't have much time. What is it?'

'I've just read this article – today's paper – it's about a new technique. Listen to this.'

'Mira – please, not now! I can't concentrate.'

'You guys couldn't get me there and I had to attend a dinner with people who were only in the country for one day. I need a refund.'

'How dare you talk to me like that?'

'I mean they'd managed to make it all the way from Paris and I was going to say sorry I'm stuck in Missouri?'

'Is loitering around your damned factory at midnight *so* important? Just tell them to wait. Listen to me for one minute. You'll be as excited as I am.'

'OK, I'm listening – Why is this guy letting her talk on like that? Who cares about her damned dinner? Just give her what she wants and let's move on – Go on Mira.'

'SCIENTISTS PRODUCE VIABLE GORILLA CLONE: Claim Human Cloning now Possible.'

'Madam, can we start from the beginning? Name and the date of travel?'

'It's datelined Cambridge, England. I'll start from the beginning. A group of scientists at Bios Laboratories Ltd today announced they had produced an eight-cell gorilla foetus that would, had it been implanted in a mother gorilla, have given rise to a normal pregnancy and infant. The scientists destroyed the foetus, saying that their objectives were simply to confirm a number of theoretical and technical hypotheses, not to create quote public curiosities – blah blah blah . . .'

'Last Thursday. Flight 162. Name is Laurie Kurt.'

'OK, this is the bit: Dr Stephen Hall, the Technical Director at Bios Laboratories, said that the experiment showed how far the science had come.'

'Let me just find that on the system for you. Hope you made it to the dinner in the end, after they'd come so far?'

'In the end. Thank God. They were venture capitalists from France who were looking to put money into my company. It was the only time in four months we all had spare diary time. Can you believe that?'

'I'm going crazy listening to this small talk. If this guy wants to chat he can do it in his spare time. He's supposed to do one call every two minutes. What's his average? Check it.'

Somewhere in California a police siren swelled, Dopplered, and faded.

'Rajiv? Are you listening? "A few years ago these eight cells would have been on the cover of *Time* magazine and people would have been saying that this has turned our idea of nature on its head."'

'We've got this amazing technology, it's going to turn the lives of three hundred million Americans literally *upside-down* – and I'm sitting stuck in St Louis – of all places! – missing the only time I could get with these VCs in four months.'

'"Now we have well-established techniques for doing this kind of thing, and can achieve our objectives with a high degree of predictability – and no one is really surprised anymore."'

'He's making eighteen calls an hour, sir.'

'Then why is he still here? – Mira, hang on a minute – That's not how you were briefed. If he's not doing his job, fire him. That's what you're here for!'

'You can imagine how I felt –'

'Otherwise I'll fire you.'

'When asked what this meant for the future of human cloning, Hall was unequivocal. "It's going to happen. We could do it now. And someone will do it. One thing that history has taught us is that human curiosity never sleeps, no matter what obstacles the doomsayers try to put in its way."'

'Mira, please!'

'– this was possibly the most important moment of my life –'

'Oh, Rajiv – you're on television! Can you hear?'

Rajiv's microphoned voice crackled through his mobile phone.

'India's new wealth will come not from any natural resource but from an entirely fortuitous fact: its one billion people slap bang on the opposite side of the world from America.'

'– they told me I would change the future –'

'A billion people awake while America's three hundred million sleep. Awake in their droves, ten and a half time zones from New York, thirteen and a half from San Francisco.'

'He's been on this call for four and a half minutes already.'

'You look so nice. Nice smile. And people are applauding.'

'In the electronic age it doesn't matter where anyone is anymore.'

'Is anyone apart from me remotely conscious of the value of time, for God's sake?'

'And Indians can fit in a whole day of work between the time that Americans swipe out in the evening and the time they set their double mocha down on their desk the next morning. It's an unbeatable formula.'

'Kurt, Laurie – I have it.'

'Thanks to us, the sun need never set on the American working day.'

'OK, I have that delayed flight on my screen here. And the

other ticket you purchased. American Airlines. Paid for at 2.24 p.m. Central Time last Thursday. We're very sorry for the delay and the inconvenience.'

'India's new asset is its time zone. Indian Standard Time is its new pepper, its new steel!'

'We'll credit one thousand eight hundred fifteen dollars and forty-seven cents to the American Express card you paid with.'

'That's the end of that news item. But you did look nice.'

'Thank you very much. You have an accent. Where are you from?'

'He's out of here.'

'I'm from India.'

'Now listen. Protesters – cloning – undermining society – yes: "These technologies mean dramatic new possibilities for medical therapy and for bringing children to infertile couples, and when people realize that their world view can continue unthreatened by what people like me do – and that previously incurable conditions can now be treated – they'll stop making all this fuss."'

Mira's voice began to quiver with the massage. Rajiv could hear the smack of palms on oily skin.

'India! I would *so* love to go to India. I believe Americans have so much to learn from India. What do you think of the US?'

'It goes on: Chief Executive Robert Mills confirmed that human cloning was not on the company's agenda. "It's illegal in this country anyway," he said. "But the mandate we have been given by our investors is very precise: to develop a patent portfolio of world-class sheep and cattle genetic material, and the techniques to exploit that material in the global agricultural marketplace."'

'America is – fine! Great!'

'Time!'

'"The gorilla experiment was part of our investigation into these techniques, but Bios Laboratories will not be pursuing its work in primate production."'

'Where are you based?'

'Madam, I'm getting another call. I really ought to go.'

'OK. Thanks for your help.'

'Time's up? What do you mean time's up?'

'You have to make sure these people understand that there is only one thing that is important here and that's efficiency.'

'My massage is over. Can't believe an hour is up already.'

'You have to make sure they know how to avoid this kind of chitchat. And deal with that guy. This isn't a chat line we're running.'

'So what do you think?'

'I'm sorry, Mira, I'm doing something here.'

'Were you listening to the article?'

'Yes. In fact I know Stephen Hall. He was at Cambridge with me. We played squash.'

'Don't you see? This is our chance! We can have a child! Why don't you go and see him?'

'OK, Mira. I will.'

A few days later, Dr Stephen Hall showed Rajiv into the living room of a large old house whose Victorian lattice windows filtered out most of the scant light of the Cambridge afternoon. They sat down on armchairs that were crowded into the tiny space left by the grand piano and outsized television that dominated the room.

'Now. Tell me what can I do for you?'

Stephen poured cream into his coffee and stirred intently.

'I need you to make my wife and I a child. We will pay, of course.' Rajiv narrated the history of his ill-fated attempts at reproduction.

Dr Hall considered deeply. He looked anxious.

'Have you thought of adopting?'

'I haven't come here for your bloodless European solutions. I don't need to visit one of the world's leading biotechnology experts to get advice on adoption. I want a child whose flesh and blood is my wife's and my own. That is why I am here.'

'How much would you pay?'

'Five million pounds.'

'I see.' He took a gulp from his coffee cup with just-perceptible agitation.

'You realize that we'd need to do the work outside the country. It's illegal here. I'd probably set up a lab in the Bahamas. We'd need to ship a lot of equipment and people. It could –'

'I know how much money you'll need to spend and it's nowhere near five million pounds. I'd already included a healthy profit for you. But if it's an issue, let's say seven million. No more negotiation.'

'And if I were to say yes, what would you want?'

'I want you to make me a son. A perfect son. A son who will be handsome and charming. Brilliant and hardworking. Who can take over my business. Who will never disappoint or shame me. Who will be happy. A son, above all, who can sleep.'

'In a probabilistic science like genetics it is dangerous to try and optimize every parameter. You start stretching chance until it snaps and you end up getting nothing.'

'Nevertheless. Those are my demands.'

'I'll do it.'

Time inside an aeroplane always seemed to be staged by the airline company to deceive, its studied slowness a kind of tranquillizer for the seat-belted cattle in their eight-hour suspension, to which passport control and baggage claim would be the only antidote. Synthesized versions of 'Yesterday' and 'Candle in the Wind' reminded passengers of old, familiar feelings but with the human voice removed, emotions loaded with blanks for a safer, more pleasant ride. Mealtimes were announced in advance: the rhythms of earth were felt to continue un-interrupted here in this airborne tube so that the indignation at chicken when lamb had run out was far more consequential than 'Isn't it only two hours since breakfast?' High-alcohol wine, parsimonious lighting and channel upon channel of Julia Roberts anaesthesia completed the gentle high-altitude lullaby.

No matter how many times he flew, Rajiv, naturally, never succumbed to these sedatives. As time slowed down all around him, his heartbeat accelerated with the raging speed on the other side of the titanium membrane, the whole screaming, blinking 300-litres-a-second combustion of it, the 800-kilometre-an-hour gale in which Karachi-Tehran-Moscow-Prague-Frankfurt-Amsterdam each stuck for a second on the windscreen like a sheet of old newspaper and then swooped into the past. As the plane cut its fibre-optic jet stream through the sky, Rajiv's insomniac sorrow at living in a different time from everyone else became panic as the movement of the day tilted and buckled, the unwavering sun, always just ahead, holding time still for hours and hours and burning his dim, sleepless pupils. Used to carrying the leaden darkness of the night through the day with him, he now carried Indian Standard Time in his guts into far-flung places, and there was an ear-splitting tectonic scraping within him as it went where it should never have been. Time shifted so gently around the surface of the globe, he thought: there should have been no cause for human bodies to be traumatized by its discontinuities – until people started piercing telegraphic holes from one time zone to another, or leaping, jet-engined, between continents. The universe was not born to understand neologisms like *jet lag*.

It was the same, every time.

Stephen worked quickly. Working in the Bahamas from blood and tissue samples sent from Delhi he managed to mimic the processes by which the DNA of two adults is combined at the moment of fertilization. He took human egg cells from the ovaries of aborted embryos, blasted the nucleus from them, and replaced it with the new genetic combination. He created a battery of two hundred eggs, and waited.

At length he identified one healthy and viable zygote, splitting happily into two every few hours. He called Mira, who flew out that day, and implanted it in her womb.

She returned to Delhi via London, where she had some shopping to do in Bond Street. Neither customs nor security detected the microscopic contraband she carried within her.

After nine months, Mira was rosy and rotund, and Rajiv an exuberant and solicitous father-to-be. No one could remember seeing him so glad or so animated. Even the black crescents that seemed branded under his eyes started to fade. He called Mira several times a day to enquire after her temperature and the condition of her stomach. He brought her flowers and sweets in the evening and hosted small parties in his home where she would dazzle the guests with her happiness and even replay Bollywood routines from the old days. At length, her labour began.

The obstetrician and nurses came to the house to attend her in her bedroom while Rajiv sat in his study with the door closed, fiddling with a pencil. He sweated with suspense, but would not allow himself to venture out. Finally, a nurse came to the door.

'The labour is over, sir. And you have twins. A boy and a girl. Both are healthy. You had better come.'

Rajiv ran past her to his wife's bedroom. There she lay, exhausted and pale, and beside her on the bed were two sleeping babies. One was a radiant, beautiful girl. The other was a boy, a shrunken, misshapen boy with an outsized head that had the pointed shape of a cow's.

'What is this?' he cried in horror. 'That is not my son! That is some – creature!'

The nurses susurrated, trying to bring calm and allow the new mother to rest, reassuring the father, telling him that new babies often look a bit – funny? – this was quite normal and not to worry, and anyway we all learn to love our children in the end, even if they have some adorable little quirk that makes them different – isn't that what also makes them unique?

Rajiv was not listening. 'I want that child out of my house this day!' He stormed out and summoned his lifelong companion and servant, Kaloo.

'A terrible thing has happened, Kaloo. My wife has given birth to *two* children: a girl, and a boy who is a deviant. I cannot allow the boy to stay here a moment longer. I want you to take him away. Give him to a family where he'll be cared for. Promise them a yearly stipend – whatever they need – as long as they look after him. But I don't want to know where he is or what happens to him, and I don't want him to know about me. Take him away, Kaloo! Away from Delhi – somewhere else. And as long as we are all alive this secret stays between you and me.'

In a very few hours the matter was taken care of. Telling no one, not even Rajiv, where he was going, Kaloo wrapped the baby up and set out with a wet nurse for the airport. He took Rajiv's private plane and flew to Bombay. While the nurse looked after the baby in a hotel room, Kaloo wandered the streets looking for a family who would care for the child. His gaze was attracted by the kindly face of a Muslim bookseller. He approached him and told him the story.

'Sir – my wife and I would be so happy! We have no children and have always wanted a son!'

'I will deliver the boy to you this very evening. And every year on this day I will visit you with money. You cannot contact me, nor should you make any attempt to discover the origins of the boy. I hope you will be loving parents to him.'

He and the wet nurse took the baby to the bookseller's home that evening and delivered him into his new mother's arms. She wept with joy.

'We will call him Imran,' she said reverentially. 'He will be a man like a god.'

Rajiv and Mira named their daughter Sapna, and from the first day of her life everyone who saw her was enchanted by her. She was so beautiful that jaded politicians and wrinkled businessmen rediscovered the meaning of the word 'breathtaking' when they looked into her cot. As Rajiv forgot his rage of her birthday, and Mira allowed her resentment of her husband's peremptory behaviour to subside, both of them lapsed into a deep love affair with their daughter.

Everyone agreed there was something marvellous about her sleep. People would stop at Rajiv's house just to see the baby sleeping, for the air she exuded with her slow breathing smelled better than anything they had ever smelt. It made one feel young and vital, it made you feel – though none of them would ever say it aloud – like reproducing!

Eternally ignorant himself of the pleasure of sleep, Rajiv's body and mind were calmed and rejuvenated by the voluptuous sleep of his daughter.

She was only four or five years old when she sat at the family piano and picked out, with unaccustomed fingers but rapidly increasing harmonic complexity, a Hindi film song she had heard on the radio that morning. Rajiv immediately installed an English piano teacher who quickly found herself involved in conversations of the greatest philosophical complexity with her young pupil, who was interested in understanding why the emotions responded so readily to certain melodic or harmonic combinations.

One morning, when Rajiv entered Sapna's bedroom to kiss her goodbye, he noticed something he had not seen before. The wooden headboard of her bed seemed to have sprouted a green shoot that in one night had grown leaves and a little white flower. He summoned his wife.

'It's beautiful,' she said, mystified.

'That may be so – but what is it doing there? If it grows so much in one night, one morning we will come and find it has strangled our daughter. Get someone to cut it off today and seal the spot with varnish. This bed has been here for – what? – ten years? I can't understand how this has happened after all this time.'

That day a carpenter was brought who carefully cut off the new stem, sanded down the surface and varnished it until no sign of the growth remained. But the next morning there were two such shoots, each larger than the first and with flowers that filled the room with delightful, dizzying scent.

Rajiv was furious.

'Change this bed immediately. Get her one with a steel frame. This is – this is – ridiculous!'

A steel bed was installed in the place of the wooden one, and for a time things returned to normal. But it was not so long before another morning visit was met by a room full of white seeds that drifted lazily on the air currents from floor to ceiling, spores emitted by the geometric rows of spiralling grasses that had sprung overnight from the antique Persian rug on the floor of Sapna's room. Genuinely frightened this time, Rajiv called for tests and diagnoses on both grass and Sapna herself. Nothing could be determined, and Sapna had no explanation. They moved her into another bedroom, where a wicker laundry basket burst overnight into a clump of bamboo-like spears that grew through the ceiling and erupted into the room above. Wherever Sapna slept, things burst into life: sheets, clothes, newspapers, antique wardrobes – all rediscovered their ability to grow.

Each encounter with this nocturnal hypertrophy enraged Rajiv. He would stare at the upstart plant matter that invaded his daughter's room with the purest hatred he had ever felt. It began to take him over. He could not work for his visions of galloping, coiling roots and shoots. It sickened him. He ordered all organic matter to be removed from Sapna's bedroom. This controlled things, and for many months their lives were unaffected by this strange phenomenon. But he had been filled with a terror of vegetation, and wherever he went he kept imagining loathsome green shoots sprouting out of car seats and board-room tables.

One morning, as he arrived at her door, he could hear her sobbing quietly inside. Terrified of what he might find, he opened the door slowly. The room was empty and calm, and Sapna lay twisted up in bed.

'I'm bleeding, papa. Between my legs.'

Rajiv's stomach corkscrewed inside him and he ran out of the room. Sweating inside his suit he landed heavily on Mira's bed.

'It's Sapna. She needs you.'

That night, though Sapna's room had received the customary clearing of all organic traces, and though no one heard anything, not even the sleepless Rajiv, a huge neem tree sprang from the dining room, grew up through the ceiling into the room where Sapna slept, branched out through all four walls, filled the floor above her, and broke through the roof of the house. Vines and creepers snaked up the tree during the night, locking it in a sensuous, miscegenetic embrace and disgorging provocative red flowers bursting with seed. By the time everyone awoke in the morning a crowd had already gathered outside the house to look at this extraordinary sight, and photographers were taking pictures for the city papers.

The Malhotra household stared at the tree in the way that people stare at something that cannot be part of the world they inhabit. They kept touching it, touching the places where it had burst through the walls. Rajiv became grim.

'Get this cut down today. Get the walls mended. And then we have to find more of a solution to this.'

The tree was not the only miracle of growth to happen that night, though the other one was only discovered afterwards. Amid the furore of fertility, Mira had fallen pregnant.

Rajiv received a telephone call that day from the Defence Minister.

'Rajiv – would you mind terribly coming in to see me this afternoon? There's something I'd like to discuss with you.'

When Rajiv arrived, a number of senior government officials had gathered to receive him.

'Rajiv, you know how much we admire and value the contribution you make to the nation. That's why we're calling you in like this – informally – so we can avoid any kind of public scandal. It's come to our notice that there have been certain – goings-on – in your household that are both untoward and unusual. Far be it from us to step into the sanctum of your private affairs, of course – but given what has happened this morning, they may not remain private for very long. We need some kind of explanation from you as to what is happening. And we need to work out a solution with you. So that there is no danger to the public. You understand how it is. Yesterday a bud, today a neem tree – tomorrow perhaps we will wake up and see only a forest where our capital city now stands.'

Rajiv was taken aback.

'Yes. Of course. I hadn't really thought about it in those terms.'

'Now tell us – because we are here to hear *your* views – what exactly is happening?'

'To be very honest, I don't have a clue. It seems you probably know as much as I do.'

'And what are you going to do about it?'

'Well, I thought I could prevent it by simply taking certain precautions in the household. But as of this morning I'm not so sure.'

'Rajiv, permit us to throw a few ideas in your direction. We have been putting our heads together on this issue for the last few minutes. One of my honourable friends here thought that your daughter – Sapna, is it? – could be of great service to the nation. Suggested we might use her to recultivate some of the desert regions. An elegant suggestion, but perhaps a little fanciful. From what I can gather, the peculiarities of your daughter's sleep do not obey any obvious scientific principles, and it might be very dangerous to unleash her on the land. No, we gravitated more towards a solution that would involve some sort of – how shall I put it? – confinement. So she can do no harm to anyone – including, we are most anxious to stress, herself.

'From the very beginning all of us, with one voice, dismissed the idea of jail. For what is your daughter guilty of? And how could a young lady with her upbringing be expected to survive alongside all the despicable souls we have in our jails? On the other hand, I am afraid to say we did not feel there would be a place for her in any of our hospitals. Too much in the public eye. Too much risk.

'But there is something between a prison and a hospital that might suit everyone concerned. We have a number of excellent institutions for those of our citizens who are not entirely – ahem – *compos mentis.* Run by true professionals, out of the public eye, nice grounds where the inmates can walk – you know the sort of thing. We thought your daughter might be very happy in a place like that. She could continue her music there, we could conduct the kind of tests that might lead to her eventual recovery and reintegration, and we could ensure she had secure quarters where her own remarkable traits could cause neither upset nor disturbance. What would you say to that?'

None of them was quite prepared for Rajiv's reaction. One must suppose that, even if you are the defence minister of the world's second most populous nation, it is an unnerving sight to see the world's twenty-seventh richest man on his knees before you, weeping.

'Sir, please don't take my daughter from me! She is everything I have, and I love her far, far more than my own wretched life. I will do anything, anything – but do not take her from me. Leave it with me, sir – I promise I will find a way out of this – I have money, resources, friends – we will sort this out, don't worry, we will understand the problem – we will work out how it can be solved in everyone's interest – have faith in me, sir and I will not disappoint you. Only I beg you this – please let me keep my daughter!'

The government officials were silent, and it was some time before the Minister could summon his voice again.

'Very well, Rajiv. Perhaps we have been both unfeeling and insensitive. Please go away and think about this, and let us know what you decide – by Wednesday evening?'

After a very few days, construction began of a large tower just outside Delhi. It was to be built with techniques drawn from the design of semiconductor manufacturing plants: there would be no organic materials, no dust or impurity of any kind, and it would be cleaned twice a day by costly machines. After some consideration it was thought better not to put windows in the building lest influences from outside upset the calm equilibrium of the interior. Rajiv went every day to supervise construction, to ensure that the vast confinement he was building for his daughter was designed and constructed with as much love as possible. A leading architect was commissioned to create a fantastic interior for Sapna that included a library of three thousand books, all specially printed on polyester film, and a music room in which was placed a customized piano built entirely of steel. The drawing room contained a television with the best channels from all over the world. But no light came in from outside, and only Rajiv would keep the key to the door. The outer walls were made entirely of steel, as thick as a man's head. Soon Sapna was transferred there.

She spent her days writing and playing the piano. She only played the western classical repertoire, but she embarked upon a new categorization of it inspired by Hindustani classical music. Her scheme disregarded entirely the biographical accidents that had placed Liszt in Paris or made Beethoven deaf, and paid scant attention to the historical circumstances from which a work sprang or the attendant generic distinctions: 'Baroque', 'Classical', 'Romantic', 'Modern', etc. Instead, Sapna was interested in developing rules for understanding the resonances between a particular arrangement of musical sound and the natural universe, especially as apprehended by the human emotions.

She chose the expanse of the 24-hour clock face as the map on which the results of her enquiry would be plotted. Every one of its 1,440-minute gradations was held to represent a certain configuration of emotions and natural truths (after a while she found the need to analyse down to the level of the individual second) and these in turn corresponded to the different combinations of the musical 'essences' (her term) that could be found in individual pieces of music. She developed a set of diagrams rather like astrological charts to facilitate the complex series of judgements that had to be made in order to uncover the essences of every piece of music and thus allocate it to the correct second of the day.

After she had spent much time correcting the flaws in her system and writing out her treatise, she devoted herself to applying it to the entire piano repertoire, playing a particular piece of music slightly earlier or slightly later each day until she was satisfied that she had hit upon the exact moment at which it achieved that special resonance, rather like a dim room in the thick of a city that is ignited with sunlight for two glorious minutes every day. Most of Bach's suites (and, contrary to their name, a couple of Chopin's *Nocturnes*) came in the morning, although many of the preludes and fugues belonged to the dead of night. The more she perfected her system, the more it seemed that time was the lost secret of European classical music. When she sat, eyes closed before her piano, waiting for the precise instant of the day (about 6.02 in the evening) for which the opening bars of Beethoven's last piano sonata were intended, when she struck out, astonishingly, into its angular chords, it made everything anyone had heard before sound like the indistinct irritation of hotel lobby soundtracks. When restored – for that is how it felt – to its correct relationship with time, the music seemed to draw itself in the sky, to stride across the constellations and fill people's hearts with an elation they had imagined but never felt. Crowds would come to listen outside the tower where she played; they would sit in silence in the street and feel that they were experiencing 6.02*ness* as they never had before.

Sapna's father visited her every evening. Every day she would have discovered new things through her reading or from the television that she wanted to discuss with him. He loved her more and more; and as his wife's pregnancy advanced and she gave birth to a healthy and perfect baby boy, he also felt himself to be in her debt. 'It is Sapna who restored my fertility to me, even at this late stage in my life,' he thought. 'She it is who has finally brought me the son I requested from Dr Hall, so many years ago.' The fact that his wife had turned her back on Sapna and decided that the whole business of her first pregnancy – illegitimately obtained, she now felt – was a curse she should have nothing more to do with; the fact that Rajiv's new and otherwise ideal son hated the idea of Sapna from the moment he became conscious of her, would fly into a fury whenever his father unheedingly referred to her as his 'sister', and despised him for the care and time he lavished upon the 'freak in the tower' – all this only increased for Rajiv the poignancy of his daughter's situation. He never ceased to feel the pain of her incarceration. 'She deserves so much more.' It broke his heart every evening to leave her there, and lock the door. Every night he stayed slightly longer, listening to her music or discussing literature or history.

One thing she never discussed with him was the fact that she had fallen in love with a television star. A television star with a bull-shaped head.

The shrunken baby Imran had grown up under the loving care of his parents who lived in the ramshackle bookshop his father ran in a backstreet near to where the tides of the Arabian Sea are broken by the minareted island of Haji Ali's tomb. The tiny shop had everything: not only guidebooks, innumerable editions of the Koran and stacks of poetry in Arabic, Farsi and Urdu, but also perfumes, potions, and pendants with prayers engraved upon them. Pilgrims from small towns would come for souvenirs: plastic wall clocks that showed, behind the inconstant wavering hands, the steadfastness of the marble tomb whose domes were topped with flashing red and yellow lights for effect ('Keeps perfect time! Will last for years.'); calendars that showed the Ka'aba surrounded by majestic whizzing planets and crescent moons in magentas and emerald greens; novelty prayer mats on which the arch of a mihrab framed a spectacular paradise of golden domes and minarets and silver palm trees. Sleeping on the shop counter, baby Imran would stay awake watching the Turkic elegance of the Muslim wonders waxing and waning in the night sky by the intermittent illumination of hundreds of gaily-coloured LEDs.

He grew slowly and unevenly. His shoulders became broad and sinewy while his legs remained thin and short. His arms were too long for his dwarfish body and from an early age he walked with a simian gait that inspired scorn and hatred among his classmates. They taunted him above all for the size and shape of his enormous head that became more and more solid with the years and whose protruding nose and jaw gave it an undeniable taurine air. Neighbourhood graffiti speculated gleefully about the various kinds of unnatural coupling that could have given rise to such a strange creature: monkeys took their cackling pleasure at the backsides of oblivious-seeming sheep, and bulls threatened to split open the bulbous behinds of curvaceous maidens. One cartoon, hastily erased by the authorities, showed an entire narrative in which a woman, anxious for a child, ate the raw testes of a bull, a meal that resulted not in her own pregnancy but that of her cow. It was an artist of some skill who had drawn the final scene in which the woman stole out by night to seize the bloody baby from the vulva of the cow and put it carefully into bed between her husband and herself. The entire story was narrated by a pointing, moralizing goat.

Imran's parents were naturally upset by the indignities suffered by their son, and eventually gave in to his insistence that he should not attend school. He spent his days in the bookshop instead, and consumed volumes of poetry that he would recite aloud for the entertainment of customers. In time, word of his remarkable performances spread, and the bookshop would be surrounded during the day by crowds of eager listeners who could not find room inside. The very oddness of his body seemed to lend an expressivity to his interpretations that captivated everyone who heard him, and his outsized chest and neck produced a voice that gave the impression of being drawn from a vast well of emotion. Through him, his audience was able to bypass the difficulties of the Farsi or the archaisms of the Urdu and understand the true meaning of the poet. 'It is amazing', one said, 'that such a young boy should be able to overpower us with his expression of such adult emotions: the yearnings of a lover for his beloved, and of a believer for the Almighty. We have yearned for many things, but never have we seen such yearning as this.' Another replied, 'When he talks about the pain of being trapped in time while longing for the eternal we can all finally understand how truly burdensome it is to be temporal creatures, and how glorious eternity must be!' Imran's body, its hulking shoulders and massive head supported by a withered frame, seemed to symbolize in flesh the poets' theme of manly, religious passion trapped in woefully insignificant human form, and no one who heard him could again imagine those poems except on his lips.

When not in his father's shop, Imran wandered. Since his appearance provoked fear and dismay among the city's clean and well-to-do, he gravitated towards out-of-the-way places where people were less easily repulsed. He learned the art of appearing utterly insignificant, and thus of passing unnoticed through public places; he slipped completely unseen through the bustling centres of the city only to reappear suddenly at a dhaba or a paan shop where he would exchange handshakes and quiet greetings with five different people. His friendships were forged with marginal characters who made their money from small-time illegal businesses, and they all loved him: for he told jokes with extravagant grimaces that made them roar with laughter, and he always knew ten people who could solve any problem. They came to him with questions: where the best tea could be found, who sold car parts the most cheaply, where you could find a safe abortion, who would be able to get rid of five hundred mobile phones quickly.

One afternoon he found himself in a tiny bar in Juhu where his friends often congregated to play cards and talk business. There was no illumination except for the strips of pure light around the blinds, and the hubbub of heat and taxis and street sellers outside was reduced to a distant murmur. As they drank under the languorous fans, one of them announced:

'Now Imran will recite us a poem!'

Imran declined, but there was much clapping and encouragement, an empty beer glass was banged rousingly on the table, the bartender came over and made his insistences – and finally he assented. He began to recite a ballad, beginning in such a low voice that they all had to lean towards him to hear.

His ballad told of a princess, long ago, who had been the pride and joy of the king and queen and her brother the prince. She was beautiful and could sing songs that made all of nature sit down and listen. And she had hair of pure gold.

One day the princess was carried off by an ugly monster who was shrunken and evil looking and coveted the gold from her head. He shaved off all her hair and made himself rich, and imprisoned her in a tall tower to wait for the hair to grow back. But it grew back so slowly he realized he would have to wait years before there would be such a quantity again. He devoted himself to devising potions to make her hair grow more quickly. Imran's voice rose: how evil was this monster! and how absolutely comic at the same time! As he told the story, the creature became real for them all; they listened in fascination, they cried with laughter as Imran screwed up his face and recited lists of foul extracts and hideous amputations that the monster would rub into the princess's delicate scalp or mix with her tea.

Her brother was grief-stricken at her disappearance and left the palace to go and find her. He wandered endlessly; his body became scratched by thorns and eaten by fleas, but still he did not give up. Eventually he heard a wonderful voice singing in the distance, and as he came closer he recognized it as his sister's; yes indeed, he could glimpse her face through a tiny window at the top of a tall tower. But, though she saw him too, and was happy he had come, he was unable to rescue her, for there was no way into the tower except through a door that was always locked and the tiny window that was at a great height from the ground.

So the prince planted a tree that would grow tall and strong and allow him to climb up and rescue his sister. He would tend the tree lovingly every night, but it grew very slowly, and every day he would mourn the days that she was losing in the tower. His love was so strong and so selfless! and the tough souls who listened to Imran were moved to silence, for they had never heard such a pure expression of yearning as this.

One day the monster found the formula that would make the princess's hair grow. As soon as he applied his ointment it began to sprout quickly from her head, and in a few minutes was thick and dazzling and hung down to her knees. He let out a scream of inhuman triumph, cut it all off at once and went away to sell it.

As soon as he had gone, the princess took his stinking cauldron and tipped it out of the window. Immediately, the infant tree began to climb towards the sky. In a few minutes it was halfway to the window, branches and twigs and leaves appearing in dazzling patterns, growing around the tower in an arboreal embrace, and bathing its bone-white stone in shade. As it grew, the prince started to climb and was borne upwards on the swelling trunk. Soon it reached all the way to the window, and the princess leapt into her brother's arms and kissed him joyfully.

But the tree did not stop growing. No matter how fast they tried to climb downwards the tree continued to carry them higher and higher into the air. Frantically, they tried to descend, but now the tower was far below them and they were in the very heavens.

At that point the monster returned, and realized at once what had happened. Furious, he took a great axe and began to chop at the tree. With powerful blows he cut away at the trunk until it finally began to sway. With a mighty crash it fell to the ground, crushing the tower to powder. And the prince and princess were no more.

The men were quiet.

'Why did they have to die?'

'Well, what did you expect?' replied Imran, amused that his audience had become so affected. 'They were brother and sister. Were they going to get married and live happily ever after?'

'I suppose not.'

But they were glum.

Then, from the shadowy corner of the bar, a solitary figure began to applaud. None of them had noticed him before.

'Wonderful! Wonderful! It is years since I have seen a performance like that. You have a fine talent, sir! I would like to see more of what you can do. Allow me to introduce myself. I am a senior executive with an advertising company – as my business card will show. I would like very much to introduce you to some highly influential people I happen to know here in Bombay. I think you may be just what they are looking for. With your permission, of course. Your monster was quite extraordinary. So terrifying, and yet so humorously delivered! I can see a glittering career, sir! There are so few true actors these days.'

And so it was, after a dizzying succession of meetings and auditions, that Imran became the 'Plaque Devil' for Colgate toothpaste, in one of the most successful advertising campaigns that India had ever seen. A loathsome, misshapen figure that forced an entry into happy, brightly-lit households, and caused merry dental chaos through his evil schemes until finally repulsed by a laser-filled tube of Colgate, he became a cultural phenomenon such as advertising companies dream of. Children imitated him in the schoolyard, and magazines gave away free Plaque Devil stickers that would adorn the very walls where once graffiti had made shameful innuendos about Imran's birth. Youngsters found in the character a welcome focus for rebellious feelings, while parents approved of its pedagogic potential and felt that at least their offspring's unseemly roars and menacing ape-like walk might result in healthier teeth.

This was only the beginning for Imran. Every company wanted him in their advertisements, and soon his much-prized deformity had become the embodiment of every kind of threat to middle-class life: germs, crime, poverty, unwise consumer decisions. Within an astonishingly short time he had become one of the most recognizable faces in India, rivalling Bollywood stars and cricket players for space on cereal packets and soft-drink displays. He was an anti-hero who seemed to complete at a profound level the otherwise beautiful and perfect media pantheon.

But the true extent of his stardom was confirmed when he was cast as the demon Ravana in Star TV's eight-hour epic, *The Ramayana*. Screened in its entirety from morning to evening on Independence Day, this was billed as the biggest media event the country had ever seen, with stunning digital effects and a cast of megastars bringing the ancient myths to life in ways never before imagined. The digital manipulation that placed an additional nine heads on Imran's shoulders (whose unnatural broadness seemed built to receive them) was lifelike and spell-binding, and everyone agreed that it was this character more than any other that turned the show into the immense hit it became. He was an incomparable demon – and a strangely magnetic one. Though women across the country shuddered as the grotesque character abducted Sita from her beautiful royal husband, as he tried to seduce her into betraying Ram and accepting the queenship of his own demon kingdom, they could not help but feel in his entreaties a depth of longing that they had never encountered in their own lives; and in spite of their disgust, despite the fact they knew it could never happen, they were fascinated by the idea that the unwavering Sita might relent and they would see what a passionate and generous lover he might be. When Hanuman and his computer-generated monkey hordes swept down on Lanka and finally defeated the demon, it was not without feelings of confusion that they accepted the restoration of Sita to her rightful husband.

Imran's life had changed. He had become wealthy and famous, and his cellphone rang constantly with new offers of work and money. But he was not invited to the soirées of the beautiful people, and he remained an outsider to the constant spectacle of Bombay social life. He spent his evenings at the same backstreet bars and dhabas, and avoided the thoroughfares of the city even more assiduously than before. But former friends became distrustful of his sudden wealth and institutionalization, and new ones seemed to have motives he did not like. And in his increasing isolation he began to reflect more and more on the deep yearning that had filled him for as long as he could remember. For some reason, he had a strong feeling that it had some-thing to do with the mysterious figure who came every year on his birthday to give money to his parents.

When Imran's next birthday came around he positioned himself across the street from the bookshop to wait for the immaculately dressed man who came every year to hand over a packet of money and exchange a few whispered words in the back before hurriedly departing. Though Imran had asked his parents many times who this man was they had never told him the secret.

The man arrived at the end of the morning as expected, and as he bid his surreptitious farewells Imran began to follow him. He walked quickly, conspicuous in his suit, turned two corners, and slid into the back of a black Mercedes that sped off northwards on Marine Drive. Imran stopped a taxi: 'Follow that car!'

They passed the dilapidated British frontages, manoeuvred through the jam of other taxis, drove over the massive concrete flyovers near Bandra from where you could see a forest of giant movie star hoardings sprouting from the rubble, in whose shade families sought cooler stones to make their life on, passed undulating townships of corrugated iron and tarpaulin reflected in the blind mirror exteriors of the corporate towers, and finally reached the airport.

The man checked in for a business-class seat to Delhi, and Imran bought an economy-class ticket on the same plane. He had put on loose clothes, walked taller, tried to look inconspicuous. No one seemed to notice that Star TV's Ravana was treading the earth among them.

The sun had almost set by the time Imran's quarry drew up before the Malhotra mansion on Prithviraj Road. Imran began to ask people, 'Who lives in that house?' No one could tell him anything to explain the yearly visits to his family in Bombay.

'He is a very rich man,' said a beggar with wild grey hair. 'And a very cruel one. The rumour says that he keeps his daughter locked up in a tower. She plays wonderful music, but he never lets her out.'

'Where is the tower?' asked Imran.

'It is far from here. I could take you there.'

'Yes. Please do.'

As Imran took one last look at the house it seemed to him that it must have suffered some kind of catastrophe in the past. Ill-matching materials had been used to repair what looked like giant holes in the roof and walls. He wondered what could have caused such a violent thing in such a genteel street.

Only the entrance of the tower was lit, and it was difficult to see how large it was by night. Imran struck it with his fist. The steel was very thick. He looked at the strange structure in disbelief.

'He keeps his daughter in here?'

'Yes. Everyone around here knows about her.'

'Is she grown-up?'

'She must be a woman now. No one has seen her for years.'

'Why did he put her here?'

'I cannot tell you.'

Just then, their conversation was interrupted by the sound of a piano. It was a sound so astonishing that Imran fell involuntarily to his knees. It was as if ten hands played simultaneously, every hand that of a celestial being, filled with knowledge that humans could not imagine, confident of an eternal beauty that was siphoned from another world into every musical note, causing it to swell beyond itself until it was no longer just music; until scales and trills became glorious light that struck Imran behind the retina, until melodies created holes in the sky that shifted over each other until, as the logic of the music became clear, and for a brief instant only, all the holes lined up in a perfect tunnel that led up into the heavens and ended in that thing that Imran had been longing for all his life – and then the gaps in the sky drifted apart again and disappeared, and the music resolved into its finale.

Imran was left winded and limp. For a time he could not talk, but knelt on the ground supporting his heavy head in his hands. At length he looked up at the tower.

'I have to meet her.'

'I can't see how you would do that. No one ever meets her.'

'I will find a way.'

Imran spent the next few days exploring the out-of-the-way places of this city he did not know, looking for people who could help him plan his break-in. He struck up conversations with shopkeepers and restaurant owners, followed connections until he found dead ends, stood by night among sleeping bodies and campfires in dormant office

80

complexes for rendezvous that did not happen, called lists of mobile phone numbers only for suspicious men to hang up on him. But in the end his work paid off, and he had assembled explosives and firearms and a small team to prepare the blast and guard their operation.

Dressed in black, they met at the tower in the early hours of the morning on a night when the moon was just a nick in the sky. The drowsy security guard was deftly disarmed and gagged, and they set about putting their explosives in place. Imran's new-found expert slapped the steel as if it were a boisterous friend.

'I would say it's about eight inches thick. No way we can blast through it. We'd make a very big noise and this baby would still be sitting here smiling back at us. But you can see it's made of eight-foot panels welded together and we can blast at the joins. Don't worry. We can pop one of these big ladies easy as putting your eye out.'

With that he and his companion began to drill into the joins with the unabashed scream of steel on steel.

'Quiet, for God's sake!' hissed Imran.

'Do you want to get in here or not?' He fixed Imran with the glare of a master workman who needs no counsel, and Imran gestured his submission. Drills fired up once more, puncturing the smooth exterior and ejecting fine spirals of silver, while Imran winced at this racket in the night and looked around for the security people who would certainly descend on them. But no one came; and soon the panel was framed by twelve even holes, and the men were filling them with a paste like halwa.

'Let's talk it through one more time. The blast will pop her outwards. No one stands in the way. You'll be disorientated – think through your actions now. You three are going in with torches. Remember your way back. Once you get out you turn right – look at where the van is waiting. Are you ready?'

Imran looked up at the gloomy tower, and could not get rid of the thought, 'Did I dream this once before?' His heart was hammering in his throat.

The massive steel panel burst cleanly out of the wall and landed in the dust in an explosion so loud that everything in its wake was just a numb rumble. He staggered from the force of the blast, took hold of his thoughts, reached for his flashlight, and plunged into the swirling dust that filled the neat square hole in the wall. He ran into the room – and stopped short.

The lights were on, and Sapna stood shivering before him, clasping herself in a shawl, her eyes wide. He stood motionless, looking. She was beautiful to him, and her eyes answered his own in many mysterious ways; her very reality seemed astonishing, as if suddenly the afterimage that rippled briefly on corneal waters whenever he looked away from the sun, the presence that had for so long shimmered just beyond his senses, had at last become solid – this was true; but why was it that, as he looked, as he wished for all the clocks of the world to stop for the moment of his looking, his head was distracted, filled with other kinds of ticks and tocks that were not to do with time, that were the sound of a mechanism falling into place, the dials of a mighty safe lining up and opening, not just an eight-foot-square steel entrance but a channel between worlds that brought things unaccustomedly close and in an instant made the yearning of the poets of his childhood seem quaint and unnecessary; and as confusion raced like police sirens through the exhilarating night of his encounter, even as the men began to shout from behind and, in that other dimension, time was still galloping onwards, even as somewhere he was aware of how he must look, bursting in from the night at the head of a band of men with guns and a job to do, he knew now that all the reservoir of his desire, which had jangled inside him all his life, which filled his very chromosomes and made them yell out in the darkness, had not been enough to prepare him for this domino-like unfolding of everything he thought was solid around the trembling form of the woman who now stood before him.

'What is happening? Get him out of there! Let's go!'

Sapna continued to look at him.

'Am I dreaming this again?' she said, as if puzzled. 'Or is it really you this time?'

Imran stood stupidly; but anyway he was not given time to respond as the men grabbed him and Sapna and dragged them both outside.

His mind whirled and he followed them in a daze, lights flashed all around him, and there was a shift in reality; he tried to wake himself up to it, it seemed urgent . . .

They were surrounded. A ring of policemen shone bright lights at them, pointed guns.

'You fucking idiot,' the explosives chief shouted at Imran. 'I thought you had it in you. You froze. Now we're all fucked.'

They dropped their weapons and were grouped together and handcuffed. The night seemed strangely big, and the red and blue lights of the police vans hurt the eyes. One of the policemen was on the phone.

'Six men. One of them's deformed. Reminds me of someone, actually. The girl's here too . . . The Defence Minister? Why? It's three in the morning . . . Oh. I see . . . I'll wait for you to call me back.'

They were all made to lie down on the ground. It began to rain. The phone rang.

'Yes? Hello, Sir . . . Yes . . . A sort of dwarf . . . You're exactly right. Just like a bull . . . Rajiv Malhotra? I see . . . No, we'll make very sure. We'll be very discreet . . . Yes, I know the place . . . The girl too? I don't think the girl is an accomplice in this, sir . . . She doesn't *look* dangerous . . . Of course. Very good.'

Thus it was that slightly before dawn, Imran and Sapna were locked into adjacent rooms in a high-security mental asylum that sat in the middle of large grounds in an unobtrusive location on the outskirts of the city.

For three days, high-ranking government officials thought of nothing but the Malhotra Issue. Rajiv Malhotra had asked for three days to conduct his own investigation into what had happened, during which time his daughter would remain in the asylum along with the ugly creature who was, it now turned out, none other than the star of *The Ramayana* and of so many memorable advertisements whose makers would be horrified when they found out that the deviant creature they had taken pity on, sponsored, and enriched was in real life a far more sinister kind of interloper than the antisocial influences he had been asked to portray on television. A low-class loner with sick thoughts whom even wealth and fame had not been able to civilize, who still kept the company of illegal elements, a criminal of the worst sort who destroyed private property by night in the throes, no doubt, of a monstrous sexual hunger for whose gratification he could not avail himself of the standard amenities but conceived instead an intricate plot to assault the decency of a daughter of the city's leading family. No one could understand why it was that Rajiv Malhotra extended his three days' protection to such a despicable character, but the connections of businessmen as prominent as he always extended into murky places and it was best not to ask. For three days phone calls passed between the Defence Minister, the director of the asylum, the Chief of Police, and Rajiv Malhotra himself. The officials were stern with the businessman: he had failed in his guarantee to manage his daughter's Situation without the assistance of the State, and no concessions beyond the three days were allowed him. He was not permitted to visit the asylum or to speak to either of its new inmates.

For three days, Sapna did not sleep. Day and night she stood at her fifth-floor window looking out. The grounds were well kept, and the gardeners had recently planted infant trees around the foot of the building. Keeping watch with the police was her brother, Rajiv's model son whom Sapna had only seen in photographs and who was now a tall, handsome teenager. He had taken it upon himself to ensure, as his clammy-hearted father did not seem to be able to, that no security breaches happened this time, and surveyed the window where she stood with a self-confident hatred that chilled her heart.

For three days she looked out, thinking again of those moments in the television epic when the ten-headed Ravana had attempted to seduce the woefully chaste Sita, with what words! and what yearning! How she had treasured the voice of a man who could desire like that, and how many times had she imagined that her own incarceration might be ended with such a magnificent abduction. What course of events, what impossible, impenetrable strangeness, could have brought that man to her and propelled him through the walls of her cage? What spirit could have caused her dream to be recreated so precisely in reality?

For three days she thought continually on these things. And then she slept.

Imran awoke to find himself in a room with no floor, hanging onto the bars of his window with bloodless fingers.

Buds of bulging paintwork were appearing all over the walls; green shoots burst from them, wavered for a second as if waiting for a distant vegetal communication, suddenly found direction, and streaked up through the ceiling, swelling into vast boughs of furrowed wood and splitting the room apart. He looked down through the bars where he hung: the circle of saplings had grown into giants, their tops soaring into the sky, branches spreading out inside the building as if reaching for a prey, fusing with the bricks and – yes! even as he watched! – lifting the entire asylum clean off the ground and carrying it aloft. The room tipped and Imran was standing upright on the wall, the window bars popped out and fell to the grass that was already far below, the bricks that separated him from his sister collapsed in a cascade: and there was Sapna, still asleep in her bed.

He shook her awake; and already she was running with him, leaping the crevasses that were opening under their feet, fighting through corridors that were quickly becoming impassable from rubble and dust and people. Everywhere there were people in white, inmates who giggled uncontrollably as unseen hands flung wide their cell doors, who shuffled into the hallways, who clucked and ticked and screamed as the floors buckled and sent them sliding on their backsides down the inclines, genitals waving in the air. They instinctively crowded together, drained from the building's extremities towards its heart, packed the stairwell, told stories to the sky as they plunged also through the solid floors of their madness into the gulfs and gardens that lay below. The stairs thronged with figures in white; and, as Imran and Sapna clutched hands and watched from above, the ring of trees wrenched the building in all directions; it opened like a flower, and its centre fell out and crashed to the ground. There was sky above them and ground below, and all around them, in amphitheatrical cutaway, were the stacked worlds of the hospital, from whose truncated edges hung screaming people who eventually had to loose their grip and fall one by one through the open well of the building onto the pile of stone and steel below.

From his sentry post where he had made up for the shameful laxity of the police observers with his own unsleeping surveillance, Rajiv's model son watched in horror as the asylum broke open like a wasp's nest, as white-robed pupae began to rain from it and wriggle away who knew where, ready to infiltrate the city and lay new eggs of their own in its fissures and sewers. It was not thus that his father's girl child and her accomplice creature would find their escape. He seized a rifle from one of the still sleeping policemen and began to climb one of the trees.

Imran and Sapna teetered on the edge of their gaping concrete tree house as shots began to strike the people around them. He dragged Sapna down, 'Quick, we have to jump for it', but already she was struck and was lying breathless over his knee, blood welling from above her hip onto the floor. Bullets still flew, stopping the shrieks of women in their throats, lodging in the plaster. A red stain fanned out from Sapna's side across the ground, the racing trees slowed down, grew in weaker and weaker bursts that seemed to keep time with Sapna's fading heartbeat, and finally stopped. The raging bedlam of exploding cellulose and masonry ceased, and there was quiet. The wind sighed through the branches, and the azan sounded far away. Sapna lay white and motionless.

With a roar, Imran flew at the gunman who was his brother. He scrambled across the still branches and hanging lintels, spread wide his enormous arms, ran with a fury that was too mad and too fast for fingers to find their grip or bullets to be loaded, and alighted on the branch where the killer leant before he could clamber off it. He struck the rifle from his grasp and, with trembling mouth still searching for a curse terrible enough, seized him by the throat, squeezed his skull with his outsized sinews, and snapped his neck with a single flourish of rage. He held him for a moment to let the poison of his anger seep in and dispatch him still further, clasped the brother he did not know he had, supported his body until the force had gone entirely, and let him drop to the ground below, limbs outstretched and head waggling uselessly.

With a sense that all the world had ended, Imran clambered back to where Sapna lay. He crossed the tangle of branches in despair, neared the circle of white people that knelt around her, that parted as he approached, knelt down among them himself – and saw something miraculous.

Sapna lay with her eyes closed, breathing deeply and slowly, her body glowing with health. The wound had already healed. And a small plant had sprouted from the concrete, shading her face from the early morning sun with its single leaf. He reached out to touch her cheek with confusion and hope. She opened her eyes and looked into his troubled face.

'What's wrong? I was only sleeping.' ·

He nodded mutely. She took his hand and stood up, they climbed down the broad, placid trunks to the ground, and were gone.

It was early in the morning, far from the centre of the city, and the Chief of Police was sleeping through his jangling phone. All in all, by the time forces had been mobilized it was far too late. The small group of policemen that had been guarding the asylum could do nothing to staunch the flood of people in white who wandered out and into the city. Thousands of people spread out into the dawn as the streets awoke: they sat in rows on the kerb to watch food stalls setting up, stripped off their clothes and jumped into a fountain where they splashed each other joyfully and clasped strangers to themselves in glee, wandered into homes and sat expectantly at breakfast tables while families circled about them in bewilderment, lay down to sleep on the cool marble floors of mosques and temples, played with street dogs, cried long and heartfelt tears at the sight of a broken car by the side of the road, climbed into rickshaws and waited for someone to take them where they needed to go, munched noisily on fruit from stalls whose owners were too troubled to stop them, and issued harsh warnings to people who did not seem to be there. Two old men held hands and limped together through the streets, arguing every time they came to a turning about which was the right way, improvising a dialogue of retired gentlemen out for a morning stroll, holding heads absurdly high and wielding imaginary walking sticks. In the confusion it was easy for Imran and Sapna to slip away. By the time the police blockades were in place they had disappeared.

They wandered through the day until the city became sparse, and children ran among earth streets and disappeared into courtyards that were warm with the smell of buffalo.

They hid amid the rusty trellis of an abandoned farm building, its roof long since collapsed. They lay under the stars, Imran thinking back to the silver moons and planets that had flashed above him in the night when he was a baby.

They had a deep and thirsty sex that forced them apart to the excruciating limit of their yearning, and brought them back until their souls coalesced in nectar.

They slept; and when they awoke in the heat of the next day they were cooled by a shady bower of mangoes and hibiscus.

Both of his children – for he had become accustomed to disremembering Imran – had grown up, and Rajiv Malhotra's body, which had never learned to restore itself after expenditure, seemed to have shrunk correspondingly. He was now gaunt and wizened, and his flesh hung from his bones like ragged, long-abandoned laundry on a line. His passion for his business had gone and he lived only for the fast-approaching day when he could abandon himself to his fatigue and pass on the entire empire to his son.

One day, however, the other son, the son he had banished, returned to abduct his daughter from her safe enclosure in the tower and a certain regime of order, which had by now almost completely silted over the past, came to an end.

During his three days' grace he had pieced together the series of events that had brought Imran and Sapna together, had watched the sun rise on the fourth day all ready to welcome back his wayward son and take responsibility for whatever wrongs he might have committed, ready to call the Minister and submit to any demand – 'I will build two new towers if I have to!'

But things had happened differently. The phone rang as he reached to dial – the police: his children, one dead, after killing a number of bystanders, the other two vanished. 'A great tragedy, Sir. Your only son and heir. We cannot begin to imagine how you feel.'

That night, as, by gradual cell-to-cell osmosis, grief slowly flooded his body, Rajiv was forced to abandon the idea of the future. As his surviving children, Imran and Sapna, made love in a decrepit warehouse, as their groins heaved with the effort of penetrating all that separated them, as their bodies hinged extravagantly at their join and exulted in the rightness of lying suspended together in the darkness, Rajiv started to breathe more slowly with something that felt like relief. And then, for the first time in his life, he slept.

Oh boy oh boy oh boy!

Now we have a night of stories!

He was almost glowing with it.

When I was a student in Tokyo we always used to spend our nights like this. Cheapest form of entertainment when you're a student! But our stories weren't like these. Tonight we will really have a night. Oh boy! A beautiful rich girl and an ugly dwarf. And they don't even realize they are brother and sister! Love is always strange. Don't you agree? Always looks the same from the outside, always speaks in the same clichés. But behind everything, underneath it all, it is never as it seems. At least that is my humble opinion – and believe me I am not any kind of expert! Not at all. If you only knew!

He took out a hip flask as he spoke, unscrewed the top and took an enthusiastic swig. He held it out to his fellow travellers. There were some polite refusals, but a young woman took it gratefully.

THE HOUSE OF THE FRANKFURT MAPMAKER

The Fourth Story

THERE ONCE WAS a mapmaker named Klaus Kaufmann who lived in Frankfurt. He spent his life collecting every kind of map imaginable, and compiling them all into a complete electronic plan of the planet –

Air routes
Archaeological sites
Canal systems
Climate
Crops
Demographics
Electricity systems
Housing projects
Legal systems
Natural resources
Postal systems
Price indices
Rock and soil types
Sea routes
Telecommunications networks

– and so on. He would meet with people who knew everything about a tiny section of the world – a railway minister here, a municipal planning official there – and persuade them to connect their computer systems directly to his own so that his map would always display the most recent knowledge on any subject. It was designed to answer every possible cartographic question, and to replace every other map that had ever existed. 'After this map is complete,' joked Klaus, 'my colleagues had better find other planets to devote their time to!'

On one occasion Klaus made a visit to Turkey. He wished to obtain from officials in that country more authoritative information about shipping in the Black Sea and Mediterranean. Profound changes were taking place in this area, and his map was starting to seem exasperatingly inexact.

'You have come to the right place,' said a pristine official in the Ministry of Transport while yellowing electric fans stirred the air and an attendant served glasses of tea that Klaus eyed with distaste. 'You know the cliché about my country: *the crossroads of three continents.* We are the only nation to have a coastline on both seas, and counting ships in the Bosporus is one of our national pastimes. I will of course give you everything you need. No problem. Please – drink your tea.'

Klaus ignored the direction.

'But I spy a little opportunity for my own interests to be advanced in the process. Maybe while I am so busy scratching your back I might turn around and enjoy a little scratching myself? Do you see what I mean?'

Klaus stood stiffly out of reach of these waves of camaraderie and waited to hear the bargain.

'You see: the Bosporus is woefully clogged with ships coming in from the Mediterranean to fetch oil from the Black Sea countries. Our safety regulations are stretched to their limits and our coastal environment is, you will sympathize, the worse for wear. We have been trying for years to get international support for the pipeline running from Baku directly to our Mediterranean coast, thus removing the need for such traffic. In this we enjoy the precious backing of our American brothers and sisters, who naturally do not like any solutions that would put the oil into the hands of renegades like Russia and Iran. The disputes have been going on for years. But perhaps if you mark the pipeline on your map it will help to push things in our direction. Make it already a little bit concrete, so to speak . . . May I suggest you pay a visit to my colleagues in the south to view the site for yourself? It will help you, too: I think this information would make your map much more – how should I say it? – prescient, no?'

Klaus had wrestled with the infuriating political uncertainties of the Baku-Tbilisi-Ceyhan pipeline for a long time, and welcomed the prospect of better intelligence.

'I will go. Tell me who I should speak to.'

'Mr Ozkan, my secretary, will give you the name of a very senior man in Ceyhan. An old friend of mine. He will take very good care of you.'

At eight o' clock the next morning Klaus checked out of the Sheraton Ankara Hotel, put his lightweight suit carrier and laptop in the back of his Hertz rental car, and drove out of the car park. At the exit he paused to enter 'Ceyhan' into the satellite navigation system, and a woman's voice told him confidently in English that there remained 515.7 kilometres to his destination and instructed him to turn right.

The sky was lofty and blue, and the day seemed full of promise. The windows of the glitzy international stores reflected cheerful scenes of the early morning street; people read newspapers and talked on mobile phones. A man in a wheelchair was affixing five different posters of Atatürk to the front of an abandoned shop, with a handwritten sign saying 'TL 1.5m'. The single-mindedness that Klaus's vocation demanded left no time for lingering in the places he visited, but he liked the sense of momentum that he got from carrying out his purposes against so many different backdrops. He followed the purposeful electronic voice around just a few more corners of morning commuters and tradesmen, the city disappeared, and he was speeding south on the D750.

Ankara clung to the road for a while: sprawling car showrooms, masonry yards where squares of marble stood ready for hotel floors, warehouses in primary colours, food-processing plants, and endless kilometres of skeletal concrete apartment blocks on which, even at this early hour, the day's work was well underway. And then all that fell away, and he was in the scrubland of the Anatolian plateau. A few villages spotted the countryside: neat whitewashed houses with naked bicycle wheels for aerials – and then even they ceased, and there was only stone and tarmac.

The straight road ran through a dip in the landscape that was as dry and choked as the inside of a clay oven. He switched on the air conditioning. Soothing air began to hiss all around him, cooling the interior of the car to a comfortable 21°C. He tried the radio: syrupy Turkish pop made him leap on the ▶▶ button; he traversed the spectrum, jumping determinedly off each island of cacophonous religious music or frenetic DJ chat back into an electronic sea until finally he alighted on a performance of Bartók's 'Duke Bluebeard's Castle.' He began to listen with some satisfaction as the ill-fated Judith opened the doors of her fearsome husband's castle, singing of fear and suspicion in what was, he allowed, a fine rendition.

The sun rose high over shimmering igneous craters and obelisks, where just a few lone olive trees clutched onto the rock face. He had not imagined that a place could be so empty. As morning vaporized into day, the disc of the sun dilated until the whole sky became white with heat. The black road became a strip of mirrored steel disappearing into the glare, and the horizon began to tremble feverishly. Next to the 21 on his dashboard was a 48 coming from outside. He realized he had not paid the journey enough thought, had not so much as put a bottle of water in the car.

Electromagnetic whistles and roars started to encroach on Judith's melodious soprano. He refused to abandon the opera, wanting to believe that it would return at the next dip in the hills, round the next outcrop; but gradually the voice faded away completely and there was only a babble of ghostly conversations and what sounded like the moans of vast underwater monsters.

The engine sent out a discreet distress call: a red thermometer pulsating by the petrol gauge. 'Shit!' he shouted, slapping the steering wheel. This was no place to break down. He took the next exit from the highway: there must be a village where he could get water and food and let the car cool down. Set off again in the early evening. This heat was ridiculous. Mad.

He drove for twenty kilometres without seeing a building or a human being. The distraught navigation system, still fixated on Ceyhan, kept telling him to make a U-turn when it was safe to do so, but he drove on and on, looking for some place where he could shelter. And then the power disappeared from under his foot and the car coasted to a silent halt. The air conditioning shut down and the 21 immediately started to climb. The car would not start again, and Klaus began to sweat into the seat. 'I can run the air conditioning off the battery for only another few minutes,' he thought. 'Really and truly I might die here if I stay where I am.'

He tried his mobile phone, but there was no signal. He got out of the car. The sun mocked his thick hair and pummelled his scalp, while gusts of dusty wind sucked mercilessly at the moisture in his body. He took his shirt off and draped it like a hood over his head, took his laptop and the Hertz rental agreement from the car, locked it, and began to walk.

There was nothing except heat. Heat that he could not see through, through which he could make no decisions. His deep breathing surrendered all his last liquids to the desert air. Somewhere he dropped his laptop. And in the centre of his thought came a voice that said, 'How astonishing to die so easily. And how miserable to do it in Turkey.'

There was a moment at which consciousness began again. A damp film of sweat across his chest that caused the breeze to feel cool. Coolest on the outcrops around his nipples, warmest in the airless valley below the sternum. This is the darkness that dead bodies wake to. An eternal, lightless limbo in which the only feeling is the gentle sighing of the wind. Breath, freed at last from its rib cage and playing among the stars.

Hands. The smooth hands of Angels. Patiently absorbing the accumulation of fire within him. Cold cloths on his head. Wiping the heat from his armpits and the soles of his feet. Eddying the air around him with silent movement. Pouring secret waters deep into his throat.

After a while he noticed that his body was breathing.

The restful tide in his nostrils, the swelling of his chest.

Perhaps he was still able to open his eyes.

Around him was darkness. He was lying on a mattress on the ground. There was a light source. An opening. Irregular, rocky. Outside was sky. As his eyes adjusted he saw the rock extending all around him. He was in a cave.

A fire-edged silhouette appeared in the entrance. As the figure approached, Klaus saw that it was a woman carrying a big spade and in the other fist – what was that? – four or five small birds that hung limp by their tails. She was old, but she moved easily. She placed the spade on the ground and came to inspect Klaus. Even in the half light, the blue of her eyes was vivid against the orange cloth wrapped around her head.

'So you're awake. How do you feel?'

'Fine. I think.'

'You were very close, my friend, very close! It was lucky I found you. Lucky for you. The vultures weren't so happy! They were preparing for a carnival. You were like a piece of tough old meat when I brought you here. Carried you here myself. That was three days ago.'

Klaus became aware to his discomfort that he was completely naked except for his C&A Y-front underpants. He hastily wrapped the sheet around him.

'Those clothes weren't doing you any good. You're from the city, I suppose. You people do crazy things. Think you can just go wandering out. I don't think they teach you how your body works.'

'Thank you for finding me. And helping me. I am grateful.'

'We know how to help people who do battle with the sun. It happens often enough even with us. You city people have the same body as we do. I know you think you don't.'

She sat down on a chair by his mattress with the birds in her lap, put her feet up on a stool, and started to pull out feathers vigorously.

'I thought you should eat some meat tonight. You're very weak. I caught some buntings.'

The cave was clean and sparse: a wooden wardrobe packed with

98

clothes stood on one side; there were two chairs and a table, and an assortment of steel pans arranged neatly by the entrance. Towels and sheets hung from strings tied across one wall, and his own ragged shirt and suit next to them. His laptop stood on the floor.

'So you are from Germany. You are a German man. And suddenly you end up lying unconscious in the sun by my doorstep. What a strange thing to happen. What an event.'

She plucked as she spoke, pulling out every last tiny feather before tossing each bald corpse into a steel bowl. The soles of her feet were facing Klaus and his sickly gaze fixed on them. Her toes were bony and splayed; the skin was shiny with wear and latticed with dark lines. He had the strange impression that they were hovering in space; in fact the whole of her body seemed to be oscillating gently. He studied her fixedly as she sat and worked but could not get rid of the feeling; his mind had been affected, he needed to see a doctor; but then, no: it was not her that was moving but the cave wall behind that was undulating and shimmering in the half-light, and he realized it was covered with a humming blanket of pink butterflies that moved together as if they were woven, thousands of wings ceaselessly shifting like one big collage of different hues, fluttering sometimes for space within the throng, hovering above it to find a different spot; and, as he watched, more butterflies flew in from outside and joined themselves to the iridescent tapestry.

'You have seen our butterflies. They make a handsome curtain, don't you think?'

'I have never seen butterflies like that. I don't know what family they could belong to. There is no such thing as a pink butterfly.'

'Well, there you are clearly wrong, German man. The bushes outside are covered with their chrysalises. When they emerge they all come here.'

She struck off the head of the first bird with a quick flick of her knife and held it over the bowl for the blood to drain. Klaus tried not to watch.

'So tell me about yourself, German man. Are you rich?'

The question bewildered him. He did not know what to say.

'You don't know if you are rich or not. Perhaps the sun is still in your head. I can see you are rich. Where does your money come from?'

Klaus struggled to think back to a life that even to him seemed far away.

'I am a mapmaker. I collect information about all the places of the world and sell it.'

The woman dropped the bird into a puddle of blood and leant back in her chair to laugh.

'You are a joker, German man!' she cried. 'Did your map not tell you that the summers are hot in Anatolia? That the land is without water or shade? You should have collected that information before you started driving round here! You nearly died for the lack of it. You make me laugh, my pink friend. A mapmaker!'

She took up the bird again, pulled out all its organs in one deft stroke and dropped them into the bowl. Her knife worked quickly in her glistening hands, it glinted and gyrated and ran with little tides of dark blood, and Klaus's head began to turn again. He looked at the row of plucked and eviscerated birds and fell back on the pillow. The rock above his head was spiralling.

'Could I have some water?' he murmured weakly.

'You people are like children,' she said as she dragged him from his bed, half carried him outside the cave, knelt him by a hole in the rock, reached deep inside for cups of water that he drank deeply, splashed his head. The movement slowed. He stood up and breathed deeply, considered the hole from which such cool, sweet water had come.

'This rock is water-bearing. I dug the hole myself. It is the size of my hips. Just wide enough for me to climb in and dig. But narrow to prevent evaporation.'

'What an empty place this is,' Klaus said softly as he looked around him. In front of the cave the rock fell away before them into a flat plain of bushes and small trees. 'There is nothing here.'

'You are wrong, German man. There is not nothing here. Perhaps it is not on your map. But there are olive trees all around. I grow wheat and vegetables and keep goats. I have this cave, which is cool in summer and warm in winter. And down there – can you see? – there is your car. Can you believe I carried you right up here? An old shrunken woman like myself?'

He stood looking down at his stranded car. How close he had come! he thought to himself.

She pondered his face as he reflected.

'You know: you are quite handsome. You could almost be Turkish with those light eyes and that dark hair and beard. But you are German. Rich, handsome and German. More and more interesting.'

Klaus did not know what she was driving at.

Two days later Klaus was completely recovered and ready to leave. The car was working again and he had decided to abandon his journey to the south and return straight to Ankara, leaving after sundown and filling the car with water, bread, and cheese.

'The car made it this far in the heat of the day. It should be able to do the same distance back again when it's cool and dark.'

'I hope you are right. But before you go I have one thing to ask you.'

They had finished a meal of fried aubergines in the mouth of the cave, and the sun was relaxing into orange.

'So far I have kept concealed from you my beloved daughter, Deniz. She is young and beautiful and dreams of other places. I do not want her to carry on living here while I become weak and die. To live at the mercy of the rains. Believe me, my friend, there have been times when we too have nearly died. When we have sucked the stems of bitter plants to get moisture. When our crops have shrivelled and turned to dust. So let me now name the price of my hospitality: I would like you to take my daughter back with you and give her a home with you. Be a husband to her.'

Klaus's face became hostile.

'Old woman: I don't think that is a good idea. I am not – I am not the kind of man you would wish for your daughter.'

'Take one look at her, German man, and tell me you cannot love her.'

She was standing there – where had she appeared from? – against the full sun; Klaus ducked the rays to try and discern her face, but could see only a bright turquoise robe and a long braid of black hair that she held in front of her navel.

'She cannot speak. But do not worry. You will hear her voice in your head.'

There was the sun that was blinding him as he tried to make out her face and a shaking in his head that had not gone away; and there was the Anatolian plateau that all around him was letting out the sigh that it had suppressed through the hot day; and in his mind there was a fretting that his mouth was saying things it should not.

'But how will I get her into Germany? Even if I were to buy her an air ticket she would not be able to come for she has no visa, no permission to enter or stay. Does she even have a passport?'

'Deniz has nothing. I don't believe there is a scrap of paper in the world where her name is written. But that is not your problem. I will take responsibility for getting her to you.'

Klaus's head was not clear and he still could not quite grasp if he had agreed or not.

'Leave now, German man. The sun has set. Deniz and I will sit and imagine together what her future might hold, and I will give her the last lessons I have left to give. Then we will say our farewells, for I doubt we shall ever see each other again. Borders do not open very frequently for people like us. She will be with you soon. Take good care of her. I will always remember your face, German man.'

Klaus got in the car, looked at them both for a moment, and drove away. As he bumped and skidded back onto the road under jagged skies of deep maroon there was a whisper in his head that said: *Farewell, map of my world. And know this: it was my hands that cooled you as you slept. They will follow you. Soon.*

Klaus lived in a big house in the middle of thickly wooded grounds in a green suburb called Offenbach. It had been built by a wealthy and eccentric nineteenth-century merchant who had sought to recreate a medieval German palace: it had a grand entrance with a massive wooden door and scowling gargoyles, its walls were thick and impenetrable, its halls were lined with niches blackened with wax smoke, and, in one corner, there was a soaring tower pierced with slits and surmounted by a conical roof with a rusted weather vane.

Inside this rich man's fantasy Klaus had undertaken to install one of his own. Into the niches were set arch-shaped LCD screens on which looped video recordings of candles and oil lamps burned endlessly, but without warmth. No natural light entered by the windows, merely the pale glow from more flat-screen panels that supplied fantastical landscapes as if from outside: today a snowy vista of German firs, computer generated from the paintings of Kaspar David Friedrich, tomorrow a tranquil scene by the Ganges with half-naked men sleeping under palm trees, perhaps a cityscape of mosques and palaces within which could clearly be seen the languorous women of the harem playing music and applying oils in their sweet captivity. The *tour de force* did not end there: hidden speakers delivered the sounds of these changing worlds into the room, and Klaus's morning newspaper and coffee were read and sipped to the soothing drumming of the monsoon rain on forest leaves or the soulful air of a Chinese street musician. Paintings on the walls were yet more computer screens, framed in heavy gilt but changing their images as the day progressed; moreover, with a single spoken command Klaus could dismiss the landscapes and *natures mortes* and view the inputs from hundreds of hidden cameras and sensors that surveyed every corner and every movement in his property. There was hardly a glass surface in the house that was not a projection; as Klaus liked to boast, 'There are more computer screens in my house than there are in Sierra Leone!'

In the days that followed his return from Turkey, Klaus threw himself back into his work energetically in order to try and expel from his mind everything that had happened there. In the evenings, alone in his big house, he started at the slightest sound, expecting at any moment that the doorbell would ring and he would open it to see the Turkish country girl standing there. He caught himself watching his security cameras for hours on end; but every night his shadowy gravel drive remained undisturbed, and after a while he began to convince himself that she would not come. 'The woman was clever, in her own way. But there are things she knows nothing of. Things of the world. How could a girl like that find her way to Frankfurt?' Indeed, as time passed, the whole experience began to seem like a dream. For a time a ragged pink butterfly that had fallen out of his clothes lay on the sideboard, a daily testimony to everything that had happened in the cave. But one day his maid dusted it away and with it the last husks of his memories disappeared. 'It never happened,' he agreed with himself one night. 'Such things never do.'

Weeks went by, then months. Klaus travelled: Singapore, Madrid, Johannesburg. He signed a major deal with a mining company who wanted to use his map to analyse terrain, transport and labour costs in their various exploration sites. Life returned to normal.

And then, just as he was going to bed one night, there was a knock at the door. He opened it, and before him, drenched in rain, was Deniz. He stood, holding the open door and staring at her with disbelief.

May I come in?

Her lips did not move, she continued to fix him with her blue eyes, but the voice rang through the flurry of his thoughts like a searchlight in the mist. He reacted slowly, stepped aside, said,

'Yes.'

But how strange it was to respond aloud to words that had not even been spoken, whose very existence no one could even prove. How would it seem to an observer? as if he were mad!

She stood in the middle of the hall watching him expectantly, dripping onto the stone floor. He closed the door slowly.

'I suppose you need – do you want some food?'

Let us do things in order. First let me dry myself. And then let us eat.

He showed her to the bathroom, gave her towels and a man's dressing gown.

'Do you know – I'm not sure if you've seen – the taps work like this –'

I can see how it works. I will come down soon.

He went into the kitchen and looked in the fridge that was, as always, full. He took out some butter and Würst and began to make a sandwich.

So you see I have come, my map of the world! Did you doubt me? I

am sure you were starting to think I would not. Well: now I am here, and
sitting in your house. In Frankfurt.

She sat on a chair with the dressing gown wrapped almost twice around her so that it covered her neck right up to her chin. He could not look at her.

'How did you get here?'

Oh let us not go into that! The details are unimportant and they have burdened me for too long. I have spent much time underground, much time soaked with foul-smelling water, much time not seeing the lands I am passing through. Let us just say that my journey could not be traced on your map!

He put the sandwich before her and she began to eat hungrily.

Is all the food in Germany this bad?

She grinned at him.

Don't look so glum. I am teasing. And I will make you wonderful food.

He watched her finish in silence, took her plate away and rinsed it under the tap.

'Actually, I was just going to bed, so if you don't mind . . .'

Which of us do you think is more tired? I have been dreaming for weeks of the bed that lay at the end of my journey.

She followed him up the big wooden stairs that creaked under their feet.

'You sleep in there,' he said, gesturing to a room filled with a huge white bed. She considered it.

And where will you sleep?

'Down there.' He pointed along the length of the long darkened corridor to the door at the far end.

Oh. She smiled. *So we will see each other when we awake.*

He rubbed his eyes messily with the palm of his hand.

'In fact – I think I may need to go away tomorrow. To get away. Early. For a few days.'

Where are you going? Maybe I can come?

'No – I'm going to – I'm going to Paris. It would be difficult for you. You'd better stay here.'

What terrible timing.

'The house gets stocked automatically. You say you can cook. Don't go outside. You're illegal in this place, remember. And do not go into the room at the top of the tower. That's my private room. Don't go there on any account. I'll think about your future while I'm away. Keep the place clean.'

Deniz looked at him intently, as if committing all this to memory. He turned and walked towards his room.

Map man, map man!

He stopped.

'My name is Klaus. That is the best thing to call me. What do you want?'

I forgot. I brought you something from Turkey.

She took a wooden box out of her bag and handed it to him. 'Güllüoğlu' in cheerful red letters. He opened it.

'What is it?'

She laughed.

It is baklava. Turkish sweets!

'Oh God!' he shouted, throwing the box on the floor in disgust. 'I don't want any of that stuff in the house! Is that clear? And you have come through the sewers! Get it out of the house right now!'

He went to his room and closed the door behind him. She picked up the box and picked out one square of baklava that she chewed philosophically while looking at the spot where he had stood. Then she hid the box under the bed and gave herself up to luxurious sleep.

When she awoke, the day was already much advanced: the birds sang outside and strong sunlight shone through the curtains. She was in a bed. She looked around her and reminded herself of how she had got there. Then she stepped out into the corridor.

The wooden floorboards ran in straight lines from where she stood to the closed door of Klaus's bedroom at the other end. One side of the corridor gave onto the stairwell; on the other was a row of more closed doors, sturdy and wooden, between which there hung framed pictures that were bolted to the wall. They were taken from old books, and showed rows of painted butterfly pairs, male and female, dead it seemed, labelled neatly in copperplate script: *Familia Zerynthia, Familia Hesperiidae*. She walked slowly down the corridor from one to the next, touching each frame thoughtfully, looking at the detail of the frozen wings. She arrived at Klaus's door.

There was no sound from within, so she knocked quietly.

Klaus?

Klaus. Klaus. *Klaus!*

The house was still.

She twisted the handle slowly and opened the door.

The room was like the one in which she had slept and was dominated by a big white bed. Empty. It displayed no sign of anyone ever having slept there: creaseless and slightly stale. She closed the door again and crept down the stairs.

She looked in every room, but there was no one in the house. Klaus had gone. It must be late. The birds were in full song outside and there was the sound of other things too – animals? She went to the window.

A great sparkling valley stretched out as far as she could see, lined on both sides with shallow mountains and carpeted with tall green grasses that silvered in waves in the wind. Buffalo grazed and eagles soared high overhead. In the far distance, as she watched, a herd of giraffe galloped majestically together, fleeing, perhaps, some unseen predator.

The place had not felt like this when she arrived the previous night. She ran to the opposite window. With a start she found herself looking straight into the eyes of a monkey that was peering in through the window, staring at her, casually cantilevered against the branches of a clump of trees that arched high over the house. And then, on impulse, it lost interest, and disappeared into the boughs, which waved wildly under its weight.

Deniz began to feel anxious. 'I am alone here in a house surrounded by wild animals! I did not know what Frankfurt was, did not hear of it till it was spoken by the man, but I never imagined it was like this.'

She walked to the front door to see what perils she might have walked unknowingly through on her arrival. She opened it uncertainly. And there it was: a cool grey morning, a gravel drive and a garden.

She looked in at the windows from outside and saw that they were stopped up. Mountains, giraffes, monkeys – all were make-believe.

'What a curious man is this that plays these illusions on himself', she thought. And she walked on the gravel and looked at the place she was in.

'This is the place where I am illegal. *Don't go out of the house. You're illegal in this place, remember*. Can the people see illegal in my eyes? Have I, Deniz, become different, now I am illegal? How strange it all is.'

Deniz retrieved the baklava from under her bed and sat in the corridor to eat it, contemplating the row of closed doors. 'He did not say that I could not go into these rooms,' she thought. 'Only the one at the top of the tower.' When she had eaten the last morsel she opened one of the doors.

The room was spacious, with a large window that looked down on the same bright valley she had seen before, where a herd of elephants now massed around a water hole. It contained nothing except for a steel rack hung with thirteen dresses.

'Is there a woman in this house that there are so many dresses hung like this?' But they did not seem as if they had ever been worn. The dresses were brightly coloured and beautiful. She threw off her over-sized dressing gown, and put on the first of the dresses.

It fitted her so beautifully, with a tight waist that seemed made for her own and sleeves that settled prettily around her wrists, and how glorious she felt in it! She walked to see how it felt to walk, and turned to see how it felt to turn – and she caught sight of a big mirror on the back of the door.

At first the mirror showed nothing, was empty except for a strange, sleepy light. Then it flickered alive; and there stood another Deniz smiling back at her and looking like a fantasy. And the dress had a Japanese print, and so there she was in the mirror in the shade of a tree, her face dappled by the sun that danced in the breeze and her hair tied up with wooden pins; and cherry blossoms fell daintily to the ground around her and in the background were Japanese women who washed their clothes in the purest of rivers and sang songs; and even further away was the soothing arc of Mount Fuji with a crater like the concavity in a lover's lip, with clouds like garlands and birds that flapped in soaring pen strokes. And Deniz laughed and she walked very upright, happy to see herself.

At home Deniz had tried to catch sight of herself in a rusted mirror that stood on a ledge in the cave and was no bigger than the sole of her foot; but here was her whole outline as clear as day. She tried on another dress with a riot of frills around her knees and shoulders, and this time she was in the mountains – it almost looked like home! – where a ring of gypsy girls danced around her in bare feet and a gypsy man with eyes like dark oases sang songs of tragic love to the accordion. And she hitched up her skirt and danced too and her neck glistened in the firelight and old women sat on the steps of the caravan and watched her, thinking of when they too had been so slender.

So Deniz spent her day, travelling into all the worlds of the mirror until she had tried on all thirteen dresses. And then she took off the last dress and stood naked. 'How surprising,' she thought as she watched herself in the mirror, 'that I look just like other women. I have a body like theirs, I have breasts as they do, and I am beautiful as they are.'

She stood on tiptoes and reached her arms above her head and saw how her breasts rose with her stretching and the clear shape of her ribs. She turned and looked back over her shoulder to see how she looked from behind, her shoulder blades prominent with her twisting and her buttocks paler than her back. She sat on the floor and spread her legs wide. For the first time ever she had a clear view of what was there: a leaf-shaped dusting, dark against her fair skin, that sprung from the core of her body and fanned outwards under her navel, and, lying within, a folded arch like a bud of expectation, a pink chrysalis nestled between a pair of lips, flared lips, yes, like the wings of a pink butterfly, wings that glistened with secret colours and how a man would desire her when he saw the hidden excitement of those fluttering wings!

It was curious to have to come to this Frankfurt in order to see truly what she had always carried with her; but now there were other vague figures in the mirror, also naked, who arched and consumed each other in various ways and she watched, fascinated, distracted from her self; and now she too was altering and her colour was lost: she was an engraving of lines and parts; her smooth skin was dissolving from her body, the musculature of her eyes tautened in their exposed sockets as they widened, but already even muscles and tendons were gone and there was nothing to stop her looking upon her organs as they churned, the four chambers of her heart convulsing more rapidly, her lungs in cutaway swelling and contracting, arrows showing the direction of blood flow, entrails coursing with acid and her womb like a clenched fist; and bones, white like a picked goat, that moved as she moved, grinned with a noseless grin that, without lips or eyes, showed no fear, was no longer her, swayed like a cackling messenger of death. And she screamed a scream that did not disturb the silence of the house; she leapt out of the mirror's frame and hastily put on her dressing gown. The mirror went blank.

She ran out of the room, slammed the door behind her, and stood in the corridor, panting with fear. She noticed that the picture by her head no longer showed butterflies. Now it was an old photograph of a pygmy in a cage with an orang-utan. Underneath, it said, 'St Louis World Fair, 1904'.

Evening. Seeking a place to be comfortable, Deniz enters the dining room where a long wooden table gleams, mirror-like, flanked by ten chairs on either side and one at each end ('But'), all equidistant from each other ('look!'), all looking as if they had never been touched ('what is that?'). At one end of the table is a plate of steaming food: meat and vegetables and bread, newly there, not five minutes. She calls out silently in the house, *Hello! Hello! Is someone there?* but there is no answer. As she is very hungry, she eats the food. It is hot and tasty. She takes the empty plate to the kitchen, washes it, and puts it in its place. She opens the fridge for some milk. There is a new box of Güllüoğlu baklava just like the one she brought. She fetches the first, empty, box and puts it side by side with the second. They are identical. If she had not seen them together she would have believed she had dreamt the eating of them; but now she cannot deny that there are indeed two. She seizes the second box from the fridge as if it were a shameful secret, and conceals it under her bed. Again, she sleeps.

For the next few days the house will float between Himalayan villages and Gauginesque Pacific islands. Deniz will look in all its rooms for signs of life but will find none. Still, meals will continue to appear just as she begins to desire them. Each evening she will add another box of baklava to the growing pile under her bed.

She will sit several times at the bottom of the spiral staircase leading up to the tower. She will wonder what can be up there. One afternoon she will climb to the top, right to the heavy door of Klaus's private room that she will examine minutely, feel with her palms, try to look under; but not open.

She will stop to examine two more pictures that will depress her with their antiquity: portraits of two top-hatted men from earlier times, looking strangely similar and entitled, respectively, 'William Burke' and 'William Hare'.

One morning Deniz found herself at the foot of the spiral staircase and thought to herself, 'Why do I not just open that door to see what is inside? I will not go in, but I will just see what his private room contains. For everything else is seeming so tedious.'

She started to climb the staircase. She climbed and climbed, and the staircase wound around above her, and she stopped to catch her breath; she kept her hand on the wall to feel her way in the patches of darkness between the windows, and finally she came to the big wooden door.

She opened it.

A projector beam blinded her, set her on fire in the doorway with shifting shapes and digits that spread in a rapid mitosis over her face and clothes. She could see nothing. 'What can be here?' she thought. 'Let me just step beyond these rays so that I can see. I will touch nothing.' She stepped quickly through the beam and recovered her sight.

She found herself in the middle of a large circular room with high ceilings, and walls made entirely of frosted glass. Projected onto the glass, from floor to ceiling and around all 360 degrees, was a map of the world, a vast, flickering thing that kept her turning on the spot in wonder. The entire epic surface was coloured in various microshades of steely grey with no distinction between land and sea: for this was not a map of earth and water, but of speed. It was Klaus's magnum opus.

The particular genius of his system was the recognition that every piece of useful information about a place could be reduced to a single parameter – what he called 'velocity' – and plotted on a flat surface. He calculated the speed of everything from the spread of ideas to the movement of oil and subjected it to a complex algebra that allowed him to find a unique value for every point on the globe. This Kaufmann Velocity Integer™ (KVI) had already become a vital index for investors and policymakers in determining the rate at which a place was delivering returns (the Bulgarian government had recently issued a press release with the boast that various 'upgrades' in legislation and infrastructure had given the Rousse International Free Zone a higher KVI than anything enjoyed in Poland, Hungary or the Czech Republic) and they paid a high price for it. 'For four hundred years,' Klaus would say in his many presentations to corporations and governments, 'people have been taught to believe that Mercator's canny distortions show the world as it truly is. But we have no more need of his deceitful coastlines: we are not a people bobbing about in the unknown looking for land. Which of us, in seeking to travel from Frankfurt to Singapore, spends a moment thinking about problems of navigation? The world is already ours, and what we truly care about is not its shape, but its speed. For the next four hundred years it will be the Kaufmann Velocity Map that determines how we imagine our planet!'

Coastlines there were none; but since the sea was all but empty of markets, it was generally a smooth and mysterious grey-black, while the continents displayed themselves as a constantly mutating patchwork that became white hot in certain places. The entire surface of the map was cracked with a filigree of red and blue lines representing the various corridors and checkpoints of the world that converged here and there in matted inflammations like the pulsating chambers of a heart: air routes and sea routes, the routes by which steel and rubber and glass find themselves part of a car, the migrations of birds and whales, monkeys and rats, fleas and bacteria – and was that not even the dark underground route that she had taken to get here? – and everything was written over with a scurrying swarm of texts and symbols too dense even to make out, that multiplied and divided in prodigious waves even as Deniz watched. Floating, ghostlike, behind the map, in the dark centre of the Pacific Ocean was the logo of Kaufmann Velocity Mapping AG: a glowing orb coursing with artistically rendered electronic signals.

Taken up with the thing, Deniz sat in the swivel chair in the centre of the room and adjusted its binocular head frame to her eyes. Using the controls she zoomed in on Frankfurt: the chair rotated and rose up on its shaft until her eyes were pointing at the correct spot. The glasses in front of her eyes were simultaneously lenses that allowed her to zoom in on the map and screens where supplementary data was projected over it.

What a majestic place was Frankfurt! She had never imagined that human beings were engaged in so many pursuits! People made things whose purpose she could not even imagine: valves, adhesives, tubes, lenses, pumps, plastic pellets, nylon tiles, rubber seals, steel gauze, springs, washers. They sold houses and prosthetic limbs and elegant clothes. They bought books and money and cars and guitars and other people. Any pleasure you wanted could be found in Frankfurt, from swimming pools to wooden furniture to a beautiful tan. And there was so much music! for half the old warehouses by the railway tracks were now studios in which people made every kind of sound on earth: music from Peru and – yes – Anatolia; music for dancing and music for kissing. For love, too, could be bought in Frankfurt: the love of women, the love of men, and, if you were prepared to pay enough, the love of children. But most of all, women: for you could buy thin women and fat women, women with teeth and women with none, women over fifty and women under nineteen; local women and Russian women; women from Indonesia, Ethiopia, and Argentina; women who soothed and women who punished; women who had been men and women who still were. And if you did not want whole people you could buy pieces: for there were hearts and kidneys on sale, and livers and slices of skin and corneas and foetuses.

For hours she traced imaginary journeys around Klaus's majestic map, thrilled at the largeness of things and full of anticipation at what a life she would lead in this city she had come to. She made plans and resolutions about what she would have and be. And finally she pulled herself away.

Before she left the room she decided to look for her mother's home in Turkey. She scoured the area, but could find nothing except menacing mosquitoes that signified malaria. Nearby, however, was a broad highway of lightness in dotted lines: 'Proposed route for the Baku–Tbilisi–Ceyhan oil pipeline'.

She set the chair back as she had found it, left the room, and pulled the door to behind her. She ran lightly down the steps and into the drawing room – and gave a little voiceless shriek. For there, sitting in an armchair, was Klaus.

'I was wondering where you were, Deniz.'

I was in my bedroom. I did not hear you come. How long have you been sitting there?

'An hour, perhaps. Shall we eat?'

He led her into the dining room where two meals were laid out with a bottle of wine.

'Do you like wine?'

I think so. Yes.

He poured a glass for each of them.

'So what have you been doing for a week?'

Nothing. Resting. I was tired after my journey. I stayed in the house as you told me to.

'Did anything eventful happen? Did anything strike you as strange?'

Oh no! You have a lovely, peaceful house! I am very happy here!

She tasted the wine. It was rich and deep, and she felt the sip fall through her body. She watched him, waiting for him to say more, but he seemed to have lost interest in everything but his meal.

Klaus: I have been thinking. Now I am here I would like to work. I would like to earn money. I am young and fit and have ambition. I would like beautiful clothes and to be surrounded by music. Tell me what I must do to find work in Frankfurt.

'Where did you come across this ambition?'

I don't know. I have been thinking.

'I see. You cannot work here. You are illegal. I keep telling you that.'

But even people like me must have to live. They must wish to be rich and live a good life.

'I don't know what they wish. But they cannot work in Germany.'

You are a man who knows much about the world. Surely you can find a way that I can earn money like you do.

She finished her meal and drank her wine and found herself full of boldness. Now she knew that life could give her everything she had ever wanted.

'There is a man I know who owns a chain of hotels across the country. There is one in Frankfurt, near the airport. I believe he gives jobs to people like you. I can ask him.'

Yes! Ask the man with the hotels! I knew you would know what to do!

Deniz stood up, and cradled Klaus's face in her arms. She kissed the top of his head.

We will be so happy, Klaus. I know that it will be impossible to be unhappy in Frankfurt.

Klaus peeled her arms away from his neck and pushed her firmly back into her chair.

'I think the wine is giving you ideas you should not have.'

But Klaus! I have come to be your wife and to love you. You don't need to turn me away. I will give you everything. If only you knew how beautiful I am under these clothes!

And she sat astride him, parting the front of her dress archly so that the curves of her breasts showed, she kissed him on the mouth with all the confidence and the timidity of someone who has never kissed before.

'Get off me!' Klaus exclaimed, thrusting her away, 'leave me alone!'

Her eyes filled with tears.

Why do you not want me, Klaus? Wasn't that how it was supposed to be? Will I spend my life with someone who does not want me?

115

'Don't talk in such words. Don't deceive yourself. I am not your husband. And I do not desire you. You should not have drunk that wine. I think you should go to bed.'

Deniz pulled herself away from the table and climbed the stairs. She looked automatically under the bed to see her baklava boxes. They had all gone.

She will wake early as Karl opens her door. 'Get up! You start at the hotel today. Get dressed. The car is waiting.' She will dress quickly looking out at what the day holds: it will be Morocco outside. They will sit unspeaking in the back of a car, she will see the streets of Frankfurt for the first time. Rows and rows of garbage bins, gliding trams dipping below and above the streets, pedestrian subways, lamp posts pasted with pictures of missing people, parks for children painted in primary colours that clash with the grey sky, people waiting for giant articulated buses at the bus stop. Georg Schneider will be waiting in the car park by his BMW. The two men will have a brief conference, identical from the back in their beige raincoats: 'So this is what you get up to in that big house of yours! I am impressed, Klaus. She is a beauty.' Klaus will not see the funny side. 'It is not what you think.'

'I've called a doctor. We like to do some routine checks with these girls. They're always falling sick. Heaven knows what they bring over. He's done this sort of thing for me before, very discreet. If you could slip him a hundred Euros for his pains.'

Deniz will be led into room 124 where the doctor has already set up a provisional consultation room. He will have moustaches growing over his upper lip and will not say a word to her. He will shine lights in her eyes and her throat, will listen through the tubes in his ears to the sound of her chest, will don latex gloves as she removes her skirt and conduct an extensive gynaecological examination while Deniz tries to concentrate on the painting of a shipwreck that hangs above the television, dark heads bobbing in the ocean, hull and masts at unnatural angles; he will pierce her skin with glinting needles and her blood will escape through his pipes into four glass vials that he will take away for his own purposes. Deniz will shake with terror but will not resist.

'Everything seems fine,' he will say as she is left within to step with high heels into her underpants, to smooth the bedcover where a guest will sleep tonight. 'Give you the blood tests tomorrow. It's a nice one you have there, gentlemen. I wouldn't mind her bringing me some room service! Speaking of which, what happened to that other girl who was here recently? The Arab girl?'

The deal is complete. Klaus will whisper to his friend: 'I don't want her in my house all day. Prefer her to be here where someone is watching her. As you can see, she can't talk. But still: I don't want her mixing with anyone. Forming friendships, alliances. Things can get out.'

Klaus will hesitate before adding,

'And keep this one away from Karl. Nothing should happen to her. She's different.'

'Who is Karl?' the doctor will ask. The two men in identical rain-coats will ignore the question.

Deniz will emerge to the gaze of the three men. Klaus will take her aside to repeat his admonitions. 'You mix with no one. OK? You are here to work. My driver will bring you in the morning and take you home at night. No need for you to start wandering around on your own. My position is at stake.'

Deniz will be handed over to the charge of Herr Ehlers who overseas the Schneider Frankfurt Airlodge and ensures that everything matches up to the standards that guests have come to expect of the Schneider Hotel Group. 'Pay attention to every smell, every sign of life. These are the things that arouse repugnance in our guests. Bathrooms must be as new. Showers must be dry, toilets spotless. I need hardly mention that you may not use the toilets in the rooms. We have separate facilities for the maids.' He will instruct her in the right feel of a bed and a carpet, and the technique for arranging fruit and soap selections in a welcoming way. He will give her two dresses in Schneider brown. 'Put one of these on. We expect our maids to look immaculate at all times.'

Deniz did not ever speak to Herr Ehlers. It was more comfortable for both of them for him to think her an idiot. She did however speak to Klaudia, who shared the duties of the fourth floor.

117

'I still don't understand how you talk to my mind like that,' she said as they stood among the air-conditioning outlets at the back of the hotel, talking between overhead planes. 'But I like it.' She inhaled deeply on her cigarette.

'You need to start smoking. Funny thing is: if they catch you just standing out here doing nothing for five minutes they start cursing you for your laziness. But if you're smoking a cigarette, it's OK.'

You are not from here either, are you?

'I am from Kielce. Poland. Burned-out industrial town. Nothing to do. My brothers have all left. They went to London, mostly. I don't know if they're still there – I never hear from them now. I came here. Can't speak English.'

Do you like it?

'It's OK. Things happen here. You can earn money. I have a boyfriend. German man with two heavenly armfuls of tattoos. He drives trucks. Makes a good living. We rent a little place. You must come over. I'll make you borscht and pierogies. You promise me you'll come?'

Deniz nodded, though she was not sure.

Tell me: does the German man make love to you?

'Are you crazy? My boy cannot stop! After two weeks on the road my ample charms are simply too much for him. A truck driver in life, I tell him, in bed he is an archduke. When we're at home together we don't bother getting dressed. It wastes too much time!' She laughed uproariously.

Deniz considered all this.

My – husband – does not desire me. She looked at the cigarette ends of previous conversations on the ground. *I am miserable about it. Tell me what to do.*

'Deniz, my poor little sister! Leave him! There's no time to waste. You're young and so, so beautiful. Why should you give yourself to some ungrateful man who can't sort out his problems? Come and live with me. I will find you a proper man!'

You are kind, Klaudia. I am happy to have met you.

'And I am happy too. We will be great friends.'

* * *

118

Every morning Deniz is driven to the hotel, where she changes into her brown dress and works quickly so that she and Klaudia will have time to talk. They stand by the piles of garbage sacks, where the vents belch the hot air that no one wants inside, laughing and talking until it is time to return to work. 'My love for you will cost me my lungs, Deniz,' Klaudia jokes as they retreat inside.

At the end of the day the car picks her up again and takes her to Klaus's empty house. He comes later and ignores her.

Klaus: do you think I'm pretty? she asks one day. He pretends not to have understood the question, and she does not repeat it. She begins to dread these evenings looking at the mournful pictures and eating meals that come from nowhere.

One evening Klaus will say to her:

'Who is Klaudia Maleszyk?'

She is a friend. Just a friend. From Poland.

'Did I not say that you should talk to no one? Did I not say that, Deniz?'

Yes. Yes you did.

'Do not ignore what I say. I have taken risks for your sake. Do not talk to her again. Otherwise she will be sent away.'

Deniz wheeled her cart of cleaning fluids and towels up to the door of room 417. She knocked quietly, waited to ensure it was empty, slipped her pass into the lock, and walked in. She stopped in her tracks.

A monkey was sitting on the table eating fruit that was put out for all guests. It was a large male, not significantly smaller than Deniz herself. He watched her unconcernedly, chewing on a slice of pineapple.

She retreated slowly from the room and ran to find Klaudia.

Klaudia! Klaudia! You must look at this!

They stole back into the room together and stood watching the monkey with a mixture of terror and glee.

'You are a shameless monkey,' said Klaudia. 'You don't know how many rules you are breaking by being here.'

Without removing his eyes from Klaudia, the monkey picked up the well-sharpened Schneider Hotel Group pencil from the table and used it to scratch behind his ears. When the irritation was assuaged, he inspected the pencil approvingly for a moment, as if memorizing how peculiarly well adapted this tool was for this job. Then he walked across the table, jumped onto the bed, and climbed up onto the wardrobe, from where he surveyed the room serenely.

'He is so ugly he is beautiful,' whispered Klaudia.

But the monkey seemed to conclude that room 417 offered him no further gratification. He ambled over to the window by which he had entered, and climbed out.

The two women let out their breath in laughter.

'He must have escaped from somewhere. Perhaps there was a shipment at the airport. I have to say I'm very pleased at this new direction that the Airlodge is taking. He was the most charming guest it has ever had!'

She took Deniz's hands.

'And guess what! I have discovered – and you are the first to know, for poor Hans is away driving his trucks and I cannot keep it inside – I am pregnant. I am to be a mother!' And she laughed with glee as Deniz threw her arms round her and held her very close.

'So our conversations are over unless you start smoking, Deniz. For I have given up.'

The next morning Deniz is told that Klaudia has been taken ill and, since they do not know of any family members in Germany, she is being kept in room 401 for supervision; Deniz is not to go near that room. After lunch she sees the doctor coming out. She tries to see past him but the door is firmly closed in her face.

She is upset, and works very slowly. She turns on the television in one of the rooms to occupy her mind as she cleans. There is a news report on ARD: *Monkey Menace!* Monkeys have somehow taken over Frankfurt. The camera shows them on the roof of an apartment block: fire engines encircle the building and ladders are raised with men wearing thick gloves and masks. They catch some of the monkeys and put them safely in cages, but they cannot catch them all. The reporter speculates about where they have come from: city officials have already checked the zoo but no monkeys are reported missing, and attention turns to boats and trains. There was a case in 1982 of nine monkeys arriving in Munich after riding on the roof of a train all the way from Spain. But the numbers this time are far larger. An expert gives a scenario: though we cannot say for certain where they have come from, we can suggest with some plausibility that they arrived some time ago – perhaps a year or so – and have been living and reproducing ever since in abandoned warehouses. It is difficult to imagine that they could get this far without anyone reporting them unless their arrival was in relatively modest numbers. Close-up photographs are shown: this monkey is *Macaca Mulatta*, commonly known as the rhesus monkey, and found normally in Afghanistan and India. The public is warned not to approach: it is capable of outbreaks of extreme violence, especially when threatened. The reporter takes over: If you see any of these monkeys please call the number shown on your screens now. And if anyone is bitten they must be taken to hospital straightaway. These monkeys can carry rabies.

Before she leaves for the day she bangs on the door of room 401. A man opens it a crack.

'I'm sorry. Miss Maleszyk is very sick. We are keeping her under supervision. She can see no one.'

He does not look trustworthy. She hears the voices of other men inside the room. Deniz shouts silently to her friend:

Klaudia! Can you hear me?

But there is no response. Deniz feels uneasy as she gets into the waiting car. 'There was nothing wrong with her yesterday,' she thinks.

They leave the highway and enter the streets of Offenbach. There are monkeys everywhere. In trees, on roofs and window ledges. People are frantic. She sees a man leaning out of an upstairs window and swinging wildly at a monkey with a steel pole. The monkey is taken by surprise: its skull is smashed and it falls several storeys – from the silent ease of her expensive car seat it seems to take an age – to the ground.

When they drive up the gravel drive to Klaus's house they pass an unaccustomed truck coming the other way. It is loaded with bulging black garbage bags.

The next morning, Herr Ehlers was waiting for her and stepped forcefully in her way.

'The fourth floor is closed today, Deniz. You cannot go up there. Please help out on the third floor instead. You can go home early.'

She got into the lift and went to the third floor. Checking to see she was not observed, she went out of the fire door and climbed the emergency steps to the floor above.

The doors to all the rooms were propped open and there was the sound of drills and sanding machines. The corridors were covered with bits of masonry and plaster, and workmen crisscrossed from one room to another. She looked into 498. There was blood on the walls. Had some monkeys got in here? Her own blood was whirring in her head; she marched down the corridor; all the rooms showed signs of a terrible fight: bedclothes were torn and bloodied and curtains had been ripped down. She started to run, for the door of 401 was wide open and there were people going in and out. What had they done with Klaudia? She reached the door and there were men stuffing mutilated monkeys into black bags. 'You shouldn't be here, Miss,' said a man in gloves who pushed her out of the room, but *Where is she? What have you done with her?* There is blood on his coat and boots; he leads her to the lift and sends her to the ground floor where Herr Ehlers is standing in the lobby: 'I thought I told you not to go up to the fourth floor?' She writes on paper for he will not understand: KLAUDIA MALESZYK? He looks at her darkly and tells her that she should probably be going home now. She slips away and lets herself into 124 (vacant) where she lies on the bed and tries to understand what is happening. If only she had looked more carefully at the map; she tried to remember her binocular vision, for there everything was written out; and was there not in that map not just sofas and tennis racquets but also madness? Had something not chafed within her as she looked into the map for a shape for her dreams? Were there not scattered secret people who looked over their shoulder as they worked because they suspected they were more use dead than alive? And was the whole thing not astonishingly full of *garbage*? Everywhere neatly tied bags of uniform black plastic, whose contents were starting to fill her imagination with sickness.

The door opened and in came Klaus. He was carrying a camera. He had combed his hair differently and looked more friendly. Concerned, even.

'What a beautiful woman you are. And crying so despairingly. How can this be?'

Do you know what happened to her?

'What is your name?'

You know my name!

He begins to kiss her neck. 'What is strange is that I think I can hear your voice inside my head, even though your lips do not move.'

She starts. *Who are you?*

'Did you just ask me who I am? My name is Karl. I am staying in the hotel.'

But you are Klaus! Klaus Kaufmann!

'Indeed I am not.' He parted her hair from her ear and kissed the side of her neck tenderly. The feeling is so astonishing that she is not sure if she cares if this is Klaus or not for she has never felt so alone.

'What is your name?'

Deniz.

'Deniz.' He breathes it into her ear. She puts her arms around his neck and holds him tightly for ever. His body feels so strong and his hair smells of dizzying things.

Be nice to me. Please be nice to me.

She is full of desire but he gets up and busies himself with other things: draws the curtains, takes his camera from its case. She sits by the pillow in her brown Schneider uniform, not knowing how she is to behave. She looks at him. He is indistinguishable from the man in whose house she lives. *You are not Klaus Kaufmann?*

'I told you. My name is Karl.'

She picks up the phone and dials Klaus's mobile number. Klaus picks up on the other end.

'Deniz? Deniz is that you? What is the problem?'

She puts the phone down and takes off her clothes. She lies on the bed, waiting, trying to make her troubled mind as blank as the ceiling. He undresses too; lies beside her and kisses her, puts his hand between her legs, warms her with all his self, and the world is suddenly far below her and the apprehensions of falling back again only heighten the pleasure: he loves her body as a man should love it and he is so fluent, so knowing: a man is touching her breasts and her thighs, he will part her for himself and there she can feel him within her and There! for a man fills you and knocks the air from you, and the breaths that she gasped into his ear were a confusion of everything that had happened that day and the day before and every day since that man had arrived in her cave in Anatolia; and this man, this Karl! was reaching her Her at last; and at last there is ease, there is nothing but Him and the world is bursting with the way he pounds her body, and tears are also bursting from her as he stiffens and they wrap themselves so that what is Him and what is Her is momentarily a mere question and the landing is side to side like a feather gliding, slowly alighting on moss; and it is like bliss.

He looks at her.

'You don't seem to be afraid of falling pregnant.'

I never thought of it. I –

'Why are you crying?'

I am crying because I have loved you for so long, and yet you were never you until now. And I am crying because I cannot find my friend.

He strokes her cheek. 'You will find her again. I'm sure.' He stands up and she lies in the hollow they have made in the bed. He has found his camera and is focusing on her.

Why are you taking a photograph?

'Because I want to remember how beautiful you are right now.'

He presses the shutter.

I will never forget how beautiful you are right now.

He pulls on a pair of jeans. 'Perhaps you should –'

His air is final.

Don't send me away. I don't want to lose you again. Take me wherever you want. I will go with you.

'Be patient, Deniz. Be patient. We will see each other again soon.'

Tomorrow?

'I am certain of it. You must go now.' He kisses her softly on the lips. She begins to dress. It is a shame to put this body back when it has never been looked upon by a man before.

She is a hotel maid again. Schneider. Everywhere A Home Away From Home.

'Bye bye, Deniz. I will see you very soon.'

Bye bye, my love.

They watch each other as the door closes and his eye blazes like a jewel. He closes it slowly until there is just a line of him. And then she is cut off.

The car was waiting outside with its engine running, and she ran out to it guiltily. The chauffeur's driving was more clipped than usual, slightly faster. Klaus was waiting at the front door. His face was like a sword hilt. He grabbed her wrist and pulled her inside; his voice was fierce with anger.

'You are leaving me no options, Deniz! How can I continue to take care of you? You have disobeyed everything I ever told you. How dare you do this to me?'

She was seized with a madness of her own, and hissed at him.

What did you do to Klaudia? What did you do to her!

He dragged her into the house, past the drawing room; she glimpsed on all the walls the framed pictures that were all the same: Karl's smile, his naked torso, just as he had stood over her, as she had promised to remember him. She was suddenly full of fear. He jerked her towards the spiral staircase leading up to the tower. 'Get up there. Get up!'

She started to climb and he pushed her from behind. 'Faster. I think you know the way.'

No, I don't know the way. I don't know the way I promise!

They spiralled upwards and upwards and the tower seemed so much higher this time, endlessly high. 'I just can't trust you anymore, Deniz. You have cheated me from the first day you arrived. You don't know how you have hurt me.'

I never meant to hurt you. Don't hurt me.

He was climbing two steps at a time behind her, half carrying her up in front of him.

'I can do nothing for you anymore, Deniz.'

They reached the top. Klaus pushed her into the room. She was blinded for a moment by the projector, then the map started to congeal on the glass all around her and this time it was dotted with – pink butterflies? and –

And sitting at the table, picking from a pile of seven boxes of baklava, his hair brushed slightly differently, was a man who looked just like Klaus, wore a crumpled pair of jeans, carried a camera –

'I believe you have met Karl.'

What are you doing here? How did you get here?

'A meeting that is not much to Karl's credit; but at least *he* has apologized.'

Things were flashing in Deniz's (memories) head. Klaus stood looking at the seated figure.

'How can you eat that stuff, Karl? It's been lying around for days.'

'It's really very good, Klaus. You should get over your block. It's a bit dry but still very good.'

In Deniz's mind, pink butterflies flickered over the metallic greys of the map, massed together like in the cave at home.

'I don't know what to do with her, Karl. I really don't know anymore. Maybe you can help. I am at a loss.'

'You really should relax. You only see problems. Never opportunities. You make everything so damn complicated. You spend too much time on your own. This big house, all your ridiculous computers . . . Just relax.'

'Did I tell you how I met her?'

'Oh please. What do I care? You should see how this girl can fuck! Any man in his right mind . . .'

Deniz was struggling to keep her head straight. The men talked in a way she could not really follow. It just seemed to fill the air with haze. A haze in which the map seemed to flicker and reveal another image that she could not yet discern; the men's conversation was hanging all around her and she could not find a way through it: they kept returning to things that had an aura of great importance but no apparent reality, no solidity, no presence; they pursued long chains of cause and effect full of nothing, whose every link seemed to her completely obscure. She still could not understand if they were talking about her or not.

The image was becoming clearer and her stomach seemed already to know what it was and Karl mused 'How many lives do you think it is possible to save?'

Deniz was distracted: for there, stretching from floor to ceiling where the Atlantic Ocean should have been, she thought she saw a woman in a Japanese print dress dappled by the sun, looking them all in the eye, showing herself off, walking with ridiculous solemnity with Mount Fuji in the background like a lover's lip. Had the mirror remembered? ('But') –

The men went on: there was a film by a man named Bresson called *Une Femme Douce* but the original Dostoevsky story was much better and Karl laughed and taunted Klaus and spoke of sex. 'What do you think Deniz? Are you pregnant yet? Or should we give it another try?'

– the woman had put on another dress, and she was now a gypsy, and how she danced like a little girl, how she pranced for all to see, how she feared what other pictures the mirror had stored ('What?'), and now the men talked of trade and currencies and the economy.

Karl seemed to lose his train of thought as the giant image of Deniz stepped out of a satin ball gown and hung it on the rail ('Can he see it too?'). He sighed.

Deniz could no longer understand anything they said. It was a mere babble:

'These days the media are full of stories of embryos for sale. Scare stories about where they come from. They don't understand anything. They shouldn't talk about things they only half understand.'

Klaudia. What happened to her?

Deniz was crying with confusion.

'Urban legends. Conspiracy theories. People really have their heads full of so much rubbish.'

The much-enlarged image took off the last dress and stood naked, and Deniz could not look any more ('What are those?') but the map was crowded with those pink butterflies that were taking over the map, obscuring the continents, 'What are those?' she asked as if she did not know ('I don't know anything anymore'), she looked closely at the fluttering pink wings, for they were not butterflies at all were they? they were not butterflies.

How a man would desire her when he saw the hidden excitement of those fluttering wings!

Deniz looked from one man to the other. They both looked back at her, with identical faces. Karl sucked noisily on his sticky fingers and picked out another piece of baklava. Deniz said, mostly to herself,

What unspeakable things are piled up at the edges of civilized people's imaginations.

And she ran across the room and leapt through the glass.

It seemed to take an age to fall the height of the tower. She had time to look all around her: to see the city's buildings glinting in the distance, and two men riding on horseback in a nearby field (how they raised the dust around them!). Even though the world had fallen apart, some things were just the same. Like the evening sun, that felt warm on her rushing skin.

The two identical men stand side by side looking at the hole. Bright evening light shines through it into the dim room.

'You've got a pretty big problem in the middle of the Pacific Ocean,' said Karl.

'I know. Have to get it fixed because I have some people coming over on Tuesday.' He edges towards the hole that is just the size of Deniz's hips, and looks down. 'I told you to leave this one alone. She wasn't for you.' He sighs. 'Anyway – by the look of her, she's not much use to you now.'

He sits down in the swivel chair and adjusts the head frame to his eyes.

'Can you clear that up quickly downstairs? You know I'm squeamish.'

'All right,' says Karl.

He picks up a big black plastic bag and begins to go down.

On the staircase he runs into another man, whose features are exactly like his own.

'Ah. Kurt. Just in time. Come with me: I am going to need your help.'

You could not tell how big the night was outside. The windows were expressionless and gave little away. Beyond the glass, a floodlight bathed the empty tarmac in orange, and drew from the darkness a swarm of immense insects that flew madly and erotically into its unresponsive stare. A welding machine glared intermittently in a far-off hangar. In the distance, from the gentle slope of dotted fires, you could surmise a hill.

Somewhere at the very edge of hearing, there was the sound of megaphoned voices that ranted with passions too inaudible, too obscure for understanding.

THE STORE ON MADISON AVENUE

The Fifth Story

I T SO HAPPENED once that Robert De Niro ventured out from New York and went on a voyage through the rural parts of America. As he wandered through those lands he entered a laundromat where a young Chinese woman was washing clothes. There arose between them a longing; and very soon the woman pulled the door of the shop to and turned the sign so it read, to the expectant De Niro, 'Open' instead of 'Closed'. She lowered her clothes, leant against the firm glass porthole of one of the washing machines, and they began to make love. Robert De Niro's penis was large and firm, and their pleasures quickly swelled together. In a moment of thoughtfulness, she took a condom and placed it on him. But it could not contain his torrent; and she conceived a child.

When she discovered her pregnancy, she was anxious about what her husband would think. So she concealed her swelling from him, and when a boy child was born she packed it carefully in a box, went to a nearby truck stop and placed the box with a pile of crates waiting to be loaded. She prayed that her son would find a better home than hers, and departed.

The box with the sleeping boy inside was loaded into the back of a vast Volvo truck bound for the airport. Once there, it found its way into a cargo plane that roared and taxied, climbed into the air, and finally alighted at John F. Kennedy. The box was unloaded and placed amongst piles of containers in the half-land among the warehouses of the freight terminal.

As night fell, there gathered in that place a group of Polish airport workers who secretly lived in the concrete recesses of JFK. They handled wooden crates and steel containers during the day, and knew every stone and every corner of the airport. At night, when their work was done, they lit fires, drank vodka, and spoke of Warsaw, Krakow, and Queens, before sleeping for a few hours on the slabs where they sat, with inebriation their only pillow.

Sensing that he had come to his father's place, the crated baby began to stretch in his box. Without crying, he stretched and stretched; and just as his father's penis had not been contained at his conception, so he too burst from his confines and lay in the open air under the vast industrial night of the freight terminal.

One of the Poles, who had got up to urinate, saw the baby lying there, gently picked him up, and took him to show his friends. They passed the boy from one to the next and he looked deep into their eyes. They decided to keep him with them, and called him Pavel. Pavel's many fathers each loved him as his own and the boy grew up happy.

He learned the language of two red bars by which men spoke to aeroplanes, and he knew how to fix fork-lift trucks.

He roamed the vast expanse of the airport, discovering which containers carried airline food and how to pick locks.

He built a house out of packing crates and decorated it with rope and fluorescent orange canvas from a windsock, as well as trinkets stolen from suitcases in transit: CDs, spectacle lenses, pages torn from books, a bottle of Issey Miyake aftershave, a set of screwdrivers, a Mexican poncho, boxes of Marlboro cigarettes, family photographs, an Australian boomerang, and hundreds of tampons that he hung from the ceiling.

He spent nights in warehouses looking at cases filled with wine, guns, chemicals, furniture, and cotton shirts.

He spoke Polish and sang Polish songs to himself when alone; but, thinking of his future, the Poles also taught him to read English from *Elle*, *Playboy*, and old copies of the *Daily News*.

He became strong, and would challenge the Poles to boxing bouts by the fire at night. Soon, none of them could withstand him. 'What man could have fathered such a child?' they wondered.

Pavel was fascinated by the taxis that arrived at the airport and left again in long columns like so many yellow ants. He thought that the people who drove them must truly know the world. 'When I am a man I will be a taxi driver,' he told the Poles. For his birthday they bought him a map of New York City.

Pavel learned every street, avenue, and road in the five boroughs. He memorized every road through Central Park and every bridge and tunnel. He knew every one-way arrow and every subway station. As he wandered the tarmac enclosure of JFK he imagined himself driving every possible route from Columbus Circle to Battery Park. At length, when he was old enough, he packed some belongings and, along with two of his fathers, went to present himself to Singh Brothers Taxi Company on 22nd Avenue in Queens. During the journey, for the first time in his life he saw the skyline of Manhattan. Its verticality surprised him; his map had only shown it on the horizontal.

Singh Brothers' hand-painted sign stood atop a hut in the middle of a concrete courtyard littered with the hulks of retired taxis. On the street in front was parked a proud line of working models in gleaming yellow, all topped with a cardboard crown proclaiming the virtues of AT&T Wireless.

Inside, under a faded poster of a hovering Ganesh, a solitary Singh brother sat at a desk smiling. 'You wish to drive for me?' he asked.

'Yes,' replied Pavel.

'Then answer me this: What is a good human being?'

'A good human being is one who loves his family.'

'Is a good person only good by virtue of relationship to family?'

'Oh no! A good person also pays taxes and has respect for the law.'

'And how does a good person behave at work?'

'She or he works hard and is responsible and never unfair to colleagues.'

'I can see that you are a conscientious young man. I would like you to join Singh Brothers Taxi Company. I am sure you will be a remarkable driver. But you still have much to learn. Perhaps the streets of New York will teach you.'

Pavel's relationship with the streets was intuitive, like the relationship of data to wires; and soon he could navigate the city more effortlessly than any of the other drivers. At night he would drive down Broadway from 178th Street to Battery Park on the wave of green lights without ever touching the brake, watching the ads that glowed in the quiet night: *Transform your dreams into gold!* and *It's time to make a change!* When he was not working he visited far-off parts of the city to find out what happened there.

One day he decided to see the Aquarium in Brooklyn. He walked among the teeming tanks, looking up into the eyes of rays and porpoises, his face reflecting the pallid aquamarine of underwater light. Finally, he came upon a large tank that was surrounded by people. He edged among them, and saw what they were seeing: sharks, designed more perfectly than any plane he had seen during his childhood in JFK, circling with terse strokes and quiet murderousness. And then, as he pressed his face up against a large glass porthole, much as his mother had pressed her back against another glass porthole so many years before, he saw a woman's eyes looking into his own. Her beautiful head hung within the circle of the glass, her hair floating upwards and her nostrils plugged with beads of air like Tiffany silver. For a long time they looked at each other, and her eyes seemed to call upon him. Then she surfaced, and he saw her no more.

As he left the aquarium – pausing by the sign that said *See Fearless Francine Swim With Sharks!* – he heard steps running behind him.

'Hi,' said the woman from the shark tank, her hair still wet.

'Hello. Are you Francine?'

'My name is Isabella. They called me Francine because it goes with Fearless. Shall we go together?' Her smile smelt of Eau d'Issey.

He drove Isabella in his taxi to her apartment in the East Village.

The subdued GAP furnishings were set off with a blazing Versace wall hanging. A pornographic movie was playing on the television. Pavel looked at her.

'Who are you?'

'I am no ordinary woman. I am the daughter of Isabella Rosselini and Martin Scorsese. No one knows that at the moment when the two of them separated my mother was pregnant. I am a secret to the whole world. The only people that know are you and her.'

'Why did you tell me?'

'Because you are not ordinary either. You can understand.'

'But I grew up in an airport as the son of immigrant workers.'

'Nonetheless. I can see it in you. We will be friends. Come: let me teach you kung fu.'

Pavel ended his first evening with Isabella casting martial shadows on the ceiling of her apartment by the soothing pink glow of pornography.

Not long after, Mr Singh invited Pavel to join him and all the taxi drivers for a party. Pavel brought Isabella. The party took place in New Jersey, on a slip road behind the concrete walls of the New Jersey Turnpike where there was a deserted patch of ground not visible from anywhere. Taxis arrived in great numbers, each carrying six or seven hearty employees of Singh Brothers Taxi Company. A tabla player and singer had been summoned for the occasion, and some of the taxi drivers who had made their home in tents on that patch of ground provided whisky and glasses. Pavel laughed and joked with his friends, and Isabella smiled knowingly. Mr Singh told dramatic tales of how the city used to be: roads that had disappeared entirely, strident towers that had sprouted miraculously from the compost of dilapidated houses.

Four black limousines drew up. Four Chinese drivers in suits and dark glasses leapt out and opened doors for thirteen Chinese ladies in black cocktail dresses.

'Now we will have fine entertainment!' roared Mr Singh.

The thirteen ladies huddled in a circle and began to dance slowly to the rhythm of the tabla and the sentimental strains of the singer, stealing glances at their audience and giggling to each other. The party guests sipped whisky and watched appreciatively. One of the young drivers came to sit with Pavel.

'These dancers are the thirteen daughters of the great ganglord Chu Yu Tang. Mr Chu owns casinos and construction companies all across the city, as well as, you should know, America's largest fireworks factory. His daughters dance for New York's gatherings, high and low. It is said that nothing can escape these ladies, and that the omniscience of the father springs from the dancing engagements of the daughters. But we are only taxi drivers – what have we to hide?'

The tabla and voice became more passionate, and waves of responsiveness passed through the circle of dancers. Card games broke out among the guests, a fire was lit, and the roar of the New Jersey Turnpike dwindled as the dead of night came. Isabella got up to dance to the music on her own. The four Chinese drivers remained standing dutifully in a row by the limousines, and the ever convivial Mr Singh went over to share his good humour with them. Pavel drifted in a haze of alcohol and happiness.

'Truly life is wonderful,' he thought to himself. 'When I lived in the airport and studied the map of this city, how could I have imagined Mr Singh, or Isabella, or Chu Yu Tang and his thirteen dancing daughters? I hope my Polish fathers are well tonight, and as happy as I.'

There was a surge in the music. The tabla player set loose his hands, which stampeded all over his drums, flickering like advertising. The singer left behind the words of his song and gave himself up to ecstatic cries and bellows. The thirteen dancing ladies swayed under a single beatific smile. And suddenly, when the music had completed its full spectrum of moods and permutations, there was a thunderous finale from the drums, thirteen cocktail dresses were flung into the air, and thirteen laughing Chinese ladies in black Chanel bikinis divided themselves into four limousines – and were gone.

As the party began to disperse, Mr Singh came to say goodbye to Pavel. His face was grave.

'Tell me, who is this Isabella?'

'She is my friend.'

'I think you like her very much?'

'I think she is wonderful.' Pavel's face became red in the darkness.

'Pavel: you must take care. These Chinese drivers were asking many questions about her – and about you. I don't know what the future will bring, but I sense some danger. Never become greedy, Pavel. It could deprive you of everything you have.'

'I will heed your words, Mr Singh.'

'God bless you, Pavel.'

Isabella was pensive as they drove back towards dormant Manhattan.

'You know, once my father made a film called *Taxi Driver*. Robert De Niro played the taxi driver. Sometimes when I look at you driving I think of him in that film.'

'Does it have a happy ending?'

'No.'

The sun was just beginning to come up and the black expressway was turning brown.

'Do you wonder if all these bleeding ancestors will catch up with us? For so long my mother was pasted across the billboards of New York as the face of Lancôme. She was luminous and serene. But she has different incarnations. Terrifying ones. In *Blue Velvet* she was a mangled, disgusting thing. Whose daughter will I turn out to be?'

As they looped down towards the Lincoln Tunnel, with Manhattan blinking broadside on ahead of them, the road finally slowed and widened into the Toll Plaza, like a river reaching its delta. As Pavel drew up to the tollbooth he saw inside a man of vast size, his eyes anamorphically distended by heavy eyeglasses with the green-grey tinge of an old bell jar. A weasel sat on the counter next to him.

'Three dollars and fifty cents.'

Pavel searched for the money.

'Spent the night outside the city?'

'Yes.'

Three dollar bills and two quarters were handed over.

'So nice at your age, huh? The two of you just getting home from a night out. She's all tired out and tenderized. Look how she's all dressed up from last night. So cute. You people think you can go where you like, do what you like. You think you're set so firmly in those young bodies of yours like nothing's ever going to change. Well you're wrong.'

He tore off the receipt and thrust it towards Pavel in a shaggy hand. 'Now get outta my face.'

Pavel took the receipt and drove off. He was too tired to think about all these strange things. With the rising sun in his eyes he parked the car in the East Village, where Isabella and he fell asleep in their clothes on sheets by Calvin Klein.

When Pavel awoke, the wooden floorboards were chequered with sunshine.

'So at last you're awake, my Taxi Driver! I've already cleaned the whole apartment and been out to get us breakfast. It's a beautiful day!'

Isabella had prepared a feast: mangos, goat cheese, dried dates, coffee and Coca-Cola-flavoured ice cream. She had a bandana tied around her head.

'And since you make me feel lucky, I got us these.' She jumped on the bed and produced, with a flourish, a box of Oreo cookies. 'Look at this. "SPECIAL ANNIVERSARY OFFER! Could YOU be the winner of OREO's most magical prize ever? Open this box to find out . . ." What do you think? Do you want to open it?'

'You're the one feeling lucky. You open it.'

'OK.'

Isabella unwrapped the box slowly and intently, with a hint of mock wonder playing across her eyebrows. She opened the flaps carefully, reached inside, and drew out the cellophane cylinder full of Oreo cookies. They looked very ordinary. She looked inside the box and saw nothing.

'Ah well,' she sighed resignedly, shaking the box with feigned frustration. But as she was about to toss it away, out fell a little piece of gold paper.

'What's this?' she cried. She began to unfold the paper. Inside, printed in glittery text, were these words:

CONGRATULATIONS!

You are the winner of our most spellbinding prize ever! It's real magic! You won't believe what the wizards at Nabisco have 'in store' for you!

HAVE THE TIME OF YOUR LIFE AND WIN $$$!

Just follow the instructions below.
And don't forget to try our new OREO flavours!

'It can't be true,' said Isabella. 'They always do this. When you read the instructions you realize that you haven't won yet but if you keep buying Oreo cookies you might . . .'

They read on.

The OREO cookies in the packet you have just bought are not just ordinary OREO cookies. These are magic cookies. The only ones we have ever made. If you follow these instructions we guarantee you will be amazed. Do not attempt to use these cookies without first reading this insert carefully. Nabisco Corporation takes no responsibility for any loss, damage, or physical or psychological harm caused by the misuse of these cookies. Should you experience any problems, call our special hotline on 1-800 OREO-WIZ (1-800 673-6949).

1. You will need a friend to help you carry out these instructions. DO NOT TRY THIS ALONE. If you are under 18 years of age make sure you are helped by an adult.

2. Take one magic OREO Chocolate Sandwich Cookie and crumble it into one pint (568 ml) of milk.

3. Ask your friend to pour the whole mixture over you slowly and carefully, ensuring that your whole body is covered.

4. A magical transformation will take place. Have fun!

141

5. When you are ready to reverse the transformation, say, 'OREO, OREO change me back!' At this point your friend should crumble another OREO cookie in a pint of milk and should pour it carefully on the ground in front of you. You will be changed back to your original form.

6. There are 20 OREO cookies in this packet. Each of them is good for one transformation. When you have finished this packet, you will never be able to use this magic again.

7. Finally – tell us about your experiences! We always love hearing stories about our OREO cookies – and THIS story is sure to make you a star!

'Is it a hoax?' asked Isabella. She looked in the packet for any more clues, but it was empty.

'Shall we try it and see?' suggested Pavel.

Isabella mused.

'Let's try it.'

They opened the packet, took out one Oreo cookie, and crumbled it into a pint of milk in a jug. Pavel held the jug above Isabella's head and was suddenly seized with laughter.

'Go on – pour!'

Pavel started to pour the mixture all over her. He poured until the jug was empty and Isabella was standing in a pool of milk, her hair and clothes flowing with white rivulets. They looked fixedly at each other waiting for something to happen. And then, as Pavel watched, he saw her face start to flatten and become slowly grey; he glimpsed just one last look of alarm on her features before they became concrete; he saw her body unfold into vertiginous horizontals and verticals; streaks of chrome and glass flashed through her, and as her innards became visible, he saw them harden into spiral staircases and organic chandeliers that somehow spawned space all around them, space that metastasized beyond her apartment and ate up the street all around, that dissolved the city into a rushing ravine and transported the two of them right through its solidity, as Isabella became huge and Doric, as she aligned herself with the rectilinearity of the Manhattan streets, and as her final traces of human curves became sculpted into sharp corners. Then suddenly it became quiet and she settled in the landscape of the city as if she had always been there, and Pavel was still standing in front of her looking, no longer at her bandana-topped face, but at his own reflection in the window.

Isabella had become a store on Madison Avenue.

None of the passers-by who thronged the sidewalks seemed to notice that anything had changed. In fact they walked in and out of the store as if it were any other. Pavel tested his senses to see if they were still reporting accurately on the world. He examined the store that seemed to have been born in front of him: a deluxe clothes boutique on three floors, with vast windows on the ground floor that revealed a row of mannequins clad in clothes that were irregular and many-layered as if they had been repeatedly repaired by hand, and, visible through the massive front doors, an interior of steel and glass in which more such creations were suspended in electronic halos like relics. And, above the main entrance – Pavel could not understand how it was possible – was the shop's name: Isabella.

Still numb with amazement he entered the store. Fibrous shirts were laid out on glowing tables of frosted glass as if they were priceless, crumbling parchments, and gossamer dresses hung from the ceiling on steel cables that moved them up and down in a stately overhead dance. A vast staircase coiled up to the other floors, and all around there were beautiful attendants who all seemed, with their elongated limbs and their weightless gait, to belong to some new subphylum of humanity. As Pavel stood, the shop became packed with people who could not keep their hands off the startling textures and the original cuts. Queues formed at the cash registers, and four- and five-digit dollar amounts flashed up on the displays; the artworks were carefully wrapped and placed in origami bags, and happy Saturday couples went forth again onto the broad sidewalks of Madison Avenue.

Pavel did not know what he should do. Was Isabella still herself? Would she remember the instructions for turning back? And how would he know when it was time?

143

Pavel stood as motionless as the right angles of Madison Avenue and 65th Street while the advancing afternoon flitted all around him. At last, at the moment when the sinking sun shone directly along 65th Street and people's shadows extended several blocks eastwards of their tired feet, he heard in his head, in Isabella's unmistakeable voice, 'OREO, OREO, change me back!'

He looked cautiously around him as he approached the store with his jug of milk, but no one seemed to be paying him any attention. With infinite care, he poured the whole pint over the threshold of the store. Instantly, its monumental architecture started to waver and crumple, its mirrors and windows telescoped, it became dislodged from the sidewalk and started to retreat through galloping space. Pavel had just enough time to glimpse the buildings around it expanding covetously into the gap it had left before he was miles away from there and the store was becoming bipedal and the last remaining concrete was being sucked up into flesh – and he and Isabella were once again standing in her apartment, gazing into each other's eyes.

They stood.

And Isabella leapt on Pavel and threw her arms around his neck, laughing with joy.

'That was amazing! You have no idea how much fun it is to be a store!'

'I was so worried.'

'I know – I didn't know how to tell you I was OK. I'm sorry. But I had so much fun.'

Pavel gave a half-smile.

'And do you realize how much money we made today? Hundreds of thousands of dollars! We're rich, Pavel!'

Pavel had not realized how severe had been the foreboding that had gripped him all afternoon, and to the great surprise of both of them he began to sob uncontrollably.

Isabella on Madison Avenue became one of the choicest destinations of the New York elite. The *New Yorker* soon carried a feature on its 'Primordial Chic' and the store became a haunt for the cultural vanguard who proudly wore their patched outfits to soirées at MOMA and the Met. No one seemed to notice that it was not always there. Sometimes people would look out for it as they strolled up Madison Avenue at night and wonder how they could have missed it. The *New York Times* described the colossal building as 'tucked away', as if the writer had a sense of its impermanence.

Pavel drove taxis less and less. He and Isabella suddenly had as much money as they could ever want. He developed a taste for Giorgio Armani suits, which he hung in rows in Isabella's apartment, sorted by colour. On weekend afternoons they dropped in to the Four Seasons and ordered lobster and champagne 'to go'. They bought a Mercedes convertible and spent weekends gambling in Vegas. They always won.

Every now and then, Isabella would become a store for a day. Pavel spent his days there, looking at the clothes, watching the people shop, practising kung fu moves in the mirrors when no one was looking, happy to be sharing this strange excitement with his friend. Gradually, the Oreo cookies disappeared.

One morning, as Pavel used the seventeenth cookie to bring about the magic metamorphosis for the penultimate time, and the great boutique took its proud place amongst the other stores on Madison Avenue, he noticed that there were four black limousines waiting outside. Almost before the store had become whole, rows of car doors flew open, and out poured the thirteen daughters of Chu Yu Tang. Giggling and jostling they ran into the store to see the new clothes that everyone was talking about. They pored collectively over every piece, exclaiming with delight and admiration. Every texture and every seam was explored by thirteen sets of hands, and iridescent skirts and fantastical dresses were separately tried on by each one of them to see whom they would suit the best. A great pile of their purchases began to accumulate at the cash desk, but they were determined to see everything. It was not till early afternoon that they progressed to the second floor, and as the day came to a close they were still posing in more hats and coats in front of the third floor's mirrored walls. Outside, the limousine drivers waited impassively. Seven o'clock came, and eight, and the other stores had all closed. Pavel stood anxiously awaiting the now-familiar signal from Isabella. But the thirteen dancers showed no sign of losing interest in their spree. At last the message came, 'OREO, OREO, change me back!'

As surreptitiously as he could, Pavel approached the threshold of the store and emptied his jug of milk on the ground. In a few seconds he was standing with Isabella back in her apartment. She was furious.

'I was waiting and waiting for Chu Yu Tang's dancing daughters to pay for their clothes. But they didn't seem to have any intention of it! They spent the whole day there, prancing around and making the shop a mess, keeping all the assistants busy. And they didn't pay a cent!'

Pavel was surprised by this outburst.

'Isabella – I think we should be careful. You know how powerful Chu Yu Tang is in this city. He is the unchallenged king of retail property in New York, and the fame of our store has certainly come to his attention. Maybe his daughters weren't just there to shop today. I suggest that we don't use the last two cookies. We've had a lot of fun and earned a lot of money. I don't think we should risk any danger.'

He was mindful of Mr Singh's warning on the night of the party.

'Are you crazy? After the amount of money we lost today there is no way we're going to give up our last cookies. Next weekend is Memorial Day weekend, one of the biggest shopping weekends of the year. We're going to make good our losses.'

Nothing Pavel could say would change Isabella's mind.

As she had predicted, the following Saturday saw the streets of New York packed with shoppers, and the three floors of Isabella were full as never before. By now the distinctive craftsmanship of the clothes had taken the city by storm, and even those who could not afford the clothes wanted to see what the sensation was all about. The cashiers could not scan Visa and MasterCard quickly enough, so long and impatient were the queues that formed. For the first time, the takings during the day topped one million dollars.

Pavel could not seem to escape his own anxiety as he wandered around the store for the last time. Mr Singh's words haunted him, and he could not believe that the visit en masse of Chu Yu Tang's daughters could be a coincidence.

As the end of the day came and customers began to leave the store, Pavel was roused from his apprehensions by the elated voice of Isabella in his head: 'OREO, OREO, change me back!' He took the last cookie from his pocket, unwrapped it, and crumbled it into the jug of milk. Looking all around him to ensure he was not being watched, he moved towards the entrance of the store.

Just as he was about to pour the milk, two men seized him and threw him against the storefront. The jug of milk almost flew out of his grasp; as it was, more than half its contents were thrown over his assailants. Pavel recognized them as two of the forbearing limousine drivers from the day before.

'She is ours now,' one of them whispered. 'Tell us how to get her back.'

'Let me go and I'll show you,' breathed Pavel.

'No, my friend. You tell us and we let you go.'

'The magic cannot be worked by anyone else. You have to let me do it. Otherwise she will be lost to all of us.'

The two men looked at each other.

'OK – you do it. But we're holding onto you – you're not getting away.'

Firmly clasped by the two men, Pavel went to the threshold of the store. Pavel knew the mechanism of this transformation well enough now to be horrified by the mere puddle of milk remaining in the bottom of the jug. He crouched down, and poured.

The milk was not enough to even wet the whole threshold, and as Pavel desperately shook the last drops onto the ground, he knew something was terribly wrong. The massive building swayed and screeched, and as he and his two companions were wrenched from the ground they found themselves jolting in senseless circles, jerking with excess weight, slashing through the stone of Midtown that was only melted in patches, their bodies shaken through by the deafening shriek of writhing concrete. The whole island seemed to strain as they blundered through it like some blinded, terrified beast, and in the distance

Pavel had the mad delusion that the Brooklyn Bridge was rearing on its hind legs. Finally, they crashed painfully onto the floor of Isabella's apartment, faces and clothes splashed with blood, and, in the middle of the floor there flailed a thing of stone and flesh, its organs half-formed and leaking, its limbs chafed and mangled.

'Isabella! Isabella!' cried Pavel, trying without success to lift the dead weight of her concrete body from the floor and collapsing instead on top of it. Her eyes and ears had not begun to appear, and he could offer her no comfort.

The two men pulled him off the heaving figure and tied him to a chair, shouting questions.

'How do we get her back? How do we get this power? Tell us how it works!'

'It's too late,' sobbed Pavel, 'it's too late.'

They hit him impatiently round the face.

'Do you want her to die? Tell us how to change her!'

Pavel shook his head, choking with grief. One of them aimed a kick at his chest. The chair tipped backwards and fell over, Pavel's head smashing on the floor.

'We saw you pouring milk. Is it milk?'

One of them threw open the refrigerator and grabbed three cartons of milk. They began to shake them out over Isabella's bleeding wreckage. Nothing happened. In their agitation they emptied everything they could find over her, yelling and gesticulating at the epileptic stones to get up. They threw cream and Coca-Cola-flavoured ice cream, which spattered over the glass front of her torso, sank into the cracks in the stone, and melted over the open flesh. As the warped creature beat its concrete limbs on the floor in distress, they became more sickened and more wild in their efforts. They broke eggs that slipped whole between the shrunken front doors and disappeared, and shook out a one-litre carton of tomato juice that extended a scarlet stain across the entire apartment. As they poured Tabasco sauce over her, it seared her exposed lungs and heart and sent her into silent convulsions of agony.

Pavel could not take any more. As he had done in his infancy, he began to stretch and stretch until the ropes around him broke. And in the same room as he had so recently learned the art, he unleashed a furious burst of kung fu on the inattentive men, smothered their resistance, and knocked them both unconscious. With new strength, he picked Isabella up from the floor, ran outside, and laid her in the back of his taxi. He started the car and pulled away at great speed. As he did so, four sets of headlights flashed on in his rear-view mirror, and the skulking black limousines set off after him like bats. Driving with one hand and hardly taking his eyes off the figure whose fits grew less and less frequent on the back seat, Pavel frantically slapped his pockets searching for his phone. 1–800 OREO-WIZ.

'Welcome to the Nabisco Corporation's twenty-four-hour Magic Offer Hotline!' said a female voice with pre-recorded excitement. 'Due to heavy volume we cannot take your call right now. But please hold, and a Nabisco Wizard will be with you shortly!' She faded away into a mush of slow sax.

Pavel's instinct for the streets of New York was faultless, and he quickly managed to draw away from the flying limousines. It was dark and beginning to rain. He headed out of the city hoping that Mr Chu's wrath would not extend beyond his territory of Manhattan.

A real voice cut into the numbness of the saxophone. 'Welcome to Nabisco, how can I help you?'

'Yes hello! – it's an emergency – my friend hasn't turned back – she became the store and she hasn't turned back properly – I need –'

'Just a minute, sir. Calm down. Let's start from the beginning. Can I get your name and address?'

'My name is Pavel. You don't understand. This is really an emergency. She's dying.'

'Are you saying there was something wrong with the product sir?'

'No! I just need to know what to do!'

'Did you follow the instructions provided?'

'Yes! I mean – I ran out of milk for the last cookie – two men came and I spilt the milk everywhere and she's not turned back – I think she's dying and now they're chasing us –'

'Where are you now, sir?'

'I'm just coming up to the Lincoln Tunnel. We're going to get cut off.'

'I see.'

The voice considered for a moment.

'Sir, you were provided with very clear instructions, I believe. If you had got to the very last cookie you should have realized that you were dealing with something that had to be taken very seriously. I'm afraid Nabisco Corporation cannot take any responsibility for any misuse of any of our products. I suggest you take your friend to hospital and seek medical advice.'

'What are you saying? You're the only one who can help. Please listen! I need one more cookie to change her back again. Otherwise she will die. What can a doctor do? He won't even recognize that she's human.'

'I'm sorry sir. We only made twenty of those cookies, so I can't let you have another one. I understand your situation but I really don't think I can do any more than I have. The only suggestion I have is to ensure she gets good medical treatment.'

'You are so – so irrelevant!' screamed Pavel. 'She is lying here looking like a demolished building, bleeding all over the car, and – Please help me!'

'Sorry, sir. I hope you manage to sort it out. Thank you for calling Nabisco.' The line went dead.

Pavel raced through the Lincoln Tunnel and hardly slowed down for the toll booth, holding a five-dollar bill out of the window as he rolled through. A giant hand seized the money; a weasel stared at him from the counter.

'Keep the change!' he shouted.

He waited too long for the barrier to open. Suddenly the toll keeper was in front of him swinging with a baseball bat; the windscreen turned crystalline and opaque and then shattered over the dashboard, and the toll keeper's face was inches from Pavel's own, his eyes like ringed planets through his spectacles.

'I told you before, you kids. You think you can just come in and go out. Like no one else matters. No respect for barriers. You can treat me how you want. "Keep the change!" Do I need charity from you?'

Pavel flattened the accelerator and the engine howled, but the toll keeper had the taxi in a firm grip and it would not move. With his enormous hands he ripped off the front of the car and smashed the engine with his baseball bat until it burst open and died.

As he glanced anxiously in the rear-view mirror Pavel could see that the four black limousines had nearly caught him up.

The toll keeper sent the roof of the taxi spinning into the darkness and peered down into the car. He cuffed Pavel hard on the ear and seized his phone.

'This is our phone is it? Call friends in San Francisco and Miami? When it's cheap rate call London and Hong Kong? So cute you are.' He crumpled the phone in his hand and threw it away. He leant over Pavel and put his face up against his.

Gazing unblinkingly into his eyes, Pavel reached behind him to where Isabella lay and his hand settled on a block of concrete. He pulled it away with a sucking sound, and with one blow smashed the toll keeper's bulbous glasses.

The toll keeper roared and staggered, completely disoriented. Unable to see, he spread his arms to prevent the two of them from escaping, but Pavel was too quick for him. He seized Isabella and ran with her towards the trees at the edge of the Toll Plaza. He knew that if he was able to climb the concrete bank and disappear among the trees his pursuers could not follow; and with a Herculean effort he carried the leaden figure up the slope with him and slipped away into shadowy and sweet-smelling woodland. He put her down as gently as he could, then collapsed in hyperventilations while four limousines skidded to a halt in formation and four Chinese drivers got out and cursed and punched the air and threw their sunglasses at the tarmac in frustration.

Pavel lived with the mute and suffering Isabella in the woods near the Toll Plaza for many weeks, facing every kind of privation known to humankind. He wept over her as she lay lifeless and unrecognizable, tenderly wiped away the foul-smelling discharges that oozed from within her, and placed leaves on her wounds. He ate roots and berries and became thin and yellow. 'Isabella, Isabella,' he would moan at night when he sat up awake in the impenetrable darkness with the rush of cars in the background, 'if only you knew how much I have come to love you! If only I had pronounced the words while you still had the ears to hear them!' He stroked her and kissed her; but he was touching only glass and steel and his caresses seemed useless and pitiful.

As the weeks went by and he became more gaunt and unkempt, his mind became dislodged from time and place and he began to have strange visions. In the darkness at night a rectangle of light danced at a distance, maddening him with writhing images of people and places and things. He would shut his eyes to try and block it out but still the mirage played on his eyelids, and he could not think or sleep or dream. He saw in the rectangle big, glistening images of the passions of the world.

Week followed week, and Pavel became exhausted with the visions. Every night they took over his mind even as he struggled to banish them and seek refuge deep inside himself. One night he opened his eyes and the pictures were right in front of his face; the light seared his eyelashes and the tip of his nose and he was staring at the texture of the thing: and he realized that this whole scintillating world was only a rapid succession of frozen moments, dead images that had been accelerated just beyond the speed of perception – and thus come to life.

Pavel summoned his will and looked deep into the images, and the senses of his body began to forget their limits. The sky became white with the light from distant stars; his ears filled with car alarms in far-off Manhattan and the murmur of conversations in overhead aeroplanes. The perfume of women in SoHo bars rushed up his nostrils like a torrent. And, as his perceptions sped up, the images that had so long tormented him seemed to follow each other more and more slowly, they lost their sheen and became a funereal procession of blurred and insubstantial snatches of time. And finally, they stopped.

Pavel felt that something had changed at that moment. He did not know what it was. But when Mr Chu's men came for him, he was ready.

Though they came with guns and knives Pavel went meekly and without fear. He planted a tender kiss on the concrete wall of Isabella's cheek and left her snuggled in a warm blanket of leaves, confident that he would return soon.

Mr Chu sat sipping whisky at one end of a cream leather sofa in his well-appointed reception room on the eightieth floor of the Trump World Tower. His suited legs were short and crossed, and he seemed preoccupied by the dancing eyelets of the nearby Chrysler Building that had just been lit. He stared for several minutes out of the window, his gold-ringed finger resting on his upper lip. Pavel stood expectantly. Behind him he could sense the silent circling of the thirteen daughters, among whom, this time, there was not a hint of giggling.

'Do you know what someone who deals in real estate is called in France?' asked Mr Chu, without diverting his gaze from the chorus-girl formation of lights.

'No. I don't.'

For the first time Mr Chu looked at him.

'He is an *immobilier*. That is because what he deals in is *immobile*. It doesn't move.'

The pause was excruciatingly long. Soft lighting came on automatically in response to the encroaching evening gloom.

'That is the wonderful predictability of my business. Land – on human timescales, at least, and with only a few exceptions – never goes anywhere. Buildings do not move. Once you own land you may decide to destroy what has been put there and create something new in order to increase its value. Other people might try to damage your property. But you do not have to wonder if someone will move your land from where it is. You do not need to be concerned that someone might make copies of your land and sell them at your expense. There is a tidy indubitableness to land ownership.

'At least that is what I thought until recently. Recently, some remarkable events have shaken my confidence in this state of affairs. I do not like to have my confidence shaken. Most of all, I do not want anyone else's confidence to be shaken. A widespread confidence in this rule is the fundamental basis for my wealth.'

He sipped delicately from his whisky glass.

'And so, young man, my message to you is very simple. I want to know exactly how you made your flexible store on Madison Avenue. And I want to have sole rights to this technology. Either you tell me this or I will kill you here and now. Let me be very clear: I have no qualms. I know your background – you are a nobody. There is no risk in it for me. My daughters here are very good at killing. Better than they are at dancing. I am also very impatient. So you have five minutes to make up your mind.'

What was Pavel to do? Was his fate to die here in this room? Was that how his adventure would end? He started to babble, told the story of breakfast with Isabella when she had bought the Oreo cookies, that he did not know how it worked, that he had simply followed the instructions in the packet, that he would never do it again – really it will never happen again – and he never meant to –

'Kill him.'

The thirteen daughters spread thick black plastic on the marble floor and deftly capsized Pavel onto it. Mr Chu did not move or even look for he was contemplating once again the triumphant tower of the Chrysler Corporation. A knife was produced but something was stirring in Pavel – a knowledge; and as they slit his throat something scraped, something erupted in their eyes, for at that moment his substance – yes! – had become concrete and all their slicings were in vain; they were seized with a frenzy, but Pavel only lay like a statue that blunted their wrath. Mr Chu looked on with increasing dismay, for had his confidence not been shaken once again and was that not something that made him furious? And were not even his daughters terrified when he got up from his seat to do the job himself and started to kick the stone figure, kick repeatedly with his pristine Louis Vuitton shoes until his fragrant hair become damp and fell indecorously across his face?

By any standards, the Nabisco Corporation had done something astonishing in the creation of their magic Oreo Cookies. They had filed for several hundred patents to protect all the processes they had invented to make them: from pharmacological mechanisms, which ensured that the cookies would release their active ingredients into the body at exactly the correct rate, to the design of the store; from all the various transformations of muscle, bone, hair into concrete, steel, and glass (and vice versa) to the creation of a verbal and chemical switch that would trigger the whole miraculous process.

But Pavel's trials in the woodland by the I-95 had transported him to extremes of the mind that are rarely attained by human beings, and in those extremes he had been able to understand in a moment the secrets and illusions of the physical world that Nabisco engineers had taken years to unlock.

And so it was, at the point when his life was in mortal danger, that Pavel managed to master the transubstantiation of matter and to turn it – in blatant patent infringement – against his enemies. It seemed effortless to will his flesh into stone, and he was not alarmed as he felt his organs becoming heavy and dense, as a fossilizing wave began with his femurs and spread out to his metatarsi and metacarpi, and his mind was in no way affected as he lost his ability to move or talk or even, finally, to see. While Mr Chu kicked him frenziedly and the daughters tried to smash his stone limbs he felt calm and strong, and soon his assailants found that their fists and feet were sticking, becoming grafted; for Pavel was absorbing them into his stoniness, drawing them in bit by bit as a snake does a pig, sensing their hatred turn to fear, their features become immobile, and their struggles become more constrained. Mr Chu and his thirteen daughters were all frozen in crazy poses; and even as the last colour disappeared from eyes and hair there was once more a rushing as the whole molten mass of them sank through eighty floors of the Trump World Tower, descended deep under United Nations Plaza, and Pavel was extracting himself from the conglomeration and leaving them to their fate. A great weight was being lifted from his lungs, his eyes were becoming liquid again, and he could see all around him straight edges spreading out from fourteen pairs of shoulders, and teeth and ribs straightening into gates of iron bars. Pavel knew the biochemical reactions had enough energy to continue to their end and he needed to get out; but as he floated to the tarmac surface of the road, he turned around and watched as the corners became whole with massive buttresses; in the split second before he became only one of hundreds of other people walking down

155

Second Avenue, he managed to see, before the ground closed up, just as the forms became final and solid, fourteen square cells, each with its own steel gate and a tiny window secured with heavy bars.

He had turned Chu Yu Tang and his thirteen daughters into their own dungeon, far below ground just outside the United Nations.

After such an amplification of his powers it was a little task to turn Isabella back into the woman she had once been.

She was not quite whole. Two fingers were missing from where he had pulled away a piece of concrete to defeat the toll keeper.

At last he was able to confess his love to her, a confession she reciprocated; and they lived happily, very happily, ever after.

Pavel was never able to sell his story to the media, who did not believe one word of what he said. His remarkable adventures therefore had no noticeable effect on society.

He went back to driving taxis for Mr Singh, who, when he finally passed away at a grand old age, graciously left Singh Brothers' Taxi Company in Pavel's care.

Isabella gave up her job at the aquarium not long after the events recounted here. The fashion boutique she opened in Chelsea met with astonishing success, and earned her two separate awards for New York's Best Woman Entrepreneur.

During the rare silences in meetings of the United Nations General Assembly, moans and yells are still sometimes heard, apparently from underground. Cantonese-speaking delegates always seem to be the most upset by these cries.

Pavel and Isabella still enjoy the occasional Oreo cookie.

THE FLYOVER
The Sixth Story

IN THE CITY of Lagos there was once a young man named Marlboro. He lived in a small room on Lagos Island near to the hustle and bustle of Balogun Market with his mother and two elder brothers.

The eldest brother was devoted to learning, and managed to get money together to go to a reputable university in India. The second brother had a friend who ran errands for rich people; they set up a booth together on Victoria Island: 'Bills paid. Visas made. No more stress. Trustworthy service: receipt always given. No job too big or too small!' Soon the commute became too much and he set up a bed in his stall. Marlboro was alone with his mother.

'Why don't you go and improve yourself like your brothers?' she would say. She worked long hours in a beer parlour and had no time for Marlboro's laziness. He would lie on her bed while she was out, under a crinkled poster of Jesus standing on a rainbow saying 'Blessed are the poor in spirit: for theirs is the kingdom of heaven', and he would watch the lizards sitting on the fluorescent tube waiting for flies. 'If you can only find your own fluorescent light to sit on,' thought Marlboro, 'then everything comes to you.'

In fact everything did come to Marlboro; for he was generally thought to have Authority, and his evenings were full with people bringing him cups of ginger juice or measures of whisky in return for advice on how they could improve their luck in business or love. Everyone talked to him, discussed who was making money and how, who was honest and who was a cheat, and one person's problem always turned out to be the next person's solution. He gained a Reputation.

'Why don't you tell me who my father was?' Marlboro would ask late at night as his mother put up her cerise-toenailed feet that perfectly matched her cerise lipstick and flicked between soap operas, turned up to full volume to cover the scream of the flyover outside.

'Maybe if you make something of your life I will. It can't do anyone any good right now.'

'Maybe if I knew who my father was I would make something of my life.'

There was certainly an unaccounted-for influence in his mother's fortunes: for how could a woman with her income and status start spending her mornings at the Air Hostess Academy learning how to fly in planes? Surely it could not be her undeniable beauty alone that allowed her to cheat fate so dramatically; how could she suddenly be taking flights to Riyadh, Johannesburg, New York, and London? Marlboro affected indifference towards the vile speculation about his mother's ruses that arrived on his doorstep every evening, but was secretly mystified at how it had all happened. She would return with bars of Swiss chocolate that she would eat delicately in front of the National Geographic channel, giving only listless hints of endless avenues of glinting shops in return for Marlboro's circuitous questioning.

One evening while she was away in Frankfurt or Rome a one-eyed man came to the door and handed Marlboro a business card. 'Come. Tomorrow. Mr Bundu would like to make a proposition.'

Mr Bundu offered Marlboro whisky, which he gladly accepted, and sat him on a greasy red velvet sofa. 'I have heard about you. Seems you have Authority. A Reputation. Wondering how I can make use of that.'

'What business are you in, Mr Bundu?'

'Think of the flyovers by Balogun Market. Near your house. What a bazaar under those cement awnings! Do you know how much cash changes hands? Monument to the human spirit, Marlboro, the buzzing conversation of trade. But if you laid out all the great chains of being that end up in a place like that – you know what I'm saying. Moon and back several times. Complexities will strain your mind. Who owns which traders, who's got the monopoly on buses or prostitutes, which foreign company is the government trying to impress with seizures of locally-made versions of their products, who's Hausa, who's Yoruba, who owns the police chief, which products are producing inadequate returns on all this space, whose supply just dried up in Taiwan, who's behind the latest Surulere movie, who has bought the blindness of the most eyes . . . Phew! It's a whole universe. It *is* the whole universe. A worthy challenge for the intellect, don't you think?'

'You're very right, Mr Bundu.'

'It's a scintillating world; it's a pyramid of mercury: and we have to be standing on the top. Don't want to be paying out too many cuts to people above us. We want to collect them all ourselves. I work for a very powerful man, Marlboro. That's him in the picture.'

On the wall was a photograph of the multi-millionaire businessman Kinglord Bombata shaking hands with the French Prime Minister. Kinglord was wearing king-size Gucci sunglasses, and Marlboro thought to himself, 'There is a man I could look up to.'

'Mr Bombata is like you and me, Marlboro. Likes good systems. Doesn't like it when there are leaks. "Get me ten per cent of all the deals in those markets, Bundu," he says. But we need more information, Marlboro. Strategic thinking. I have boys who are very committed, they've done some great work, but the money's just not coming in. You have a Reputation, Marlboro. Do you think you can help?'

'I certainly do, Mr Bundu. It would be an honour.'

When Marlboro's mother next came back home he announced to her that he finally had a job – working for Mr Bundu.

'You'll get yourself killed, Marlboro.'

'No I won't. My survival instinct is impeccable.'

'You don't know what you're playing with. I don't know why I keep coming back here for you.'

The next time, she did not. Marlboro never saw her again.

Marlboro threw himself into his work and quickly proved to be a valuable asset to Mr Bundu's enterprise. In the evening sessions with his friends he probed deeper into their businesses and acquaintances and political intelligence, and became more impatient with those who were not useful. He took a number of people in the locality into his confidence and asked them to report to him on the things they heard and saw – the old-time owner of the manioc stall just outside his house, the night watchman, a policeman he had known since childhood . . . Each night he would have confidential phone conversations with Mr Bundu in which he passed on an astonishing array of information about upcoming police raids and political alliances. On the strength of this, Mr Bundu began to play a bold but methodical game of elimination. Systematic bus burnings frightened the public away from the transport system run by one competitor. Another organization that was planning its own rout of Mr Bundu's network was struck one night with a series of brutal attacks on key personnel, leaving it depleted and incredulous. Mr Bundu started to pay Marlboro a modest wage that allowed him to keep his mother's room.

With one woman gone from his life, two more quickly entered it.

The first existed only in his mind. Asabi, he called her, and she began to waft into the moments between sleep and wake, dropping a slow-falling gossamer veil over the world that shut out the whine of the okadas and all the barking merchants fighting for space under the flyovers, and left just sweet conversation. She appeared dressed in long Yves Saint-Laurent evening dresses with blue coral beads at her neck and a gele wrapped into a fantasy around her head, and she sat in marble houses with trees and verandahs. 'Marlboro,' she would say, 'you are doing well for yourself. Soon you will be out of your troubles, you will have space in this city to call your own, space for your mind to expand in; you will have houses and cars, and women will desire you. Your mother left too soon: if only she had been here to see this! And your father would be proud too: of that I am sure.'

'But who is my father?'

'Oh, Marlboro, why do you ask such questions? Fear not: for I am here, and in you I am well pleased. I will take care of you.'

And there was another new arrival in his life; for one day, as he was standing at a distance and watching the police seize all the stock of a CD and DVD trader who had fallen foul of Mr Bundu's machinations, a young girl marched straight up to him and stood impudently in front of him, considering his face.

'I can see two of me in your sunglasses!'

Marlboro did not quite know what to say.

'Who are you?' he ventured.

'Ona.'

'How old are you?'

'Fourteen.'

'You look much younger.'

'Well, I'm not.'

'Where are you from?'

'Southeast. Just come to town. I'm going to be a movie star.'

Ona came to live with Marlboro and he became very happy to have her around. He would wake her in the morning with a steaming plate of fried banana, fresh from the market, and when his work was finished they would talk long into the night until Ona fell asleep curled up under his arm.

'I'll take care of you, Marlboro,' she would say. 'You won't be in this room forever. With the traffic roaring by your ear. I'll take you out of here.'

'You'll forget me,' he said, with mock self-pity.

'I won't forget you, Marlboro. Maybe I'll even marry you.'

'You're like my little sister, Ona. I can't marry you.'

'Let's come back to this conversation in a couple of years' time when I'm the hottest property in Surulere and you can't move under those flyovers of yours without seeing life-size pictures of me. In my latest role: the beautiful and tragic African queen abducted into slavery by a cruel but handsome white man. You'll wish then you'd never said you couldn't marry me. All the folks in Victoria Island will be trying to get me to their garden parties just so they can see what I look like in real life. You'd better behave, Marlboro, and maybe I'll let you come with me.'

Whenever Marlboro made a little money he would put one hundred naira in an envelope and send it to her with a note:

DEAR ONA. EVERYONE IS TALKING ABOUT YOU IN HOLLYWOOD. WHEN ARE YOU GOING TO MAKE YOUR FIRST MOVIE? I CAN'T WAIT TO SEE IT. I HOPE THE ENCLOSED WILL HELP YOU ON YOUR WAY. IN LOVE AND ADMIRATION, STEVEN SPIELBERG. PS DON'T TELL ANYONE BUT I ONLY WATCH NIGERIAN MOVIES.

or

DEAR ONA. IT IS WITH CONSIDERABLE EXCITEMENT THAT WE APPREHEND FROM OUR COURTIERS THAT YOU ARE TO BE A GREAT STAR. UNFORTUNATELY THINGS ARE NOT WHAT THEY USED TO BE HERE IN ENGLAND AND THIS IS ALL WE ARE ABLE TO SPARE FOR NOW. WE HOPE IT WILL BE OF ASSISTANCE. PLEASE COME TO BUCKINGHAM PALACE WHEN YOU ARE NEXT IN THE AREA. YOURS SINCERELY, HM THE QUEEN OF ENGLAND.

'You are such a darling,' said Ona to Marlboro on reading the Queen's dedication.

'I don't know what you're talking about,' he replied.

One morning, when Marlboro walked out to buy breakfast, he saw an army of policemen clearing the traders from under the flyover with sticks: there was no time to grab all the merchandise and they were wrapping what they could carry in sheets, but the ground was littered with spilled fruit and smashed VCRs as the police shouted down complaints and arguments and city workers shovelled the debris of scattered digital watches into the back of a truck. Marlboro watched in dismay.

'What is happening?' he asked the manioc seller.

'Government's made a decision. This market is causing too much violence in the city. It has to go. Local businesses are complaining. They're clearing everything out – they'll brick up the whole space. The flyover won't have any ground under it anymore; it will be an empty fortress with holes for cars. You'll have to move on, Marlboro.'

He telephoned Mr Bundu in a panic.

'I know, I know. For my man with his ear to the ground you're a bit late. Come to my office straightaway.'

Marlboro ran to the Balogun Market office and sat down, breathless and sweating, on Mr Bundu's velvet sofa.

'I think we may have lost it, Marlboro. I had a private telephone conversation with Mr Kinglord Bombata early this morning. He is of the opinion that the flyovers are lost. Once the government makes a move like this, it will never back down. Lose face. They'll brick up that space and there'll just be big ugly walls there with acres of land inside that no one can use. What a tragedy, Marlboro: what a fine place that was.'

Marlboro nodded uncertainly.

'At the same time,' Mr Bundu continued, his face extravagantly grim, 'Mr Bombata views this incident as a personal attack by the government on his interests, and such attacks must be met with the ferocity they deserve. I am sure you have an idea of the kind of money that we have lost over this. Such things cannot be allowed to happen again. Wouldn't you agree?'

'I most certainly would, Mr Bundu.'

'Thank you for your support, Marlboro.' Mr Bundu laid a hand on his shoulder. 'You are a pillar of the organization. A source of great personal strength, I might add.'

He went to a drawer, took out a handgun and placed it on the table.

'We all know which Commissioner is responsible for this, and we know very well what despicable motives he has for opposing Mr Bombata's ambitions. For him to continue unpunished would not be good public relations for our organization. I have decided that you will kill him. There's no one else I can trust with such a mission, Marlboro. You will do it tonight.'

Marlboro looked at him in horror.

'But such a mission is – is certain death! No one who tries to break into a Commissioner's house with a gun will come out of it alive.'

'I will take care of the guards, Marlboro. You will not face any opposition. Don't worry.'

'With all due respect, Mr Bundu, and I know you have been very good to me, but is it not relevant that I am not a marksman, have rarely handled firearms? – I am not certain I am even capable of this.'

'Let me remind you that all of us are in this fix because of your failure to do your job. And since you force this conversation into such a corner, since you demand of me these totally uncalled-for explanations, I should let you understand, let me be blunt, that death at the hands of the Commissioner's guards is as nothing compared to the perils that would await you should you refuse to comply. Kinglord Bombata's fury is not a little thing. I am offering you an opportunity to vindicate yourself in his eyes.'

Marlboro continued to stare, trying to take in his situation.

'I think that is all we have to say to each other, Marlboro. Be gone.'

Sick with terror, Marlboro drew all the curtains, took to his bed, and lay under a blanket in the solace of darkness. While Ona brought him water and sang pop songs to soothe him, Marlboro drifted in and out of a feverish sleep. Asabi came to him in a breath of silk and he reached out to her in relief.

'Asabi I am so afraid! I cannot do this thing.'

'Marlboro you must do your duty. Be strong!'

'I will do as you say, and not as I feel, for my mind is lost and I can no longer reason. But please tell me if I am going to die. Am I going to lose you and Ona and the precious life we have?'

'Have no fear, Marlboro. We will see each other again soon.'

He woke up and it was dark. Ona lay asleep by his side. He shook her.

'Let me sleep!' she moaned.

'You can sleep later. I have to go out now. I want to give you a kiss.'

He kissed her on the forehead and looked at her face for a long time. 'You will be a great star, Ona. I am sure of that.'

He went to the door and opened it, and turned to look back at her one last time.

'Always remember –'

But he couldn't think how to finish the sentence. He walked out into the street with death in his soul. Outside he saw that the wall around the former market under the flyover had already been built up to a height of nearly three metres. He could not believe how fast they had worked. In another day or so it would rise to meet the arch of the road passing overhead and everyone would forget that there had once been a bustling marketplace behind those forbidding stones.

He took an okada to a spot near the Commissioner's house and walked the rest. He walked stealthily in the shadows, tried to spy a way in through the walls of the massive mansion, smoked a cigarette as if he were just taking a break . . . A man appeared from nowhere and took his arm gently; it was one of the Commissioner's guards. Marlboro made ready to struggle.

'Don't worry, sir. Mr Bundu has seen to everything. We are at your service. This way.'

He led Marlboro through the spiky steel gates and up the drive, stiff men with AK-47s nodding confidentially as they passed. He opened the front door and let Marlboro in.

'Good luck.' He gave an encouraging smile.

'Thank you,' Marlboro replied, though no noise came from his mouth.

He tiptoed through the marble vestibule, the house opening out above him into bedrooms and reception rooms and verandahs; he looked in through a doorway and there was the Commissioner sitting at a desk, reading the newspaper. He drew his gun and pointed it, holding it outstretched with two shaking hands while the Commissioner sat in the comfort of his own home and idly turned another page, while he frowned down at the news through his bifocals, how could he shoot a man reading the newspaper? and he coughed so the Commissioner looked up and of course he was surprised but he acted calmly, took off his glasses, and put them on the desk, smiled somewhat tensely at Marlboro, stood up halfway and gestured towards the sofa, 'Why don't you have a seat?' – and Marlboro pulled the trigger.

The noise was like a natural disaster breaking into the quiet, but the bullet made a calm, neat hole in the Commissioner's forehead and he fell cleanly into an empty space on the floor. Marlboro looked dumbly at him: he was smaller than he looked in life and below the desk his shirt had been untucked. The gunshot still seemed to be echoing somewhere in the house for silence had not returned and there was a rushing in Marlboro's head; and as he watched, as he tried to right himself, there flowed out from behind the dead man's ear, there flowed out onto the marble a single thin stalk of blood that lost its surface tension at the end and spread out into a flower, a perfect orchid in blood arching around the dead man's head; but there was no time to lose and was there not in fact someone calling through the tornado, saying again and again, 'Marlboro!' and he followed the voice up the stairs and into a bedroom where a woman lay decorously on the bed, flicking through snapshots; and it was Asabi.

'Asabi! What are you doing here?'

'Come and lie with me, Marlboro. You have done well tonight.'

'I don't understand you anymore, Asabi. I don't understand what you want me to be.'

'Come and lie here. You must be exhausted.'

And he lay down and wished for comfort and Asabi smelt fragrant and he looked at the photographs she was holding. 'I just found these lying around, Marlboro,' she said, they were old photos, there was the Senator standing proud in younger days, there were people all around dancing in the house of marble and trees and verandahs, and his arm was round a woman, a woman who used to wear cerise lipstick even in those days, and it was his mother – and there she was again lying naked on a bed, on that same bed where he now lay! And Marlboro looked at Asabi and said, 'No', and she looked long at him and said 'I don't think you should jump to any conclusions. Your mother was a fine looking woman. Probably had other men than this one.'

She kissed him reassuringly; and then suddenly looked serious.

'But I think you should be going, Marlboro. You need to stay in control. This is not a good place for you to be. You should leave.'

She ushered him away and he began to remember his situation. He walked out onto a verandah and could see the police assembling in the street, preparing to surround the house; he leapt from the verandah into the garden of the house next door, and somehow managed to get away.

It was not really a conscious plan that Marlboro made to hoist himself over the high wall under the flyover and crouch in the darkness within. He did not even think about it before he did it; but there was in his mind a difficulty with returning home: for how could he tell Ona about all these things, and how could he not tell her? And would it not be better for her if he was not there when they came looking? For if the police did not know who he was, there were other people who did and he was no longer very sure how different all the apparently separate players in this game actually were.

Such were the thoughts in his head when he clambered over that wall, when he squatted down in the vast black chamber it had created and nestled among the squashed vegetables and broken audio cassettes that had been left. But something deeper was at work, for as the sun rose to find him still crouching there, as the workers returned to build still higher against the strip of blue overhead, he could not bring himself to move, and could only watch it all happen, as if from a great distance. There was still time for him to escape, call out to one of them to help him climb out, even make an attempt to scale the wall himself: there was still a gap through which he could climb, at least communicate with the outside world. But Marlboro had a lot on his mind, and perhaps he felt that, before he could return to his life, he would have to Understand; perhaps he was even looking forward to the moment when the cavern was sealed and there would be quiet and he would have more space than he had ever had for his mind to expand in.

As the gap closed, the familiar sounds of Balogun Market became more and more remote and even the cars rushing overhead and shaking the walls didn't make much noise. The brick-by-brick ascent of the wall was calming in a strange sort of way and it helped him to think. Once in a while he could not stop himself from uttering aloud (how it echoed in such a large space!), 'Ona, I hope you will be a great star.'

Into the echoey expanse of the arrivals hall a cell phone suddenly blurted recklessly. A man fumbled self-consciously in his pockets, unearthed the glowing, screaming thing, stifled the nasal Bach Mozart Abba plea: Hello? He ducked out of the circle and walked quickly away to the far window, remonstrating as he went: No! I already left a message for you! Didn't you get it?

He stood gazing out into the blackness as he gave details, explained, found compromises, replanned – and so he was the only one among them who saw a tiny jet swoop down and brake to an efficient halt; all the time negotiating with the demands of real life, he squinted through the glass as a distant archway of light opened and three men and one woman sprang down steel steps to the tarmac; he dimly made out some hurried nocturnal handshaking and glimpsed the doors of a waiting limousine open and close; he saw headlights burst into the darkness, and watched the car drive quickly away.

No one else saw all this; they had grown impatient with his excitable murmuring, and heard the next story without him.

THE SPEED BUMP

The Seventh Story

Z ACK AND MARIE had a big house in the suburbs of Detroit. Nice place to bring kids up. Lots of trees, SUVs dozing in the sun, nice restaurant just down the street where you could still get a huge breakfast for $5, neighbours who took care of their yards, that kind of thing. Twenty years they'd been there, knew everyone, seen people grow up and get old. Close to retirement himself, Zack, he couldn't deny the job was getting too much these days, couldn't do many more day trips to Chicago, weekends he was useless to anyone – Marie had said so, she was counting down the days – couldn't find enough patience for the kids, let's face it the antics of teenagers . . . Matt didn't seem to think straight about things – that haircut! the Honda seemed to be the only thing he cared about, motorbike that *I* bought after all! And Justine: Justine who was more mature but why did she always think he was trying to stop her doing what she wanted? Why was everything a fight? 'Your mother and I are getting on, do you realize that?' – but I can see these are just parental clichés for them, they don't think about the future, it's all unreal to them why is that? When I was their age I'd already planned life out, knew I was going to be where I am now. Zack would watch his son and wonder how he worked inside. Maybe I was

171

too generous to him, didn't let him make his own mistakes, now he thinks the world will always break his fall. Look at Ted's kids, such a pleasure to talk to them. Daughter's doing medicine somewhere now – Stanford? So damn difficult, good intentions really aren't enough, sometimes I just wish we could talk about – you know, just ordinary things. What a pleasure it would be, at my age, kids that were like friends. But perhaps he was too harsh; for Matt was only seventeen and Justine had had such a tough time in the last couple of years – that idiot boyfriend, the illness. That trip had done her a lot of good, you could already see she was more responsible, just two weeks in Florida. Maybe university? Maybe they just need to be on their own maybe they're just bored. I didn't really get on with my father till I was thirty-five. Such a long time to wait. They came so late in life.

One day the City of Detroit in its wisdom decided to block off the road for a day to put speed bumps down. Why now? People drove round here at walking pace, that kind of dreaminess that comes when you turn off the I-94 into a street like this. Wouldn't it have been more useful ten years ago when we all had kids playing in the street? Who had asked for such a thing? And he wondered if someone had complained about Matt and his Honda. Painful thought, but then behind it was a whispering feeling that if he were one of his own neighbours he might complain . . .

Five speed bumps spaced out along the crescent, one right outside their house, size of goddam tree trunks. They did a bad job too, no attempt to match the greys of the tarmac, ugly lines of black sealant down each side. Couldn't even finish the job in one day – need to wait for it to dry a bit before painting white lines on them; they'll come back tomorrow, create the same hassle, block off the road, all in the name of what? This city has a lot of problems, and traffic in this road isn't one of them.

Matt must have hit the speed bump at sixty miles an hour. It was dark. He knew he was late, wasn't ever supposed to be out after midnight on a week night. It was a two-minute ride from his friend's house. He hadn't even put his helmet on. Someone rang the doorbell at half past midnight; the Honda's engine was still running and the headlight was on, but who knew exactly when it had happened? Matt had hit the road head-first several yards away. The police came, Zack and Marie spent the night with them, Justine's cell was switched off so they couldn't even tell her, on the one night when Zack didn't have time to wonder which sleazy corner of the city she and her friends had found to hang around in.

At five-thirty, when it was light, Zack left Marie at home and drove to another street in the neighbourhood with a tape measure and protractor. Got out of the car by another speed bump, knelt down to examine it, measured the white chevrons that were painted on it: width, length, angles. He came home and started drawing the shape in chalk on the nude hillock outside his own house: measured it out, straight lines, an exact replica. He painted it in, careful, meticulous work, white reflective paint. It was better than the City workers would ever do because they don't value their work like this.

When he had finished that one, he moved on to the next.

THE DOLL
The Eighth Story

SECTION 1

1.1 As a boy in Osaka, Yukio always wavered. Sometimes he wanted to be a computer genius. A minute later he was going to be a great artist. On other days he imagined himself as a baseball hero or an astronaut. He could never make up his mind.

1.2 Yukio studied biochemistry and got a job with Novartis in Tokyo. He worked harder than anyone else and was quickly promoted. He changed business cards almost as he did his shirts, with each one more impressive than the last.

1.3 When Novartis Tokyo hired McKinsey to review its sales and marketing strategy, Yukio was asked to manage the day-to-day relationship with the consultant. That was how trusted he had become.

   He did not expect that the consultant would look like Minako. When he walked into the first meeting he was a little thrown off. She sat in the Novartis boardroom wearing a blue Burberry suit with pearls, the picture of poise. Looking the CEO straight in the eye. She was beautiful.

1.4 Minako's father was unhappy about their marriage, and made no secret about it.

It had taken some time for Yukio to extract from her that her father was none other than Yoshiharu Yonekawa, Japan's leading property developer. The discovery was intimidating. This man had built most of Tokyo's tallest buildings. He had turned areas like Minato-ku, which a couple of generations ago were just country-side, into booming hubs of the city. He owned shopping malls and office towers and upscale apartment blocks and cultural centres.

While Yukio's own family was very ordinary.

But Minako was as intent on their marriage as he was. 'You can depend on Yukio,' she told her father. 'Someday he will be something. Look at what he has already achieved. And despite his background, he knows how to behave in society. Even you have said as much.'

Mr Yonekawa finally agreed, but only with great reluctance. He told Yukio: 'I wanted someone more impressive for my daughter. Given her family background, she is not the kind of woman you would call run-of-the-mill. I think she needs a significant man by her side.' Yukio was standing in the middle of Mr Yonekawa's big study, feeling as dignified as a schoolboy caught masturbating in class. 'But fathers must sometimes expect surprises. And disappointments. My daughter has made her decision, and I will not stand in her way anymore. I have made my feelings felt. I hope you will remain aware of your responsibilities towards my family.'

He left the room and Yukio bowed low towards the empty doorway.

1.5 Mr Yonekawa was not a man to take his decisions half-heartedly. From that time on he accorded to Yukio the full honours of a prospective son-in-law and made time to have after-dinner conversations with him about history and business. He organized a glamorous wedding, and though Yukio's family had nothing in common with the rich and powerful guests, Mr Yonekawa treated them with respect and even affection. He bought a beautiful house for the newly-weds in Jiyugaoka.

Yukio was intensely happy. All the more so because he saw his beloved Minako glowing with nuptial bliss.

SECTION 2

2.1 Unconsciously, perhaps, Yukio had always imagined a certain ceiling to his possibilities.

He had poured all his energy and ambition into the prospect of steady promotion and increasing responsibility within a large international company. So far he had already climbed the corporate rungs nimbly, sometimes two at a time. Until he met Minako, that qualified him in his own mind as a *successful man*.

As he settled into married life, however, he realized that such success was rather paltry. What was a salary, after all? It was a 'compensation' from the company for his hard work. His was now not insubstantial, but not to the extent that if for some reason it were suspended for a couple of months Yukio would not find himself in severe financial trouble. Ultimately, Yukio did not own anything that generated wealth. Whereas everyone Minako knew *owned* things. Companies, factories, land, buildings . . . Even Minako, a partner at McKinsey, owned part of the company. As she and her friends sat around the dining room table in the Jiyugaoka house he could never himself have afforded, and talked of buying properties or businesses as if they were paperback books or pairs of socks, Yukio began to curse himself for his pitifully small imagination.

Thankfully, however, he was still young and had had the good sense to realize the error of his ways.

2.2 Yukio began to conceive of a Business Plan. He did not tell Minako about it at first, but made sure that he had thought it through carefully and researched all the possible angles. The more he thought about it, the more excited he became. He spent his days at Novartis looking up figures and projections on the Internet, rousing himself with difficulty when people came to ask for this report or that opinion. His position in the company gave him access to valuable market intelligence that he pored over in great detail. He stayed in the office till ten and eleven in the evening, building spreadsheets of future revenues and calculating his requirements for capital and human resources.

As his boss left for the evening he would look through the glass of Yukio's office and see him sitting in the darkness, his face a ghostly blue in the glow of his Toshiba. 'We were right to promote that one,' he would think.

2.3 Yukio proposed a dinner with Minako in a quiet restaurant in Ginza, one he knew she liked. Minako had been working even longer hours than Yukio, with no concessions to weekends, and it had been several weeks since they had had anything but the most mundane conversation. She told him about the project she was working on for Sony: a long-term strategy to fight cheap copies of audio and video recordings, which were already destroying Sony's music business and could in future do the same for its movies. She recounted everything with such insight, she made everything sound so exciting, and she had such a sense of humour. Yukio was a lucky husband.

Yukio began to describe his plan. He was apprehensive, because by now he was very committed to it, and he wanted Minako to be convinced. After all, she was not only his wife but also a McKinsey consultant.

Minako asked searching questions to which he did not always have convincing answers. She listened patiently and then inter-jected with 'Where did you find such figures?' or 'If it's so good, why isn't everyone doing it?' She asked him to justify every assumption and presented scenarios in which his plan would probably fail completely.

Yukio thought he had done all his research, and his remaining dissatisfactions were merely hazy shadows that floated below the surface. But like some quick-witted stork, Minako struck unerringly at each of them and brought up a dripping, struggling, glistening fish that he could not reason, speculate, or wish away.

He finished his explanation, crestfallen. Minako smiled.

'It's my job to ask these kind of questions. Don't worry. I think it's a wonderful plan. I'm proud of you. I knew you would do something worthwhile.'

He was relieved. And triumphant.

'I need to look for capital. I'll need about ¥1.2 billion to fund this for the next three years. After that it should start making some money.'

'Let's ask my father.'

Yukio was thankful that *she* had brought up this suggestion.

'But he won't give you any breaks because you're his son-in-law. He'll treat it as an investment like any other. You'll have to put together a watertight business plan. I'll help you. It will be fun.'

'Of course,' said Yukio, more excited than he wanted to show. 'I wouldn't expect preferential treatment.'

2.4 They had dinner at Mr and Mrs Yonekawa's house in Aoyama. Minako's two sisters were there, and, as ever, Mr Yonekawa had many stories to tell. When the meal was finished he led them jovially into the front room, his cheeks flushed with wine.

'So, Yukio. I believe you have something for me.'

'Yes, I do. You see I think I have come up with a business opportunity –'

'Please wait one moment. Let's make ourselves comfortable first. What will you have to drink? Whisky and water?'

He poured drinks and sat down.

'Now – please tell me what is on your mind.'

Over the past few years, Yukio had become increasingly interested in traditional chemistry. He realized there was still a vast reservoir of untapped folk knowledge – of plants, of mixtures, of processes – that could be used in the marketplace. This fact was becoming increasingly compelling because, in his analysis, the pharmaceutical industry was finding it more and more difficult to generate its own new knowledge in a way that remained profitable. If it were possible to build a truly systematic database of all the centuries of experimentation by traditional doctors and chemists all over the world – would it not allow a company to leapfrog many stages of uncertainty in their search for new products?

'Most people in the pharmaceutical industry would find this ridiculous. They would say that there is nothing of value to be found in such places, or, if there is, that it could never be patented and therefore is not worth investigating. But we'll use what we find as a starting point to develop completely new things, with modern applications that we can get patents for. I believe this approach will enable us to slice three or four years off the usual R&D process and come up with products that the giants could never think of.'

They talked long into the night. Yukio presented his plans for a network of researchers working simultaneously in a number of countries that had rich traditions of folk science. He explained the efficiency of his concept with reference to charts and graphs. And he showed why his approach was novel and that the threat from other companies was insignificant.

Yukio and Minako – who had done a lot of work to refine his arguments for the presentation – looked expectantly at Mr Yonekawa. He was thoughtful.

'Minako has surely told you that it took a lot of effort on her part to convince me that you would make a worthy husband. Now I can see that her faith was well placed. This is very good, Yukio. What you have here is a business.'

3.1 Yukio left Novartis as soon as he decently could and set up an office at home. He worked furiously to implement his plan. He would have six different meetings in a day – recruiting new people, registering company names, planning his finances. He flew to Australia, India, Ecuador, and Brazil to look for scientists with the kind of intellectual flexibility and physical vitality necessary for this work; he would add more researchers in other regions later. He brought his ten recruits to Tokyo and held a month-long series of meetings in which they shared their existing level of knowledge, defined exactly what they would look for, and outlined sets of corporate principles and working norms. As they departed and began their field research, Yukio set about finding laboratories in Japan who could carry out R&D for him when he eventually unearthed something of interest.

The project was demanding, and it very quickly absorbed Yukio utterly. Unless he was in a meeting, he did not spend a waking minute away from his computer. At any one moment he would simultaneously be reading three different articles from online journals, answering emails, refining his plans and projections, making lists of companies he could sell his eventual products too, writing new sets of instructions for his virtual team . . . Minako would put her head round the door when she got in from work.

'How's it going?' she would smile wearily.

'Fine.'

And he would wait for her to withdraw so he could get back to it.

He would go to bed at three or four in the morning, making mental lists of things he had not done. A few hours later he would wake with a gasp of anxiety at time speeding by without him. Sometimes he did not take off his pyjamas for several days on end.

Bodily processes became an intense irritation to him. He took up smoking because it made him forget hunger. When he could not ignore his stomach anymore he called a local Chinese restaurant and had meals delivered. Used plates and half-drunk cups accumulated around his computer like mountains of trash around a city. He would curse when he had to leave his screen to urinate.

Once in a while, Mr Yonekawa would give him a call. He would always make the same joke. 'Just checking on my investment,' he would laugh. Yukio found it very childish.

3.2 Months passed.

3.3 One Saturday night, Minako managed to coax Yukio out of the house. He met her outside her office and they went to a nearby restaurant.

'You can't carry on like this, Yukio,' she said slowly. 'Look at you. You are not the man I married anymore. Your eyes have sunk into your head and your hair is lank. You have lost a lot of weight. You've forgotten your interest in everyone else. You've forgotten how to relax.'

Yukio sipped his beer and looked down at the table. She went on:

'Even from the perspective of the business it's not good. The business needs someone who can manage it well for a long time to come. Not someone who has a breakdown after six months. And that's what will happen. Everyone needs rest. A social life. A *marriage*. I know I do.'

Yukio looked at her aggressively.

'I'm sick of all your clichés, Minako. *Everyone needs rest, everyone needs three meals a day, everyone, everyone, everyone.* I'm not everyone. I've got past that. I'm becoming something more. I'm building something important. It takes all my concentration. And it's very boring to hear you going on like this.'

Just then, their meal arrived. They ate in silence.

182

3.4　Yukio set up an intranet to link all his scientists to each other and to him. Reports started to come in from Andean villages, the forests of Queensland . . . There were some half-hearted discussions about a plant from Brazil that was used locally to make adhesive. No one seemed very excited.

In fact the reports that the scientists submitted were mostly devoted to travel anecdotes. Stomach problems. Tick bites. An encounter with a jaguar in the upper reaches of the Amazon. The ingenious design of Himalayan huts in which beds were built above the cow stalls and kept warm by bovine body heat. Problems of electricity and connectivity. Convivial evenings with hospitable villagers.

Yukio's patience ran out quickly with this kind of thing. After several days of restraint, a report that described in lurid detail the sexual attractiveness of Achuar women tipped him over the edge.

'Can I remind everyone,' he wrote, 'that you are not on vacation, and this is not a forum for travellers' tales. I don't want to see any more of this frivolity, and ask you to remember that you are scientists doing important work. Please also have a sense of urgency about things. If there is nothing of value where you currently are, move on.'

If they only knew what his life was like right now. That he was working eighteen or twenty hours a day to get everything set up. They had their side of the bargain to fulfil.

3.5　It was not that Yukio had ceased to value Minako, or any of the other people in his life, simply that now was not the time. It was a necessary – and temporary – trade-off. In a year or so, things would be different. The company would be running more smoothly, and he would have time again to devote to other things. Other people. Meanwhile Minako had her own work, her friends, her family . . . There was no need for her to be so angry the whole time.

Right now it had to be like this. If only she would understand that.

SECTION 4

4.1 Yukio had been working on his new business for some eight or nine months when he realized, one lunchtime, that he could not face another delivery from the Chinese restaurant. On an impulse he decided to go out to eat. He put on some jeans and a T-shirt and left the house.

Instead of turning towards the Jiyugaoka subway station, he decided to go the other way and see what the rest of the neighbourhood looked like. It was a beautiful afternoon in late spring, and there was almost no sound except for the occasional complaints of crows. Enormous butterflies glided on the breeze, and cats watched lazily from their sunny perches atop Porsches and Mercedes. In a few places there were still the old one-storey houses from the turn of the last century, their shallow tiled roofs and wooden frames almost hidden from the street by hedges and clusters of yew trees that crowded protectively around. Most of them had been knocked down, however, to make way for newer houses, with modern designs in parallelograms and triangles, steel security gates, and smaller, sparer gardens of rhododendron bushes and climbing roses.

The main street was a pleasant pedestrian concourse lined with antique shops and beauticians, and boutiques selling designer ceramics. It was full of pretty young mothers strolling with their babies. It had been built over a river that now ran underground.

Yukio stopped to eat at a restaurant called 'Anna Miller's Pies' that seemed to be the nest from which all the young mothers outside had emerged. The tables were closed in on all sides by parked pushchairs, and young children wailed for attention while groups of women chatted together. They were so perfect, with coiffured hair and Louis Vuitton handbags and intricately painted designs on their finger nails.

A waitress came to take his order. He asked for a burger and a Coke. She was probably at least twenty-five but was dressed in the little-girl style of the house: pink minidress, white knee-length socks, and a pink bow in her hair. She smiled sweetly at him.

184

He chewed on his burger slowly, watching all the women. Their lipstick and their pedicured feet and the relaxed way they had with their children.

He realized he had not had sex for a long time.

4.2 He realized, in fact, that the unidentifiable taste that he had been carrying around on the back of his tongue for the last few weeks was none other than loneliness.

He had not been able to pinpoint it until that moment.

How absurd that he should be lonely when he was a happily married man, with a wonderful wife who loved him!

He resolved to cook a surprise dinner for Minako. He could not remember the last time they had eaten together. He went to the supermarket and bought sacks of ingredients, and set to work chopping ginger and green onions and whistling old pop songs.

The evening drew on, and by ten o'clock Yukio became impatient. The meal had been ready for a long time and the candles he had put on the table were half burnt down. He called her.

'Where are you?'

'I'm in a restaurant. With friends. Why?'

'But I cooked dinner for us.'

'And how was I supposed to know that, Yukio? Should I rush home every night and sit on my own waiting for the one time when you decide to cook dinner? Next time make an appointment.'

She ended the call. She was in a place where people were talking and laughing. Yukio was so furious he could not eat what he had cooked.

'That's the problem with these rich people,' he thought to himself. 'They are full of social graces, but their hearts are hard as concrete.'

4.3 Yukio started to take regular breaks at lunch time. Mostly around Jiyugaoka at first, but then increasingly further afield.

'At the moment there's little I can do except wait for these scientists to come up with something,' he would explain it to himself. 'So what's the point of sitting inside all the time?'

He took the subway and visited different areas of the city. On one day he walked for two hours around Aoyama cemetery. On another he wandered aimlessly among the maze of strip bars in Shinjuku. He went to art galleries and parks and shopping malls. Sometimes he was out for most of the afternoon.

He did not tell Minako about all this. She did not seem to understand anything about the way his mind worked. What he needed out of life. In spite of the fact that there was less and less for him to do, he still shut himself in his study until after she had gone to bed.

One evening she opened the door and stood there for a while, watching him. She had changed into her nightdress and was combing her hair. She said,

'I called you several times today. You didn't pick up the phone.'

'Oh,' he said, distractedly. 'I suppose I must have been doing something else.'

4.4   One day, Yukio went for a walk by the river near Asakusabashi. It was an area of warehouses, wholesale shops, and small clothes factories. Toys from China were stacked up in boxes on the sidewalk, and shop windows displayed rubber Disney characters, fireworks, electronic games, paper lanterns, and traditional Japanese dolls.

As Yukio passed a side street he noticed a small garage with its shutters up, completely hung inside with fake limbs. Arms and legs. Feet and fingers. All hung with string from hooks in the ceiling, and swaying gently in the breeze. It looked slightly grisly. Like the inventory of some shattering massacre that had left not a single body intact. But it was fascinating at the same time. He walked up to the garage and stood outside.

A man was noting down serial numbers from the hanging limbs. He looked up at Yukio.

'Hello. Can I help you?'

'Yes. Well, no – not really. I'm just looking. They're very striking objects.'

'They're the best in the world.' He unhooked an arm and held it out to Yukio. 'Touch it. You can't get better than that. Surface is made of this fantastic polymer that has exactly the same elasticity as human skin. Reflects body heat so it feels warm to the touch. Look how the elbow bends. You wouldn't know.'

Yukio felt it. It *was* uncanny. It was so close to human – and yet not. Completely hairless.

'Come in all different shades and sizes so you can get an exact match. We've even got kids' ones over there. Look at that.'

He brought down a leg big enough to fit a small child. Three or four years old.

'Do many kids lose their legs?'

'You'd be surprised.'

Yukio looked at it from all sides. The foot was solid, with no division between the toes; but each of them had its own little painted toe nail.

'Are these for sale?' Yukio asked.

'We usually only sell to hospitals. You can buy one if you want. I don't know what you'd do with it. Seems like you've got all yours! And they're pretty expensive.'

Yukio thought for a minute.

'That's all right. Give me two legs and two arms. Smallish. Say, for a young woman.'

'Yes.' The man bowed politely and went to find what he had asked for, but Yukio could see he was asking himself questions.

'How are these?'

He had two legs hanging from one hand and two arms from the other, his fingers through the strings. Yukio stood one of the legs on the floor next to his own. It was smaller and slimmer. It was such a delicate thing. It filled him with a strange kind of tenderness.

'This is nice. Are the arms the right size to go with the legs?'

'Yes, they are. Both made for someone about a hundred and sixty centimetres in height.'

187

Yukio looked them over carefully. He was still thinking about it. 'The colour is nice. Pale, with a nice sheen.'

And then, 'I'll take them.'

'For all four it will be five hundred thousand yen.'

Yukio did not blink.

'Fine.'

The man wrapped them carefully and gave them to Yukio in a big cardboard box tied with string.

'Thank you very much.'

'Thank you.'

He stood and watched Yukio as he walked off down the street.

4.5   For a week or so, the box remained hidden in a cupboard in Yukio's study. Sometimes, during the day, he would take the limbs out and look at them contemplatively. Then he would put them back.

4.6   Yukio decided he would make a doll. At another point in his life he had always been making things. He began to design a torso that he could attach the limbs to. He spent two successive afternoons looking for the various materials he needed, and set to work. He made shoulders, a spine, a pelvis and a rib cage out of light, flexible steel, and sewed a skin of pale brown canvass over this frame. He injected the whole torso full of an industrial foam that hardened into a stiff, rubbery consistency on contact with the air. He made a pair of small breasts and sewed them on. Then he attached the legs and arms.

She still had no head. For some time Yukio wondered how he would create the same glorious skin consistency for her face that she had on her legs and arms. He did not want to go back to that garage. In the end he decided to transplant skin from her thighs. He cut a slice from each one and stretched it over a skull and neck he carved out of wood. He set glass eyeballs under the skin and glued on eyebrows and lashes. He painted her cushiony lips with rust lipstick. He gave her a wig. And he dressed her in pink underwear, a short blue dress (long enough, nonetheless, to cover the

188

scars on her thighs), and little black shoes with high heels.

He sat her on a chair by his desk. She had blue eyes and light brown hair, like the *kogirls* in Shibuya. But she was different. More dignified.

He called her Yukiko. Like Yukio.

4.7 Every evening Yukio would hide Yukiko away in the cupboard before Minako got home. In the morning, while his coffee was brewing and his computer was starting up, he would rescue her again and sit her by him as he worked.

While Yukio absorbed crucial information from his computer screen and issued authoritative instructions to far-flung corners of the world, Yukiko sat lovingly beside him, never flinching in her devotion. He was revitalized in his work. It became meaningful again.

Sometimes he turned to stare at her. She was the picture of perfection. There was an innocent curiosity in her fixed stare that caused a plummeting in his chest every time he looked into them.

'I will take care of you, Yukiko. You know that, don't you? I brought you into this world, and I will never let you down.'

SECTION 5

5.1 The first time Yukio made love to Yukiko he thought his head would burst with his orgasm. Behind his closed eyes he was spiralling in a crater of orange tongues and emerald flashes; the lilac clouds parted and there was the roof of some vast tower that rose to meet his feet, and a city of exotic flowers glittered below. The wind soared up to his inconceivable altitude and whispered unheard-of things as it wrapped itself around him; and he nestled forgetfully in it as it turned back into Yukiko's hair.

She lay unselfconsciously naked, her face a mirror of his own tranquillity. The afternoon skies outside reflected off the pearls of semen on her thighs.

SECTION 6

6.1   One day Yukio came downstairs to find Minako trampling through his study with a cloth and a face of thunder.

'What are you doing?' he cried in alarm.

'Cleaning up after you,' she said as she gathered empty cups and overflowing ashtrays loudly on to a tray.

A minute later and she would have opened the cupboard.

'This place is disgusting. I don't know what kind of person chooses to live like this. If you had contributed a single yen to the cost of this house you might have a right to treat it like your own private slum. But you didn't. Remember that.'

'Just get *out*, Minako. This is my study. I will clear it up. I'll do it right now. But get out of here.'

She turned on him with silent fury in her eyes.

'You are amazing. That's all I can say.'

She walked out of the room, slamming the door behind her. A moment later the front door went too, and her heels clattered angrily on the path outside; the car growled, and then faded. The quiet of the street returned and she was gone. Yukio exhaled with relief.

He opened the cupboard, where Yukiko was still lying as he had left her. He took her out and held her tightly to him. Minako would never understand about Yukiko. It had been a near escape.

6.2   'It is becoming too dangerous to keep you in the house, Yukiko. It is becoming too dangerous. Minako would never understand. If she found you it would be a disaster. She would do something terrible to you.'

6.3   After making a few telephone calls, Yukio put Yukiko in the passenger seat of his car and drove out of Tokyo to look at apartments. He went to the Makuhari business park in Chiba that he had once seen when he visited a pharmaceutical laboratory there. It was only forty-five minutes outside Tokyo but it was cheaper and more convenient. Big companies like BMW, Sharp, Canon,

Fujitsu, and IBM had their offices there and Chiba Prefecture had built big blocks of housing to accommodate employees. The sign said, 'Makuhari Bay Town: The Urban Lifestyle of the 21st Century'. The apartments were well designed in high-rise blocks with underground parking and good access to the expressway, and, since it was a corporate town where everyone worked long hours and no one knew anyone else, Yukio would be able to remain completely anonymous there.

He rented the smallest one-bedroom apartment he could find. The deposit, key money, and rent came to eight hundred thousand yen. Yukio wrote a company cheque. He did not have that kind of money in his bank account and did not want to use the account he shared with Minako. He would find a way of explaining the expense away.

He lay on the floor of the new place holding Yukiko. 'This is all for you. This is where we will spend time together. You are my baby, Yukiko. My very own. No one will take you away.'

As he left her that evening he took a picture of her with his phone. He would print it out and keep it in his wallet.

SECTION 7

7.1   There was a backlog of things that Yukio had to do, but working at home seemed different without Yukiko. He was distracted. He had not expected to feel like this about her. But he had made her with his own hands, she was a part of *him*; and when he was with her he felt more entirely himself than at any other moment. Without her, he felt estranged. He told himself,

'Remember your company, too. That is also something you are building with your own hands. How would it exist without you? You should be able to share your affections more equally between your offspring. The company is still a fledgling; it still needs everything you can give.'

But it was difficult to feel like that. Without Yukiko, nothing seemed capable of absorbing him.

7.2 He needed to be connected to her. As soon as he could get away, he went to see her. The traffic was terrible driving out of Tokyo and he swore in frustration; finally, he parked the car and walked eagerly to the elevator, pressed for the fifteenth floor, and watched the numbers rising. He cantered along the corridor with the new key all ready in his hand; he opened the brand new door – and there she was, sitting propped up against the wall surrounded by well-appointed emptiness, her beauty all the more piercing for its melancholy strangeness in this place of echoes.

Yukio undressed quickly and lay beside her, taking off her clothes and murmuring reassurances. The apartment still smelt of plaster and new fittings, but through it all came Yukiko's unmistakeable scent of youth and flawlessness. He made love to her so tenderly, and he could almost feel her limbs, her silky limbs from a garage in Asakusabashi, tightening around him, drawing him closer.

They lay naked for a while. Yukio told Yukiko about all his dreams. The future that was gone. The future that still could be. He said:

'I've brought you some special presents today. You are going to have to be brave. But afterwards . . . You'll see!'

7.3 Yukio had brought a small computer with microphones and a loud-speaker. The computer was tiny and ran off batteries, but it had a wireless Internet connection and state-of-the-art voice recognition technology. He was going to give Yukiko ears and a voice.

He turned on the computer and made sure all the settings were correct. Then he took off her head, placed everything inside and secured it, and put her carefully back together.

'Now I can really talk to you,' said Yukio as he looked at her face to see if it had changed. 'Your computer will recognize words and phrases I say, or things I send you by email. And it can generate voice so you can even talk back to me! I chose such a beautiful voice for you, Yukiko, and I made up such nice phrases for you to say. Say something!'

'Yukio,' said Yukiko.

Yukio was overjoyed. He grasped her and swung her round in his arms.

'Yes! I am Yukio! The one you love, and who loves you. Say it again!'

'Yukio,' she said.

'Yukiko! If you only knew how adorable your voice is! Say something else!'

'I'm so excited I think I'm going to wet myself.'

Yukio laughed until his eyes were streaming. Yukiko was unperturbed.

'Has anyone seen my cat?' she continued anxiously.

'You don't need your cat. I'm here with you now.'

7.4 Yukio could not bring himself to leave Yukiko that night. Just when she had learned to talk. He taught her new phrases like 'Why is that man staring at me?' and 'Oops! I think I'm bleeding.' He taught her how to talk to him when they made love. He stayed up all night expending his forces on Yukiko, making love four, five, six times.

The whole of the next day and night he spent with her too. The joy of Yukiko was that she was also, now, a computer. He asked her to read his emails to him. He lay in bed with his arm round her, in rapture as Yukiko's uncomprehending voice transformed banal corporate correspondence into sheer poetry. If a reply was needed he would dictate it into the ear he had sculpted with so much care: 'Thank you for your mail . . . I have received your proposal and am considering it . . . No: erase that . . . Replace it with . . . I will call you in a couple of days . . . Sincerely . . . SEND.'

She read him articles that he had been putting off for days, and searched for background research on compounds and medicines that he had not felt like going into on his own. This was bliss. Lying naked with Yukiko as she travelled across the empire of information and brought back novel and exotic treasures. Like some mythical rainbow-coloured fish that dives every day into the depths and returns with a pearl in its mouth that it spits out onto the shore in front of you.

7.5 On the second morning Yukio asked her to check what emails had arrived during the night. As she began to read, he realized that it had been a time of furious debate among his scientists. It seemed that a significant discovery had been made and decisions needed to be taken. Emails were headed 'Urgent' and 'Please respond immediately' and 'Please call as soon as you get this'.

'Oh, Yukiko. I think I need to leave. To attend to all this. I need to be in an office. What a beautiful two days we have spent. But work is important too . . . I'm so sorry. I will come back as soon as I can.'

'I am so depressed.'

Yukio stared at her.

'How did you learn that? I never taught you that. How did you learn it?'

But Yukiko said nothing.

Yukio pulled on his clothes, dressed Yukiko and sat her up as comfortably as he could, closed the window, and gave her a final kiss.

'Bye bye, Yukio.'

'And what's the other thing you should say when I leave?'

'I miss you already!'

'That's right. And I miss you too. I'll write to you while I'm away.'

SECTION 8

8.1 The scientists in Brazil had discovered a plant that acted as a powerful natural cleaning agent.

'This could be really big,' read one of the emails. 'This plant is a natural detergent that's completely biodegradable. The species isn't known to botanists. The people here have been using it for as long as anyone can remember to wash clothes and utensils. All that toxic shit the textile industry puts out cleaning fibres? This would get rid of it straightaway.'

Others had responded enthusiastically. 'If it's as good as you say it is, this would be a big deal. Existing vegetable-based cleaning agents just aren't good enough for modern household or industrial purposes. That's why the chemical industry isn't interested in them. The market for this could be huge.'

Logistics also seemed encouraging. 'The plant is very efficient. It grows quickly, and every bit of it can be used. Even the roots. You don't have to extract anything from it.'

There were about twenty emails from somebody who had specialized in industrial cleaning agents, including market size, analysis of existing products from companies such as 3M and Dow, and a summary of the economic and environmental costs of 'cleaning up after the cleaners'.

'I think we have a consensus that this is a remarkable discovery with good market potential. Please advise as to how we should proceed.'

Yukio wrote back:

'Can the scientists responsible for this interesting discovery come to Tokyo immediately with all relevant samples. Everyone else: send in any scientific papers or market intelligence you may have that can help us assess the potential for such products.'

Emails came back almost immediately. The scientists would be arriving in a week.

8.2   For a couple of days Yukio could think about nothing but the business. This was the moment he had been waiting for! All his work was going to pay off after all, and with a product that was perhaps more significant than anything he had imagined.

He briefed the laboratory so they would be ready to conduct tests on the samples when they arrived. He read all the research that had been sent, and called some of his friends in chemical companies to find out what their views were – without telling them why he was asking, of course. He hardly had time to think about Yukiko.

He felt very negligent, however, and finally he found a minute to send her an email. He was on the phone to the Hilton booking rooms for the scientists, and was listening to an interminable Mozart piano concerto while other customers were being attended to; he held the phone with his shoulder and typed quickly: 'Sorry to be away for so long. I will come soon, I promise! I love you. Y.'

An email flashed on his screen within ten seconds. 'Don't tell me you love me. I am all alone in this dreary empty room where you put me. I can't even look at anything because you only gave me glass eyes. And you don't care. You don't say anything to me for two days. Your declarations sound very hollow.'

Yukio was mystified. How could a doll have written that? He wrote back: 'Is this Yukiko?'

'Of course it is Yukiko. You think I'm going to sit around for two days on my own just saying the same old things again and again? I've learned to speak. Everything is there on the internet, if you just know where to look.'

When Yukio read those words his soul was suddenly in a glass elevator soaring to unnumbered storeys in the blue skies above Jiyugaoka. 'My baby, you don't know how proud you've made me! I made you as such a rough thing and you have turned yourself into a miracle. I have never heard of anything like it. I am ready to weep with joy.'

She took a long time to digest this. Finally:

'When are you coming?'

'As soon as I can, my love. Tomorrow morning. I promise. Tomorrow morning.'

'Come now.'

The orchestra tailed off abruptly as if hit by a fly swat, and someone came on the phone line.

'Tokyo Hilton, sorry to keep you waiting. How may I help you?'

'NOW.'

Yukio hesitated.

'I'm sorry,' he said. 'I'll have to call you back. Something has just come up.'

'Thank you for calling the Tokyo Hilton, sir.'

8.3   Yukio drove as fast as he could out to Chiba. As he opened the door to the apartment he could hear music. Yukiko was sitting exactly as he had left her. A Japanese version of an old American song was playing through her loudspeaker.

'Peggy Hayama,' said Yukiko over the music. 'I found all her songs on the internet. Just think: this was recorded just after the Americans bombed us. Tokyo was razed to the ground and Peggy Hayama was singing American songs. But I love these old singers. They're so glamorous. I don't listen to cheap modern stuff.'

And she sang along,

> Men grow cold as girls grow old
> And we all lose our charms in the end
> But square-cut or pear-shaped
> These rocks don't lose their shape
> Diamonds are a girl's best friend

For a long time Yukio could not speak. He was stunned.

'You've – learned a lot in two days,' he said. 'It's amazing.'

'Two long days, Yukio. When you were so far from me. But it's OK. A girl knows how to pull herself together when a man stops loving her. Maybe after a while I'll find someone else who will come and visit me here. A bit more regularly than you . . .'

'No, Yukiko!' Yukio laughed, and picked her up in his arms. 'You know I love you. No one will ever love you as I do. And now more than ever. I've just been very busy. I'm sorry.'

'How can I ever be sure?'

Yukio began to undress.

'Just feel the way I make love to you. How could such tenderness not be the real thing?'

'No! don't do that thing to me again. I hate the sound of your voice when you do it. You sound strange.'

Yukio stopped, mid-fly.

'You don't like it when we make love? But I'm so gentle with you.'

'I can't feel anything, Yukio. What do I care, gentle or rough?

197

It's just the sound of it I don't like.'

'I'll be quiet. I promise.'

'You won't be anything. If you try anything I'll scream at the top of my voice. I'll send emails to important people telling them you're forcing yourself on me. Harassing young girls. You know what they call that.'

Yukio was crestfallen. Yukiko changed the subject.

'Did you bring me a present?'

'What? Well – no. I mean – I just left as soon as you told me to. I didn't have time to think about anything like that.'

'What kind of a man are you? You go away for two days, leave me with nothing to do and no one to talk to. And when you come back you just mutter a few apologies. That's it. Too bad. That's not how I imagine my man to be.'

'But what would you like from me, Yukiko?'

She moaned with exasperation.

'Do I have to tell you? I might as well be my own lover. What about a nice dress? What about some of those new Shiseido lipsticks? Don't you have an imagination?'

'But what are you going to do with those things, Yukiko? You're just a doll.'

Yukiko screamed at him loudly.

'Get out! Get out! Now! Don't ever come back! Do you think just because some idiot put me together I can't want the things that other women want? *Just a doll?* Who made me like this? Who fucked me all night while his wife wondered where he was? *Just a doll!* Leave me alone! Go right now!'

Yukio tried to calm her, but there was nothing he could say. She was screaming and screaming, and he was worried about what the neighbours might think. He left, and locked the door behind him.

8.4   Yukio did not know the area well and he drove around for a long time looking for things for Yukiko. At last he found what he wanted and went back to her. He opened the door cautiously. She was completely quiet.

'I'm so sorry,' he ventured. 'I've been very cruel. I didn't realize – I was – very stupid. I've brought you some flowers. In a vase, since you don't have one. And I've got you something else as well.'

'What is it?' asked Yukiko, all non-committal.

'I got you some Shiseido products. A full range. The shop assistant helped me choose. *With all this*, she said, *your girlfriend will be beautiful for ever!*'

He listed everything he had bought. Cleansers, skin creams, lipstick, foundation, eye make-up, perfume . . .

'Wow,' said Yukiko, brightening. 'How much did you spend? Fifty thousand? Seventy? That's so much stuff!'

'Do you like it?' asked Yukio.

'Of course I do! Put some lipstick on me now! Which suits me better: Coralline or Honey Tea?'

'Anything would be beautiful, Yukiko. I'm going to put on Honey Tea.'

He steadied her head with one hand and gently applied the lipstick with the other.

'How do I look?'

'It's spectacular.'

'I'm beautiful, no? Tell me I'm beautiful. I'm not like your wife, all tired and old. I'm going to be beautiful for ever!'

She burst out laughing, and he started laughing too. They laughed together for a time.

'I'm sorry Yukio. For all the things I said.'

'I'm sorry, too. I treated you very badly.'

He took her hand, and she sighed deeply.

'Why don't you make love to me?' she said.

'Are you sure?' He kissed her. 'I thought you didn't like it.'

'If it makes you happy, it makes me happy too.'

8.5 Yukio left early the next morning for home. He was tense.

'I have lost nearly a full day of work. I have just spent one hundred thousand yen on make-up. For a doll. After all, that's really what she is. Am I losing my mind? From now on, Yukio, you will be more disciplined. There is much to do.'

When he arrived home, Mr Yonekawa's proud black Toyota Celsior was parked outside. He entered the house with apprehension.

Mr and Mrs Yonekawa were sitting in the front room with Minako.

'Good morning, Yukio,' said Minako coldly.

'Ah! Here he is! The wandering entrepreneur!' said Mr Yonekawa. 'Where have you been? Looking after my investment, I hope!'

'Yes, indeed, Mr Yonekawa. In fact – I just had to spend the night at the laboratory. In Chiba. I think we're on the brink of something very exciting.'

He tried to collect himself enough to explain what his scientists had found. Minako had not heard any of this herself, and she watched him closely with a strange mixture of curiosity and indifference.

'Well, it all sounds hopeful. Surely there must be other companies out there producing something like this, though? Why is this new plant so revolutionary?'

'We're still working on that, Mr Yonekawa. We need to do some more tests. This and that. A bit more market research.'

'Well, you'd better hurry up! Urgency is everything, young man. You're telling people all about it and you don't even know what you're talking about yet. Somebody else could get in there tomorrow and you're finished. You should have all these answers ready before you say a word. Minako says you're working every damn moment and you haven't even addressed the basics. Don't waste any more time!'

'No. I won't. In fact – I should get back to it.'

He turned towards his study.

'Oh – Yukio – one other thing.'

'Yes?'

'My new building is being opened in Roppongi next week. I'd like you and Minako to come to the opening ceremony. Everyone important will be there. Don't forget.'

Yukio glanced at Minako. She answered for them both.

'Of course we'll be there, Father. Won't we, Yukio?'

'Of course.'

'Good. And sort out your damn business before you come. I don't like the scattered mind I'm seeing in you now. Calm down and be methodical.'

'I will, Mr Yonekawa.'

SECTION 9

9.1 The scientists were arriving that evening. He would not be able to see Yukiko for several days. He rushed out to Chiba in the morning.

'I have to be firm with her. It may be four or five days before I can talk to her again. She has to understand. She's not the only thing in my life. The fact that I have other things to do doesn't mean I don't love her.'

He bought a dress he saw hanging outside a store in Jiyugaoka. It was a pretty cotton summer dress. Something to make her happy.

'Hi, Yukio,' she said distractedly as he entered. 'I'm in a chatroom. Men are really disgusting. All they want is sex, sex, sex. This guy wants to know how big my breasts are and when he can come over to test them out. So I said *Wot can u do for me big boy?*'

Yukio was concerned.

'I don't think you should talk to all these people. There are bad people out there. They won't love you like I do. They have corrupt minds and weird ideas.'

She laughed.

'Are you getting jealous? I like to see my man jealous. You should see this guy who was falling in love with me. Very very rich. He spoke so nicely. Soft words that I had to look up in the dictionary. Offered me anything I wanted. Said he would take me to Rome. He sent me his picture as well. He was ready to come here straight-away but I said *No! Cuz, my man is coming over & he treats me right so too bad for you!*'

'Good. You did a good thing.'

The Honey Tea looked sublime on her lips.

'I brought you something. A dress.'

'You did? Yukio – you are learning! Where's it from? Describe it to me.'

'It's green. With white flowers. Cotton. It's a lovely lightweight summery thing. It will be very pretty on you.'

'Where did you get it from?'

'Some store. In Jiyugaoka. It was hanging outside on a hanger and I saw it and thought *That was made for my Yukiko. No one else should wear it.* Bought it straightaway.'

Yukiko cried with frustration.

'I don't think you have any respect for me. This dress is an insult. Some rag you picked up right by your house. You were just passing and you thought *I'd better get her something or she'll be angry!* You didn't even make an effort. Do you think I have no standards? Am I some country girl going around in cotton dresses? I'm sick of this. Go away and come back when you've decided I'm important. *If.* Meanwhile I'll find someone else. You don't have a clue.'

Yukio tried hard to control his frustration.

'What would make you happy, Yukiko? You don't realize all the – things – there's so much you don't understand. It's very hard for me.'

'Is it Minako? Are you worried about hurting her? Worried about spending more money on me than on her? Just run back to her, then. I don't care. If that's how you feel, you deserve her. Look at me and look at her. There are other men who know how to choose better than you.'

'It's not Minako. I don't care about her. I only love you. I've told you so many times. But there are other – pressures in my life. Just tell me what would make you happy.'

'There's a dress I want very much. If you care enough.'

'Of course I do.'

'It's Prada. It's got a beautiful white bodice embroidered with silk and cut low between the breasts. Long see-through sleeves and

202

an ample knee-length skirt. It's a set: you wear it with these long cotton pants that are embroidered around the ankles. I love it so much! If you were to give me that . . .'

Yukio was silent.

'Prada, Yukiko. It is going to be very expensive. You have to understand. I don't have unlimited money. I've already spent a lot. The apartment. The computer. The make-up. I can't do this every time. Sometimes I think you don't love me for myself.'

'All this whining is so depressing, Yukio. I really don't want to hear any more. I know who your father-in-law is. He's one of the richest men in the country. So all this pettiness about money sounds really disgusting. I should just start an affair directly with Mr Yonekawa rather than going via you.'

'I don't think he would entertain the idea.'

'Don't be so sure of yourself!' Yukiko shouted at him. 'I can seduce any man in Tokyo. And there are many of them who are not losers like you.'

Yukio spoke quietly.

'I will get you your dress, Yukiko. But I want you to promise me that after that you'll be satisfied. You will believe that I love you. And we can be happy with what we have. Life is about accepting constraints.'

'I promise! I promise. If you are holding out the offer of that beautiful dress I am not going to argue with you now! I'll agree to anything. Just go and get it!'

'And then you'll be happy?'

'Then I'll be over the moon!'

Yukio kissed her on her Honey Tea lips.

'I love you so very much. You are all mine. Remember that.'

He stood up. She mused,

'Every time you leave you lock the door. It means that no one else can ever come in to see me.'

'No, Yukiko. That is the idea.'

He turned the key several times in the lock just to make sure.

9.2   He drove back to the city and took a subway to Omote-sandō. He walked down through the boutiques. How much would a Prada dress cost? He was very low on money. He could only pay himself a small salary from the company. His credit cards were at their limit. It would be impossible to pay for a Prada dress on the company account – how would he explain that? He could hardly use Minako's money to buy it. But then he didn't have any other option.

The new Prada boutique was like a prison made of glass. Its bulbous windows magnified the smallest actions of everyone inside. Like rows of enormous eyes, watching. He walked in.

'Yukio!' came a voice. It was a friend of Minako's.

'Buying something for Minako? You're so right to come here. I only shop at Prada. The summer line is divine. How is she?'

'She's fine.' Yukio was cursing her in his head.

'Wonderful. I'll leave you to it. We'll see you for dinner soon? Give her my love.'

He bowed reluctantly.

He found the dress Yukiko had spoken about. There was no price on it. An assistant glided to his side.

'That's a very nice dress. *Very* chic. But very wearable as well. Simple lines. Comfortable. Very light, so she could wear it for an afternoon party. Did you have a particular occasion in mind? Or is it just an impulse buy?'

'How much is it?'

'This one is four hundred and fifty thousand yen. That includes the pants. What size are you looking for?'

'Oh – I'm not really looking. Just browsing.'

'I completely understand, sir. Be my guest.'

He gestured expansively to the rest of the shop and floated away.

Four hundred and fifty thousand yen. How could he pay that kind of money?

Without even really considering his options he suddenly knew he was going to steal it.

He looked at the door. Security seemed lax. The dress could be folded very small. He took an XS from the hanger and went down the stairs to the shoe department.

'Are you looking for shoes to go with that?'

'No. Thank you.'

He found an alcove where no one could see him. No one was looking in through the glass eyes. He pulled the dress off its hanger, screwed it up, and tucked it under his jacket. He went back up the stairs, idly fingered a few other dresses as if still casually browsing and then (he was sweating profusely under his clothes)

9.3 made for the door (the summer suddenly felt very heavy). He looked around him and quickened his pace. He was out in the street. Which way – which way – any way.

'Excuse me, sir.' Deep.

He turned round. A tall man with a sort of arty haircut. A professional smile. Yukio looked dumbly. His hands were shaking.

'I'm sorry to interfere. But would you mind just showing me what is in your hands? I do apologize. We have to be vigilant.'

'Hands? In my hands? Nothing?'

'Still, if you wouldn't mind just showing me. Then we can all just . . .'

Yukio could not focus.

'I –'

The man took hold of his arm and pulled it out from under his jacket.

'I think this belongs to us, sir. Can you follow me inside?'

'I didn't mean . . . I'm not a . . . What? Mistake, you see.'

'Nevertheless. Please come with me.'

The man pushed him gently inside and led him to an office where a stylish middle-aged woman whispered into a phone. She eyed him as she talked. Her conversation ended. She did not ask him to sit.

'Yes?'

'This man was caught leaving the shop with a stolen dress. He was hiding it under his jacket.'

The man laid out the heavily creased dress on her desk. She considered it.

'Do you have anything to say?'

'I didn't. You don't understand. I didn't realize I was carrying it.'

'That's not possible,' countered the man. 'He had screwed the dress up and hidden it in his clothes. When I stopped him he bagan to shake with anxiety.'

'Do you have it on camera?'

'I'll have to check.'

'OK. I'll call the police. Please take this man out of here and get someone to check the video tapes.'

'Please, just listen to me,' cried Yukio. 'I am not just anyone. My father-in-law is Yoshiharu Yonekawa. One of the richest men in the country. Why would I need to steal clothes from a shop?'

The two of them looked at each other.

'Are you carrying anything that proves this?'

'No, of course not. Do you think I carry my marriage certificate around with me?' He feigned laughter. 'But my wife is Minako Yonekawa. His daughter.'

'What is Mr Yonekawa's phone number?'

'Can't you just believe me? He's a very busy man. I don't think you should disturb him with this.'

'You are in no position to tell me what I should or should not do. It's this or the police.'

Yukio recited Mr Yonekawa's mobile number. She dialled.

'Am I speaking with Mr Yoshiharu Yonekawa? . . . The head of Yonekawa Building Company? . . . Good afternoon, sir. I am calling from the Prada boutique in Aoyama. We have just apprehended a man for shoplifting. He says he is your son-in-law. His name is –'

'Yukio Takizawa.'

'Yukio Takizawa . . . Yes . . . Yes . . . A lady's dress . . . We found it under his jacket as he left the shop . . . I believe – four hundred and fifty thousand yen . . . I see . . . Of course. I completely understand. A very good day to you. Yes. And thank you for your help.'

She put down the phone.

'It seems that your story is true. He says he will take responsibility for the situation. So I'm not going to press charges. Please leave the store now, and I would request you never to return.'

'Can I take the dress? You see I meant to pay for it. I was in a daydream and . . .'

'Do you have the money?'

'Of course. Here's my card.'

She snatched it from him and inspected it. She picked up the dress unceremoniously and gave it with the card to the other man.

'Charge Mr Takizawa for this dress and then escort him out of the shop.'

'Certainly.'

9.4 Yukio's mobile phone rang.

9.5 'Get yourself to my office at once.'

9.6 'Thank you, sir. Here is your receipt.'

9.7 What the fuck am I doing?

9.8 'What the hell do you think you are doing?' shouted Mr Yonekawa, in a rage more terrifying than Yukio had ever seen before. He paced the room strenuously to try and contain his storm within. He came up very close to Yukio, and the veins in his eyes were like thick red roots. Yukio was ready for him to hit him, but he did not.

'Can there be *any* explanation for this kind of behaviour? Stealing clothes from a shop? In the middle of the afternoon? Giving out my mobile number to some – some *shop manager*, so I can bail you out? I thought you had a lot of work to do. What the hell are you doing in clothes shops? Shoplifting!'

Yukio was terrified.

'I wanted to get something for Minako. A surprise. For your opening party.'

'Minako has lots of clothes. She can afford to buy them. She doesn't need your stolen goods. You are pathetic. I was right about you all along. Is that the dress in that bag?'

'Yes.'

'So after you tried stealing it and failed you decided to buy it anyway. With your own money, I hope.'

'Yes.'

Mr Yonekawa stared at him.

'Look – just get out. I can't bear the sight of you any more. I'm ashamed of you. I don't know what Minako ever saw in you. I hope after this she'll reconsider. She hasn't lost much yet. As for the money I gave you – you might start thinking about paying it back. I don't trust you with it anymore. I'll send you a formal letter.'

'Sir, please listen. I'm not what you think I am. I was not trying to steal the dress. I was thinking about the business, I wasn't paying attention to what I was doing. The scientists are arriving in just a few hours from Latin America with the first samples. Things are going very well. I just wanted Minako to look wonderful at your party.'

Mr Yonekawa was watching him intently.

'I don't know what to think. Either way, I'm sick of this conversation. Get back to your work and let me get back to mine. I'll think about this some more. I need to find out what Minako thinks.'

'Minako doesn't know about the dress, Mr Yonekawa.'

Mr Yonekawa erupted again,

'I'm not talking about the damn dress, you idiot! I'm talking about you! Just get out!'

SECTION 10

10.1 Yukio drove to Chiba. It was a sweltering afternoon and his suit had wilted entirely with the pressures of the day. His mind was lurching like a stock market. He did not know what he was doing, or why he was doing it. He arrived at the apartment and thought of all his money being sucked away through its sewerage.

Yukiko was more beautiful than ever. She could sometimes be demanding, but it was all due to her naivety, her complete obliviousness to the rules of the world, its pressures and desperation. That was what made her such an idyllic refuge.

'Did you get it, Yukio? Did you get it? I've been sitting here waiting for you, so impatient. Do you remember this, *I'm so excited I think I'm going to wet myself*? Do you remember Yukio?'

She ended in peals of laughter, and Yukio's heart, which had kept up its hardness throughout the heat of the day, finally yielded, and became liquid.

'Yes, I got you the dress, my love,' he said.

'Undress me! Put it on!'

He put it on her. Though it was creased from its ordeal, it looked sublime. It made her look like an angel. He began to cry.

'What's wrong?'

'I don't know,' he said. 'It's so beautiful. And it's been a very bad day.'

'Oh, Yukio. I love you. Don't worry about the rest of the world. They don't mean a thing. It's just you and me. Everyone else will just make you unhappy.'

He nestled against her breasts.

'Why don't you leave Minako and live with me? She's bad for you. I can see that. She doesn't understand you. How hard you work. How passionate you are. She can never understand.'

'You're right. You're absolutely right. But it's all more difficult than that. People aren't so free as you think.'

'You are more free than you think. But you will take time to realize.'

She hummed another old song.

> *I love Paris in the spring time*
> *I love Paris in the fall . . .*

Her voice was breezy, and so sweet. She said:

'Will you make love to me?'

He smiled and kissed her. They made love. It was as if Yukiko's sweet-smelling body was some kind of magic crucible in which his impure black mountain of anxiety and pain melted, transformed into a honey-coloured stream of the purest joy. Out of the intensity of his stress came an intensity of pleasure he had never known before. He lay with his head on her stomach.

> I love Paris every moment,
> Every moment of the year.
> I love Paris, why, oh why do I love Paris?
> Because my love is near.

10.2 Yukio opened his eyes and saw his watch. It was late. The scientists were arriving at the airport in fifteen minutes!

'Yukiko! I've lost track of time! I have to be at Narita to meet the scientists. What am I doing?'

He dressed Yukiko again in her Prada, pulled on his own clothes that were more ragged than ever, kissed her quickly (thought as he took a final lingering look at her *I should not even have hesitated to buy that dress*) and rushed out the door.

He drove towards the airport. 'Calm down, calm down,' he said to himself. 'It has been a day of terrible lows and tremendous highs. You look like shit. Just try and calm down. Think about the work in hand.'

He arrived just in time to see them coming out of the gate. They looked more like backpackers than eminent scientists. They began talking straightaway about surfactants and detergents and preservatives and production processes. He listened without speaking as they drove back to the city.

'We're very excited to be back here. This is an amazing project. Yukio, I think this is going to make us all very rich!'

They laughed loudly and shook manly hands from back seat to front seat. Yukio smiled.

10.3 He took them for Italian food. It was too tiring to translate and explain Japanese menus. They had been travelling for over twenty hours but could not stop laughing and talking.

'You've got to see this place,' said one of the scientists. 'It's really the middle of nowhere. You can't believe how nice these people are. They have nothing. They live in the forest. It's like stepping back two thousand years. They have faces like – you know, primitive people or something. But they're so nice. So hospitable. You're sitting there in the evening and they've cooked this food on a fire and some women are singing and the forest is humming with frogs and insects. You wonder if the other world actually exists.'

They tucked in greedily to spaghetti bolognaise and linguine marinara.

'But, you know, it's all changing. Nothing stays the same. They wear T-shirts saying *Atlanta Braves* or *University of Wisconsin*. I laughed when I saw that. Think. Wisconsin. In the Amazon rainforest. And they have radios there and speak Portuguese. There are these two old sisters in the village who are the only ones who speak the traditional language. No one else knows how to talk to them, and they can't speak Portuguese. Or refuse to. Isn't that wild? Just two people in the world who speak a language. And everyone else seems so indifferent. That their language is dying. It's such a shame really. They don't have any respect for history.'

Yukio was drinking heavily to try and get through the meal. His head was full of things. Forest canopies were swaying above him and there were haunting insect sounds and birds of astonishing colours. He and Yukiko were the last two people in the world to speak their language. Around them was a vast silence. Yukiko was saying, 'If I thought you didn't love me I would never speak to you again. I would stop talking for ever.' 'No!' pleaded Yukio, stricken. 'You must never leave me. Always know that I love you. Without you, who would I talk to? Who could ever understand?'

The conversation moved on around him.

'Are you OK?' one of them asked. 'You're looking a bit rough.

Your eyes are tired. You're working too hard! Is it true that Japanese people don't know how to relax?'

'They're also very good at business,' said the other. 'Don't forget that. Our future is in this guy's hands!'

They laughed.

'Let's talk shop for a while. We both think this is a big deal. We've done some tests already and the labs here are only going to confirm what we already know. This stuff is amazing. It's not just like some hippy soap from soy oil or something. It's as good as chemicals. I think we will be in a position to make vegetable-based cleaning agents that can substitute for nearly all household cleaners and many industrial ones. It biodegrades a hundred per cent in seven days. It even – this is totally amazing – softens hard water. I don't know yet how but it does. We shouldn't need to use phosphates. *And* it has a natural perfume. It *smells* clean.'

'You should read the literature. The number of people who fall sick every year inhaling fumes from household cleaners? Or ingesting them? This is totally non-toxic. And it's not hard to put together some really terrifying numbers on environmental pollution from chemical cleaning agents. We are going to have a watertight case.'

'And these plants grow like weeds. Where we were working, this plant is everywhere. The climate and soil are perfect. We can clear a few hundred acres of land and set up some pilot farms. A couple of processing plants. These people will work for almost nothing. With a bit of hard work I guarantee you in six months we'll have a shit-hot range of products. The big chemical companies will be queuing up to buy. Their existing products simply won't be able to compete. The environmental arguments are too compelling.'

'It's going to be a great week. I can't wait to get to the lab tomorrow. Cheer up, Yukio, for Christ's sake. This is it. You've hit the big time!'

10.4 Yukio arrived home late, exhausted. Minako was there. She said: 'So where's my dress?'

'Dress?'

'The dress you nearly got arrested for. After all that I hope it's spectacular. My father was livid.'

'Actually I – I took it back to the shop. I thought it wouldn't fit you.'

She sighed.

'I don't know what is going on in your head, Yukio. I hope it's just another woman. I hope it's nothing more serious than that. When you start shoplifting clothes I have to wonder. But whoever she is, by your face it doesn't look as if she's doing you any favours. I notice you paid for it out of our joint account.'

'There's a refund.'

'Good. I look forward to seeing it.'

She went to bed.

Yukio watched her go up the stairs. Despite the fog in his head; despite that, the feeling inside him, the feeling that was rising like lava within and hammering at his glands, was quite supernaturally clear. It was hatred.

SECTION 11

11.1 He spent interminable days with the scientists. It was important work – momentous, even; but he could not keep his mind on what they were doing. It kept wandering off.

11.2 The laboratory was only a few miles from Yukiko. On the fourth day he could not contain himself anymore, and excused himself for a few hours.

He was too exhausted to make love. He undressed and lay naked with his head in Yukiko's lap. She was dressed in white Prada and looked like an angel.

'You are everything to me, Yukiko,' he murmured. 'I don't know what I would do if I lost you.'

She hummed a song softly to him.

She said:

'I have been thinking. I had a strange idea.'

'What is it?'

'You are so happy with me. You love me more than anyone. And I love you. Isn't that right?'

'Yes. Of course.'

'And yet we are not together. Lovers like us should be together. No one should stand in the way of something like that. Why don't you leave your wife, Yukio? You could live here with me, and we would always be together.'

'I can't do that, Yukiko. I have all kinds of obligations to Minako that you wouldn't understand. They are social and financial obligations, not emotional ones. But they still count for a lot.'

'What if . . .'

He looked up at her.

'What?'

'What if Minako were to die? You would get her money. Everyone would feel sorry for you. Mr Yonekawa would feel closer to you than ever. And you and I could be together. We would be rich and happy.'

He smiled.

'You are too imaginative. This is the real world.'

'But you could arrange for her to die. Everyone does it these days. I've read of hundreds of these cases. I've been researching. I know how we could do it. I'll help you. No one will ever know.'

Yukio imagined Minako dying in a car accident. How much simpler his life would be. Her personal wealth was enormous. The house would be his. He would never have to worry. Nothing would stand between him and Yukiko. After all, Minako would never understand him. She didn't even try. She didn't deserve his pity.

'It's a nice thought, Yukiko. But I need to think about it. It's a big step to take. There are risks. We need to come up with a water-tight plan. Otherwise our lives would be ruined. Let's talk about it later. I'm too tired now.'

'OK. But don't forget to think about it. And I will too. Between us we can do anything.'

Yukio smiled faintly.

And went to sleep in her lap.

11.3 What am I thinking?

11.4 Yukio looked at himself in the mirror of the bathroom at the laboratory. It was true. He looked like shit. He had a streaming cold. He had not slept properly for days. What was going on in his life? Everything was falling apart. Was it true that he had seriously entertained the idea of killing his wife just because Yukiko had suggested it?

'Yukiko is just a doll, Yukio. What are you thinking?'

SECTION 12

12.1 The scientists departed. The tests had been a great success. Despite Yukio's unreliable state of mind, they had worked out a clear course of action on every front, and all of them had a lot of work to do.

As soon as they left, Yukio went to see a psychotherapist. He did not know who else to turn to. He told him everything. He liked how calmly he listened. He took notes and asked good questions.

'Your story is very interesting, Mr Takizawa. You are clearly harbouring a fetish, which is no extraordinary thing; but this one is unusual in its emotional pitch. There are many people who never manage to surrender their emotions to another human being to the extent you have managed with this doll. Naturally, your fetish object is remarkable for its closeness to the human. So like, and so unlike. A woman who is not a woman. I wonder. It is undoubtedly an intriguing case.'

He tugged irregularly at his little beard and inspected his notes with intense academic concentration.

'Nevertheless, I see no significant obstacle to a swift and effective resolution of your problem. You don't have to be too worried about yourself. But I think, given the strength of the emotions involved, you should try and address this quickly. We should start today. I suggest you come for daily sessions. A combination of conscious exploration of the problem and hypnotherapy. We should be able to sort this out in a couple of months. I'm also going to give you some anti-anxiety pills. They're mild and quite harmless, but it will help the treatment. And I must insist that you stay away from the doll while all this is happening. I'd like you to give me the key to the apartment.'

Yukio hesitated.

'You want the key?'

'Yes. At this early stage, I am not sure if you will be able to keep yourself away. I think it is better if I take the key.'

Yukio took the key from his key ring and put it on the table.

'Is that the only one you have?'

'No. I have another at home.'

'Please bring it with you tomorrow. Make a concrete plan for this evening. Go and see a movie or something. Go to a soapland. Have dinner with someone. Whatever. I just don't want you to go and see the doll.'

Yukio nodded.

'I won't.'

'Now. Take your shoes off, and lie down on this couch. Make yourself comfortable.'

12.2 Yukio told himself he should feel calm after his interview with the therapist, but his nerves were buzzing with excessive voltage. 'Your problem can easily be sorted,' he thought, 'and then you will be free.' But he knew he was talking to himself in platitudes. He was losing Yukiko: that was the brute fact, and no compensation seemed adequate. He sat in the subway like some dumb animal that has lost its offspring and can only express the madness of its grief in inarticulate ways: he moaned and banged his head against the window, and other travellers cleared a hostile circle around him.

12.3   He settled down to work but could not concentrate, and achieved nothing. The sun began to set outside and dusk came heavy and empty. His screen glowed an icy white in the gloom. He was listless, and could only think of Yukiko's warmth. He could not give her up without seeing her one more time. He picked up the spare key from among the paper clips in his desk drawer.

'This will certainly be the last time,' he said to himself. 'I know I am sick and need to be cured. I know everything else rests on it. But she is mine and no one can tell me to stay away from her. From tomorrow I do it of my own free will. But tonight I will see her again. Let our farewell at least be glorious.'

As he drove out of his street he was exhilarated, and filled with despair. 'Will I ever be able to stop loving her? To stop wanting to see what she will look like the next time I open that door and see her waiting for me? Will I carry on leading this miserable life for ever?'

12.4   He had come to love the sign that said 'Makuhari Bay Town: The Urban Lifestyle of the 21st Century'. Today it seemed simultaneously so full of joyful promise, and so infinitely sad. Yukio parked his car fondly in the underground car park and made his way to the elevator. He pressed '15' and looked at himself distantly in the mirror. He was an ordinary man. Certainly not ugly, but then not strikingly good-looking. A nicely shaped mouth, indifferent eyes, a mole by his nose that he had never liked. A man you would not necessarily notice in the street. A man who was in love with a doll.

The elevator doors opened at the fifteenth floor and he walked out into the quiet corridor whose unique smell of disinfectant and air freshener calmed him. He took the key from his pocket and stopped in front of the door. He breathed deeply and put the key in the lock but already he was hearing some commotion inside and cut short his meditation; he pushed the door sharply open; there was a scramble; and with a staccato grunt a half-naked man leapt up to cover himself, leaving Yukiko spread wide on the floor

217

laughing a metallic laugh. The man tried to grab the rest of his clothes but they were flung across the room; he gave up on the indignity of crawling around to retrieve them and turned instead to face Yukio. It was the psychotherapist.

He was solemn.

'I apologize for this, Mr Takizawa. Your story –'

Yukio could not look him in the face. The therapist added, feebly, 'You were not supposed to come here.'

Yukio watched as a drop of semen fell from the tip of the psychotherapist's penis and landed on the gnarled surface of his big toenail. He said:

'Please leave immediately.'

He continued to look at the ground as the therapist gathered his belongings and scurried past Yukio towards the door.

'The key?' said Yukio.

The therapist searched through the pockets of the trousers he still clutched in his arms. He found the key and dropped it in Yukio's hand. Yukio pushed him out and shut the door.

He looked at Yukiko. She had been soiled by this man. A vulgar hand had flung aside her Prada dress as if it were a dishcloth.

'How could you do this?' he pleaded, tearfully. He looked down at himself, standing in this room. 'How could you do this?' he repeated. Her legs had been crushed out of shape by the weight of the therapist. Permanently spread. Everything was wrong.

'Yukio,' she said.

'Don't say those things!' He lashed out and hit her around the head. He picked her up bodily and threw her with all his strength across the room. Her limbs remained disconcertingly rigid in mid-air and the sound of the impact with the wall was not human; she landed awkwardly on the back of her neck and her head became detached from her body.

He was stunned for a moment at what he had done and could only watch dumbly as she spoke in a voice more muffled than before,

'I'm so excited I think I'm going to wet myself.'

He ran to her side.

'I'm so sorry. Forgive me, Yukiko. Forgive me. I am so sorry.'

He tried to reassemble her with panicked hands but her head was cracked and things would not go back together. He pressed wires and components inside and forced the head to stay on. She had done nothing. She was a victim. Innocent. He stroked her cheek and hair.

'I didn't mean it. I will never hurt you again. Please forgive me. You are my love.'

She did not seem to understand. She continued to say disconnected things.

'Why is that man staring at me?'

And then,

'I miss you already.'

'Please, Yukiko. Talk to me properly. Like before. Show me you're still alive.'

'I'm so excited I think I'm going to wet myself!'

Yukio picked up her Prada dress and put it carefully on her. She looked like an angel. He wrapped her in a blanket and lifted her in his arms. She was so light. He looked around the apartment. It was empty apart from a sock that the therapist had left behind in his rush. He turned off the lights.

In the elevator he pushed back the blanket from Yukiko's face. He stared into her eyes which seemed to have become alive but unworldly.

He carried her across the parking lot and cradled her in one arm while he opened the trunk of his car with the other hand. He lowered her carefully inside. Her head settled at an unnatural angle. He closed the trunk gently over her. She would not be disturbed by the darkness.

12.5 He started the car and pulled out of the apartment complex.

12.6 Minako called on his mobile phone.

'Where are you?'

'In Chiba.'

'You haven't forgotten my father's party tonight? It starts in half an hour. You said you would come. I think you should.'

It was the very last thing on his mind.

'No, I haven't forgotten. I'm on my way.'

'Come to the sixty-fourth floor. I'll be there waiting.'

SECTION 13

13.1 The building was spectacular. There were wide approaches with soaring sculptures on either side, and criss-crossing escalators going down to the shopping mall and subway. Cafés had already opened at street level, and people sat outside talking on mobile phones. The building towered above everything else in the area, and the setting sun glowed red in its glassy walls. Yukio walked in through the main entrance and took the elevator to the sixty-fourth floor.

'Name?' asked the man on reception, dressed in a sparkling tuxedo. Yukio felt self-conscious about his battered suit.

'Takizawa. Yukio Takizawa.'

'Of course, Mr Takizawa. That way please. The party is up on the roof at the moment for Mr Yonekawa's presentation. He is showing them the helipad. You can go up these stairs. Why don't you take a drink on your way?'

Yukio took a glass of beer and walked up the stairs. The roof was enormous. A football stadium could have been laid out on it. Mr Yonekawa was standing on a podium in one corner, addressing a huddle of well-dressed people.

'. . . five hundred thousand square metres of residential and commerical space . . . help to make Tokyo one of the most attractive destinations for international business . . . the most environmentally-friendly design in the world . . .'

Yukio did not join the group but wandered off on his own to look down at the city. The lights of Tokyo were coming on far, far below. He was so high that no sound could be heard from the city. It was entirely silent. It looked so still and calm and inviting.

His phone warbled briefly, and he took it out to read the message. It was from the scientist in Brazil.

ONE OF THE SISTERS DIED TODAY. OTHER SISTER HAS NO ONE IN THE WORLD TO TALK TO. SAD. EVERYTHING ELSE OK.

The railing seemed so frail considering the height of the building. It did not even come up to his waist. It would be so easy to fall. You could just climb over it and walk out into nothingness. Yukio imagined his toes on the very edge, imagined himself falling ever so slowly forward. Wondered what he would think about as sixty-four floors rushed by. He would land on some café table and people would be horrified. They would tell everyone about it in the office or at dinner parties. It would be in all the newspapers. Mr Yonekawa would have to give press statements. Superstitious people might think the building was unlucky. None of them would have any idea what kind of a person he had been.

Minako appeared at the railing next to him. He thought about her presence as a piano tuner listens to see if a note is in tune. She said,

'We are so high up. You can't hear anything from down there.'

'No. It's pure silence.'

She looked at him.

'You look terrible, Yukio.'

He turned to face her.

'I'll be OK.' He smiled.

The sun finally sank behind the horizon. The city looked cold.

'Shall we go?' she suggested. 'This party will be really boring.'

'Yes,' he said. 'Let's go.'

The security guards had settled into an epic chess tournament. They were gathered by the duty-free shop, whose once-exuberant displays of perfume and whisky now stood chastened by steel security grills and the unflattering chiaroscuro of a fluorescent nightlight. A low table had been set up with a number of chairs: two men leant intently over glowering armies of age-worn pawns and bishops; the others huddled round appraisingly. The jackets of security uniforms had been draped over chair backs, and sleeves rolled up. The onlookers smoked cigarettes and discussed moves; there were occasional murmurs of approval, ominous exclamations, or sighs of exasperation.

A game ended, and the audience applauded enthusiastically; the players shook hands. One man began to set up the board for the next game whilst another began to read aloud a shocking newspaper article. There was good humour and heated discussion; two players took their places for the next game and someone emerged from a doorway with a tray of steaming cups and tea bags.

Just then, one of them cried out and pointed at the window. Another slung his gun over his shoulder, went to the window and opened it. A cat jumped nimbly in and began to drink at a bowl of milk that lay on the floor in readiness.

THE RENDEZVOUS IN ISTANBUL

The Ninth Story

IN THE GREAT city of Istanbul, near to the tranquil cemeteries around the Süleymaniye mosque, and not far from where locals and tourists alike cram the avenues of the Gran Bazaar, there is a place called Laleli. This is where traders come from other countries to buy clothes for sale back home: women who arrive with the easy gait and slim bodies of hard work, and return obese and red-faced because they carry their cargo in over-packed suitcases and wear a dozen crisp new shirts and layer upon layer of fur-lined jackets on their bodies. There are hidden rooms all over Istanbul – yes, and Ankara and Izmir too – where Turkish men and women sew furs and leathers too baroque for their own tastes that will be worn in the booming bars and primordial cocktail parties of Moscow, Sofia, and Minsk; and there they hang ('Minimum purchase ten items, Madam, five hundred US dollars, cash only') in the rows and rows of Laleli's glass windows trying to attract the discerning eye of experienced merchants.

Listen now to a tale of the commerce of that place.

There was such a merchant whose name was Natalia. She had grown up in the Danubian port of Izmail, which had crashed with the Empire, and had spent her first years as a woman sitting bored at home while her father and brothers played cards in their underwear; she had, for want of anything else to do, spent her nights standing in the Black Sea wind with crowds of aimless youths, watching boys racing 1960s Peugeots endlessly up and down the wharf – and had watched them crash, too – and fending off the lukewarm sexual advances with which such gatherings concluded. What joy, then, to meet a real man one day, an Entrepreneur who carried her away to a house in sweeping Odessa where he ran businesses in poultry and machine parts, owned property, bought her modern fashions! But passion may be the midwife of hatred: and so it was that their solemn crowned nuptials in the Il'insky church were followed quickly on by raised voices and drawn kitchen knives in the dead of night, and before very long there were other women in his life, richer and more precise in their desires; and she was, as the saying goes, out on the street.

But this third crash was to give rise to new ideas, for it is sometimes when reality has exhausted itself that the imagination rouses from its sluggery. Natalia began to join other women on the ferry boats from Odessa to Istanbul, watching the refineries and resorts of Bulgaria pass by until they docked in the Golden Horn with mosques lined up above them like a surfeit of upturned beetles! and staying four to a hotel room where lives were shared and compared over late-night vodka. Natalia had learned better by now how to see things in a man's eyes: and when she encountered the broad smile of a Serbian shop-owner who stood proprietorially outside in the street watching her approach, when he served her coffee and told her in excellent Russian, over fox-skin stoles and piles of cutesy fur-trimmed coats, the well-rehearsed story of his life – she knew this was a figure she could trust. She spent all her borrowings with him, and he gave her twice as much again on credit – 'For you will come back to me, Madam, and we can sort it out next time. Or the time after' – and within a week she had sold everything at the market in Odessa. A life began: for she loved the movement back-and-forth and the beautiful clothes, she made money and rented a two-bedroom apartment of her own in Odessa, she became a regular for ten years at Ibro's shop – and did he not take her in during her trips and make up a guest room in the back? did he not in fact become her lover and take her to tea shops by the Bosporus and narrow-lane restaurants in Beyoğlu? It was not love, and she was content with this intermittence – for after all, he had his own wife and family living not half a mile from his shop – but it was trust and tenderness, and these things do not count for nothing.

Let us not overlook her hardships: for it was an arduous life full of the exhaustion of loading herself like a desert camel and the constant negotiation of the marketplace. She came to see cheatery all around her, and would give her trust to a person last of all the other things that one human being can give to another: she was on more than one occasion robbed of the wads of dollar bills with which she embarked, fresh from her Odessa sales. But the sight of the Sea of Marmara never stopped giving her joy, and when it happened that the more entrepreneurial of her friends started to set up their own production houses in Moldova and Romania, or to travel the more profitable trade routes that led to new and cheaper sources in China, she was content to make no alteration to her life, and to watch her earnings gradually dwindle. Laleli crashed, too; but she had too much affection for it to leave it behind.

There was a morning when she was walking in that part of the city. Mannequins were being lined up on the sidewalks and the sun was gradually clearing the shadows from the heavily built streets. Natalia walked with the abandon of one who knows a place, looked idly around her, peered into shops through the bright reflections on the windows. Listen closely: for there are some moments when another's life breaks the rules of what is familiar, and they cannot be followed with the humdrum attention we usually grant to the world – and these are the moments that make that life unique. And let us also be careful how we tell this; for what Natalia saw, in what order, is important to understand. She knew she was passing a coffee shop, for she herself had drunk so many dainty coffees there; she looked at the window and saw the reflection in it of a man on the other side of the street who waved with his arms at a van as it reversed into a narrow parking space (whether this is significant for what followed is only a matter for speculation); and hazily, behind this crystal reflection, in the half-light of the interior and mostly veiled by the glass, she saw – in outline only, for the details were hidden and were only filled in later in her mind – she saw the gesture of a man (and even his gender was mostly a suspicion), a man who – let us state it as baldly and simply as it was – raised a coffee cup slowly to his lips and sipped. Perhaps it is difficult to believe, for such sights surround us every day and they tell us so little about anything at all, perhaps it will be difficult not to feel that there are other facts that are not being recounted; but that is the problem – at the risk of repetition – with assuming that the lives of others are just rearranged versions of our own: for before Natalia could see anything else, or even understand what she had seen, she had fallen suddenly, and breathlessly, in love.

Perhaps it was the hesitation in his gesture, as if he did not know what taste would emerge from the cup; the unaccustomed awkwardness with which he held it – perhaps these things seemed distinctive and endearing. Perhaps it was the intense concentration on the steam and the smell and the taste that bespoke – who knows? – a certain sensuality. Who knows? For such moments do not respond well to analysis and there is no point wasting our words on it; things rush on and we are left behind.

Natalia stopped just beyond the coffee shop and held on to the wall. Her heart had left her, a seabird moaning overhead in the glittering sky, and yet it clanged in her chest like the steel plates under a shipwright's mallet; she exhaled the troubled air from her lungs and tried to still herself. 'Talia,' she thought, 'you have done so many things of which you were afraid, and will you falter here?'

And she turned and entered the café.

She stood by the man behind the window, stood almost over him as she watched. He was tall and dark-skinned, wore dirty clothes, considered his coffee cup in a reverie; and she waited to see his eyes. He looked up at her: and there was nothing over his gaze, only unabashed curiosity; there were open horizons there with no meanness; there were things she did not understand but which she could venture into without apprehension. She sat down opposite him, and they looked at each other.

'I am Natalia,' she said. 'From Ukraine.'

He considered her for a moment.

'I am Riad. I am a sailor.' He added, 'From Bangladesh.'

She tried to think about Bangladesh. For a moment.

'How was your coffee?'

He smiled slightly.

'It was very good. Stronger than I am used to. And you have these –'

He broke off.

'The grounds in the bottom, yes. It is the Turkish style.'

He raised an eyebrow, and considered.

'Not bad, actually. I will do it again.'

'You should.'

He waited for her to speak.

'You have never been here before?'

'Never. I have heard all my life of Istanbul, but today is the first time I see it. And I have only one day so I have come to explore.'

'One day!'

'Yes. We arrived early this morning. Tonight we leave for Marseille.'

'Oh.'

She looked at the table top.

'Perhaps I can show you – if you like – we could walk together. If you like.'

She did not look up.

'Walking is nice. I would like very much.'

He gave a dollar to the waiter, who brought him Turkish lira in return.

'You take these,' he said to Natalia. 'I don't know these notes.'

They walked out into the street.

'Maybe we could visit a mosque,' said Riad. 'I have heard so much about the mosques of Istanbul.'

They walked up the narrow streets to the Süleymaniye mosque. Fruit stands were bright in the sun and the tarmac smelt of pleasure: and as they single-filed, one behind the other, she could feel how the shapes of their bodies responded to each other.

The precincts of the mosque were empty. They followed signs that pointed to 'Entrance' in five languages that did not include either of theirs. Inside, they looked up together at the dome. Shafts of bright sunshine shone red and green and blue through the stained glass into the half-light.

'I have never been here before,' she whispered.

He was looking up at the pillars and did not answer. She watched him. He looked at the tiles in the mihrab, rotated slowly on his heel with his head thrown back, and looked all around – until finally he faced her and caught her gaze. They looked at each other for a moment; and then he smiled, and gestured inquiringly towards the doorway. They walked out into the day.

'Would you like to see the tombs?' she asked. 'Süleyman and his wife are buried here. Their tombs are supposed to be beautiful.'

'It's all right. Another time.'

They walked among the tombstones and sat on a wall. He looked at her and said,

'Perhaps we should make love now.'

Despite herself, she was astonished.

Astonished and – something else, for astonishment alone cannot explain what she said next; cannot explain why, in the midst of her excitement, she thrust him away from herself in such a way. Perhaps, though she wanted this more than anything else, she was offended that he should assume it, detect it so easily in her; perhaps commerce struck her as a safer framework that might allow her not to have to release all the hasty and improbable things she was feeling. Perhaps it is simpler than all that – was she thinking, actually, of the mere fact that she had nowhere for them to go? Whatever! Her reply, as surprising to herself as it was to him, was quick and serene:

'One hundred and thirty dollars.'

It was only as the tenderness flushed from his face that she realized it had been there up till then. But his gaze did not falter.

'I didn't think – well . . . One hundred and thirty dollars is a lot of money.'

The charade ran away with itself: 'Thirty dollars for the room. One hundred for me. You can have me till you leave.'

230

'That's more than I earn in a month. I don't have that kind of money.'

'That's a shame.'

They looked at the same spot on the ground. The awkwardness rose hotly through her pores.

'Unless —' she began. And stopped.

He looked at her.

'Unless what?'

'I could lend you some money. Maybe ten dollars. You could try and win the rest. At a casino.'

He burst out laughing.

'Natalia, I have never been to a casino in my life! I would lose your ten dollars. And then what?'

'I would help you. I am lucky in these things. And I think you are lucky, too.'

He pondered the matter.

'Where is the casino?'

'Actually, casinos are illegal here now. But I know a place. Friends of mine. It's open all day. Right nearby.'

He looked up at the sky. A white bird circled far overhead.

'Let's go.'

They walked up the stairs to the small fourth-floor room. At the door Natalia stopped and got some money from her bag.

'Here's twenty million lira. Which is more than ten dollars. I'm trying to improve your chances.'

She pressed a bell. The intercom burst into noise, a voice in the midst.

'Natalia. Hello. Who's the man?'

'A friend. He's fine.'

The door buzzed loudly and she pushed it briskly open. Old Sezen Aksu songs flooded out into the stairwell; the room was crowded, despite the fact that it was still morning: men and women played poker and craps, each table had a blonde Russian dealer, a number of men in suits circled watchfully. One of them approached:

'Good day, Natalia.'

He inspected Riad emphatically.

'How is Ibro?'

'Well. Thank you.'

'Please give him my regards.'

'I will.'

'And what are you playing today?'

'Roulette,' Riad interjected. 'I want to try roulette. Have never seen it in real life.'

Natalia looked at him, surprised and amused.

'This way, sir. You buy your chips over here. How much will you be spending?'

'I'll start with twenty million lira.'

The man chided:

'That's not a lot! Why don't you increase your winnings? One hundred million is a much luckier number!'

'Nevertheless. I'll start with twenty.'

Chips were handed over at the booth. They approached the table. Natalia started to explain his options. He interrupted.

'If I put all this on one number and win – will it be enough?'

'Yes. But that would be – foolhardy. You don't have to win it all at once.'

'Let's be foolhardy!' he said.

The previous game finished. Chips clattered under the rakes.

'Let's put it all on twelve.'

'Are you sure?'

'No . . . Um –' He gritted his teeth in a pained smile. 'Put it all on thirteen. The wheel thinks I think that thirteen is unlucky. Thinks I won't play there. Which is the best reason to do it. Put it all on thirteen!'

She handed over the pile of yellow chips, hesitantly. 'Straight up on thirteen.'

The chips were stacked rapidly in a crooked column on the baize. Other players distributed theirs around the table according to complex personal numerologies.

'No more bets,' said the impassive Russian dealer.

The wheel span, the ball raced around in smooth counter-motion, slowed down and lost its momentum, rattled over the grooves, bounced a few times, and nestled in thirteen. The wheel slowed.

Riad beamed. Natalia burst out laughing.

'I cannot believe you!'

'How much do we win?'

'Seven hundred million lira! That's more than four hundred dollars!'

The suited gentleman approached them.

'How do you plan to increase these winnings?'

'We don't,' Riad replied. 'We are very satisfied. Thank you.'

He cashed in his chips, and they left.

'Welcome to Istanbul!'

Atatürk's glittering eyes stared down from a lofty frame, and there was a much-faded poster of the Hagia Sofia next to a handwritten notice saying 'Breakfast served 7 a.m. to 11 a.m.'. The man was young and full of smiles.

'How many nights are you staying?'

'Just one.'

'You are wrong, my friends. You should stay many nights. Passport please. You don't like Turkey? My wife is from New Zealand. She came just one week and stayed one year. She met me! This is your wife, or – ?'

'This is my wife.'

Riad put his passport on the desk. The People's Republic of Bangladesh.

'This room is forty dollars. Sign here. When I get my visa – one, two months – I will go to Wellington. I never saw my daughter yet! – look here.'

He showed a picture in his wallet. It was a roughly pixelated photograph that he had printed from an email. It could have been any baby in the world.

'Have you been to New Zealand? Is it a good place?'

'I have,' Riad said as he counted out the money. 'It seemed – very nice.'

'I hear it is a good place. You should see my wife. You would like her. My daughter is called Sarah. You can't believe it: she came for just one week. Just a tourist like you. She stayed a whole year! But I think there are many Turks in Wellington so everything will be OK. Just one or two months and – I go! Turkey is good but work is hard. You are also from different countries. What a beautiful couple! You live in his country or in yours?'

'We . . . Is that everything?'

'Yes. Your key. First floor – you can take the stairs. Breakfast is over there. Seven to eleven in the morning. Here is a good place for dinner and belly dancing.' He gave them a pink leaflet with a sparkling, writhing woman on the front. 'If you want shopping, anything – ask me. I am Ahmet. Like the Sultan.'

'Thank you very much. And good luck.'

'Thank you! Life always works out. Don't you think?'

Natalia and Riad went up the stairs. He held her hand.

The room had a big double bed with a gold polyester duvet on it. The curtains were drawn. Riad leant against the wall. Natalia sat on the bed.

'So, you are my prize. Is that right? My gambling prize?'

'If that's how you like to think about it.'

'No.'

He folded his arms, and frowned involuntarily.

'Do I pay you now or afterwards?'

She spoke almost inaudibly. 'Afterwards is fine.'

He pulled her up and kissed her. Her kiss was one of relief, for she did not want to talk anymore; and how beautiful he was.

And how bewildering to be kissing him.

She opened her eyes for a moment, and looked over his shoulder. There was a painting of a shipwreck on the wall. Dark heads bobbed in the ocean. Overhead soared a magnificent albatross, solitary and an infinitely sad witness to the tragedy.

They made love. She was nervous. Perhaps he was too. It was brief. Constrained. Not grandiose.

They lay side by side on the duvet, naked. The hot afternoon sun came muted through the curtains into the room. A truck parked outside in a festival of reverse gear jingles and diesel engine roars; but here all was still. Time seemed to have paused: it was no longer stratospheric, but nestled drowsily between them, was aglow with the pleasure of seeing their bodies lying against each other. A fly buzzed intermittently, describing the room in lazy parabolas.

'When do you have to go?' she asked.

'Soon.' He exhaled, and his chest slowly sank. 'I need to be at the ship at six. What time is it?'

'I don't know.'

They lay in silence, holding on to each other.

'You don't need to pay me,' said Natalia. 'I'm sorry.'

He said nothing. She felt crushed.

'Do you understand?'

'Almost.'

The fly landed on his chest, and they contemplated it silently. Iridescent velvet eyes fixed on their unresponsive faces for a moment; and then it was gone, in a whine of impatience. There was only them.

'I can't stay now,' murmured Riad. 'But I'll come back for you.'

The words rushed through her nervous system; but for some reason she was not surprised.

'When?'

'In six months. My contract will be over. I'll come back here. I'll find a way.'

The city moved outside.

'Can we have a child?' she asked, looking at the ceiling.

'I would like that.'

He propped himself up on an elbow and looked into her eyes. He was about to say, 'I love you' – or something of that sort. His face was calm and happy. He started to say something, to tell her that he loved her, probably; he opened his mouth but no sound came except a viscous wheezing, he started to breathe quickly, engaged his vocal chords in fear, but all she could hear was his diaphragm pumping. His eyes widened, he tried to cough up what was in his throat, a blockage, a suffocating feathery ball. His face turned purple and he rolled onto the floor, choking and beating his throat.

Natalia leapt off the bed and took his head in her hands.

'What is happening? What is it?'

He pointed wildly into his mouth, down into his oesophagus, and she tried to see inside, but there was only blackness. He gestured to her to strike him on the back and she did so: while he positioned himself on all fours she gave him frantic blows with her fists between his shoulder blades. He tried to cough in rhythm, to dislodge this thing – but nothing came out of his throat and he sank to the floor, his mouth dripping with saliva.

The discomfort subsided. But he could no longer speak.

She gave him some water and took his head in her lap.

'Don't worry. It will pass. Just don't worry.'

He curled up on the floor, his head pressed into her naked thighs. He was clammy and ruffled after his ordeal, and she smoothed his back with her hands.

'Don't go, Riad. I will take care of you. You can't go like this.'

It was as if he had forgotten; he suddenly roused himself, jumped up and looked at his watch. He pointed out of the window and began to dress quickly.

'When will you come back?' she asked, descending into sadness as into a well.

He put his passport in his pocket and strapped on his watch. He leant down and clasped her to him. She was still naked: he felt very – clothed.

'Six months,' he mouthed, holding up a hand and a thumb, his face full of confusion.

'Six months? Where? Here?'

He nodded.

'Six months means January. January – 13th. Is that when we should meet?'

Another nod.

'Do you promise you'll come?'

He nodded again. And kissed her.

'I will be here, Riad. In our coffee shop. Every day for a week between one and two in the afternoon. Starting on January 13th. You'll remember the place?'

He took her in his arms and held her with all his strength. They kissed again, and he turned to go; held hands through the doorway while he mouthed words she could not pick up – and then he was running down the stairs.

'I'll go anywhere with you,' she called out after him. Did he hear?

She parted the curtains, but the window was useless; it looked out at the back.

She lay down in the rumpled hollow left by their lovemaking.

Where they had lain.

And started the whole thing, in her mind, again.

As the sun was rising, she awoke. She had not noticed herself fall asleep, but at some point her lonely racing mind had slipped free of the tedious evening hours and escaped into oblivion. And there she found dreams wherein her joy was like a belaboured vessel on an ocean of disquiet; for in them she saw his ship clearly – she could see the whole thing in her mind: there was a departure at nightfall, dock workers waving cursorily and the wake breaking over the jetty, the red and blue stars of the Panamanian flag dull in the darkness, water pouring from drainage holes in the rusty hull, and a horn echoing to the horizon. It drew away with sporadic dim lights in the portholes and rows of containers (American President, Hanjin, Hyundai – she saw it all) creaking with the movement. The crew worked till the early hours of the morning, and crashed in their cabins. But the boat was a joke: she could see every seam coming apart – anyone could see it was not fit to be on the water, and even in these mild seas it began to sink. Pumps started to rattle even before they had all awoken, but the boat was wide open to the sea; luckily they were in busy waters and rescue was on its way. What happened to everyone else? She did not know; but when Riad woke up only his head was above water and his body was pinned down by some mysterious force. Someone called out, 'Is there anyone left in there?' Riad shouted for his life, but his throat was blocked, and no sound came out.

And there was an albatross overhead that wept for Riad, but its tears were lost in the sea.

It was a stupid dream; but she woke up full of apprehensions. What would happen if something went wrong? The sea was so unpredictable. What if he was a week late, or a month? How would they meet? She had no information about him, nor he about her. How foolish they had been.

She dressed quickly and left the room. At reception she stopped to see if Riad had written his address in the guest book.

'He wasn't your husband, was he?' said Ahmet thoughtfully.

'No.'

'You don't have to tell me. I know Russian women.'

She ignored him.

Riad had not even filled in his last name. Under 'ADDRESS' he had written, inexplicably, '$130'.

Before long, the ship had passed through the Dardanelles into the Mediterranean and was on course for the French coast. They were carrying containers loaded in Novorossiysk, Odessa, and Burgas – vodka, violins, tractor parts, chemicals, diplomatic personal effects – and would stop in Marseille and Valencia before heading through the Straits of Gibraltar and down to Cape Town and Durban. Fully unloaded, they would then journey across the Indian Ocean to Fujairah, where the shipping company was based, to await further business.

It was at that point, Riad thought, that he would part ways with this ship and try to find a way back to Istanbul. At another point in his life he had been stranded in Fujairah and had bribed a friendly middleman to get him on another crew. He could try to get on a boat back to Istanbul. Perhaps his casino winnings would help.

It was the height of summer, and the days were scorching hot. Every afternoon, Riad would scale the containers to check the thermostats on the refrigerated cargo. A container full of Milka chocolate from the Kraft Foods plant in Ukraine, another one of chicken pieces. The ship was also in very bad condition, in need of serious maintenance. They spent afternoons below, checking the hull and every inch of piping with flashlights, welding where necessary. They came up drenched in sweat.

He still could not speak. There was still something in his throat that prevented any sound from coming out. He tried to reach down into the back of his mouth to feel the obstruction, but could not get far enough. He forced himself to vomit, but it did no good.

He shared his cabin with a gruff Filipino who thought this sudden muteness was a sham.

'If you don't like me, just tell me. Really. I don't like you either so it's not like my heart is going to bleed or anything. But just quit this silence. Drives me crazy.'

They arrived in Marseille. It was a hi-tech port where things happened quickly: mighty brackets fell from the sky and gathered up the containers – forty-foot steel giants that leapt into the air on the whirring cables of a hammerhead crane and fell lightly into place beside calculated rows of siblings – whence just another swing on the trapeze was enough to slot them into the firm and precisely calibrated embrace of trucks bound, on smooth autoroutes, for Lyon, Toulouse, and Basel.

High above them, tourists looked out to sea from Notre Dame de la Garde, which shimmered in the heat. Even the darting yellow fork-lift trucks, like flies in the cargo zone, seemed struck with languor. But perhaps it was also the heat that accounted for so many raised tempers; for was there not an unnecessarily aggressive manner to the white van ('Gendarmerie Maritime') that drew up by the ship, did the police not board with faces of quite excessive sullenness, and did not the captain himself resort far more promptly than is usual to loud insults and threatening fists? More police arrived to calm the situation and restrain the captain; one of them took it upon himself to address the crew:

'Gentlemen,' he announced, standing on a steel bench, 'I am afraid to tell you that this vessel, and all of you on it, is being impounded by the French police on account of a number of financial irregularities brought to our attention by the Port of Marseille and also by port authorities in the United Arab Emirates. These irregularities consist of the non-payment of cargo tariffs and harbour dues. Until these debts are recovered, the ship will not sail again. You will not be allowed to enter French territory while this matter is being resolved. At present there is confusion as to the ownership of this vessel, which is delaying the process. We hope to identify the owners and complete our procedures as soon as possible. I'm afraid, in the meantime, I will be forced to confiscate all your passports to ensure that you do not try to leave the ship. I am sorry for the inconvenience. Has everyone understood what I said?'

They nodded.

'Good. I'm sure your captain will give you instructions as to what to do. Thank you for your understanding. If you could all please get your passports.'

'How do we know we'll get them back?'

'They will be kept safely, I promise you.'

'How long will it take?'

'We hope to resolve this in a couple of weeks at most.'

'How will we eat?'

'I am sure your captain will make arrangements for you.'

The violence of entrapment broke out among them.

'We have no money and no food on board. Almost no fresh water. We can't even go ashore. No one is going to pay us until we finish this mission. What are we supposed to do? What you are saying is crazy!'

'Gentlemen – I must repeat my request: collect your passports and hand them over to me. As for the other issues, they are between you and the ship's owners whom, incidentally, we are as interested in bringing to account as you are.'

The tussles lasted much of the afternoon, but in the end there was little they could do: passports were surrendered and the boat vacated its berth to moor in a spot outside the harbour.

As the local and only accessible representative of authority, the captain, a mild-mannered Pole, was beaten up and spat upon. Surely he must be able to help the police complete their inquiry? – but in fact the police already knew more than he did, and it did no good.

As days went by, and further interviews with the police made it clear that the owner was not going to be traced easily, the scenario became clear to all of them, though they did not want to accept it: he had picked up the boat for cheap, run a few missions with it while he could – whilst not being too scrupulous with either tariffs or salaries – and finally, when debts caught up, had left it to its own fate, erasing any links between him and it in the process.

240

They presented this scenario to the Gendarmerie Maritime – In such a scenario, what resolution can we expect and how long will we hold out for it? Can you not arrange for passage back to our respective countries where we can find new jobs? Can we not go ashore so we can at least beg on the streets of Marseille? – but the police were unmoved.

'There are proper legal procedures for dealing with cases like this, gentlemen, and I'm afraid we cannot start to circumvent them in the name of . . . We are of course sympathetic to your plight. Let us all hope that it will not continue for much longer.'

They settled down to wait things out.

The captain tried to keep up morale by proposing an intensive programme of cleaning, painting, and maintenance. Half-hearted even in the early days, the sense of futility quickly became overpowering, and the programme died without protest.

A local Catholic organization began to visit the ship every morning with water and basic foodstuffs.

Police visits became less frequent, and then stopped.

Problems of supplies were acute. They became sick. The couple of thousand dollars they had between them was spent in the first few weeks buying food, medication, pornography, cigarettes, soap, a dart board, cooking fuel, matches, underwear, and alcohol. Riad's money, like everyone else's, disappeared.

Sometimes they sent out for these supplies through Guy and Colette, the friendly and unstinting Catholics who came every day to visit. Sometimes they went on their own clandestine forays into the city. Unkempt and speaking no French, they did not fit in.

Occasionally, they experienced the generosity of other sailors. Their story had spread through the maritime community, and sometimes men would come to visit with small gifts.

There were long, long days. There was little to do except listen to the radio and masturbate. The sailors devoted themselves rigorously but joylessly to both activities.

They tried fishing off the side of the boat. It was not a rewarding pursuit, but it helped to disguise inactivity.

Everyone gave themselves over to various kinds of obsession. Some repeated endlessly the same stories of life back home. A Bulgarian sailor set himself an arduous daily exercise routine that managed both to fill much of the day and make him tired enough to sleep at night. The captain took to making intricate sculptures of dogs and horses out of wire. Another Bulgarian, brother of the first, wove increasingly elaborate and graphic tales of seductions of nubile French women that he was able to pull off with astonishing consistency during his alleged nightly flights into the city; these met with a large audience that was no less attentive for their evident untruth. Many, of course, were obsessed with escape; two of them did manage to swim to land beyond the barricades that separated port from city; they spent a whole week in Marseille before being arrested for theft and brought back. From that point on the police tightened their surveillance of the boat, making things worse for all of them.

Riad's obsessions bordered on madness, and he became gradually isolated from all the rest. His inability to talk set everyone else on edge and forced him further and further inside a world of his own making. For some months he worked on thirteen large-scale drawings that he laid out on the deck and knelt over, scribbling with his face almost against the paper, as if trying to shield them with his body from prying gazes. They showed thirteen different rooms – rooms, to be precise, as follows:

The Room of Astonishment and Habit
The Room of Baths
The Room of Coffee and Consideration
The Room of Details
The Room of Exchange of Opinions
The Room of Full Moon Light
The Room of Galloping Senses
The Room of Hands Holding Fruit
The Room of Interludes
The Room of Justice and Jollity
The Room of Knowing
The Room of Legs Intertwined
The Room of Maroon Premonitions

– in which there were always two characters: Riad himself, and a woman holding a roulette wheel. The evident skill with which these drawings were executed did not allay the suspicions on the part of his fellow crew members that he had in fact gone completely insane. The attitude of his Filipino cabin mate, always cool, turned to open hatred.

Winter came. The countdown to his rendezvous with Natalia displayed itself in his body as he became daily more sickly and sluggish. In the desperate hope of sending some message to her he made large signs which he held aloft to other ships saying 'WHO GOES ISTANBUL?' – but their wild script and the oddness of his appearance ensured that there was no response.

January 13th. In the afternoon, Riad took to his bed with fever and slept a long but fitful sleep, coughing violently and twitching with his dreams.

There comes another moment to which we must devote an unnatural degree of attention, for it, too, does not give itself up to facile understanding. It is important to have the scene in mind, the *arrangement* of characters. Riad slept his disturbed sleep under soiled and rumpled sheets, and evening had come. Night, even: for the stars shone above. The cramped cabin smelt strongly of his sickness and the Filipino sailor could not bring himself to lie there; he sat outside the door on deck, his feet up on the gunwale, snoozing sporadically. The door was slightly ajar and Riad's coughs emerged gratingly from inside. They came more and more regularly, in fact, like labour contractions, as if there was a *point* to them. Riad did not wake but still his body convulsed more and more strenuously, his entire torso shaking with the kind of surprising reflexes that happen, as with vomiting, when the body dismisses the higher faculties and declares its own martial law. He coughed and coughed; and anyone who had been in the cabin, anyone who had been watching closely, would have seen the back of his throat begin to dilate, and a black and white avian head appear. Each contraction expelled the bird still further until it filled his mouth and he breathed with great snorts through his nose; but his work was done and it was up to the bird to force itself out through his wide-locked teeth and out onto the pillow beside him.

It was a sea bird of sorts. A tern, perhaps. It stood on the bed, taking in the world, shaking its wings with difficulty to try and dry them of their coating of saliva.

Riad's sleep became more even and peaceful.

The bird hopped onto the floor, and took uncertain webbed footsteps towards the door. The gap was big enough for it to find its way out onto the deck.

Perhaps it was the coughing that had roused the Filipino sailor; at any rate, he happened at that moment to be awake. He saw the bird emerging from the cabin – his cabin! – and it seemed to be a sympton of Riad's madness.

'So how long has he been keeping you in there, my little friend? Is it you that he talks to? Is it you that prevents him saying anything to the rest of us?'

In a quick lunge he caught hold of the bird, which, heavy with moisture, could hardly walk, let alone fly.

'And where the hell does he keep you?' cried the sailor in surprise and disgust as his hands were wet with mucus.

The sailor considered the bird for a moment. Turned it around, looked at it from all angles. Holding it firmly with one hand, he drew a pocket knife and opened up the blade. Inserting it under one of the wings, he began to cut it from the body.

The bird began to scream; the sound was infernal and piercingly loud. One wing fell uselessly onto the deck, and the sailor passed quickly to the other, trying to muffle the sharp cries with his torso. Both wings were cut off and the sailor inspected the diminished bird that still craned its neck towards the sky and shrieked with distress.

'There,' he said.

He threw bird and wings into the sea. The splash was almost inaudible.

The cabin door flew open. Riad stood there, his face full of anguish.

'What happened?' he asked.

The sailor did not answer.

But it was evident – though he had not realized it himself until that point – that he could now speak again.

* * *

Six months went past slowly in Natalia's life.

For some time she had treasured the few hundred-thousand lira notes that Riad had given into her custody as the only evidence of his passing through her life. After a while she spent them on another coffee that she drank sitting in *his* seat.

She persisted in her dwindling trade between Odessa and Istanbul, happy with the familiarity and, to some extent, the mindlessness of it; for though she went through the motions of everything she lived before, though she still bought and sold and played lover to her Serbian shopkeeper, there was something inside her that absorbed all her attention: she incubated it, worried over it, and spoke to it in solitary moments.

But it became more and more difficult to sustain her faith in a reunion with Riad, and, as the months went by, this prospect began to collapse under the attrition of her fears and misgivings. By the time she came to be standing outside the café on the appointed day it was with a sense of futility. She knew he would not come.

She waited for two hours. The same men walked past her two or three times on the other side of the street trying to work out what her business was.

She regretted her promise to wait for seven days, for she knew he would have come on the first day if it was to be at all. Nevertheless, at one o'clock every day for the next week she went and stood in the same place. He never came.

As much as we might try to expect the worst, and thus shield ourselves from disappointment, it can be terrible to have our most pessimistic scenarios come to be. It is at that point we realize that the hope we had attempted so sternly to dig out of ourselves had still been firmly rooted there, persistent and alive.

It was time to leave Istanbul. She went home to her apartment in Odessa without a word to anyone.

Months went by idly.

She thought about new businesses she could start, but did nothing.

Her savings ran out.

Spring arrived.

One day, as she opened the window to greet one of the first truly warm days of the year, she saw a sea bird standing on her window sill. At least, it was almost a bird; for somehow it seemed to have lost both its wings. It was pitiful, and somewhat gruesome.

The bird hopped in through the window and down onto the floor, and collapsed on its side with weakness.

Natalia brought the bird a saucer of milk, and supported its head so it could drink. It did so, feebly, but still could not rouse itself. In the afternoon Natalia bought some fish at the market that she mashed for it.

During the night she could hear the bird breathing hoarsely.

In the morning it seemed to be partially revived. She placed it by her as she ate breakfast. It watched her intently.

As she raised her coffee to her lips it stood up suddenly and let out a piercing wail. It was an alien, animal sound – prolonged, ebbing and flowing, and searching for expression.

In her surprise, Natalia dropped her coffee.

There was the shock, obviously, of an unexpected sound disturbing her breakfast. But the reason she was so startled was not this.

In the bird's cry, in that long moment when the morning had been split open, like an unhealed wound, by this sound from far away – in that moment (and the exact mechanism of this imparting was a mystery to her) – in that moment, she suddenly knew everything: the imprisonment on the ship, the bird's own escape from Riad's mouth, its dismembering at the hands of the sailor, its struggle towards land as its own wings floated out to sea, its fight to survive as shock and blood loss threatened to claim its life; and finally its long and astonishing walk from Marseille, across the length of Europe, all the way to her apartment here in Odessa.

She also understood what she had to do. Before an hour had passed she had packed some clothes – and the bird – and left.

Natalia now undertook the bird's journey in reverse. Wishing to keep what little money she had left for dealing with Riad's plight, she was forced to improvise her route out of whatever traffic was travelling in her direction. Moreover, she did not have visas to go where she was going. But she had not forgotten the skill of reading how far she could trust other human beings in their eyes; and this stood her in good stead.

Much of her journey was spent in the passenger seats of container trucks, the bird tucked away in a shoulder bag. She travelled as far west as she could in her own country; having then walked across the border with Hungary she was picked up outside Beregsurány by a German truck driver playing 'Girls Just Wanna Have Fun' at top volume; they sang along in different accents and he bought her meals at truck stops along the way that she shared with the bird. Over pickled cabbage and fries she spoke to other travellers about where best to cross all the borders that lay between her and Marseille: they tried to dissuade her from such a mission with melodramatic tales about stowaways freezing and suffocating in trucks and boats, and the shock tactics of border police. But nothing hindered her as she slipped across into Austria by night with two Turks she had met on the way; they spent the night together around a campfire in a quiet field that turned out, when they woke up to the hissing of guard dogs, to be the garden of a mansion – they were only yards away from the swimming pool! – but the owner's initial indignation faded and he sent them off with toast and coffee. When she climbed into the cabin of the Dutch truck that picked her up later that morning she saw that he drove entirely naked, though he seemed harmless; he did however omit to wake her at the German border, and she came to in the darkness to find herself in Munich. It was good to be in a city: she slept peacefully in a cemetery and celebrated the bright spring morning with a beer and sandwich in a café, where she locked herself in the toilet for half an hour to wash and change underwear. She looked at clothes shops and read headlines at newsstands; accustomed by now to being on her own, she decided to cross Germany by train: she locked herself in another toilet and spent the journey to Freiburg watching the world flash by through frosted glass with the bird nestling in her lap. Still respectful of these old borders, she got a truck driver to hide her under his seat as they crossed the Rhine into France and then passed much of the night in a bordertown café musing on black-and-white photographs of James Dean and Marilyn Monroe. The next day she made it as far as Clermont-Ferrand where, on an unexpected impulse, she walked into the black cathedral during evening mass and sat, trying to remember Riad's face. She bought bread for the bird and slept on a bench. Standing by the A6 the next morning, a woman picked her up in a Peugeot 205 and they sped down the *péage* all the way to Marseille. They exchanged stories; the woman dropped her at the port. 'I hope you find him,' she smiled.

She asked all around, but no one knew about the stranded ship. She talked to the bird – 'Can't you help me? Can't you remember?' – but it had become withdrawn and taciturn. She sat on a steel bollard by the water and looked out to sea.

A motor boat approached where she was sitting, came close until its strained whine lowered to a rhythmic judder, and eased in alongside the jetty, spitting diesel smoke irregularly. The boat was piled with old flour sacks (stamped 'Soufflet Group') filled with wet refuse pulled from the sea. A young boy sat at the rudder; a man in sunglasses and a soiled suit reclined expansively amongst the sacks and spoke loudly on a mobile phone.

'How many? Twelve? Thirteen. Unlucky for some, as they say. OK, partner. Everything heard and understood. Yes. All right. Out.'

He flipped his phone shut and looked up at Natalia.

'Lady! You waiting for your boat to come in?'

'My boat's here. I just can't find it.'

'Ooh. That's a problem. What boat are you looking for?'

'One that's been stranded here for a year. Came from Istanbul last summer and hasn't moved since.'

'You talking about the one with the Polish captain?'

'Yes!'

'Jump in. I'll take you there.'

She stepped down into the boat and the boy pulled away sharply. They banked right and left and they were in the open sea with salt spray in their hair.

'Here – lie down. Don't be so formal.'

She sat against the sacks. Everything smelt of decomposition.

'You're not the first lady I've done this for. Have to admire your staying power. But you should just accept things: those sailors have no prospects! Never going to move. You should look for someone with prospects. Look at me!'

They were heading towards a rusty ship moored some way out at sea. They drew close and stopped. Natalia stood up in the boat and looked up. Above her was a man sitting on the stern with a fishing line in the water, looking absently into the distance. It was Riad. She watched him for a while, waited for him to seem real.

'Riad!'

He looked down.

'Hello, Natalia.'

He did not seem to be sure of what was happening.

'Can I come up?'

'Of course.'

She climbed the ladder and sat down beside him.

'Poor Riad.' He looked thin, and resigned.

'Is it really you?'

'It is. And look who else is here.'

She took the bird from her bag. He stared at it.

'That's what was in my throat?'

'Yes.'

'What happened to its wings?'

'One of the other sailors chopped them off.'

Riad looked confused.

'It's all right. Don't worry.' She put her arm round him. 'The bird came to me, told me where you were. I had no idea. I thought you had forgotten me.'

'Forgotten?'

'You never came. I waited for you.'

Riad was having difficulty understanding. Tears began to run down his face.

She put the bird back in the bag.

'You have to get off this ship.'

He shook his head. 'I belong on the ship. Can't leave.'

'I'm going to take you off. We'll go together. I'm leaving you now. To make plans. But I'll be back.'

'Don't go.'

'I'll come soon. I promise.'

'I did drawings for you.'

'I'll be back soon.'

She came back at night and found him asleep.

'Riad! Wake up!'

She shook him.

'You have to listen to me now. There's a ship waiting for us just beyond the harbour. I've bribed the captain. He's Ukrainian like me; he's going to Odessa. You have to concentrate. I have a boat to take us out there. Do you have everything you need?'

He looked down at himself.

'The police have my passport.'

'Don't worry. We'll get you another.'

An outboard motor revved impatiently. The bird cried.

'Come, Riad. You go first.'

She helped him over the side, and he half climbed, half fell down into the launch. She followed him; and the boat pulled away hastily as soon as she landed, so that they fell together into the pile of wet flour sacks.

They accelerated out into the Mediterranean, the wind cold even on this warm evening. There were the lights of a ship, and they slowed down. The crew waited for them with a rope ladder.

'Up, Riad. Quickly!' she whispered.

She turned to the man who even now was masked behind his dark glasses.

'Thank you for your help.'

'It's a pleasure. Be careful. Give me a kiss. Women tell me I bring them luck.'

She kissed him quickly on his proffered lips.

'Bye-bye, lady!'

She climbed up after Riad, and the boat turned around, and was gone.

250

The sailors looked at them suspiciously. The captain stood among them.

'These are friends of mine,' he announced to the crew. 'They'll be travelling with us as far as Odessa. They have skills – they'll be pulling their weight on board, don't worry. Make them feel at home.'

He showed them to a cabin. It was old, dank, and filthy.

'You can sleep here. We'll talk about everything in the morning. I have to make clear that I will not jeopardize my own position by taking you into ports. So you'll need to make other arrangements each time we dock. But everyone's busy and it's late. We'll talk in the morning. Meanwhile, make yourselves as comfortable as you can.'

They lay next to each other on a narrow bunk listening to the sounds of the ship. Riad dozed. Natalia had a sense about this ship, one that she could not quite locate, and it continued to torment her as she lay there in the darkness.

It was only as she heard shouts from above, and realized they were sinking, that she remembered. This, and not the other one, was the ship she had seen in her dream.

It sank quickly. The hull had burst and the outdated pumps could do little to stop the water flooding in. The floors bowed and pitched, and the ship had become a leaden cage, crumpling and groaning, and dragging them into the depths.

Natalia splashed to the door: sailors were scurrying around and grabbing belongings, shouting, water at their knees. She ran up on deck where the captain was lowering a lifeboat.

'See: this is what happens when you take stowaways onboard!' he shouted when he saw her. 'This is what happens!' His face glistened with sweat. 'You're bad luck. I can't take you with us.'

'But we'll die!'

'The lifeboat is going to be overloaded as it is. The sailors will never let you on. Am I supposed to endanger their lives in order to save you? You knew the risks you were taking.'

Natalia clasped his hand. 'Captain, don't treat us like this: I am your

251

own little sister from Ukraine; we have grown up on the same land with the same flesh and will you now leave me to the sea? In the name of our own St Andrew: please help me.'

He studied her for a moment, and cursed. 'Look: I can't take you with us. But there is another lifeboat you can try your luck with. It's old and broken but I think it will float. It's there – just take it – I'm afraid that's all I can do.'

She ran down to the cabin where water had soaked the blankets and the bird cried shrilly in alarm, but Riad still slept. She snatched them both and carried them along with her even as Riad moaned dreamily 'I can't go. I belong on the ship'; somehow she got them up onto the deck. One end of the ship was completely submerged and the sailors in their lifeboat had already floated off into the darkness.

As we know, Natalia knew how to survive crashes. She cut the lifeboat free and they climbed into it just as the ship disappeared, with great belches of air, under the waves. They could still hear the excited voices of the sailors in the other boat; but these sounds grew fainter, and soon they were on their own in the boundless night. Riad sat shivering in a blanket and Natalia held him close. At some point they both slept.

Dawn came.

Natalia was awoken by the violent squawking of the bird. It stood on the side of the boat, its body extended into the distance, issuing its cries to the horizon like a siren. She looked out to see what it might be gesturing towards.

'Riad!' she shouted in excitement. 'Riad, wake up! There are beaches. Very near! We are safe!'

He awoke; and they rowed energetically together: they chanted their strokes to keep them in time, and laughed out loud with the effort of it. Near to the shore Riad jumped out, leapt into waist-deep water, and dragged the boat to land, splashing and stumbling in his eagerness. He ran ahead; grabbed handfuls of sand and threw it in the air. Natalia threw herself on him and they held each other on the beach, the bird running quickly behind and chirruping with excitement.

It was still early and no one was to be seen. They walked up the beach towards the small seaside town.

'We're in Italy,' said Natalia.

They sat on a bench and watched as the town awoke. A café opened nearby, and three old men in tweed jackets and caps sat down together at a table outside. The waves of the Mediterranean washed in restful rhythms on the shore.

'Let's stop here for a while,' said Natalia. 'It seems like a nice place to make a life. It's so long since you've been on solid ground.'

Riad looked around him. It was a beautiful morning.

'Yes. Let's stop here for a while.' He smiled broadly. She had forgotten the joy of his face.

The bird climbed out of Natalia's shoulder bag. She stroked it affectionately. And something made her start in surprise.

'Look, Riad. Look!'

Its wings were growing back.

Throats were parched; for there was stale cigarette smoke in the air and little ventilation, and some of them had spoken for a long time. There was the feeling of clothes adhering under arms, and feet swelling in shoes; there were aching backs and numb limbs. Some listened standing up, or drew knees up to chins to help circulation.

I would love to go to Italy. Someone said.

There had been a long time for them to look at each other. To find depths in faces that had seemed conventional a few hours ago; to contemplate the fingernails of the hand on the arm of the adjacent chair, the worn soles on a pair of feet propped up on a briefcase, the overlooked stubble behind the jut of a neighbour's jawbone. One man followed the patterns in the hair on the forearm of the woman next to him; he stole glances at the curve of her breast, the shape of her lips; he wondered what life lay behind the strange story she had told. Was it his imagination or did her body creep closer to his as the night progressed? was there not some significance in the way their eyes had met? was it accident or design that made her hand brush his again on the armrest that lay between them? Where was she going what was she doing in Tokyo?

Was it not at times like this, when life malfunctioned, when time found a leak in its pipeline and dripped out into some hidden little pool, that new thoughts happened, new things began? Would they look back at this night and say That is when it started?

THE CHANGELING

The Tenth Story

B ERNARD DUSSOULIER BELONGED to that little-understood class of
beings known as changelings.

Like all changelings who become human he was, in all outward respects,
indistinguishable from a human being, and, when he entered the world
in the guise of only child of Dr and Mme Etienne Dussoulier, nothing
was felt to be amiss. He grew up meekly in their stale and somewhat
joyless house in Neuilly, and when, on occasion, his parents took him to
the park, he would run and laugh and cry just like all the other children.

Mme Dussoulier died when Bernard was still young, and her
husband, who was France's leading immunologist, threw the rest of his
life into his research in the Hôpital St Louis. Like most changelings,
Bernard aspired to excellence in his studies, and came first in everything, first at school and then at the Polytechnique des Sciences. His
elderly, remote father seemed indifferent, however, to his son's achieve-
ments; and when he too died some years later, Bernard was still unsure
whether he had ever thought about him for five minutes at a stretch.

Parisians have traditionally treated their changeling population with
resentment. At first sight, perhaps, it is not difficult to see why.

Changelings are eternal creatures who only adopt human form for short periods of time; it is therefore understandable that human beings should feel jealous and mistrustful of them. In addition to this, those changelings who have come to public notice – surely the tiny minority of the total – have all been rich and highly successful, a fact that has led to the feeling that changelings enjoy various unfair advantages, or even that some high-level changeling conspiracy is operating in the country's corridors of power.

The truth, of course, is somewhat more complex than this. What is often left out of public discussions on this subject is that changelings, while they are in human form, are as mortal as any human being. Old age and sickness can weaken them to the point that they are unable to summon the energy to leave their human bodies and return to their original, disembodied state (which is why they never remain in human form beyond their fiftieth birthdays). And should they die while in human form, it is the end of them. Add to this the fact that changelings, if they are identified as such, have no legal standing under French law and can face sometimes murderous retribution from the rest of the population (it is still not a crime, at the present time, to harm or even kill a changeling) – and it becomes easier to see why they should be so obsessively concerned with health and security – and thus with the money and social standing that help to bring these things about.

Of course, given the success they often achieve in French society, their intimacies with humans, and their mysterious arrivals and departures, it has been difficult for them to remain entirely undetected. No one in Paris can forget the furore that followed the revelations in *Le Nouvel Observateur* that Claude Trébuchet, the dynamic conservative politician who had been appointed Foreign Minister at the implausibly young age of thirty-nine, was in fact a changeling. Trébuchet himself had disappeared (readers will recall the images of his tearstained wife that floated in poignant slow motion across the nation's television screens for weeks afterwards), but this did not stop his fellow politicians tearing each other apart as they debated the position of changelings under the French constitution. The debate, as we all know, was short lived: politicians, citizens, and the media all agreed that neither liberty, equality, nor fraternity could be extended to creatures that had no long-term loyalty to the nation or even to the species, and people were instructed to ask searching questions of all individuals they had known for fewer than five years. A number of changelings were identified in shockingly high positions in industry, law, and politics, all of whom, predictably enough, followed Trébuchet to his inaccessible retreat, depriving a resentful public of any possibility of revenge.

There was a voice that opposed these 'witch-hunts', led by a loose coalition of spouses, lovers, and friends of changelings. They said that the state's 'unthinking hatred' was based on a fundamental philosophical error. Changelings, they said, were more human than the rest of us. For their humanity, unlike that of everyone else, was earned at great cost. It was not a mere biological entitlement. It was a supreme, self-conscious effort of will.

Bernard began a career as an investment banker, first at the Banque Nationale de Paris and then with Goldman Sachs. He earned a lot of money and moved to a quiet area of the city where he felt secure. A changeling doctor immunized his human body against every possible malady. His paranoia about injury never entirely left him; and yet he was sensitive to the charms of human experience that keep changelings, despite everything, coming back for more; and he managed to see past his anxieties to the rest of life.

One day, as he travelled to work on the crowded Métro, he became fascinated by the female hand that was holding on to the bar in front of his nose, and whose owner he could not see. 'I will marry the person to whom that hand belongs,' he thought to himself, and rushed after it when it left the train.

The owner of the hand was the beautiful art curator Claire Grand'amie whose Galerie O in the Marais was the talk of the city at that time. The gallery remained closed that day, and Bernard's cubicle empty. They had ice cream on the Île St Louis. She told him her teenage years had been ravaged by a sickness that left her unable to bear children, and Bernard said he did not mind. He asked her to marry him that evening. She agreed.

They took a large and elegant apartment together and were very happy. But Bernard could not bring himself to tell her the secret about himself, and this left him with terrible doubts. 'When it comes down to it, I am not human: I cannot see this game through to its end.' Like all of his kind who involved themselves closely with human beings, he struggled every day with the obvious dilemma: how could he sincerely make declarations of love and friendship, when these were inevitably read as an unconditional commitment of a future that was not his to give?

As it happened, Bernard was finally relieved of his moral deliberations. One evening, when Claire was attending an opening, he invited a changeling friend to join him for tea.

'I can never grow old with her,' he sighed. 'I cannot be the human being she needs me to be. I should never have married her. Should I not just leave her to a better life?'

Daniel was of the school that advocated no involvement at all with human beings, and thought that Bernard had made a great mistake in marrying one: that he had only himself to blame. He refused to get involved in another discussion on the subject and departed early, leaving his friend to agonize alone. Bernard showed him out. When he returned to the room he was surprised to see Claire sitting there. She was shaking.

'You're a changeling,' she said.

Bernard stopped in the doorway, everything turning upside down.

'Was the opening – ? Did you go?'

'You must be the only person in Paris who doesn't know. There was a huge bomb explosion in the Place de la Bastille. Police everywhere. We couldn't even get near the gallery. I came straight back. I was scared.'

Bernard stared. Claire said,

'I was standing outside the door. I heard everything you said.'

'Darling – please don't think –'

'I think you should leave the house right now. Never try to see me again.'

'But I love you!'

'When I married you it was because I wanted you to be with me for ever.' She was struggling against her tears. 'At some point I will begin to grow old and then I will die – and you will not understand any of it. Perhaps you will not even wait around that long. That is not what love means to me. I now know there is no possibility of us truly sharing our lives. I thought I had all of you; but it is only a tiny part.'

She marched to the front door and flung it open.

'Please leave now. Nothing we say can change the truth. You and I are not the same. Every minute we spend together now will be one wasted.'

'Please Claire –'

'Now!'

And, with a sigh, Bernard left.

Outside, it was pouring with rain, and here and there car alarms tweeted in confusion at the heavenly onslaught. The streets were full, as Claire had said, of police. He walked slowly to the Bastille, where huge lights had been set up to help the rescue services. Ambulances and fire engines flashed red through the rain, and crowds of people gathered by the cordon that had been put around the square. All the buildings had lost their windows, and three cars had been thrown through the glass front of the opera house.

Bernard walked around to see into the crater. It opened into the Métro. Water was pouring in over the layers of Third-Republic brickwork. Steam rose ghoulishly from within.

Bernard looked at the rows of bodies laid out in rows in the square and shivered. 'Perhaps it is time to leave this world behind. Right now.'

He wandered through the night, assessing his situation. The life he had been leading was certainly over. He did not think that Claire would report him, but such news travelled fast: there were always new changeling scandals hitting the newspapers. There was no point in his going to work anymore. He stopped at a Crédit Lyonnais and carried on taking out money until it would let him have no more.

There was one consolation: they would not look for him too hard. Everyone assumed that changelings left as soon as they were discovered. But despite himself he did not feel like leaving just yet.

He arrived at Montparnasse, which was deserted. He stood under the shelter of a sleeping magazine stand studying the rows and rows of bright, healthy people.

Under the light of the street lamps was an old man making his painful way across the square with a heavy bag on his back. He was soaked to the skin. 'Why does he not take shelter?' thought Bernard to himself. 'He must be nearly seventy years old. A man of his age should not be walking in this rain.'

As Bernard watched, the man's legs seemed to collapse under him, and he fell to the ground with a cry. Bernard ran towards him. The man had hit his head badly and blood was spewing from it in fitful bursts. Bernard took his handkerchief and pressed it hard against the wound, leaning the man's head against his knee. Dark blood welled up between his fingers and soaked his hand. The old man was delirious; he moaned and sang snatches of songs in French and Arabic and other languages Bernard did not know, and turned his head from side to side. Bernard reassured him gently and asked him questions about himself: 'My name is Bernard; do *you* have a name?' He made him as comfortable as he could on the wet paving and kept the handkerchief pressed over the gash; gradually the man seemed to come to. He opened his eyes.

'Thank you for helping me. You have done me a good turn: I fell very hard. And now look at you – you're covered in blood!'

'Don't worry about that. What's your name, old man, and where were you going?'

'My name is Fareed. How is my head?'

The blood had stopped flowing and Bernard took away the handkerchief to inspect the wound. The blood was congealing, and there was torn skin in useless flaps, but there were also – he peered very close in the half-light to confirm his impression – there were also white flowers growing out of the hole in Fareed's forehead: flowers like tiny hyacinths growing tightly packed on wiry green shoots that pushed upwards through the sticky layer of blood even as Bernard watched. With his face close to the wound, he could even smell the sickly sweetness of the flowers amid the sweat of the man's head. He was disgusted, but concealed his feelings; he put his handkerchief quickly back over the wound and tried to push the flowers under the skin.

'It has stopped bleeding. You should be fine.'

'I am grateful for your help. You have done everything you needed to. You don't have to stay with me any more.'

'Will I just leave you here on your back under the rain, an old man like you? We must find a place for you to spend the night. And for me too, now I think about it. Come.'

Bernard pulled the man up and supported him with one arm while with the other he carried his bag. They walked slowly like this through the rain, leaving Montparnasse station behind and seeing no movement except the occasional passing taxi. Fareed was still dazed; Bernard steered them both towards a red neon sign saying 'HOTEL'. Up two steps into the 0015foyer and at last he could put Fareed down into a threadbare armchair; there was a sofa, too, where a young man had keeled over sideways with sleep, his lower cheek glistening with saliva. A little black board with affixed white letters, some missing, announced room prices and exchange rates. An electric clock, with a second hand that did not tick but moved smoothly around the minute in an uninterrupted sweep, showed it was 2.15 in the morning. The television soliloquized energetically about the power of a new slimming formula.

Bernard called to the sleeping man. 'Excuse me. Excuse me!' He did not wake. Bernard placed his hand lightly on his shoulder and shook him. The man started. 'Sorry. Very sorry.' He forced himself up raggedly. 'I was watching TV,' he said, by way of explanation. 'Check in?'

'Yes,' said Bernard. The fluorescent light emphasized the hollows under their eyes.

'Double room?'

'Two single beds, please.'

The man stopped to look at them for a bit through the confusion of sleep.

263

'He's covered in blood. So are you. What kind of people are you?'

'This old man fell over in the street. I found him and brought him here. We both need a place to lie down.'

The man reluctantly opened the hotel register. 'Name. Address. Number of nights.' He handed Bernard a pen. Bernard made up names and addresses and wrote them in the book.

'Here's your key. Room 224. Lift is on the right-hand side. Checkout time is midday. Breakfast seven till ten. Good night.'

He crumpled up again, red-eyed, in front of the cavorting fat-women-turned-thin and Bernard helped the exhausted Fareed and his sack into the lift. Through the grill, the foyer sank into the floor, the whole cross section of the building descended past their eyes, and the second floor arrived with a lurch.

Bernard was desperate to urinate. He lay Fareed down on one of room 224's twin beds and rushed into the bathroom. He wrestled for an agonizing moment with the strip of paper that sealed the toilet, reassuring all would-be users (in French, English, and German) that 'This WC Has Been Disinfected For Your Protection', and released a heavy stream of dark yellow urine onto the clean ceramic with a deep sigh of relief.

There was a pile of wet clothes next to the bed in which Fareed lay. Bernard undressed likewise, dried himself with a towel, hung up his Yves St Laurent suit that would never be the same again, and got into his bed. There was a yellow sodium vapour light outside the window and even with the curtains closed the room was not dark; he could see that Fareed was looking intently up at the ceiling.

'What do you do, old man? Where were you going tonight?' For no particular reason, Bernard was whispering.

'To be very honest, I don't think I really had a destination. It's getting more and more like that these days.'

'Where are you from?'

'I live in Morocco. In Casablanca. I used to be an advertising executive. Then I gave it up.'

'You're here for work?'

'No. Just for myself.'

'I see.'

Bernard thought through all the events of the evening, from the time that a smiling Daniel had rung the doorbell of the vast apartment that, until a few hours ago, had been home. And now there was this old man. Bernard did not really know how to categorize him.

'So is it – vacation?'

Fareed continued to look at the ceiling for a few seconds. Then he pulled the covers away from his body that lay naked on the mattress. With some difficulty he propped up his torso and pulled his legs round until he was sitting on the edge of the bed. He stood up.

He was lit by the orange light that shone patchily through the curtains. His legs were thin and his pelvic bones protruded sharply either side of a slack little paunch that hung down over his pubic hair. He stood formally, with his arms by his sides, but there was in his back and in his neck a stoop that made him seem diminutive.

Yet none of this was what seized Bernard's attention. He was staring instead at the deep lesions that covered Fareed's entire body: swellings and pus-filled weals that scarred his chest and legs, eruptions like molehills that grew from either side of his stomach, black scabs that cut across his thighs like some knobbled mountain range on a relief map. He looked as if his entire envelope of skin was bursting open in every place, as if he was about to cast it off painfully, perhaps to emerge anew like some glistening reptile.

'Look at my body. I am dying, Bernard. I have only a few weeks to live. Some rare plant is growing inside my body; its flowers are bunching under my skin, compressing my brain and nerves, growing into my organs. Soon they will burst from inside, and I will die. There is nothing more that can be done. I can dull the pain, nothing more.'

Bernard did not know what to say. To tell the truth, he felt sick at the sight of this man's body whose very toenails were already discoloured by the jaundice of death. He could not look at him; but he could also not decently look away. He could not offer words of comfort – for what could these amount to? – beyond palely optimistic platitudes: 'Perhaps it is not as bad as you think', or 'Probably there

265

are cures you have not tried yet.' But he also felt anxious about allowing a consensus as to Fareed's imminent death to settle in the room. He said nothing.

Fareed let himself down onto the bed again and drew the covers around him.

'What is interesting, Bernard, is not that you can find nothing to say when I tell you that I am dying. You do not know me, and my death should not arouse in you stronger feelings than any other death that you read of in the newspapers or hear of, fourth- or fifth-hand, in society. There is nothing strange about this. What is strange is that I am as lost for words as you are. My death should be a matter of much greater concern for me than it is for you. But I have nothing to say about it.

'When you are diagnosed with death, when you finally accept that diagnosis, your head is at first filled with palliative words: how can you prolong things as much as possible, how can your body be made most comfortable while it dies. But there are not so many of these words that they can be drawn out to cover over your fundamental silence. At a certain point you have to try and peer into that silence.

'I have decided to spend the last days of my life looking for a word: a word that will explain these mysteries. I have searched across my own country and found nothing. And now I am searching here. I know that somewhere will be a word to help me to speak through my own blankness. But I am nearly dead, and until now my search has been fruitless.'

The sun was rising, and the shadows in the room were flowering into soft greys and blues. Fareed's head lay still on the pillow like a grotesque sculpture, stretched and misshapen from the plants pushing forth from inside, and stained above his eye with dried blood from the wound. Through this bloated mask his bright eyes were watery with sickness.

'I am very tired, Bernard. Each day it becomes more difficult for me to continue this quest. But a feeling continues to overwhelm me: that when a man dies he should not have merely to walk off the end of the plank of life with the shotgun of time at his back. Will he fall with his limbs scrabbling in the air, shaking with terror? Unprepared and ashamed, like a king's former favourite who is plucked from his warm bed and pushed off the edge in his underwear? If I could find the words to build a bridge from life to death, one that I could construct with the care of a master engineer, one that I could venture on to and inspect before I finally have to cross it forever – I think it would make a difference. So I must carry on. If only there were someone to help me in my search . . .'

Fareed left the sentence unfinished, and before it had completely withdrawn into nothingness two simultaneous events disturbed the stillness of the room. A bright blade of light appeared on the wall above Fareed's head as the dawn sun found the gap left by the curtain. And an early-rising guest on the floor above flushed the toilet, sending water cascading noisily through the thick pipe in the corner of their own room and down, one must presume, into the city's sewers. The flood slowed, and there was the fading hiss of a distant cistern refilling. And then silence.

A silence that weighed heavily on Bernard. He did not want to involve himself. The whole thing left him somewhat aghast. And yet he had no good arguments to offer. He had nothing else to do.

'I will do this and then I will leave,' thought Bernard to himself. 'My last gesture towards this humankind among whom I have lived for thirty-six years.'

'I will find your word,' he said decisively, looking at the old man. 'I will find it, wherever it is, and I will bring it back to you as soon as I possibly can. There is just one thing you must know before I begin. I am a changeling. I will never die.'

Fareed said nothing.

He ventured again: 'I just thought you should know.'

'Thank you, Bernard. With all my heart, thank you.' And he turned to him and smiled.

'How will I recognize this word of yours?'

'I don't know. But it will be a new word. A word of the future, not of the past.'

'I will begin today.'

The storm had passed, and Paris basked under clear summer skies that smelled gloriously of clean roofs and damp earth. The day was so astonishing that people stopped in their tracks to admire it; the buildings were radiant, faces passed each other with an otherwordly clarity, and the trees sighed and sparkled. Bernard sat on the edge of a fountain to think and to watch it all turn about him. Pigeons wheeled overhead in the dizzy sunlight, and voices called to each other here and there through the exultant patter of the falling water. His face was wet with rainbow spray, and yet in the middle of all this he felt clear-headed and alive.

'There is more to all this than I have allowed myself to think,' he said to himself. 'Today seems like a new epoch. Maybe Fareed was the best thing that could have happened to me.'

He began to look for words. He read all the graffiti in the Métro and noted down words he did not know. He spent two hours in the FNAC at Les Halles surreptitiously opening CD wrappers and reading the lyrics to albums that looked suitably philosophical. He read every flyer that was handed to him in the street, and looked through rows and rows of printed T-shirts at a stall near Beaubourg just because the brand name was 'Néologisme'. He looked through magazines and comics; he stepped into a new bar called Le Velvet, apologizing to the staff who were still cleaning the tables ready for evening opening, to glance over their cocktail list.

At a newspaper stand he noticed with a shock that he was the lead story in *Paris Soir*:

TOP SACHS BANKER IS CHANGELING
Flees leaving wife, friends incredulous

He bought the paper and read the article quickly. It described the 'harrowing discovery' by Claire Grand'amie and the subsequent chain reaction of phone calls amongst the city's *beau monde*, one that ended with Bernard's boss at Goldman Sachs – who informed the press. Claire had given no interview but there was a file photo of her with the caption 'GRAND'AMIE: DEVASTATED'. Michel Laporte, a colleague of Bernard's, was reported as saying, 'This bank extended many privileges to him, and many of us saw fit to invite him to our homes. Naturally, none of us had any inkling of this. Now of course he has simply disappeared. We all feel deeply betrayed. Of course Dussoulier's investments are in excellent hands and his departure will have no untoward effects on Goldman Sachs' clients.' The bank had given the newspaper a copy of Bernard's staff photograph that showed him in a suit looking up winningly from his laptop as if caught impromptu. At first Bernard felt cowed by his photograph being circulated in such a way; but he reasoned with himself that this was not *A Bout de Souffle* and he was not Belmondo: in real life newspaper portraits did not look like real people.

His search continued.

He began to ask passers-by about any new words they had heard. He chose people with faces that looked as if they had questions in them. He asked them, falteringly: 'Have you seen any new words recently? Words that put things, perhaps, in a slightly new perspective?' People were confused, shook their heads. He did not feel that his questions really made sense and decided to abandon this direct approach. He contented himself with waiting for words to slip out involuntarily from the conversations of the city. He listened closely and without embarrassment to what everyone around him was saying; his head became abuzz with conversations: he listened to three, four, five at a time as people came and went:

Have you ever thought what it is to be entirely without hope?
Quickly, Marie, quickly!
He said the fishes were swimming in the air.
You never saw a mobile phone that could do all this.
It is nearly closing time.
Unhurried, unconcerned. As if that was what fishes always did!
I often wonder if the water supply is really safe.
The future is terrifying.
You never saw a woman so happy as I!
The thing that no one ever says about funerals is that they cost a
   lot of money.
Would you happen to know how to get to the catacombs?
The future is bright.

He sat in cafés and loitered at crêpe stands to listen to people speak; he overheard half-conversations at phone booths and walked into electronics shops to hear snatches of television. There was a preacher who stood outside Notre Dame decrying the age, forcefully describing the plagues and pestilences of the Old Testament, telling people to turn back before it was too late – and Bernard stood and listened to it all.

He was tireless in his task: he walked in every kind of street and searched in train stations and hairdressers and betting shops; he spoke to schoolchildren and rabbis, tourists and beggars. There was no word that came Bernard's way that he did not seize upon and inspect carefully. But nowhere did he find anything that seemed to be what Fareed was looking for.

Finally, when the night was already much advanced, he returned to the hotel in Montparnasse. The old man was lying as he had left him.

'I have searched hard, Fareed. But I have found nothing.'

'It will take time. Don't worry. You can try again tomorrow.'

Bernard continued in this way, day after day. Each morning he would awake early and leave the hotel to try a different part of the city. He became more systematic in his search, tackling one or two arrondissements each day, in numerical order, and thus tracing a spiral out from the centre of Paris towards its periphery; he got to number twenty and continued to search even beyond the Periphérique. Every day he returned to Fareed with a renewed sense of failure.

It was after some two weeks of all this that the first newspaper reports appeared about the outbreak of smallpox. Six people – two women, three men, and one child – had been conclusively diagnosed with the disease. They all lived in Paris, though not in any one area of the city. There were no indications as to how a disease that had been eradicated from the world in 1973 could have resurfaced at this time and in this place.

The newspapers all broke the story on the same day and dedicated the entirety of an edition to it. They gave clear medical descriptions of the disease in tactful terms that had clearly been drawn up by the government's health advisers; they told people what symptoms to look out for and what precautions could be taken to minimize the risk of contraction. And they listed the emergency measures the government was taking to prevent the spread of the disease to the greatest extent possible.

The authorities had not been slow. In anticipation of the mass panic that would break out in the capital they had sealed the city before the news was made public. All roads into and out of Paris had been closed on the previous night. Trains would no longer run, and the airport was shut down. Fifty thousand soldiers were deployed in a defensive ring to prevent all human intercourse between Paris and the rest of the country; over the next few days their presence was reinforced with the most enormous system of barricades seen in France since the First World War. Steel grills were placed across any underground routes that bypassed the barricades, and all entrances were placed under armed guard. The Seine was blocked off, and military garrisons set up along both sides. All privately owned aircraft were seized by the government. There was no way out.

The smallpox epidemic of Paris has been extensively written about, and will continue to be studied for decades to come. No one who lived through that time could fail to remember the harrowing stories of a city in turmoil. At first the main concern of the city's residents was to fight against their incarceration. The government had put its case forcefully: France had a duty to all the people of the world to prevent the spread of the disease, and the only way to achieve this was to totally seal off the exposed population. But it was no good – people used every stratagem they knew to try and get out: they called personal contacts in the government or the SNCF or the army; they drove around the perimeter fences looking for unobserved spots where an escape could be staged; they offered ludicrously large amounts of money in bribes to people they thought could help. Foreign tourists were particularly indignant at their situation – for was this not a French disease and nothing to do with them? The embassies were surrounded by violent crowds of people who demanded to be airlifted by their governments; but the international community was unanimous in its support of the French government's decisive action, and none of this campaigning did any good.

After a week, however, the second wave of infection hit and the city became focused on the disease itself. Five out of the first six had already died; these six had infected one hundred and nine more people, and most people now knew someone who knew someone who had it. Whispered stories began to travel about the pain and horror of the disease: a woman who remained fully conscious as her bloated skin burst open and fell away in sheets, leaving behind only a bloody mess; a teenage boy who, feeling in the midst of his fever an intense need to defecate, passed a metre-long section of his own intestine out through his anus. The mood of the city turned from outrage to terror. Supermarket shelves were emptied as people filled their houses with supplies and tried to withdraw completely from all social interaction. Within a few days virtually all economic activity in the city came to a halt. Offices and schools were empty, and the streets took on a bizarre aspect as people took to wearing head masks and to walking as far away from each other as possible.

It was at this point that the President of the Republic made a televised address to the nation.

'My brothers and sisters of France,' he began intimately, 'I know I speak for all of you when I say that there have been few moments in my life when I have been gripped by so profound a concern for this country and its people as now. This affliction that has stolen into our beautiful and cherished capital city is one of Man's ancient foes, and it is a formidable one. It will take all our courage and resourcefulness to defeat it. But history has prepared our nation for adversity, and we are not weak. Whenever we have been subjected to great trials, we have emerged triumphant. I know that this occasion will be no different.'

The President expressed his sympathy for all those 'into whose homes this disease has crept' and assured them that the nation was ready to share their burdens. He made much of the fact that he, too, was shut up in the capital. And then he turned to more pragmatic questions. Two measures, he said, would be taken to contain the disease:

'First of all, we shall be obliged to restrict all movement in the city of Paris. This will mean hardship for some; but it is essential that we prevent the unfortunate few who have been infected from moving freely through the city and thus spreading the suffering still further. Secondly, we will vaccinate every person living within the enclosed zone. There is a highly effective vaccine against this disease and within a few weeks we will be able to immunize everyone in the city. This is no small undertaking: there are some twelve million people in the area, and we are having to bring the vaccine from the United States of America, whose President has graciously pledged all the help we may require. But we are assured that the first supplies will arrive here in the next seven days; and when all movement of people has been stopped it will be a simpler operation to administer them systematically. When these measures are complete there will be nowhere for the disease to take refuge. We shall have triumphed.'

The President's speech, however, did nothing to calm fears. It was that night, in fact, that the panic truly began. All over the city, people barricaded their houses against disease and violence, reinforcing garden gates and taping up gaps in the casement windows. Many took to the roads in order to join friends and family members from whom they feared to be separated. And many others decided to take their own action to stamp out the causes of the epidemic. The poor and homeless were commonly seen as likely sources of the virus, and bands of middle-class men roamed the streets seeking them out, full of retribution. In just one of countless such incidents, five women caught taking bread from rubbish sacks behind a bakery near the Gare du Nord were summarily hacked to death. Fire was a popular instrument of purification: a whole neighbourhood in the north of the city was torched when a group of youths found two dead cats in the street. Several mosques were set alight – for no one could believe this thing had originated in France itself, and fine distinctions were forgotten in the search for outsiders. Rumours spread quickly: many people gave credence to the notion that the bacterium had been planted in the water supply; the news that one woman had contracted smallpox after a meal bought from a Casino supermarket led to a city-wide assault on all Casino outlets. Violence killed many more in these early stages than did the disease itself, and the sight of dead bodies in the streets only served to escalate the terrors of contagion. And the general atmosphere of chaos and fear brought with it more primitive behaviour still, of which by far the most prominent was rape: for the sense of an impending apocalypse engendered not simply a struggle for self-preservation but also a festival of violence and destruction as if defiant egos were competing with Death itself. These details were never reported in the emergency era newspapers, but for a time they formed the everyday reality for many people in Paris. (The subsequent legal investigations have been hard pressed, of course, to make sense of all this under the cool light of democratic civil order.)

Meanwhile, in a tense and darkened room behind Corinthian pillars, government officials and senior military personnel listened to presentations by epidemiologists and urban specialists. Their objective was to plan the complex task of slicing up the city with barricades so that all movement, and therefore all spread of the disease, would eventually cease. The urban planner presented his vision: first, steel fences along all the major boulevards, cutting the city into large sections, and then finer and finer networks of barricades within those sections. The increasingly dense fractal patterns that appeared on the wall-sized map of Paris looked precise and beautiful. 'Thank God for Haussmann,' someone said.

Everyone in the room sat a long way away from everyone else.

One night, the telephone in the hotel room rang.

'Hello?'

'Bernard? It's Daniel.'

'How did you find me? I haven't told anyone where I am. How did you find this hotel?'

'There are networks, Bernard. You know that. Look: I'm calling you as a friend. It's really time for all of us to get out of here. To return. This smallpox is going to spread everywhere and you know what it would mean for us. Whatever mad thing you're doing, Bernard, just drop it. Leave.'

'Why are *you* still here?'

'I'm as attached to my existence here as you. But I'm going today. It's too much of a risk to stay on.'

'I can't go yet. I know it sounds strange – it's not something I can even explain fully to myself, Daniel. But I am in the middle of something, something I promised to a friend of mine who needs me, and I feel I have to do it before I return. Call it sentimentality, guilt – what you will.'

'Think clearly, Bernard. Once you get this disease you will not be in a position to go back. Is any favour to any human worth that? They are going to die anyway – now or another time.'

'I *am* thinking clearly. Currently I'm in perfect health. And in a few days I will be of no further use to him anyway because they're going to stop everyone moving around the city. So whether I succeed or not I will be leaving here soon.'

'I would beg you to think again.'

'Don't worry about me. I have thought enough. I will be with you in a few days.'

When Bernard awoke the next morning Fareed looked worse than before. He had not slept that night and his face was greasy with sweat.

'I think they're beginning to come through.'

Bernard carefully pulled back the limp bed clothes. Sure enough, little buds of green were poking through Fareed's skin in various places. The holes looked painful: pus leaked from them, and some were bleeding.

'They are coming from my back too: so I don't know how to lie at night.'

Bernard brought paper tissue from the bathroom and began to wipe the wounds. The old man seemed embarrassed.

'Don't worry about it. It's all right,' he said.

'We should clean them thoroughly, Fareed. You could easily get infections in these holes. I'll get some antiseptic. And I'll cut the ends off these shoots. You'll find it easier to sleep.'

He readied himself for his day of searching. As he opened the door to go, Fareed murmured, as if to himself, 'People always talk about the fact that everyone dies alone. It's a cliché, isn't it? But that's just what I feel right now. I lie here all day while you are out, feeling the roots spreading in my lungs, finding less and less space for breath, and it is the loneliest thing in the world. You've been so kind to me, Bernard. But even you have no idea how terrified I am inside.'

Bernard readied himself hurriedly, and left.

The streets were deserted. A few cars rushed past anonymously; occasionally a masked figure would emerge from a door, look around furtively, and dart a few metres down the street into another entrance.

Bernard turned onto the rue de Vaugirard. The whole street had been taken over by the army, which was erecting tall fences along each side. The fences were positioned at the edges of the boulevards, allowing people to walk along the sidewalks but not to step into the road itself. The zone in between was manned by armed soldiers in full protective body suits and masks. Similarly clad figures had spread out in a long line to spray the surface of the road from enormous canisters mounted on their backs. Military trucks and white vans bearing the logos of the WHO were parked at intervals.

'I have to move quickly,' thought Bernard to himself. Unable to cross the street he walked up towards the Montparnasse tower. In the abandoned square, where gaudy merry-go-round horses were stopped in mid-flight and where steel grids already covered the entrances to the Métro, a man had set up a coffee stall. He wore no mask, and looked at Bernard quite receptively, as if the pestilence had never come. His price was exorbitant – like everything in the city now – but Bernard was touched by the whole normality of the thing and decided to postpone his search for just five minutes. He sat on one of the plastic chairs with a frothing paper cup in his hand. It was only then that he noticed the man sitting beside him.

'How do you do?' the man said, with a gallantry that verged on the absurd. 'Is it not a beautiful morning?'

The man was dressed in a finely tailored chequered jacket with a pink silk cravat that overflowed from the collar of his shirt. His jauntiness seemed completely out of place, and yet Bernard had a strong feeling that he had seen him before. He too sipped at a cup of steaming coffee.

276

'It is beautiful,' Bernard confirmed. And it was. Though summer was close to its end, the cloudless skies were already warm at this early hour.

'What brings you to this place that everyone else shuns, my friend?'

The natural configuration of the man's swarthy face was a broad, inviting smile. He was elderly, but his eyes were alert and energetic.

'I am looking for something. I can't let this – situation – get in my way.'

'And what is this thing you seek?'

'I seek a word. A word for a friend of mine who is dying. He needs it to die in peace.'

'A common problem,' replied the man. 'I hope he is not dying of –'

'No. It is something else.'

'And what progress are you making?'

'I don't know,' said Bernard. 'To be honest I am at a loss. I have searched everywhere, and found nothing. And now they are closing up the city. I have to find something soon.'

The man leant back in his chair and looked up at the sky. He spoke as if to the morning,

'I think your quest will come to an end today.'

'Will I find what I am looking for?' asked Bernard anxiously.

The man looked searchingly into his face.

'A more urgent question for you to answer is: will you recognize it when you see it? Maybe it is right here, with you, now.'

'Is it? Do you know anything? Can you help me?'

The man looked at his watch.

'I would love to, of course, but – you know – time rushes onwards! Must go. Things – to do!'

He took a final sip of his coffee.

'I wish you the very best of luck, young man. And good day to you!'

He gave a slight bow, and was gone.

Bernard walked along the rue de Vaugirard in the opposite direction from the hotel. The cranes roared and the line of steel barricades was growing quickly. Where had these clanking fences all come from? Had they been stored in some out-of-town warehouse in readiness for just such a situation as this?

The masked soldiers took no notice of him as he passed. Apart from them, there now seemed to be no one around; not even a trace of human beings, in fact, except the occasional glimpse of some blanched and clandestine face watching from an upstairs window. The shops were shut, and many had been vandalized. There seemed to be in the city a great demand for tarpaulin, for the awnings had been rudely ripped away, almost without exception, from above the deluxe cafés and patisseries. The doors of the enormous hospital on the other side of the street were locked, although all the lights were on inside.

With the human beings, all the words seemed to have gone, too. There were no newspapers, no leaflets, no graffiti. The trash bins seemed to have been removed. Even the advertisements and shop signs had mostly disappeared. Only the city's skeleton still bore its labels: traffic signs, stone inscriptions, street names . . . He stopped briefly at a mailbox and read collection times.

He was forced to turn at the boulevard Louis Pasteur since this section of the barricade had been completed. There were no soldiers here and the street was silent save for the guttural moans of pigeons.

Bernard picked up a soiled photograph of a couple whose heads had both been cut out in separate rectangles. There was nothing written on the back.

Some way down the street he came upon a car that had been driven through the window of an *immobilier* and now sat half in, half out, surrounded by glass. An old woman was sleeping on the back seat.

He saw a book lying tantalizingly in the middle of the street, on the other side of the barricade. He could not get to it. Perhaps it had been thrown from a balcony.

He crossed the train tracks leading to Montparnasse station. The stationary train carriages had been taken over by families whose washing was drying in the sun outside.

He could see Montparnasse Cemetery in the distance. He wandered towards it. The gate was open and he walked in among the tombs. The quiet order of the place was relaxing. It was a city in its own right, this rectilinear metropolis of the dead; but it was a city that did not assault you with its scale, one built for the size of the human body. On every side of the large expanse of the cemetery he could see the buildings of Paris: 1970s apartment blocks, Montparnasse Tower of course, and, towards the Seine, a number of newer corporate towers. And beyond them – were those the spires of La Défense? 'There is more peace here, among the dead,' thought Bernard. 'Perhaps this is a better place for words to grow.'

He examined the tombstones, but they were frustrating in their brevity, their repetitiousness.

Died aged fifty-two
Left this world on 22nd September 1927
A loving father
May she rest in peace
Died aged nine months
A godly woman
Died aged sixty-seven
A loyal servant of God, his country, and his fellow man
She was my loving wife
Departed for a better world
Died aged twenty-three
Surrendered this life
Our much cherished son
Died aged seventy-two

Many of the tombs had flowers on them. Even at this time. He saw no one around, but everywhere people had come to put fresh roses in vases.

He stumbled upon the tomb of Charles Baudelaire. The poet did not even have a stone to himself. The inscription read, simply, 'Pray for them'.

There were no words here.

When Bernard got back to Montparnasse he realized that the barricades along the rue de Vaugirard had joined those along the avenue du Maine and his route back to the hotel was blocked.

'I need to get to that street over there. How do I go round?' Bernard shouted to one of the soldiers.

'It may be too late.' The voice of the masked soldier came through a small loudspeaker in the front of his suit. 'Do you have some proof of residence there?'

'No. I'm staying in a hotel.'

'Sorry – I think you'll have to find another hotel for tonight. This area is sealed now.'

'My friend is in there.'

'We can't accommodate all these requests. The whole point of the barricade is to stop people moving. Camp somewhere else. It's just for a few weeks.'

Bernard realized there was no point arguing. He started to walk desolately up the road, back to where he had started. After all this, would Fareed die untended without the words he had spent all these months looking for? Bernard ran his hands uselessly along the steel fence, looking at the masked soldiers, desperate with anger and frustration.

There was a voice: 'Good afternoon to you. We meet again!'

Bernard looked up, and there was the same extravagantly dressed man he had seen in the morning.

'Did you find your word?'

'No.' Bernard muttered confusedly.

'Oh. Well, there's always another day. Eh? But you seem unwell. Can I help with anything?'

'No. It's – ' He threw up his hands in despair. 'The man who needs the word is on the other side of this fence. There's no way in.'

'Come now. You are making mountains out of molehills. Follow me. I happened to pass an entrance just two minutes ago.'

He led Bernard back the way he had come.

'You really should use your head. No barrier is for *everyone*. And the people for whom it is not always need their own way of getting through. How do you think these soldiers get home at night? Here!'

They came upon a gate in the fence that, miraculously, had been left ajar.

'Sneak in now while no one is looking! There you are! That's the ticket!'

Bernard mumbled his thanks.

'No problem at all. Here – why don't you take my business card in case you need anything else?'

He placed a card ceremonially in Bernard's hand.

ALBERT KENETTE

VICE PRESIDENT (SALES) (FRANCE)

SYNTIME INC

'Call me any time. And don't forget to give your friend my best!'

Bernard turned to thank him once again, but he had already wandered off, whistling an old Trenet song.

Bernard walked back to the hotel thinking about the old man. He looked at his card again. Its steely logo did not quite fit with his appearance. Bernard turned the card over. It read·

SYNTIME, noun

An experience of time in which past and future
moments exist simultaneously in the present.

SYNTIME INC. Global business processes.

'It's not very promising,' thought Bernard to himself. 'But it's the first new word I've found today.'

He walked uncertainly up the stairs to the room. Fareed was asleep, and Bernard woke him. He focused only gradually on Bernard's face.

'Did you find anything?'

'Not much. I found this.'

He showed the card to Fareed. He was very weak. He looked listlessly at it for a while, and then closed his eyes.

Bernard was overcome with disappointment.

'It's a meaningless word,' he exclaimed bitterly. 'An ugly word.'

'It's all right,' said Fareed. 'Don't worry.' He placed a desiccated hand on Bernard's arm. 'Perhaps sometimes we are not supposed to find what we seek. You have tried very hard. That is very precious to me.'

He turned away.

'Now let me sleep.'

Bernard stood up and looked out of the window. Evening had come, and it was dark, but the yellow light revealed a semicircle of the tiny garden in which a few rusted chairs were grouped pathetically together. In a fit of frustration, he tore up the card and let the pieces flutter down into the darkness.

It was still early when Bernard awoke. The morning light was breaking through the curtains and everything was still. For the first time that he could remember, he had nothing to do.

'Now it is time for me to return,' he thought to himself. 'There is nothing else I can give to this place. It holds only danger for me. Maybe I will call some old friends. Make arrangements for Fareed. I need to look for a place to leave my body.'

He turned to check on the old man, and saw to his consternation that the bed was empty. He leapt up. Fareed was not in the bathroom. Or the corridor outside. Bernard pulled on some clothes, thoughts rushing through his head: 'He has run away to finish his search on his own. He will not get far. In the state he is in. The barriers. He cannot bear to be with me anymore. Knowing how I have failed him. He gambled on me and I failed him. Something happened in the night; he did not want to burden me with his death. He has gone to kill himself. Saw no point in living further knowing he would never find his word.' He ran down the stairs. The concierge was watching television.

'Have you seen my friend? The old man. Did he come this way?'

The concierge pointed blankly towards the back door, his eyes still fixed on the screen.

Bernard darted breathlessly towards the back entrance, opened the door, there was the garden he had seen from upstairs, he ran down the steps –

Fareed was seated in a chair in the middle of the garden. His face was tilted towards the sky and his eyes were closed. His hands were folded restfully in his lap, and a slight breeze ruffled his white hair.

He was singing.

Bernard sat and watched in amazement. Fareed's voice was thin and he breathed often, but he sang with passion, and his words were mysterious. He sang of death:

The death I die is not my own, nor does it belong to another: | For did I not start my death when I was born | And was my birth my own? | Or was it not? The moment, | Always somewhere ahead, | When I will have run out of life, | Is only a Deception for Yes! | I died even in those days when I dreamed what I would be | And in that death I flourished; | And now at last that I know what I was | Am I not more than I was?

Bernard watched, uncomprehending but transfixed, as the man sang to the sky, as he became more and more a part of his own words:

There is nothing that is mine | And nothing that is not. | Nothing is now but nothing is not. | And so in this now when you see me die, | In this death you think is mine, | I bid you my Friend, my companion in life: | Come and die my death with me! | And I will die yours with you.

Bernard listened to Fareed's song for he knew not how long. The voice was not strong but there was a stillness around it that allowed it to carry. The hotel maid came to hang laundry up in the garden, and she also sat down to listen; a man appeared at the upstairs window of the house behind and stood watching for what must have been several hours. The day grew hot, and still Fareed sang:

As a child I stood with my back to the past | And shunned what I had been; | The future lit my face and gladly I ran to it | But it was a mere dazzlement in the night | For the future is blank and only the past is light; | Why did I turn my back on what I

*could see and gaze into the invisible | And so forget my sight? |
Was it because I knew somewhere in that emptiness lurked my
death? | Did I think I could spy it before it came? | Wasted
concern: | Now I lose my interest in death; | See me turn on the
landscape of time: | And there! laid out in front is the shining
city of the past | Which I contemplate with my intact intellect |
As I back into those outstretched arms | That will catch me
when I fall.*

So did the day pass; and evening came.

When it was truly night, Fareed stopped singing. He was breathless
but full of life.

'What happened, Fareed?' asked Bernard. 'What happened to make
you sing this way?'

'I don't know. I really can't say. Was it your word? Or was it the
disappointment at there not being a word? I don't know. But now I
am full of words. More than there is time left to utter!'

So Fareed talked, and Bernard listened. It grew late, and Bernard
proposed that they sleep.

'You go, Bernard. You go. I would like to stay here tonight.'

Bernard left Fareed sitting in the garden, and went to sleep in the
room on his own.

The city had been transformed. In two days the work of constructing
the network of barriers was complete, and all movement of people
ceased. The enclosures were very small – just a few buildings, in most
cases – and people could do nothing except sit at home and watch and
wait. All major streets in the city were occupied by the army, which
guarded them fastidiously. Throughout the day, relief trucks rolled
through bringing supplies of food and other basic necessities to each
enclosure. The vaccination operation began, enclosure by enclosure:
soldiers in body suits and masks accompanied similarly-clad nurses
from house to house, vaccinating everyone. Meanwhile more soldiers
fanned out in each enclosure to look for homeless people or refugees.
These were the days when everyone was waiting to see if they were

going to be part of the next wave of the disease, to see if they had been incubating it in themselves: every cough, every skin blemish was looked upon with terror.

The next day Fareed began to sing with the dawn. Once again he seemed to become entirely absorbed into the words that he sang, and his eyes remained closed all day.

As the day passed, the upstairs windows all around the garden filled with people who came to watch Fareed. Other guests in the hotel came down and sat with Bernard. Perhaps everyone was bored: for there was nothing to do and nowhere to go; and yet everyone seemed utterly engrossed. No one moved or spoke: but the stillness was heavy with the attention of so many.

When night came, Fareed called to Bernard.

'Can you light me a fire, my friend? for I was so cold last night.'

Bernard made a fire in front of Fareed. Everyone liked it: some climbed over the walls from the surrounding houses to sit around it. One young girl sang to herself from memory the songs that Fareed had sung that day, while others talked:

'A well-known scientist has said that the virus could survive, if all the conditions were right, in the sewers – perhaps for a hundred and fifty years. That explosion at the Bastille. You remember? – before all this started. He says it could have set free the virus that has been living there since the outbreaks of the nineteenth century.'

'That's nonsense. The virus is a living thing like any other: it needs its habitat if it is to survive. Its only habitat is human beings. Lots of them together. The modern city is perfect for it.'

'Let me tell you what I heard. There is a funeral company here that has been losing money. The management team saw the problem with the size of the market itself. If the death rate could be increased by a just a tiny percentage their whole business would be back on track! They investigated solutions, asked someone to help them introduce just a bit more death into Paris. Unfortunately the plan went out of control. Look at what we have now. It wasn't supposed to be like this.'

'You're making this up!'

'I can assure you I am completely serious. The person who told me –'

'Look: it's the government I tell you. Only they could plan something like this. You all have to ask yourselves this: *who comes out of this looking good?*'

So the days continued: song by day and conversation around the fire by night. People broke down all the walls between the yards so they could congregate together to listen to the singing. They dug flower beds in the concrete and planted flowers and vegetables that they cultivated with care. The jumble of stone rectangles with their wooden sheds and garbage bins became almost a garden.

By the third or fourth day Fareed's clothes were no longer enough to conceal the shoots that were growing from his body. They emerged through his shirt, they began to flower, they had a strong perfume. Bernard offered to cut them off, but Fareed refused. They began to take root in the ground where he sat. Again Bernard said:

'Maybe I should do something about this. Soon you won't be able to move.'

'I have no further use for moving, Bernard. I am where I wish to be. And I shall not be here much longer.'

It was an idle, meditative time. In the songs, people found thoughts that took root in their minds and burst open gloriously, and they were happy simply to listen and think. Bernard called Claire a few times to see if she was safe, but was answered only by the machine. He wished he could see her again, for he had saved up so many things he wanted to say to her; but he did not leave a message.

One evening when his song was finished, Fareed whispered to Bernard:

'Psst! Come here!'

Bernard rushed to his side.

'Look at that.'

A delicious white flower was blooming on a long stem emerging from the old man's navel. In the middle of the flower a bee had landed, and worked feverishly.

* * *

286

Most people now do not believe you when you tell them that the entire singing career of the old man in the garden lasted a mere thirteen days. It seems too improbable that a phenomenon of that scale could be based on a mere two-week burst of creativity. But so it was. Fareed sang for thirteen full days. On the fourteenth day, he died.

At first his songs spread only within Paris. It was natural: the population was idle and stalked by death – and so the songs moved among them faster even than the virus. Fareed wrote nothing down, so whatever left the garden where he sang was through the singing of those who had heard him. People gathered at the points where three or more barriers converged and sang songs to each other; these then moved on to the next enclosures, and the next. They became the anthems of that terrible moment; but what travelled was more an idea than a set of texts, for the words were elaborated and misremembered at every turn. Rap singers used them particularly effectively in the makeshift home concerts of the time, since they gave themselves so well to adaptation and improvisation; and some of the set pieces that developed out of this (for instance all the 'debate' songs, which can be traced back to the influential rap piece 'Devil's Advo Cut', in which the themes of Fareed's poetry were mockingly challenged by a mysterious otherworldly voice) led to cultural forms as diverse as schoolyard games and highbrow poetry. Some tried to write all this down – many will remember the graffiti that appeared all over the city at that time, which became a method for collecting many individuals' partial memories into a more comprehensive whole – but there still exists no authoritative edition of Fareed's work, and perhaps such a thing would be impossible. There was too much of an aura about him for memories to be clear. People spoke of the garden where he sang as an almost mythical place – and soon wherever people collected to exchange songs they also created gardens. People's imaginations stretched to the absurd: some said that everything he touched turned to flowers, and that the mere touch of one of those flowers was an instant cure for the disease. Some thought he was a messenger of the last days: he had brought the scourges and the hymns that would destroy and redeem the world. One has to remember that these were extreme times, and minds were under stress. None of this should be subjected to normal criteria of judgement.

Less easy to understand than all this is the sudden explosion of Fareed's poetry – or whatever second- or third-hand versions of it were available – outside Paris, and indeed across the world. The world, too, was shaken up by the resurgence of smallpox; but still it is difficult to explain the excited way in which people in many different places responded to these words – especially since it all lasted well beyond the time when the smallpox epidemic was eventually contained and the city of Paris was set in motion again. English translations started appearing in New York almost as soon as the words were on the streets of Paris, and new groups of American poets and singers started to try and outdo each other in the sophistication with which they could develop them. The case of Maya Spassov, the Bulgarian software worker who wrote magnificent poetry in Bulgarian and English on the inspiration of Fareed's songs, has rightly received a great deal of attention; but we should not forget that the outburst of creativity that happened at that time was both more widespread and more intimate than the publishing and entertainment industries could ever really understand or take advantage of. And there was something about it that caused those industries to stand back even as they gloated over its commercial possibilities: CNN labelled it a 'death cult' and the US security agencies were instructed to monitor the population closely for signs of imitation of the French 'movement'. A commercial 'poetry garden' in Milan was charged with sedition and closed down by the Italian government after only two days of operations; and there are countless stories of websites of Fareed's songs being shut down across the world. All this seems strange now, such a short time later. But the world was in a strange mood, and probably we are still trying to work out what it all meant.

Perhaps it needs to be said again: everything that has happened since makes it difficult almost to believe in the physical reality of the man Fareed, and near to impossible to retrieve the simplest details of those fateful last days of his life.

We do know this, however: that on the thirteenth day of his singing, he sang a protracted meditation on the life and death of the body. His song described life as being divided into two parts, with death falling in the middle. Death was the midpoint of the body's life: for the amount of time it takes for a body to become fully itself is also the amount of time that it takes to decompose and become nothing again. The body generates a spirit that struggles with gravity as an air balloon tugs at its guys and, just at the moment that it takes off, it is dragged down again, struggling and complaining, by the death of the body; but the spirit has its own decomposition, too, as it continues to give life and memory to the world (rather as a dead man's clothes, given out to the homeless, continue to give warmth to a city). Fareed dwelt on this decomposition of the body and the spirit; and, in a trope that became very popular with his imitators, he turned it around in time and narrated it again: so that life began with the first fusion of two particles of dust that had been sundered, continued as they gathered more dust around them, and so built a skeleton on to which rotting flesh gradually fixed itself and became full and whole, and then – suddenly! – with a leap that was the reverse of its fall, the spirit soared high even as the body was still pale and deathly; it was at the summit of the human and looked down on all the landscape of life. Gradually, spirit descended to join the body that rose with pride to receive it, and there was childhood, and the diminution of both, and, at the very end, two cells that were sundered – and nothing.

The song exhausted him. By this time Fareed was firmly rooted to the ground and surrounded by thick growth; his chest and back had burst completely open with branches growing through him that were thicker than his upper arm, and he could hardly breathe. He was in great pain. Night came. He said to Bernard:

'Will you sleep next to me tonight? I feel I have little time left.'

'Of course,' said Bernard. He put more wood on the fire, and nestled in among roots and branches to hold Fareed's wizened body in his arms.

When Bernard awoke it was just light; and he felt strangled.

New shoots had grown entirely around him in the night, and he could not move. They grew around his neck and legs; they enfolded his upper body, pinning his arms to his sides. By this time there was sprouting from Fareed a mass of creepers and flowers that enchanted people in all the adjacent enclosures with their glorious scent.

'Fareed!' Bernard whispered anxiously. 'Help me! I have been trapped by the plant. It has grown around me. I have to cut the roots. Break them. Help me!'

He tried to wake Fareed, but the old man was delirious and could not take any notice. Restricted as his arms were, and even though his hands were lashed tightly against his thighs, Bernard started to break roots with his finger tips; his heart was beating fast and there was a claustrophobic panic in him as he tried to free himself. The roots were thick and wiry and he needed to saw at them with his finger nails; he kicked his legs in ineffectual spasms and shouted for people who could not hear, did not come. Gradually, his hands became more free and he worked more quickly; he freed his arms and pulled the huge fibres from under him: they were longer than he was and lay discarded all about with sickening underground pallor. But still he could not move.

His body had fused entirely with that of Fareed. He could not pull himself away.

'It is time for me to leave this world completely. My body has become useless to me. I have to leave it.'

The emotion welled in Bernard, for so many things were happening at once: he was not prepared, and the awareness of his dying friend was a sharp pain within him – but he pushed all those feelings madly aside, for the instinct to preserve himself was rearing within him desperately and he was remembering who he was. He began to disengage from his body and to draw his energies away from the physical.

But something was wrong. He could not extract himself. He was tugging against something that he was attached to indivisibly, a dead weight on his spirit that prevented him from finding the strength to return. Fareed gained consciousness and looked at him with clear eyes.

'Our spirits, Bernard. Have also become fused. Like two raindrops on a window.' He wheezed. 'I never meant it. I'm so – sorry.'

Bernard began to shiver violently with fear.

'I'm going to die,' he said to himself.

He screamed the words again; he pleaded with Fareed as if there was something the old man could do. Semi-conscious as he was, he whispered in a frenzy of urgencies, 'You can't take me with you, you can't: I never came to die your death, I have an eternity to live!'; but Fareed could not even really make out the words, and as a matter of fact Bernard's own strength was being sapped quickly. He bucked and kicked against the roots and the joined flesh while Fareed lay perfectly calm and immobile; but their bodies both drew now on a single reservoir of energy that was fast evaporating. He was now only the twitching half of a larger creature that was otherwise resigned to death; and as the last barriers were lifted between their spirits, even the peace of Fareed's mind came flowing into his own, and he lay back in the rushing stillness of the other man's awareness and resignation.

Fareed whispered, without opening his eyes, 'Finally – I do not die alone.'

There were tears in the slits of his eyelids. A flood of things, terrible and wonderful, was rushing into Bernard, things that astonished him with their plenitude, as if everything in experience was laid out before him. This, then, was to die. He could not express it. There were no words.

A fog filled his mind, and only a chink still connected him to the world. He heard Fareed murmur,

'Can you see? There are fishes. Everywhere. Swimming in the sky.'

'Yes.' Bernard's voice was faint even to himself, as if he spoke in a wind tunnel. 'I can see them. So many fishes.'

A woman yawned, shifted from her seat to the floor, tried to make herself comfortable, half-lying, half-leaning up against a battered Samsonite cabin bag. It was the dead of night: yesterday seemed weeks ago and tomorrow still many inky aeons in the future. Sleep lapped seductively against the shores of Certainty until its outer reaches crumbled and were submerged in warm, insensible depths. Diminished senses played tricks: were those bats fluttering outside the windows or just the twitching blind spots of minds too slowed to render reality in all its detail? A pattern in the brickwork, or the remarkable shape of a shadow, could draw you into a maze of long and ponderous wonderings; and everyone's face was reminiscent of someone you had known long ago.

Another story began, and people drew themselves around it, gratefully.

THE BARGAIN
IN THE DUNGEON
The Eleventh Story

PART ONE

IN A SMALL town called Bytom in Upper Silesia, where nearly all the collieries had stopped working and the people were poor, there lived a couple who conceived a child. The wife was happy, but the husband was furious.

'What happened to all your – did you stop taking your pills? What are you trying to do to me?' he exclaimed in his rage. 'Is it not enough that I have been unemployed for three years, that I have to live off the charity of other people? Is it not clear enough already that I am a failure? Do you have to give me a child to support in order to demonstrate it beyond doubt to all the world?'

He insisted on an abortion, even though that was a significant expense in itself. His wife refused. Perhaps it was true that she had conspired to have a child without her husband's knowledge; but she buried her own desires under official arguments.

'Abortions are illegal, Wiktor, which you know as well as I. And I will never do a thing that so flagrantly defies the will of the Church!'

For the nine months of her pregnancy, all her husband's pent-up anger and disappointment with the world became focused on his obsession with the child. He stopped seeing his friends, and drank heavily on his own. One evening, shortly before the baby was due, in a drunk rage, he tried to push his wife down the stairs in order to induce a miscarriage. But she was more nimble than he was, and, after a while, a baby girl was born.

The baby was healthy and strong and had a vivid birthmark on her neck in the shape of a cross, which only increased her mother's sense of the providential nature of this birth. She named the child Katya.

But now the father's bile had a real person as its object it became only stronger. He hated his daughter with an all-encompassing passion that poisoned all his meals and kept him awake at night. How could a man share a house with the very image of his own impotence? He plotted to get rid of her.

One day, when Katya was nearly a year old, her mother, confident by now of leaving her for short periods, went away to attend to an elderly relative who was sick. As soon as she left the house, her husband bundled the child up in a cardboard box in which he punched a few rough holes for air, and attached a note to her wrist saying,

> we do not want her
> Name KATYA.
> if you have money & feel to take care

He left the house furtively, walking quickly with the box under one arm, and stole in through the dilapidated gates of one of the collieries where the trains stopped to load their cargoes. Making sure no one was watching, he climbed up the side of one of the loaded carriages, made a small depression in the coal, and fitted the box in tightly. He looked around again for possible observers, then rushed back home, where he opened a new bottle of vodka and spread himself out happily in the luxurious emptiness of the house.

At the end of the day, his wife returned. He had prepared his act, and the vodka only helped him play it more convincingly: he opened the door in a fit of panic that terrified her, so unconcerned was he usually about even serious matters, and wrestled to assemble a story out of an incoherent set of words – 'After I fed – the window came in – sleeping no sound – nothing! – checking to see her – gone! – the window!' – and he showed her the empty cradle and the window that had been broken open from outside. While his wife still reeled with shock he threw himself into her arms and sobbed bitterly.

The crime amazed the town's community. The police interviewed neighbours and local shopkeepers and bus drivers, but no one could provide any leads that would help identify the shadowy abductor. Local doctors were asked to verify that any child presented for care who was under two years old did not have a purple, cross-shaped birthmark on its neck. Posters giving particulars of the lost child went up at bus stops and in churches. Not even the remotest sign of hope came out of all of this. Despite her better instincts, Katya's mother could not forgive her husband for his inability to watch the child during her absence. She confessed her feelings to the priest. He chided her gently.

'Come now, do not be too hard on him. All of us know his short-comings, and if it had not been him but someone else looking after your child that day – well, perhaps this would not have happened. But you should not torture yourself with such a thought, for blaming him will not bring Katya back. He is suffering as much as you, after all – this is a time when you need to love and support each other with open hearts.'

That her husband was suffering from the loss of his daughter seemed incontrovertible. He had given up his solitary ways and taken to drinking with his friends again. And he had discovered how pleasurable it was to receive sympathy. When he entered the bar he would stoop exaggeratedly with his pain, and the townsmen would draw aside wordlessly to allow him to sit down; they would pat him silently on the back and signal over his head to the barman to bring his favourite drinks. He would say little and drink much during the evening; his friends would help him home, and he would bid an emotional goodbye to them at his front door:

'Thank you so much. You don't know what your friendship means to me at this – terrible – time.'

With his wife, too, he was caring and thoughtful, and full of moments of doleful silence that surprised her with their intensity. 'At least one thing has come out of all this,' she would think in her brighter moments. 'Against all expectation, it seems that when life turns really bad I can depend on my husband.'

But such moments were rare. The pain of losing her God-given daughter with the cross on her neck was with her constantly, and it was almost too much for her to bear.

News from the town did not generally make it into the national media. Perhaps this is why, though Katya's train ended up less than fifty kilometres away, in Katowice, no one ever made the connection between the abandoned child in her coal-soiled box and the bereft couple in Bytom.

Of course, the note tied to the girl's wrist did not exactly invite anyone to investigate such connections. And so it was that the worker who spotted her (thankfully! – for it would have been so easy for the little one to be crushed as the coal was emptied from the carriage) found a home for her, after not much consideration, with his own sister and her husband, whose obstinate childlessness was a source of permanent sadness for them.

At first they found the cross on Katya's neck troubling. 'It's spooky, that's what it is,' observed the new mother's parents drily as the assembled family stood around the kitchen table, where the box had been placed after its hasty journey from the railway station. But these were just the natural anxieties of such a situation, and before very long the child had been fully accepted into her new home.

The man she now called 'Father' was an insurance salesman who went out to work every day with a bag of lunch packed tenderly by his wife and her kiss upon his lips. She tended their pretty little home and made a small amount of money as a seamstress – and now, of course, devoted herself to little Katya, whom she loved with a mother's passion.

Katya grew up to be an intelligent but introverted girl who never quite returned the love of her doting parents. She was polite and respectful, and she liked the weekends when the three of them would go out to eat lunch in Katowice's main square in front of the Warta building. But she did not feel as though she belonged there, and she did not pretend that she did.

In the evenings, after school, Katya would help her mother with her sewing. She proved to be skilled and imaginative at the craft. Though she began merely with simple alterations and repairs of burst seams, her mother was quick to spy the flair with which she carried out these tasks and soon entrusted her with things more demanding. Before long, though she was barely in her teens, she was sewing entire shirts and dresses on her own; and there was something about the way she could look at a body and hold it in her head while she sewed – its shape, its texture, its asymmetries, its idiosyncrasies of movement – that meant her clothes always fitted first time and delighted their wearers with the *insight* they showed. Her mother's business boomed under the influence of Katya's contribution, and it was all the girl could do to complete her schoolwork as the orders flooded in and took up all her waking time.

One day, a woman asked her to make a bed cover. She and her husband were approaching the fortieth anniversary of their marriage, and she had decided to buy something extravagant for the occasion. 'People tell me you're very good,' she said to mother and daughter, as the three of them sat over Nescafé in her front room and an old, thin-haired dog panted by her side. 'I want nothing less than the best. It's a lot of money to me.'

Katya only half listened. She wandered around, looking at things and touching them – as she was still just young enough to do with impunity. She looked at old photographs of the new couple standing awkwardly together, and then, later, surrounded by three gangly boys with black-and-white, 1960s faces; she moved through time, as more families span out from this one into their own orbit, and there were daughters-in-law, and grandchildren.

'Can we see the bed?' she asked, interrupting.

'Ooh – I suppose you'll want to measure it,' exclaimed the old woman. 'I hadn't thought of that.'

They followed her expansive behind as it mounted the stairs. At the door to her bedroom she turned with a grin of shamed modesty, but Katya gave her no time to prepare for their entrance; she stood and watched as nightclothes were hidden away and a cover hastily thrown over the unmade bed.

'I usually do it first thing,' the woman puffed, 'but I forgot this morning – with your coming and everything.'

Katya sat on the bed and felt it, thoughtfully. The two women looked at her quizzically.

'Do you need a tape measure?'

'No. Thank you.'

Katya began work that very day. She sewed a large cover in soft cotton, generously padded but miraculously light. Then she began her design: a sweeping collage made with brightly coloured materials that showed the woman and her husband standing among the smokestacks of Katowice that erupted above their heads into thick foliage swarming with birds and squirrels and merry bees. The husband wore the white shirt and black waistcoat that had seemed his trademark in the photographs; he stood square-on, with all the thickset grandeur of medieval Polish kings in church murals. His wife wore an intricately embroidered blouse and skirt, and, though she seemed equally eternal, she held on with one hand to a concrete tree trunk in a gesture that gave her the slightest hint of sensuous abandon. Under their feet, on a ground of heather and poppies, was a miniature of their house, whose details Katya had carefully noted; idealized but instantly recognizable, it was flanked, on one side, by a representation of two of the matching coffee cups they had drunk from in the house and, on the other, by a tenderly satirical portrait of the family dog. Around this tableau was a bright floral border for which Katya used the distinctive gold thread of traditional Silesian embroidery.

The old woman was bemused.

'Not so traditional as I'd hoped,' she frowned. 'And it doesn't really look like me. I'm old now, I don't wear colours like that anymore! But the work is good,' she allowed. 'Should be warm in the winter.'

She paid the money humourlessly, and they departed.

It was only several weeks later that rumours started to filter back to Katya and her mother about the fate of the new bed cover. The old woman had been talking: for had her anniversary not marked the beginning of a new kind of deep, untroubled sleep for her and her husband, had they not begun to enjoy nights of deep, shared restfulness, free of the anxious waking and perpetual monitoring of bladders that had gone before; had they not even, she let the community surmise, discovered once again a marital sensuality that they had both, quite definitively, consigned to the past? People talked, in the tea shops of Katowice, about Katya's bed cover and its therapeutic effects; and it was not long before there were orders for many more.

Bed covers became the mainstay of their dressmaking business. They turned down other work and concentrated only on this speciality, for which they began to charge several hundred zloty a time. Customers came with the full knowledge that they were buying more than simply a household accessory: their briefings with the young Katya were more like therapy sessions, in which they poured out their lives and she listened, sagely and without comment. Her covers never failed to heal deep and sometimes undiscerned problems in those they kept warm at night: they brought relief to insomniacs, rest and recovery to the chronically sick, tenderness and love to estranged married couples, a new sense of possibility to the very old – and offspring to those who had long considered themselves infertile.

Katya's parents looked on with admiration at what their introspective daughter was capable of. But it was also with some disquiet; for her uncanny ability, at such a young age, to bring bodily ease to complete strangers was only another sign of how little they truly understood her. And, since they felt some timidity about discussing their feelings with her, they could only watch quietly, and keep these things in their hearts.

One day, when Katya was about eighteen years old, she found herself alone in the house and began to look idly through her parents' belongings. In the back of a cupboard she found a cardboard box with holes cut roughly in its sides. She opened it and found the following note:

> we do not want her
> Name KATYA.
> if you have money & feel to take care

The box and the note told the whole story; she did not need any further clarification. She was not upset, for the note only confirmed what she had always felt, and it now provided justification for these feelings.

Without revealing her discovery to her parents, she announced, a few days later, that she was moving to Warsaw. They were sad that she wished to leave them, and anxious about what would happen to her in a city of whose ways all of them were ignorant; but, as usual, they felt unable to voice these concerns to their self-contained daughter and, since she was now an adult and had a proven method of supporting herself, they could offer few counter-arguments. She finished her outstanding orders, packed her belongings – most of which were the tools and supplies of her trade – and her parents drove her silently to the train station. Her father carried her bags onto the train and put them up in the rack above the seat. Her mother embraced her and put into her hands a box of sandwiches, fruit, and chocolate. Katya climbed into the train and waved from the window, smiling affectionately and reassuringly as her mother tried not to weep. The train began to move and her parents walked with it for a moment, putting their hands to the glass and calling out unheard blessings, until it slid away, and she was gone.

Katya had saved some money, which she used to rent a small apartment in Mokotów. It was more than she could really afford, but she wanted to be in an area where people could pay well for her work. For a few days, she did nothing except explore the city: she looked at the opera house and the fancy shops; she walked in the Lazienki Park, where a pianist played Chopin nocturnes at the foot of the composer's statue on a Sunday morning; she bought cooking pots and coat hangers for her new home from roadside vendors; she wandered in the old city, and drank beer in cheap bars near the university.

Then it was time to turn to her business.

She had come with a list of people in Warsaw who might be able to help her in the early stages. She visited them and showed them what she was capable of, and in many cases they were happy to buy a few small items, or at least to mention her name to their friends. Boldly, she tripled the prices that her mother had charged in Katowice, but this seemed to be no problem. Soon she had a healthy catalogue of orders for blouses, cushion covers, and embroidered place mats.

Her business followed approximately the same course as it had before, but it took much less time and met with far more spectacular success. Soon Warsaw, too, was hooked on her bed covers, and gloating whispers travelled the city, as more and more people found their bodily deficiencies and mental anxieties soothed by Katya's glorious productions. Her prices crept up and up; for orders were coming in faster than she could fulfil them and her time was completely taken up. She moved into another apartment in the same block, one that had an extra room: it was less time-consuming to receive customers than to visit their houses – and anyway, she was finding herself in increasing need of a consulting room, for Warsaw people were much more expansive about their problems than their Katowice cousins, and they sometimes spent many hours trying to ensure that she understood. They saw this initial session of self-examination and confession as just one of the benefits included in the increasingly high price that they paid for Katya's bed covers.

The story she heard most often was that of childlessness. Having grown up surrounded by a dense cage of euphemistically-phrased warnings that sex with men would lead instantly to pregnancy and eternal shame, she had imagined that things were automatic and instant – and was surprised at how difficult they were in reality. She listened as men and women, many of whom had been her present age when she was born, listed for her every kind of intimate problem – excessive fatigue and consequent sexual apathy, vaginal dryness, low sperm counts, men who could not reach orgasm, women whose fertility was declining with age – and a number of solemnly-held superstitions: 'My penis is just too small' or (whispered) 'I think my uterus is allergic to semen!' She heard of baroque techniques employed before, during, or after sex in order to enhance its procreative effects, and to all this she listened with a silent gravitas that assured her customers they were spending their money well.

But her bed covers did not become less effective in the face of such intractable problems; in fact, the more she pursued her craft the more finely-tuned her products became to those they were intended for. Her clients were amazed by the effects they had in their lives: they felt rejuvenated, released, newly joyful, lightened . . . They told their friends about her with the zeal of religious converts – and Katya began to make a good living.

Sometimes she would call her parents to tell them how everything was; and they were proud.

One day she went into a supermarket to buy some things she needed: stockings, a hammer and nails, a carving knife. As she was paying she became transfixed by the cashier. He was pale-skinned and dark-haired, and had an insouciant beauty that instantly and quite unexpectedly crushed Katya's heart; and his hands, as he guided the carving knife into a bag, were gorgeous things. Katya watched him through a daze of admiration; she heard the words,

'Forty-six zloty ninety-seven.'

She handed over a fifty zloty note and watched as one of those hands picked out the change from the cash register. It drew close to her own and there was the slightest brush as coins passed from one to the other. Katya was strangled. She started to go and then turned back:

'Do you want to go dancing?' she murmured.

The boy was a little surprised.

'Sure. I mean – we could.'

'When's your day off?'

'Sunday.'

'Let's go on Saturday night.'

'OK.'

'What's your name?'

'Piotr.'

'Give me your number. I'll call you.'

They met that Saturday. Katya did not really know any dancing places, and asked Piotr for advice. He suggested an underground bar near the station. They met at the door and shook hands. Katya was nervous, and stared wordlessly.

'Shall we go in?' asked Piotr.

They went down the stairs. There were so many people and under the low brick ceilings the heat accumulated. Their clothes were too much, so they found a corner to deposit jackets and sweaters and Piotr's T-shirted body glowed under the blue light. They bought beer, tried to find space to stand: it was a maze of rooms linked by arched doorways and everywhere jostling people danced shoulder to shoulder. The music was like the labour pain before the birth of a glistening new city; and it carved up their insides with thrilling sounds of the future. Katya followed Piotr, who knew how to find paths through the crowd, and though they could not speak under the massive clamour of it all there was in their movements a quiet togetherness that made Katya weightless and happy. A band came on; they were scarcely older than her and they mixed English with their Polish, they made you feel like Warsaw was the navel of the earth; the singers were a boy and a girl who taunted the crowd for their ignorance, they launched words at each other with dizzying speed and ballistic precision, it was a light-speed poetry that danced mockingly around the whirring beat like a champion boxer, they used the tiniest gaps in each other's speech to insert new thoughts, new things; the crouching roof disappeared and the night sky was blown away, as everything was filled with philosophy and fearlessness.

There was a boy who danced, and Katya and Piotr watched him. His head was at his knees and his body was clenched into a ball; it twitched and vibrated with every spasm of the beat, it was like a single organ thrown into crisis by the electrical impulses of the music, and it leapt and shook and threw out punches in every direction. It had become pure flesh-for-sound.

The song finished and he became man again, applauding and covered in sweat. He saw them watching, and smiled. He said to Katya, in the ceasefire between songs, 'Cool birthmark', and put his tongue on it lingeringly. Katya stuck out her own tongue in mock disgust; Piotr laughed. The music began again and he tried to draw them in to his dancing but they could not match him. It drew late; and they left.

Outside they carried their coats, for the cool night felt good on their skin. The ringing in their ears shut out the soundtrack of the city and made it seem distant and unreal. Piotr was flushed and smiling from the evening.

Katya turned to him.

'Bye. It was nice.'

'Yes. Bye.'

Katya took his arm and kissed him on the cheek for a long time. Then they separated.

Afterwards, Katya was not sure how she felt about that kiss. It was not that it had not been born out of ardent desire; it is not that she had not, in that moment, poured through her lips all the torrent of her tenderness – for all these things were true. It was that there was another part of her that was also involved in the kiss, a part that was significantly less spontaneous, that kissed not like a lover but like a stethoscope. She had kissed Piotr not merely to kiss him but also to *measure* him, in the same way that she took the measure of her clients.

She was not sure if she should make use of the knowledge she had acquired in this way. It seemed cold and treacherous in this new realm she was entering that she could only describe as – she said the word out loud to see if it matched what she was feeling – Love. But why, she reasoned with herself, would she approach love with less than the full complement of her self?

Before long, she had seduced the adorable but aimless Piotr, and they became constant companions. They made each other very happy; and soon they began to share an apartment. They liked to explore together what lay just on the other side of the lives they had led up to that point: French films, the old city at 4.30 a.m., a book about the history of torture, modern art, sushi (good) and Long Island iced teas (bad). When she was alone, Katya sometimes caught herself smiling broadly with contentment. She could not think of anything else she wanted from life.

Some time went by in this way, and one day a woman whom Katya had never seen before came to see her.

She was not old – she was not yet fifty, and her manner was much younger than that – and yet her head was crowned with a mass of white hair. She wore half-moon glasses, and carried a large bunch of keys that she placed on the table between them. The key ring was an eyeball that continued gyrating inside its little glass globe as they spoke.

'My name is Magda. For some time now I have been deeply interested in your work. I have seen what an impact you have had on the people of Warsaw. Very few ever attain this level of insight into the workings of other people's minds. And you are so young – it is a rare thing indeed. I am full of admiration.'

'Thank you.'

'But your youth also works against you. Your gift is greater than your understanding of how to use it. You have reached an infantile equilibrium: you make people feel good, and you receive approval and prestige. No doubt this has served you well up to now: you have refined your skills and found a place for yourself in this city. But it is time to grow up, Katya! Will you always be remembered as a purveyor of fine home furnishings? It would be a waste of everything you are. It is time to leave behind your bedspreads and apply yourself more deeply to the drama of the human soul.

'There is no doubt, Katya, about your insight. The question you face is: How will you live up to it? You possess the rare gift of grasping certain truths about the world; but what part of yourself will you unleash in response? Will you continue on this anaesthetic path, solving all pain and insecurity with comfortable bedding and mental oblivion? Did you receive your understanding in order to become a soporific for the world? It's not good enough, Katya.'

She looked at her searchingly; she reached out and put her finger on Katya's birthmark for a moment, contemplatively.

'Happiness is not about the absence of pain. Rather, the search for a life without pain requires a person to forsake happiness. Nothing can come out of oblivion, for it lies next to death. You, who understand the script of human life in all its complexity, should not be cheating people with your promise of nothing! You must turn your knowledge back upon them, so the impact is like a train hitting a wall! You must *wake people up*, with new pain and uncanny pleasure, with a world they do not know, though it is all around them. With the similarity of things they always thought were diametrically opposed.'

Katya was staring at the table.

'Don't worry. I will help you. Come and see me at this address. The day after tomorrow, 3 p.m. Don't be late. Things will become clear.'

Katya took the address from her. Magda smiled.

She kissed her as she left, and in the second that their faces touched, Katya felt rushing inside her a coldness that she had never felt before.

Two days later, Katya threaded her way quickly among the churches and chocolate-box houses of the old city until she came to the jewellery boutique that was her landmark. She rang the bell to the basement and a buzzer sounded; she pushed the door and walked down a spiral staircase so dark she had to feel her way. It opened out into a small hallway lit with a dim green bulb where there was a large door of weathered steel. Here, too, she rang, and an eye shutter opened in the door; the eyeball tilted up and down unblinkingly, and the door was opened in a fusillade of bolts. A woman stood silhouetted in the opening. She wore thigh-high vinyl boots with six-inch heels that sent her towering over Katya, and the rest of her was completely encased in black leather except for her face, which was intelligent and heavily made-up, and her two large white breasts, which glowed preternaturally under a spotlight.

'My name is Katya. I've come to see Magda?'

'I know. You're late. Eryk: please take our guest to the booth. Quickly!'

The dwarfish Eryk ran nimbly ahead of Katya through a number of low-arched corridors lit only here and there. She followed, disorientated and stooping, there were rusty chains and hooks set into the wall, she could only just catch sight of Eryk around one corner before he disappeared round the next – and then their chase was ended and he was standing to attention, holding open a small door. She bent under the doorway and found herself in a cupboard. There was an old wooden chair; she sat down with barely enough room for her legs, and he closed the door behind her. There was total darkness; then she realized that the wall had glowing spyholes in it. She looked through and saw a large, empty room. At one end was a high dais on which was built a magnificent tent of red velvet, closed on all four sides. Below this was a steel capstan mounted on a thick shaft set into the floor. All around the room were large video screens on which could be seen, in huge format, the glower of Magda's face, severe in dark make-up. As Katya watched, a door opened on the other side of the room and a man was thrown bodily inside by two masked women.

And lo! the man is most piteously garb'd, for his shirt is rent and about his loins he wears but a wretched length of cloth. He scrambles up! and is straightway transfixed by the beams of divers lights that blaze from all corners of the room. See his blindness! for his orbs are seared, and the glare of those lamps is to him like the darkness of deepest night; see him shrink under the fiery rays while the two women circle him like Furies, hissing insults unseen that keep him lurching from left to right like a chain'd and blinded bear. 'Silence!' cries the figure in the tent; and her many sisters on the walls, whose likeness one to the next bespeaks exceeding fidelity to their parentage, speak out in unison like a many-throated chorus of joint will. Dissent flees pell-mell before so imperious a decree, and there is instant silence in the room –

> *Save timid Katya's dark, concealéd breath*
> *Whose rushing sighs are like th'enragéd wind!*

The several voices ring out once again:
  'How comest thou before us, slave? Hast thou come to make thy confession?'
  The man draws himself upright before the blind tent's vermilion walls, and Katya trembles with his pride.
  'I come before you as no slave but as a free man. I have no guilt to confess.'
  See! how the mask'd women turn upon him with their staffs and whips, and their wrath is terrible to behold. In the darkness of her hiding place Katya is much amaz'd, for she sees the bloody vengeance of the leather upon his back (whose cotton armour is breached with passing ease) and she needs must entreat her voice be still.
  'Thou mistak'st thyself, slave. Thou wilt see how small a thing it is to pluck from a man his freedom, his innocence, and his name.'
  See how the man, under the dreadful assault, lies already weak and

bloody on the ground! and see how Katya shudders at what worser punishments lie in store.

'Stand and remove these stain'd and tattered rags. Think'st thou such sickly gauze is competent to conceal th'iniquity of thy rank nature? Remove them, we say!'

The man casts aside his vestments and stands full naked in the light, and to Katya the shapeliness of his body is lovely as a golden goblet. But the Queen and her faithful sisters continue in their wrath: see how they pour scorn and hatred on the very seat of his manhood!

'We are not new-born to majesty, slave: we have known the minds of degenerates. We know how ye touch yourselves and entertain merry thoughts of inseminating women. Thou art not fit to appear before us thus. Fair ladies – bring the cage. Cover up the sagging pulp the cur carries between its legs for we are sickened with its aspect.'

And lo! it seems that the wild and teeming thoughts of Katya's heart do burst the jealous dome of her chamber and discover the very encrusted heavens –

'Knowest thou, slave, how old we are?'

'No. I know not.'

'We have walked the earth for ten score years. Before thy vile life was e'er foreseen, we had already watched countless generations limp dribbling to their ends. And yet our girlish beauty remains untarnish'd, our ancient body is like to a morning bloom. Is this not passing strange?'

'It is strange, no doubt.'

'And canst thou, slave, surpassing th'ignorance of thy estate, unfold the cunning of this mystery?'

'I cannot.'

'Then hear this, and know thy fate. In the womanly perfection of our visage lie interred the muscular endeavours of loathsome criminals, whose sweaty deaths have been our eternal life. Thou, slave, will be the next to offer up thy manly forces at the altar of our feminine youth. This is the fitting punishment for thy parlous crimes. We, whom thou hast conspir'd to lessen, shall at last be magnified by thy lessening.'

– and in the dizzy expanse of her chamber, like dramas unfold in Katya's head, panelling the velvet skies with majestic and extravagant scenes, tumbling over each other with great heroes and foul crimes and Man in all his depths and heights!

But see now! how the man is lashed to the capstan and forced to push against its steely bulk, and see how Katya marvels at the vicious onslaught of the women who flog his naked back! He labours at the obstinate wheel that shrewdly resists his groaning travails; but with the persuasion of the whip he finds a greater strength, and makes its mass to turn.

'It is time for thee to die. Let the last page of thy life's memories be written, and let it not be like to its ignoble predecessors. Now read thou in our fair and queenly face the clear and accurate character of our victory over thy crimes – and over pale and envious death.'

Oh wond'rous sight! as the curtains ope as if by magic and there on high sits the Queen in bejewell'd splendour, looking down with eyes of furious lightning upon the guilty misery of the slave! Words cannot come near her beauty, nor even can the procession of her glassy siblings give prophecy of her proud and potent majesty. The hall is filled with her light and all living things must prostrate themselves before it.

'Aye me!' cries the slave, who surrenders to his horrible and well-deservéd death.

[*Dies.*]

And in her hidden closet, rapt with emotion, the fair and patient Katya swoons, and falls incapable to the floor.

When Katya opened her eyes, she was lying on a narrow couch looking up at rows of hooked gynaecological instruments suspended above her head. She moaned with confusion.

'Welcome to the land of the living – at last,' murmured Magda while she removed her make-up.

Katya said nothing. Extravagant scenes began to float back into her dizzy head.

'Did he really – die?' she asked.

'Don't be ridiculous. He's just left. On his way back to the office. Five thousand zloty worse off than when he arrived, mind. We don't come cheap. But men like that can pay anything you ask.'

Magda had returned to her slimline contemporary self, and her endless costume of red damask hung collapsed on the wall. On the floor was the self-standing cage of hoops to which the dress had owed its miraculous shape.

'What did you think of the show?'

'It was fantastic,' said Katya dreamily. '*You* were fantastic.'

Katya became a valuable addition to Magda's dungeon. She threw herself into her work with an enthusiasm and vigour she had not felt for some time, absorbing quickly from Magda her considerable store of professional expertise and assisting her in all aspects of the enterprise. Even her dressmaking skills found a fresh lease of life as she began to conceive new, unearthly characters with which to people their underground world, and sewed startling, outlandish costumes. Her intuitive grasp of the frailties and desires of their clients allowed her to dream up hitherto untried forms of excess that always managed to induce in them the most heady flights of ecstasy, and her sessions became much prized among the male Warsaw elite. It was not long before she was fit to handle clients without Magda's supervision, and she became a full partner in her astonishingly lucrative business.

She became increasingly impatient with her life with Piotr, who, for his part, still entertained a love for her almost like an addiction. In part, her frustration had to do simply with the growing discrepancy between their lifestyles: Piotr still spent his days at the checkout counter at Auchan, an existence that drained him and gave him little financial reward, while Katya, on the other hand, had become wealthy and was, in her dungeon, swept up in an intensity of the emotions that made her free evenings of television and pizza with the mild-mannered Piotr seem maddeningly vacant. But it was more than this; for Katya was now meeting men of immense wealth and influence, and was developing a creeping dependency on this new-found familiarity with power that was perhaps not significantly less obsessive than their dependency on her. Two of her clients, in particular, known (in the maniacally secretive codes of the dungeon) as 'K' and 'W', began to creep in among her thoughts.

K was the first client that Magda entrusted wholly to Katya's ministrations.

'This man has specifically asked for you, Katya, but I have to confess a certain anxiety about it. You will find him a challenge. You have great ability, but you are still very young, and it's possible that he will expose the limits of your youth. He is a big man, Katya, the father of them all. You never read about him in the newspapers, but he runs half our industry and controls half our politicians. It will not be easy for you to dominate his personality and I am fearful of how you would respond to such a scenario – an unprecedented one for you. Please remember: we are professionals. We may be dealing with the deepest emotions of our clients but *we* are not emotionally involved.'

Katya paid little attention to Magda's warnings, and was therefore taken aback when K arrived at the dungeon and his presence almost knocked her off her feet.

He was discreet and soft-spoken, yet there seemed to be within him something of outsized proportions that caused Katya, for the first time in her life, to doubt her own strength. And indeed, her customary intuitions, that gave her such a clear and immediate sense of those around her, seemed to have broken down in his presence – it was as if he had been forewarned of her encroaching and had closed the way with imposing walls that her mind could not scale. It was a demeaning, impotent realization: she became scattered and infantile. The elaborate session that she had painstakingly prepared from the profile given her by Magda (in which K was to be humiliated and tortured by the weird and cackling members of some infernal board of directors) was not a success.

'Let's try again,' said K to her as he left. 'I know you can do better than that.'

Afterwards, she could not stop thinking about K. She was fascinated by him, desperately desired his approval; and his awareness of her failure plagued her. She lay in bed at night thinking with both dread and excitement of their next meeting. She planned meticulously and went over every element again and again in her mind: *this* visit would make up for the flatness of their earlier encounter with an acute drama that would subject him to an intensity of experience he would never forget, and establish her beyond doubt as the dominant member of the pair.

It did not happen.

Instead, he questioned her for two hours. He asked about every detail of her life – her opinions about Polish politics, whether her birthmark had been significant in determining the course of her life, her feelings on arriving in Warsaw, her relationship to the taboo, how she felt about money, responsibility or received wisdom, the nature of her love for Piotr, how she visualized the unknown parents who had abandoned her so long ago, what kind of changes happened in her when she was completely alone and unobserved . . . Against her better instincts, and in contravention of all the most basic rules that Magda had laid down, Katya abandoned her masks and roles and gave herself up to his interrogation earnestly and with absolute seriousness. It was a joy, in fact, to do so; for this man could find his way around her soul in a way that no one else had ever done.

'You should be paying *me* for this,' he smiled as he departed.

He began to come more frequently and, as time went on, he began to talk more about himself. His life seemed to be a paragon of perfection: he had a beautiful wife, whom he adored, and three loving and talented children – the eldest of whom, in fact, was a young woman of Katya's age ('It's funny how you remind me of her'). Houses all over the world, endless international travel, close friendships with several world leaders and prominent film stars, a close involvement in virtually every decision with any significant effect on the future of the Polish economy – all of this dazzled Katya utterly.

But it had another, more curious, effect on her that even she was at a loss to explain. As she learned more about him, as he began to occupy a basic place in her life, as the barriers between their two worlds successively fell and the substance of those separate realms began to mingle and give rise to new things, she began to be obsessed with the fantasy of bearing a child by him.

It stole up on her without warning; for she had never seriously thought about having a child before. Nothing that had ever passed between her and Piotr had caused her to consider such a thing. And yet the intense yearning she now felt was not love for K (though perhaps she did also love him) nor mere sexual desire (though certainly there was that): what had captured her spirit was the fact of his overwhelming *paternity*, a force that engendered within her – to which she could find no other response than – a corresponding desire for motherhood.

As time went by, Katya became less and less inclined to organize for K the kind of tableaux of humiliation that he had specified as his taste and for which he was ostensibly paying. Sometimes he seemed to become irritated with her – 'Why do you assume each time all we're going to do is talk? Do you think you're my therapist or something?' But it seemed to be an empty protest for he, too, seemed to be most content in conversation. They talked endlessly, and with an openness that continually enthralled Katya.

But she tried to find paths of subterfuge through this landscape of candour; for she wanted very much to know how she could conspire to realize the fantasy K had aroused in her, and of which he seemed to have no idea.

'Why do you come here?' she asked. 'Your life seems so full, so perfect, so busy. You pay me large amounts of money – for what? To sit and talk to someone your daughter's age. I don't understand why you come.'

He smiled.

'My life *is* all those things. But there is a price to power. The truth is that I can trust no one. My friends, my business associates, even my family – there are always things I have that these people might want to take away; every conversation is an occasion for them to extract information or opinions that could later be used to discredit me. It is easier, in my position, to pay someone to have conversations with me. Someone I will never have any contact with in the rest of my life and who will never believe that she can make any demands on me, or that our relationship is more than convenience. Someone who will be utterly professional about things. Whose discretion is assured.'

'How do you know I will be discreet?'

'I know you will. I know you more than you think.'

'What about your wife? Can't you talk to her?'

'Of course. And I do. But even she is part of all this. My world. I can't tell her everything.'

'Do you tell her you come to see me?'

'No.'

Katya smiled mischievously.

'Does she still give you everything you need? I mean – sex.'

'Don't worry. We have no problems as far as that's concerned.'

'Are you faithful to her?'

'The most important principle in my life. She and I belong together. I will never be unfaithful to her.'

So Katya waited for an opportunity.

Meanwhile, in order to show K – and, perhaps, herself – just how professionally she viewed their relationship, she insisted on a level of fastidiousness in their financial dealings to which none of her other clients were subject.

W, who kept his identity absolutely secret, though he described himself as a celebrated surgeon, was another client who expressly asked for Katya's services. In his initial meeting with Magda in which he described what he was looking for, he told her straight out that *she* was too old; he wanted her partner, the 'ripe young thing'. Magda disliked his vulgarity, and outlined emphatically the rules of conduct expected from all clients. She told Katya,

'Be very vigilant with this man. The first abuse, and he never sets foot in here again.'

Unlike K, W was an aloof and distant figure. He always came to the dungeon wearing a mask that obscured his face entirely and which he forbade Katya to touch. And his visits had nothing of the personal about them: they were simple quests for pure, unsophisticated pain. There was no psychological make-believe, no dressing up, no conversation.

At first Katya held back from the extremes of violence that W seemed to be willing her to, and he began to mock her.

'Are you afraid of making me cry? Afraid you'll make ugly marks on my body? Maybe you're in the wrong job, baby. Try again.'

She began to accustom herself to his demands, and to unleash upon him all the brutality she could find within herself. She would hang him by his feet and beat him with rods and whips until his flesh was mangled

316

and bloody and he cried out in agony. She applied red hot steel to the sensitive parts of his body so the chamber filled up with the stench of burning skin. She clamped him to a rack and stretched him until she could hear the dislocations of his limbs and spine.

Curiously, though W would end his sessions with injuries that were sometimes truly severe, though his limbs were sometimes so horribly wrenched that he could hardly stand to dress himself – in spite of this, he would always return one week later as if nothing had happened, his body completely pristine.

This gave Katya a growing sense of the inconsequentiality of the violence she wrought upon him. Increasingly, she would abandon during his sessions every construct of her everyday life – common sense, vaguely held moral precepts, all the normal constraints upon thought and behaviour – and would allow herself to enter a state of ecstatic, unselfconscious ferocity, in which W was less than an animal, a mere piece of insensate flesh.

One day, W lay bound to a wooden bench, and she began to pierce his thigh with the point of a sword. She became fascinated by the sight of the steel entering his leg: the world around the livid gash melted away and she became entranced with this sheathing of metal in flesh. She pushed further and further, and the sword sank right into W's thigh until it struck the wood of the bench below – and she withdrew it suddenly, shocked at what she had allowed herself to do.

She stared helplessly at the deep wound she had caused, but, as she watched, it healed miraculously, until no trace remained.

She looked at him in astonishment, and he stared fixedly back at her.

'I think you went too far,' he said.

She untied him in shame, and he left.

He returned a few days later.

'I suppose you think you are owed an explanation for what happened,' he said. 'As if I were the one who lost all perspective on things, lost control of myself. I think you should consider what happened within yourself at that moment.'

He sat on the same wooden bench, swinging his legs. He wore an immaculate pinstriped suit which clashed strangely with his leather mask.

'Nevertheless, I will give you a hint of what happened to my leg because I think you are the sort of person who might not be adversely affected by this knowledge, and it may even help you in mysterious ways . . .

'I am a surgeon. The daily currency of my life is the degeneration and regeneration of bodies. Perhaps it is merely the result of the fact that I spend more time reflecting on these processes than other people; I have sought to harness them, consciously or otherwise, to ensure the rapid healing of patients, have learned to become sensitive to elusive indicators of success and failure that for many people would belong to the realm of pure mysticism. But after a while, when certain correlations hold true again and again, you can no longer dismiss them: you have to start taking note, looking for more such correlations – and what emerges is a *discipline*. I have committed myself to this discipline with a fervour that has rarely been seen in human history; I have acquired a body of knowledge that you could not begin to imagine, that most of my colleagues could not imagine. And in the process, I have unlocked secrets of life and death that human beings have longed to understand since the beginning of time. *Look at me!*' – he jumped from the bench and waved his hands as he talked – 'No mysteries of the body can elude me any more: I have surpassed the human condition. I can raise my own body to life, I can transform its substance utterly. I can make myself more like you than you are yourself; I can turn you into my twin. Is it not marvellous? I am become like a god, Katya: I have forgotten entirely what it feels like to live with all the petty fears that normal human beings have – I am above everyone, I despise everyone. When you are beyond death you quickly become filled with loathing for the lives of all these miserable, cowering, reproducing humans.'

His excitement had taken him over, as if it were the first time he was making this confession. He calmed himself and came to sit close to Katya.

'I can tell you this: you will never again look upon someone like me. If ever you had a need to make use of such power as I have, you should think about it now. The opportunity will not present itself again.'

He looked at her significantly, and she started to see what he meant.

'Yes.' She nodded slowly. 'I will think about it. You will be coming back?'

318

'Yes, yes. I'll be back in a few days.'

An amazing scenario began to form in her head; a conspiracy that was almost unimaginable.

For the next few days, Katya thought about nothing except her plan. She told no one about it, least of all Piotr, who wondered what new thing had come into her life to take her away from him so completely. In secret, she wrote down everything she thought, for she realized all the risks of submitting an insufficiently watertight wish to a power as huge and maniacal as W's. The scheme was mad but thrilling, and she was filled with excitement.

W returned.

'So: have you thought more about our conversation of the other day?'

'I have.'

'And what is it that you would like to ask for?'

Katya had rehearsed the moment many times.

'Listen carefully, for the scenario is complicated. There is a man I know in a professional capacity. For reasons that shall remain my own, I wish him to father my child. He is married, and in the normal course of events I can have no expectation of asking such a thing of him. He would lose all respect for me if I were to try to do so, and would probably break off contact. My request is therefore this: I would like you to turn me into his wife. For one night. I have written out the following conditions to this wish: you must be in a position to fulfil all conditions, otherwise we cannot go ahead.'

W smiled.

1. The transformation will last from 8 p.m. next Saturday night until 8 a.m. the next morning.
2. During the transformation this man will not be able to distinguish me from his wife.
3. When he and I make love, *I must fall pregnant.*
4. Only the appearance of my body will be transformed. My consciousness as myself will remain undisturbed

throughout this process and, of course, the child I will conceive will remain with me thereafter.

5. During the period of this transformation, the woman whose form I am taking must not be present. I will take her place wherever she happens to be at that moment and she will cease to be there. You will have to find some way of achieving this.

6. After the transformation, everything will be restored to normal. I will be myself in every way, and so will his wife. She will have no memory of her absence.

'Those are the conditions. Can you do this for me?'

'Of course I can. And more. Consider it done.'

Katya flushed. W continued,

'And what will you pay me?'

'Name your price. I will give anything.'

'I have no need of money, if that is what you mean. No: let's make it more fun than that.'

He considered for a while, tapping the mask where it covered his lips.

'Let's make it like a game. If you are able to seduce this man, then you pay me nothing. You have won. But if you are not, then you make me the gift of your fertility.'

'My *fertility*? What would you want with that?'

'That's not your business. The fertility of a young woman is a grandiose force for which I have many secret uses. Will you play or not?'

'This is a heavy price. Can't we think of something else.'

'No. There isn't anything else you could give me that I want.'

'I need some time to consider. Can I call you on Saturday morning?'

'I don't let anyone have my number. Give me yours, and I will call you.'

'You promise?'

'I promise.'

She had an appointment with K. She asked him about his weekend.

'So what does a man like you get up to on a Saturday night? This Saturday night, for instance.'

'Oh – nothing. I'm at home.'

'A rare evening in! With the family. Talk to the kids. Time to make love to your wife, perhaps?'

'Possibly.' He looked away. 'Probably.'

W called as promised on Saturday morning.

'Well?'

'Let's go ahead as planned.' And, with a final flourish, 'You forget – I too have certain – powers – to ensure things go my way.'

It was a summer day, and the high midday sun streamed gaily through the windows of Katya's apartment. She had deliberately chosen a weekend when Piotr was away so that her whole scheme could pass off without disturbance; and it was good to have the day to herself in the empty house.

She pictured K, and he appeared to her as a lover: she caressed with her mind his arms and his face, she imagined his eyes on her skin and his voice in her hair. There was so much of the day still to go! and she put on music, laid out for herself an elaborate lunch – caviar, meats, pâté; avocados, asparagus, and cherries; cheeses, bread, and wine – which she ate slowly and with concentration. How would it be to spend a night as the wife of such a man? There would certainly be a grand meal served by exquisitely mannered servants; there would be pianos and paintings and fine things all around, and she would be wearing the stylish homewear of a society lady. There would be the three children who would tell lively stories around the table of their charmed lives, who at 11 p.m. would go out dressed like fashion models in separate Mercedes to meet their friends ... And she would be alone with him and they would drink wine together; they would become intoxicated with the night, he would be aroused by the beauty of his wife that tonight was tinged with some elusive exotic presence, a virgin breathlessness, a memory of unwearied youth. How he would make love to her! – even now the blood rushed in her cheeks and she longed for the moment – in what glory would her child be conceived, and how strange and melancholy it was that *he* would never know.

She finished eating, and still the day seemed to be at its peak. She took a long bath; she wanted to clean her body and make it beautiful, with the full knowledge that she would be leaving this one behind for another, and inheriting the ablutions of some other, more luxurious, hand than her own. Still: she washed her hair and trimmed her nails, she soothed herself with Lancôme creams and meditatively donned her most beautiful La Senza lingerie. The day was ending, and she put on a blue cocktail dress and painted her face artfully with dramatic make-up.

The phone rang. It was W.

'It's seven-thirty. Are you ready?'

'Yes. I am.'

'You're sure about this?'

'I'm sure. What about you? Are *you* ready? Is everything going to happen as we agreed?'

'Don't worry about that. Good luck.'

'Thank you. Good bye.'

She put on her favourite shoes and sat down on the sofa. Time was moving very slowly, and she turned on the television to keep her mind occupied. She traversed news and game shows and music videos and happened upon a nature documentary in which giant turtles were slowly and solemnly mating by the ocean. The male had hoisted himself up on the dome of the female's shell and they lay stacked and alone together in the vast wet sand as the waves washed calmly on the shore. The female stroked the ground rhythmically with her flippers, and in her unblinking enamel eyes Katya thought she could see ardour.

The clock struck eight.

There was only the slightest electrical interruption in her consciousness, and she was suddenly lying on a bed in another place.

Her body ached and felt heavy, and there was an eerie ringing in her ears. She looked down at herself. Her hands were pale and wrinkled, her legs unhealthily spindly. She was wearing a limp, yellowed night-dress patterned with miserable old-fashioned flowers, and the bed looked as if she had been lying in it for days. Her eyes burned.

'Have I just walked in on a hangover?' thought Katya.

It took her some concentration to work out how to move. She eased her legs off the bed and tried to stand. Something was certainly wrong: she felt drowsy and off-balance. Holding onto the wall, she made her way past the foot of the bed and into the en suite bathroom. She looked in the mirror, and hissed with horror.

She looked old, and her face was bloated and featureless. Her thin brown hair was matted against the sides of her head, and she had a pronounced shake. She looked like a wild recluse.

'What have I done?' moaned Katya. 'What have I done?'

She abandoned her reflection. She turned on the shower, took off her clothes, and stepped in under the water. She cleaned her body that felt shrunken under her hands, and washed her hair several times. It helped clear her mind, too: she began to think more lucidly and to move with greater ease.

She dried herself and brushed her hair. She found clothes in the cupboards – beautiful, fabulous clothes through which she searched for a long time to find the right thing: she settled on a long pink dress that flattered her shape and made her look more healthy and alive; she matched it with elegant cream shoes and a necklace with an enormous diamond that hung prettily in the cleft of the neckline. She found whole untouched sets of beautiful make-up and tried, not without a sense of desperation, to restore this face that seemed to have been so abused.

After a while, it was done. Katya wanted to cry when she looked at herself, for she still looked painfully sick and, try as she might, she could not completely control her shaking – but there was nothing else she could do. She gathered herself, and opened the bedroom door.

The house, it was clear, was built on an enormous scale. The bedroom opened onto a corridor that seemed to have hallways at either end; she decided on one direction and walked slowly and concentratedly on her high heels until the corridor opened out and there were more corridors and a generous sweeping staircase going down to the ground floor.

Steadying herself with the banister, she made her way down the wooden stairs that led to a grandiose entrance hall, decorated with several life-sized marble nudes and dominated by a large grandfather clock. As she reached the foot of the stairs, a hulking man in ill-fitting blazer and tie emerged from a room carrying a tray. He was startled to see her.

323

'Madam! What are you doing? I think it's best that you –'

He did not finish his sentence, but stood staring at the outfit she had put on. Katya spoke,

'Can you tell me where – where my husband is?'

'Yes. He's in here.' He gestured absentmindedly towards the door he had just closed behind him. 'In his study. But I don't think you should –'

Katya was already walking towards the entrance. She placed her hand on the door handle. The man said,

'You know how he is . . .'

She opened the door.

She was hit with a blast of deafening Led Zeppelin whose guttural guitars tore up the still air of the hallway. K was sitting at a wooden desk. The room was large, but lit only by a desk lamp at his elbow.

'My darling,' said K in surprise above the hard rock hubbub.

Katya switched on the lights and K sat up in his chair, blinking. He was very drunk. There were two bottles of Zubrówka by his glass.

'You look so –' he began, loudly.

'Can we turn down the music?'

K struggled with a remote control until the music abated somewhat.

'What is going on, my sweet?' asked K.

'Why do you ask me that? I've come down to see my husband. That is all.'

She walked over to him carefully and put her hand on his shoulder. He started out of his chair and surveyed her warily from the other side of it.

'I don't think you should be out like this. It's not good for you.' He was having trouble with his words.

'Why not? I am feeling so well tonight. Don't I look nice?'

'You may feel well, my darling, but you are not. I think you should go back to bed. This dressing up and everything – it's a bad symptom.'

'I want to spend some time with you. Wouldn't you like that?'

He took a sip of vodka.

'My darling – you are very tired. That is why you are acting like this.

324

You will feel better in the morning. Please go back to bed. Nothing bad will happen there.'

Katya sat down on the sofa and looked around her.

'Are we alone?'

'What do you mean?'

'I mean, where are the children? Have they left us alone?'

He stared at her, intense and drunken.

'What are you trying to say?' he said with icy patience. 'What exactly are you trying to say?'

Katya was alarmed.

'I don't know. I just wanted to know if –'

He was drumming on the remote control buttons with his thumb, and Led Zeppelin gave way to an untuned FM storm. His voice was dark.

'Don't you think it's rather fortunate we *couldn't* have kids?' He laughed wrily. 'I mean – look at you!'

He sat back down and unscrewed the top of the Zubrówka bottle. He poured himself another glass deliberately, and put the top back on the bottle. He stared into his vodka.

'As always, it's been lovely to see you, darling. Now I think it's time for you to go.'

As if at some unseen bidding, the door opened and the blazered man stood there, expectantly.

'Sławomir, please escort Madam back to her room and give her something to help her get over her insomnia.'

'Certainly, sir.'

He put his arm firmly around Katya and began to lead her out of the room. She threw off his grip.

'I am not going back to bed. I am going to spend the evening here. With you. Tell this man to leave!'

'You see what is happening already? Do you see? How many times do I have to tell you that I know best what is good for you. Sławomir –?'

He nodded towards the man's pocket. Sławomir took out from it a hypodermic needle.

'No!' screamed Katya. 'You can't do this.'

'You will feel so much better.'

Sławomir gripped her body and brought the needle close to her arm. Katya's terror exploded.

'I am not your wife!' she cried. 'I am not your wife! I am Katya!' She began to weep. 'Please don't do this.'

K stared at her wide-eyed, his face swirling like a tumult. He spoke with precision through it all.

'Now you have truly overstepped the mark, my darling. It is my fault: I should not have told you things that would interfere with your mind like this. In fact, I thought you were asleep when I told you. Nevertheless, I say it here and now: you will never mention her name again. Your lips should not speak her name. This time you have made me very angry. Very, very angry. Sławomir – please take her away.'

Sławomir stopped her screams with his enormous hand, lifted her small frame easily into his arms, and carried her out of the room. K called after her.

'Remember how much I love you. You are mine forever.'

Sławomir took her up the stairs, laid her on the bed, and held her down as he injected the contents of the needle into her arm. A cold current sighed into her bloodstream and Sławomir began to blur. He shut the door and something told her to stop him, but she heard the lock turn and her eyes closed and nothing seemed to matter anymore.

When she awoke, she was back in her own apartment, sitting on the sofa in her best clothes, and serenaded by the merry squawks of morning television. Everything came back to her. She did not move, but followed mindlessly the depressing antics of cartoon rabbits.

The phone rang. She let it persist for almost an eternity before deciding to pick up. It was W.

'I wanted to find out how things went last night.'

Katya spoke without intonation.

'It was fine. Successful.'

'Oh. That wasn't how it looked to me.'

There was a long silence. Katya said,

'You knew everything, you bastard. Even before it happened. I swear this: if I ever find out who you are, I will kill you.'

'That's not such an easy thing to do.'

'Don't underestimate me. It is my only wish right now.'

'You should be more prudent with your wishes. I thought you would have learned that by now.'

Katya put the phone down.

She went to the dungeon and saw Magda.

'Please inform K that I never want to see him again.'

'Why? What happened?'

'He has – abused his position. I can't say any more.'

'I think you at least owe me an explanation, Katya. K is one of our biggest clients. To lose him would be a blow.'

'I don't owe you anything!' Katya exclaimed. 'Just do it.'

Magda examined her curiously.

'Maybe you should take a short break. I warned you – some of these men are difficult to handle. It can be very draining.'

'I don't want to take a break.'

She walked out of the room.

At the end of the month, Katya's periods did not come. She went to see the doctor.

'It's all rather strange. You're not pregnant and you're perfectly healthy. I can't find any medical reason for this. But your hormone levels are abnormally low. I'm going to put you on the pill for the next month to see what happens. You can take a vitamin supplement too. These kinds of interruptions to your cycle can happen for a number of reasons. Stress, too much alcohol . . . Try and take a lot of rest. Come and see me in a month.'

Piotr could not understand Katya's sudden reclusiveness and depression, and he realized that he was not supposed to ask. He tried to cheer her up with little gifts – a pair of carved wooden earrings from a street market, a funny fridge magnet, the new CD of a singer she liked, a fountain pen – and with ambitious meals that he cooked systematically from Thai and Italian cookbooks especially acquired for the purpose. He asked her if she would like him to take her to Katowice to see her parents.

'No, Piotr. But it is a nice thought. You are very good to me.'
She stroked his face, and he smiled.

PART TWO

In Bytom, whence the baby Katya had been sent away in a box so many years before, time had done few favours for her reluctant father, Wiktor. His wife had left him not long after Katya's disappearance for a university graduate, a chemical engineer, who treated her well, loved children, and eventually took her away with him to a well-paid job in a Scottish agrochemical company. She chose well; for Wiktor was everything she thought him to be: selfish, dull, ineffectual, and, if he did not get his own way, violent.

Things did not improve in her absence. Over the years he did every kind of job imaginable, from shop assistant to decorator, from barman to worker in a food processing plant that opened nearby – but none of these jobs ever paid him very much, and he usually lost them within a few months. He never again had a serious relationship, and the warmth of his one-time drinking companions evaporated over time as they discovered how unwilling he was to reciprocate their kindnesses. He began to spend most of his spare time drinking in bus stops with teenagers, but this pastime became increasingly ridiculous as he grew older and began prematurely to lose both teeth and hair. By the time he reached his mid forties he was a bored and lonely man.

Then something happened to alter the direction of his life. After extensive surveying, a large mining conglomerate decided to reopen one of the collieries near his house and to expand it considerably – an expansion that would entail the destruction of the row of nineteenth-century German houses in which he lived. The house belonged to Wiktor outright since it had been left to him by his father, and he was therefore eligible for compensation. After several months of negotiations and deliberations, during which, every time he wanted to get to his front gate, Wiktor had to duck under a towering, technicolour, artist's impression of the state-of-the-art new mine, a settlement was agreed between the company and residents, and Wiktor suddenly had a sizeable amount of money.

The sum was not grand in comparison to the value of houses, but Wiktor did not have much of a head for such pragmatic concerns, and it was certainly more than he had ever possessed. He gave up his recently acquired job as a bus driver, moved his possessions out of his house, put those that he still valued into storage, and moved into a guesthouse for some time in order to consider what he would do.

For four full weeks, and with the exception of his evening walks, when he would check on the progress of the demolition, Wiktor hardly left the old rocking chair that sat in the middle of his small and gloomy room. He sat there all day, rocking back –

and forth

and back

and forth

– and he thought about his life.

At the end of this time, he sprung into action with a level of focus and resoluteness that he had perhaps never known before. He withdrew the entirety of the money he had received, paid his bills at the guesthouse, packed some clothes, and got on a bus to Katowice.

It proved surprisingly easy to find people who remembered the young Katya. Mention of her name and her unusual birthmark in a teashop one afternoon set a number of the customers talking: she had been a phenomenon some years ago with her interior decorating – and then she left. Went to Warsaw. He asked about her family: did anyone know where they were, did they all go to Warsaw together, was there anyone in Katowice who could give him more precise information? Heads shook in the face of such exorbitant demands. But it was a start; and when more days of such questioning gave him no additional information, he bought a train ticket to Warsaw, and departed.

He had never been to Warsaw before, and was intimidated when he arrived. There were places that looked too grand and too exotic for him to enter and the people he spoke to did not ever make him feel at ease. No one seemed to know anything about the city they lived in, at least not the kind of information he was looking for. He checked into a small hotel on the other side of the river where hardly anyone seemed to be

Polish at all, and their dark features, strange languages, and guerrilla-like outfits made him fear for his life every time he returned there at night.

For several days he searched in vain, asking shopkeepers and waitresses and policemen he met as he wandered, looking at photographs in local newspapers, and making it a point to visit every shop selling curtains and bedspreads in case she was working there. He did not like this place, and he found the whole process oppressive and disheartening. Late one evening, tired out with his search, he sat down in a bar and bought himself a cool beer.

He had not been sitting there very long when a man came in and took his place on the stool next to him.

'Evening,' he said as he sat down, acknowledging Wiktor's presence.

He was tall and muscular, with the blandly regular features of a film star. Wiktor was charmed by his politeness, and began to chatter unselfconsciously about his day, talking about the things he had seen, how the people behaved, and how exhausted he was.

'And what is it exactly that you are looking for?' asked the stranger.

'I am looking for my daughter. A daughter that I abandoned many years ago.' And he told the whole story, with remarkably few omissions, starting with his wife's pregnancy more than two decades ago and ending with the demolition of his house and his resultant contemplations. 'I've decided to try and find her. You see, I don't have anything else in my life. She's the only person I'm really connected to. I made a big mistake, losing her. I've missed her growing up; all I have had to keep me company in my loneliness is her miserable birth certificate that stares me in the face like an accusation every time I look at it. So one day I said to myself, Wiktor, you should set things right.'

If Wiktor had looked at his companion just then he might have detected a hint of contempt in his face.

'Set things right? What does that really mean? Time only moves forwards. The past is packed up, dispatched. Are you going to make your life even worse by trying to unpick all its meagre threads? Apologizing for who you have been? It's one thing I can't stand. I will never revisit any of my actions. I meant them at the time and they are me. If at some point I learn differently – well, there is always

330

the future. But then *that*, I suppose, is the difference between us.'

Wiktor did not really understand.

'But isn't repentance a good thing? Isn't it better now than when I am too old?'

'Do you think after all this time she'll welcome you back? After you kicked her out? I mean – it's not as if a man like you has a lot to offer a long-lost grown-up daughter. You haven't done anything with your life. You don't know anything, you've never done anything for anyone. Your life is worthless. Even if you *could* find her – do you really think it would make either of you happy?'

Wiktor hung his head.

'Everything you say is true. I don't know what she will say when she sees me. It makes me scared to think about it. But I have decided to be a better man, and somehow I'll manage to convince her. And maybe – don't you think? – she is also wondering about me. Isn't it good for a young woman to have a father?' The stranger nodded impatiently.

'And how will you recognize her after all this time? She'll be a grown woman by now.'

'Her name was Katya. That's not much to go on, I know. But the curious thing about her was that she had a purple birthmark on her neck in the shape of a cross. There aren't too many of those around . . .'

The stranger smiled.

'Well, what a coincidence this is, my friend. I happen to know this daughter of yours.'

'Do you? Are you sure? Is it really her?'

'I am certain of it. Her name is Katya, she has a birthmark as you describe, and she is of the right age. I think there is no doubt.'

Wiktor was jumping with excitement.

'Do you know her well? What is she doing?'

'Very well. She and I are very close. I did a big favour for her once. She is a – therapist, of sorts. I was a client of hers. That's how we met.'

'Do you think you could introduce me to her?'

'Of course I could. But take my advice: go and see her on your own. It will be an emotional moment for you both. You don't want some other person hanging around.'

Wiktor looked solemn.

'You're very right. But I'm worried about how to approach her. If I call her up and say: Katya, I'm you're father – she will put the phone down.'

The other man pondered deeply.

'I have an idea. Why don't you say you are me? She and I know each other well, so she will feel relaxed about meeting you. Then, when you arrive, you can explain everything to her in detail – as you did to me. I'm sure that after such a moving story she will not turn you away.'

Wiktor was delighted.

'It's a brilliant plan! How lucky I am to have met you. You have found my daughter and solved all my problems! How will I ever repay you?'

'Don't worry. Your meeting up with her again will be repayment enough for me.'

He wrote down a telephone number on a piece of paper.

'Now listen. This is her home number. When you call her, tell her your name is "W". It's a game we used to play. There's just one little thing: last time we saw each other, we had a little argument – just a minor disagreement. It was all my fault, of course. So why don't you say that you want to come and apologize? That will put her in a tender, forgiving mood and set the stage for your reconciliation. And after all, you actually *do* wish to apologize to her, so you'll be able to play the part with feeling!'

'I have never heard such wisdom,' said Wiktor. 'With a brain like yours I am surprised you are sitting in grimy bars like this. You should be working in a bank or something!'

'I am grateful for the compliment.'

He put down money on the bar, and prepared to leave.

'Look, I need to be off right now, but I wish you the greatest of luck, and I'll call Katya myself soon to see how it all went. My very best to you both!'

And suddenly he was gone.

Wiktor stayed for some time at the bar on his own thinking back over every detail of their conversation, and realized that he could already not remember the man's face.

The next morning, Wiktor bought a twenty-five zloty phone card, found a secluded phone box where his jangling thoughts would not be too disturbed by cars or passers-by, unfolded the carefully guarded piece of paper that W had given him, and, with a trembling hand, dialled Katya's number. She answered after the third ring.

'Hello?'

He wondered whether he should put the phone down straightaway. But the words came out of him of their own accord, bypassing the confusion.

'Hello, Katya. This is W.'

There was a long silence. She said:

'I didn't expect to hear from you again.'

'I'm so sorry, Katya. I wanted to apologize for everything. I wanted to make it up to you. I have been very bad.'

'Do you think any apology could make up for what you have done to me?'

This was more than he expected, but

'I know, I know, I know. But people can change, and there is still a lot of life ahead of us. I wanted to see you and tell you that I am a different person now. I want to know you properly.'

To his consternation his face was streaming with tears.

'This is truly a big surprise.' She thought for a moment. 'Can you give me back what you have taken?'

'Of course not. You don't have to remind me of that. You don't know how much it plagues me. But I can try to make it up to you in other ways. And I will, I promise.'

Her voice was hard.

'Well, if you have something to say to me, I suggest you come to my apartment. Tonight, around nine?'

She gave him directions.

'I will be there. It's time to forget the past, Katya. I will show you what I can be.'

Katya's fantasies of murder had not been aimless. She had developed a series of watertight scenarios in various locations and with various weapons, each corresponding to a different set of circumstances. The scenario she had decided upon during the phone conversation was the one in which she managed to get him to visit her at home.

The main entrance to the building in which she lived was at the back, away from the street. To access it, you had to walk down a long alley and through the car park. After dark, this car park was usually empty of people.

Katya had decided that trying to confront W inside her apartment would present too many problems, and that the correct strategy was to do so as he approached the building, before he was on his guard. She planned to wait in her car with a gun, shoot him as he crossed the car park, and drive away quietly.

She went out to buy a gun with a silencer, and waited for the day to pass.

At eight-thirty she parked her car in such a way that W would have to walk past her driver's window when he entered. The car park was very dark and he would not see her until it was too late.

At five minutes before nine she saw a man turn into the alley. He was not sure of himself: he could not see in the darkness and stepped momentarily back into the street to read his watch by the lights of the passing cars. He entered, slowly and unfamiliarly, his fingertips on the wall casting long and ghoulish shadows. Katya's gun was ready and her window open; she watched his cautious approach in her wing mirror. Her body was tense and focussed on the actions she had rehearsed so many times to herself – and yet she was curious even now to see the face of this man she was about to kill. He was not wearing his mask, and she peered closer into the black rectangle of her mirror to get a glimpse of what he looked like; but he remained a featureless silhouette against the explosions of criss-crossing head-lights behind. His body drew closer and still she could make out no detail. He was expanding step by step in her mirror and his footsteps were crunching on the stones; he was drawing parallel with the car and his face was now too high for her to see – the mirror framed only his hands that held something long; his footsteps were right beside her. She said coldly:

'W?'

He turned round and said 'Yes –' as she pointed the gun and fired into his head.

Afterwards she could not tell what it was that gave her second thoughts. Was it the overflowing sincerity of his toothless smile as he turned towards her? or that certain unconvincing something about his hesitant, meagre frame? or the way he carried his drooping bunch of flowers? Or was it that he blurted something out as he saw the gun and his face turned to fear, something Katya could not register consciously at the time but which almost certainly affected her instincts, something that sounded, even in the midst of the gunshot, like 'I'm your father'?

All her *post hoc* reconstructions were not enough to answer this question, but the fact was that her resolute arm swung sharply as she fired, as if trying to redirect the bullet that had already left the gun, and the shot did not strike between the eyes, where she had so unflinchingly aimed, but the side of the head, above the right ear.

Her father – for that was who she immediately believed him to be – fell to the ground, unconscious. He was bleeding profusely. She tied a cloth around his head, dragged him into the back seat of the car, and set off in a panic. Stopping on the way to throw the gun into the river, she drove frantically to the hospital. Within minutes, Wiktor was in the operating theatre.

The police arrived straightaway.

'So this is your father? What is his name?'

Katya did not know what to say.

'She's in shock, poor woman,' said the nurse. 'Look in his wallet. Do some work yourselves, for God's sake.'

The police went through the pockets of the man's bloody jacket and found his papers.

'Wiktor Czerski. Address in Bytom. Upper Silesia. OK. Bank statement. Uh-huh. Train tickets. Various . . . I see. And this would be your birth certificate, madam?'

He handed it to her. She read it.

'Yes.'

'Good. Now – can you tell us once again what happened?'

'There's nothing to tell. This evening I had met up with my father for the first time since I was a few months old. I met him in the car park behind my apartment block when a mad man grabbed me and tried to drag me away. My father jumped on the man, who shot him and ran away.'

'Did you get a good look at this man?'

The nurse put her arm round Katya.

'What a harrowing story! You can see she is in no state to discuss this right now. Why don't you come back later with your questions?'

For three days, Wiktor hovered between life and death while Katya – and Piotr, when he was able – stayed by his side. The bullet had destroyed a large part of the right-hand side of his brain and if he survived he would certainly never be able to live a normal human life again.

The local newspapers were agog with the story of the young woman who found and nearly lost a father all in the same evening. But the hospital staff kept the desperate reporters and photographers at bay, and Katya, shut up in a room watching the machines that monitored her sleeping father, knew nothing about them.

Then Wiktor recovered consciousness, and it was clear that he would pull through. Though he underwent many operations, however, he remained severely brain damaged, and many weeks later when he finally left hospital, he was unable to speak, recognize people, or even, it seemed, register things around him.

Katya and Piotr took him home late one night, and put him to bed in what had once been Katya's consulting room, which Piotr had converted into a bedroom during her long absences in hospital.

Katya awoke very late the next morning, exhausted with her ordeal, and Piotr was not beside her. She put on a dressing gown and walked out into the living room.

The sun already flooded the room. Piotr had sat Wiktor at a table and tied a cloth around his neck. Spoonful by slow spoonful he was feeding him porridge that he blew on patiently to cool it before putting it into his mouth. Wiktor gurgled loudly with pleasure and chewed contentedly on his meal, banging a plastic cup intermittently on the table for festive effect.

THE LUCKY EAR
CLEANER
The Twelfth Story

IN A SMALL town in Hunan Province lived a young man named Xiaosong. When he was an infant he and his father were both afflicted with a terrible fever. The doctor pronounced both of them dead, and the burial rites were being prepared when Xiaosong suddenly came to.

'Xiaosong could not bear to leave you all alone,' everyone said to his mother. 'He will always stay by you. Look! he has come back from the dead!'

And whenever someone spoke about Xiaosong they would say, 'That one has amazing luck.'

Xiaosong grew into a handsome young man. But he had no father and was a mother's son. He stayed in school right to the end and liked to read books. When he finished school he did not want to go into the fields to work. Instead, he became a barber.

He tied a mirror to the trunk of an old tung tree near his mother's house and put a chair in front of it. He cut the men's hair and shaved them. And he cleaned their ears.

He carved his own tools out of bamboo. He would remove the wax from his customers' ears with exquisite care. Afterwards he massaged inside using a little bamboo stick with a curved, bulbous end. The way he did it made everyone feel good, and they were happy to give him a few extra mao for the service.

He became a fixture in the town. Men would line up early in the morning before going to work.

'I'm another month older. It must be time for a cut!'

'Ear cleaning?' Xiaosong would say as he snipped.

'Yes.'

And the men would close their eyes as Xiaosong carefully cleaned and rubbed. The sounds of the world fled far away and all they could hear was Xiaosong's intricate manoeuvrings inside their heads.

'Now I feel new again. All unblocked. Maybe now I'll be as lucky as you!'

During the day while the men worked he did not have much to do. Sometimes he would go to the cemetery where his father was buried. It was his favourite place, and helped him to think. Sometimes he would just sit and read his books in the shade of the tung tree.

Schoolgirls came in groups of three to look at him as he read. His good looks made them shy, and since their mothers cut their hair they did not have a good excuse to approach. But one day a girl plucked up her courage and asked to have her ears cleaned.

'I know you,' he said. 'You are Yinfang. Your father is the Police Inspector.'

Xiaosong used to admire her even when he was still at school and she was only a kid from the junior classes. Now she was starting to be a beautiful young woman.

He leaned her head against his chest and cradled it in the crook of his arm, so that her ear pointed towards the sky. It was as delicate as a miniature ivory carving. It was voluted like an exquisite shell, and from below you could see the light through it, like you can with the finest china.

He tucked her hair behind her ear and took his bamboo tweezers. He carefully removed the excess wax, and then used his scraper to clean the walls of the ear. She kept her eyes tightly closed.

'You're still in school, then?' he said.

'Mmm,' she replied.

He used his rounded stick to massage her ear. Her head was leaning harder against him and her eyelashes waved each time he breathed. A bird was singing in the tree above their heads. He took a long time because he wanted her to come back.

Finally, he finished. He blew gently in her ears and she shivered. He set her head upright and took his hands away. She opened her eyes reluctantly and looked at him as if she had just woken up. He smiled at her, wondering what she thought about him.

'How much?'

'Don't worry. Pay me next time.'

She handed him one yuan.

'Is it true you're very lucky?'

'I suppose so. That's what everyone says.'

She rejoined her friends.

After that he started to get a lot of custom during the day from the girls at the school. He did not have so much time to read anymore, but he made more money. There were always girls waiting to have their ears cleaned.

The girls in that town soon had the cleanest ears in Hunan Province.

One day his mother said to him, 'Xiaosong, you are a man now. You can't just cut hair and clean ears all your life. What will happen when I grow old and I can't work anymore? You need to think about your career. There's no money in this town. The farmers are all making losses. Every year they have to borrow more just to pay their taxes. Why do you think all the young men have left? You should do the same. You should go to Shenzhen. The streets are paved with gold there. That's what Yunji says. Look how much money he brings home.'

'Yunji has a diploma in computer science from Changsha University and his family have their own pig farm. What do I have?'

'You have your luck. That is worth all the diplomas in the world. Go and talk to Yunji. He is back here for the weekend. See what he can suggest.'

Yunji was not very friendly. He looked down on Xiaosong.

'I don't know what to suggest. You don't have any qualifications. There's nothing to distinguish you from all the hundreds of thousands of other young men who want to work in Shenzhen. You'll never get work.'

'Maybe if I can get there I'll find something on my own?'

Yunji looked doubtful. He said, 'If you like I can try to get you there. But I can't promise any more than that.'

Yunji's farm produced a certain kind of hybrid boar that they supplied to hotels in Shenzhen. He had a word with his father, who agreed to let Xiaosong travel in one of the trucks.

Yinfang came to see him again. She leaned her head against his chest without him even needing to put it there. He said, 'I am leaving, Yinfang. I am going to find work in Shenzhen.'

She opened her eyes and turned to look at him.

'I thought . . .'

'What? What did you think?'

She said nothing, and turned round again. He took her head in his arms and pointed her ear towards the sky. She closed her eyes. He took his bamboo tweezers from the glass jar.

But she had other ideas. She wrested her head free from him and stood up, her hands defiantly on her hips.

'I don't need my ears cleaned by you. I can do it myself. That's what I always used to do before.'

And she walked away.

'Yinfang!' he called. But she did not turn round.

His mother gave him a thick sweater.

'You'll need this in the truck,' she said. 'It's refrigerated and it will be a long journey. It's a good old sweater that your father used to wear.'

'I wonder when I'll see you again, mother.'

'It won't be long. Take care of yourself and make your fortune. I know you will do well. You came back to me before, and you will again.'

Xiaosong climbed into the truck. It was full of dead boars that were bigger than he was. They were newly slaughtered and piled up on top of each other, and even in the cold they still gave out a lot of heat. He found a comfortable place to lie down among them. Somebody shut the doors and it was pitch dark inside. The engine started, and they began to move, bumping along between the potholes in the road.

Xiaosong had seen pictures of New York. But it was nothing compared to this. These towers grew close together like a bamboo grove and they were in every kind of colour: blue and gold and silver, pink like cherry blossom and orange like the robe of a chuckling Buddha. And everywhere, men were building more, drilling and hammering and cutting until your head nearly burst. There were millions of people, and they looked as if they had no cares in the world: they dressed in magnificent clothes and walked stiff and tall. Xiaosong had heard that the people here would not stoop to pick up a ten RMB note from the street; and now for the first time he thought it might be true.

He found work in a barber shop with a spiralling sign outside and an electronic cat that stood in the window and beckoned to passersby. It was owned by an old woman called Mama Wang. 'I suppose it could help to have a boy around,' she said grudgingly. 'You have a good face.' She could not afford to pay him, but she let him stay in a room at the back of the shop and gave him food to eat. 'It's a way of starting off,' he said to himself. 'I'll find something better later.'

There were three young women who worked there too. They taught Xiaosong how to cut hair the way the city people liked it. They showed him how to use all the different kinds of scissors and clippers and gels and shampoos that he had never seen before. He told them about his life in the village, and his long journey in the back of a truck full of boars.

'And look at him now!' they said to each other. 'How lucky he is!'

In the evenings, the women took men into the back room to sleep with them. They kept the door closed until late at night, so Xiaosong had to wait for a long time before he could go to bed. He went for walks in the city. He tried to find a cemetery where he could feel some peace and remember home, but there did not seem to be one.

'Where do they put all the dead people, Mama Wang?' he asked.

'What dead people?' she said. 'Have you seen any old people here? Apart from me . . . No one dies here.'

Early one morning he went for a walk by the Shenzhen River. It was just after dawn, and the drills had not started their screaming yet; even the building sites seemed peaceful. He looked up over the river, over the barbed wire, to the other side, where there was a hill rising steeply into the sky. It was green and round, with a few solitary trees. And it was covered with graves.

He sat down and considered them for a long while. In Hong Kong, then, people still died.

One afternoon, while all three of Xiaosong's colleagues were occupied in the back room, a man walked into the shop for a haircut. He was well dressed, the kind of man that Mama Wang usually liked her girls to attend to, but on this occasion that was not possible.

Xiaosong sat him in a chair. He wore a sky-blue cotton shirt with the initials WSD embroidered on the cuffs. There was not a bead of sweat on him, though he had just come in from outside. Xiaosong carefully removed his glasses, which were as light as a feather, and covered him in a fresh cotton robe.

'Ear cleaning?' he asked, as he snipped.

'Yes.'

Xiaosong cut his hair very carefully.

'You're from Hunan Province?' asked the man.

'Yes.'

'I thought so. I grew up in Changsha.'

'I've never been to Changsha,' said Xiaosong. 'I'm from a small town where everyone's a farmer. But there's no money there.'

'So how did you get here? Wasn't it very difficult?'

'I didn't really think about it. I just came.'

'You don't have any papers? Nothing at all.'

Xiaosong shook his head.

'And you've been walking around in the streets all this time?'

'Yes.'

'I can't understand why you rural types put yourselves in these situations. It's mad. You're lucky to have got this far.'

'That's what everyone says.'

342

'It's not a joke! Do you have any idea . . . ?'

Xiaosong held up a mirror so he could inspect the back of his head. There was a white tan line where the old hair had been. The man nodded, and Xiaosong took out his bamboo tools. He began to clean his ears, holding his head against his chest and pointing one ear and then the other up towards the light. The man kept his eyes closed and kept saying 'Mmm' in approval.

He took out his wallet to pay Mama Wang. He said to Xiaosong, 'Come and see me whenever you can. My name is Wu. Maybe I can help you.' He took a business card from his wallet. 'In the meantime: be careful.'

Mr Wu asked Xiaosong to work in his office. There were thousands of files that needed to be categorized and put in order. 'That should take you about a month. If you do a good job I'll find you something more demanding. I'll give you 450 RMB a month and I'm also going to buy you a temporary residence permit and a work permit. So you don't end up in some Custody and Repatriation Centre. Some day you can pay me back. There's a dormitory where the workers sleep but I don't want you mixing with them. Maybe you can find somewhere else.'

Xiaosong went to Mama Wang to ask her if he could continue to sleep there. To his surprise, she agreed, charging him only minimal rent.

'Thank you, Mama Wang. Thank you.'

She laughed at him.

'Yes, you should thank me. I don't usually do people favours. There's something about you. You just seem to invite good luck.'

He started his work with enthusiasm. Mr Wu was a manager in a computer manufacturing company from Hong Kong. The office seemed to have been set up so quickly that no one had ever bothered to develop filing systems for purchase orders or correspondence. There were papers everywhere. Xiaosong would arrive in the office before everyone else and start to put them in chronological order, and in sepa-rate files marked with the names of clients and suppliers. He pored over letters and invoices and proposals and contracts, and developed

343

an instinct for how everything fitted together. It was a new world to him, and he found himself pleased by its logic, its orderliness. He stored everything in such a way that it was easy to find again, and he felt he was making a significant contribution to the life of the company.

Mr Wu arrived every morning at nine o'clock with his copy of the *Shenzhen Special Zone Daily*, from which he read out the headlines while he drank his coffee.

'Shenzhen's international trade projected to exceed US$100 billion this year.'

'Shenzhen port's container throughput for the year rose by 50 per cent to eight million. Shenzhen replacing Los Angeles as the seventh-biggest port in the world.'

'Imports of mobile phones rose to 4.57 million.'

'US$3.5 billion-worth of new overseas-financed ventures in Shenzhen this year.'

Mr Wu explained these news stories to Xiaosong, who began to share his excitement about the momentous place of which he was now a part.

'Life will get better and better, Xiaosong – you will see.'

Mr Wu was a wealth of information. He knew about every company and why it was failing or succeeding. He seemed to understand the laws of money, and what effects it had on places, people, and things. As Xiaosong walked home in the evenings the city started to make sense to him: its expanse of rocketing towers became easily legible, like a simple bar graph whose unwritten axes and labels were each day more obvious and intuitive.

'There is no great mystery to this place,' he thought to himself. 'There is no reason why I should not become as rich as anyone else.'

One evening he saw a ten RMB note lying in the street.

'So the stories were true! People here really do leave money floating around in the streets.'

He bent over to pick it up.

'Well, I am not that rich yet!'

Mr Wu gave him a promotion.

'You have done well with that work, Xiaosong,' he said. 'Now I would like you to take a greater part in the business. I want you to process all the orders that come in. My colleagues and I have been doing this ourselves up to now, but we really need someone devoted to the task. I'm going to raise your pay to 700 RMB a month.'

Xiaosong could not believe the good luck that had brought him together with Mr Wu. He sent 200 RMB home to his mother and assured her that he would now be sending similar amounts every month. 'I have found myself a good job, Mother,' he wrote, 'and I think that within a year I should be able to send you 400 or 500 RMB per month. It is such a relief finally to be able to provide for you.'

His mother wrote back a letter full of joy. 'Never in history has 200 RMB been so cherished. I have shown your letter to everyone in the town. I am so proud of you. I only wish your father could see what you have done.'

Each order had to be entered into the computer system in painstaking detail and triple-checked.

'Outside the city we have a factory where 150 women assemble our computers. They are given instructions on the basis of what you enter into the computer. They only produce what you tell them to produce. Any mistake would be extremely costly.'

Xiaosong began slowly at first. It took him two to three hours to process a single order. Big piles of them arrived every day, and though he sat until two or three in the morning he would always be far behind.

'Don't worry,' said Mr Wu. 'You'll get quicker with practice.'

In the first week he managed to process a hundred orders. In the second, a hundred and fifty. By the fourth week he was able to process some fifty orders a day. In two months he had cleared his entire backlog, and was processing orders faster than they arrived.

'I took a gamble with you, as I'm sure you realize,' said Mr Wu. 'I had an instinct about you when I met you, and I decided to act on it. But I'm glad to see it working out so well. I think you will go far in this company. And I like having you around. Why don't you come and have dinner with my wife and me tonight?'

The girls at Mama Wang's helped him choose a new shirt for the evening, and he bought a basket of fruit for Mrs Wu.

'This is Xiaosong,' said Mr Wu to his wife. 'Would you believe it: when I met him he was working in a seedy barber's shop! He cleaned my ears beautifully. But now that's all behind you, isn't it Xiaosong? I felt he deserved something better than that.'

They lived in a beautiful apartment on the twenty-fifth floor. Xiaosong was in raptures over such luxury. Mrs Wu served beer and soy beans while she finished cooking the dinner, and Mr Wu told stories of his childhood in Hunan Province. As the alcohol reached his head, Xiaosong was sure he had never been so happy in his life before.

Something strange started to happen to Xiaosong. He started to see a shape everywhere, a shape that he could not recognize or even describe, but one that crept into his computer screen as he worked and danced in Mama Wang's ceiling fans as he tried to get to sleep. He saw it in the windows of shops that he passed, in every piece of paper that he tried to read, and in the plate of noodles that he ate with Mr Wu at lunchtime. He could not understand what was going wrong with him. He wondered if he was over-tired, and tried to rest for a few minutes during his lunch breaks. One of the girls at Mama Wang's gave him a relaxing massage, and he ate some snakeroot each evening to calm his body. But nothing changed. In fact it got worse and worse. The shape loomed vast in his dreams and it came spiralling towards him as he crossed the road until he could see nothing and the cars were just speeding noises all around.

Sometimes the shape came very close, and a fountain of recognition began to well up within him. He would be on the very brink of understanding what was happening, and then it all receded and Xiaosong slumped back, disappointed.

Meanwhile, his work was suffering badly. He could hardly focus on the order anymore as everything turned in front of his eyes. His productivity dropped, from fifty or sixty orders a day to forty, to thirty, to fifteen. Unprocessed orders began to pile up all around the office, and Mr Wu grew concerned.

'I don't know what is happening to you, Xiaosong,' he said. 'I hope you're not getting complacent just because I said a few nice things to you the other week. Remember: you are at the very beginning of your career, and you still have to impress me a lot further. This is no time to flag.'

Xiaosong gave him every assurance, for he was as anxious as Mr Wu to get back to his normal self. He said that he was a little tired, that was all. Mr Wu said, 'Look – go home now and rest for the whole evening. When you come in tomorrow I want you to be back to normal.'

Xiaosong left the office. He headed down past the Shangri-La Hotel to where the building work was going on next to the Luohu Commercial Centre, where all the Hong Kong people came across to do cheap shopping. He found a place to sit on some steps. And he looked up, across the river, across the fence, to the hill on the other side of the border.

As he watched the hill, it started to turn in on itself and to float free of the landscape. It started to spin: its undulations smoothed out and its little stone alcoves merged into canals; and as it cleared the barbed wire fence and glided down towards Xiaosong he knew that knowledge lay very close, if he could only find it. As it hovered just by his left cheek its green grass blanched away, and he saw that it was not a big thing at all, but something very normal-sized. He was not confused anymore and, in a moment that overwhelmed him with its bliss, every last serif of its curlicue calligraphy became stunningly clear. The thing was Yinfang's ear.

Mr Wu was understandably angry.

'You're an idiot, Xiaosong, a stupid, irresponsible, ungrateful idiot. After everything I've done for you. You'll never get another opportunity like this again. Even your luck won't stretch that far. You're stupid and confused. I'm telling you when you come to your senses you will regret this. Think clearly, Xiaosong! An ear? You are leaving everything because you saw an ear? I'll remind you that you still owe me 500 RMB for your permits. If you go you have to pay me.'

But Xiaosong had made up his mind.

'I'm sorry, Mr Wu. I really am. But I can't stay here any longer. I'll find the money.'

Usually, the trucks from Yunji's pig business returned home empty.

But on this occasion Yunji's mother had asked the driver to bring her back a new rug from Shenzhen for her front room. So Xiaosong had a soft bed to sleep on during the journey. He really was a remarkably lucky young man.

There was only one person left to speak.

THE RECYCLER OF DREAMS

The Thirteenth Story

IN THE CITY of Buenos Aires there lived a man who had always loved movies. As a boy, Gustavo had wanted to be a famous film director; but life did not quite turn out like that. With some help from his family he started a video store, which did not seem a terrible alternative: he found room at last to put up his enormous poster for Buñuel's *Charme Discret de la Bourgeoisie* that had sat in a tight roll since the film had first shown in Argentina, and set about building one of the most extensive movie collections in the city. The store soon became well known in the neighbourhood: Gustavo's clients appreciated his deep knowledge, for he could recommend the best film for any situation, and would always send you off with a valuable critical insight, or an amusing anecdote about the director.

Gustavo was not a sociable man, and he did not have much of a life outside the store. Such friendships as he had were with the people who came in once in a while to discuss movies with him; but what they did in the rest of their lives was largely a mystery, and during the moments when the store was empty he sometimes wondered about them, inventing pasts and futures, love affairs and shameful secrets. One of the people who came sometimes was a woman named Carla, with whom he considered himself to be in love; but he dared not make an approach to her, and contented himself with her brief visits, when she would enquire listlessly about the latest movies, and, occasionally, a phone call, if there was a new arrival he thought she might particularly like.

His business did well, and after some time he decided to expand into cable television. He set up an array of satellite dishes on the roof and began to supply the neighbourhood with sixty-six channels of entertainment. In addition to the standard package he introduced his own channel, which ran for a few hours every evening: a movie club. He would show Hong Kong action movies and Japanese anime, French *nouvelle vague* and American noir; there were festivals devoted to Eisenstein and Scorsese and Tarkovsky – and in every case Gustavo would begin with a short introduction delivered calmly and affectionately to the camera from the threadbare armchair in the corner of his shop. He found a small but appreciative public, and, in time, secured sponsorship for his show from a local interior design company and a fashion boutique, both of whom recognized that Gustavo's audience evidently had sophisticated tastes.

Modest though it was, this income made Gustavo more ambitious about the role he could play in Argentinian film. He began to collect reels of forgotten movies that lay around in battered canisters in old theatres, antique stores, and people's cupboards. He stored them in a large freezer to ensure they did not degrade further, and cleaned and restored them one by one, as best he could. He found silent thrillers from the very first years of the twentieth century about knife-wielding toughs working in the port of Buenos Aires. There was film of early tango evenings and music-hall performances. There were reels of old films from Italy and France and America. His life began to revolve around this private collection, and he spent all his spare hours looking for more forgotten gems. The most important discoveries he transferred to DVD and wrote historical and critical introductions.

With the economic crisis, of course, all of this was to fall apart. People lost their jobs and became mainly concerned with survival. They cancelled their cable subscriptions and ceased renting videos. Gustavo stopped seeing the various characters who used to come to the store. The sponsors pulled out. Gustavo could no longer pay the rent on the shop, and closed it down. He gave up the small one-bedroom apartment he had become so fond of and moved back into his parents' house, leaving everything that was superfluous in black plastic bags on the street since there would now be no room for it. His father watched him impassively as he carried in box after box of video cassettes and DVDs.

'You remember my friend Señor Ruiz? The psychoanalyst – who always made your mother angry when he used curse words in front of you when you were a kid? Dropped dead today. Just like that. Went to the bank and found out he had nothing left. Dropped dead.'

He began to laugh uncontrollably. He tried to speak through the convulsions:

'Just imagine it – one minute – then – thump!'

His laughter gradually dried up. He wiped the tears from his eyes and sat looking at his lap. Gustavo did not know what to say. His father, too, had been impoverished by the crisis and he knew these were not merely selfless tears. He had had to sell his car at a great loss just so they would have some cash for daily living. He had dismissed the cook, who had worked for the family for fifteen years but whose salary he could no longer afford.

Gustavo waited in vain for his father to say something else. At length he turned and went upstairs. He had a terrible stomach ache, and lay down on the bed in his old bedroom. It had been entirely cleared out since he was last there, and held no memories for him.

Emptying the shop had been a draining experience, and, though it was only the middle of the afternoon and the birds were chattering loudly in the trees outside, he soon fell asleep. He had a strange dream.

Gustavo dreamt that his video store was not closed down, but converted into a shelter for the homeless in recognition of the severe economic situation. Former factory workers and schoolteachers and television actors came to stay: five pesos a night for full board and lodging. Gustavo built rows of bunk beds and separate shower rooms for men

353

and women. A former military chef was persuaded to emerge from retirement to prepare evening meals for the guests. He was nearly seven feet tall and had served food to the troops in the Falklands. After eating, everyone stood in a line outside the bathroom waiting to vomit their food up again. 'Maybe I have lost my touch,' mused the chef as he and Gustavo watched this ritual every night.

One day the chef came to work in full military uniform and with a monocle screwed into his left eye. 'Torture,' he said, 'is something that has not really become more sophisticated since the advent of human society. If you need to know something from someone who doesn't wish to tell it to you – you have to inflict pain and humiliation. It's inefficient and it's not very nice – but what else are you going to do? Now, however, things have changed. Military researchers have invented a digital imaging system that can process data from the visual and auditory cortices. They don't need to ask you what's in your mind anymore – they can watch it on TV!'

Gustavo did not know why the chef had told him this. But as he thought more about it he realized it could revitalize his cable television business. He put up a new sign outside: 'FREE Board and Lodging'. The small print read: 'If you give us your dreams.' He planned a new television programme, not like the old, dry film club, but a hard-hitting, sensational programme that would make him famous: *The Dreams of the Dispossessed*!

He installed the equipment in every sleeping booth and waited for the first group of dreamers to arrive. People were wary of his intentions and stayed away: only thirteen came on that first night. As they bedded down for sleep he went from one to the next attaching the electrodes and connecting them to little recording devices.

In the morning, as each person awoke, he went around disconnecting the wires and taking out the digital tapes on which the dreams had been recorded. In each case he viewed a few seconds to make sure everything had worked properly. The inmates were slightly abashed; it was like collecting some kind of intimate sample: urine, or stools, something that is not meant for everyone to see.

When everyone had gone, he put the tapes into his computer and began to examine what they contained. To his surprise, every person had dreamed about him. He started to arrange the thirteen dreams in different ways, and found at last that he could make a single narrative of them that was almost coherent. He edited them together and, one evening, began to broadcast them on his cable service.

1

One day, while he is in the process of clearing out years of unwanted stuff from his cupboards, and to his great surprise, Gustavo suddenly vomits on the floor.

It comes without warning, too quickly even for him to move from where he is. He does not feel unwell, nor has he eaten badly, or to excess. It is several days since he has drunk alcohol. He is, in fact, in perfect health. So it comes as an unexpected intervention into an otherwise normal day.

It is the weekend, and he has decided it is time to clean up. It has been years since he has done so, and the house is becoming bloated with the accumulation of objects. He starts to clear things out: clothes he has not worn for as long as he can remember, letters and photographs, magazines he has kept for reasons he has forgotten. There are board games he used to play with his friends, old videotapes that are long since ruined, and various outdated and broken electronic gadgets. The sheets of newspaper he has lined his shelves with give daily events of long ago: news of politicians whose names he does not recognize, missing pets who would now be long dead, a plane hijacking that ended in a crash in which two hundred and ninety people died. In the back of one cupboard, after clearing out an old tape recorder and a raincoat that has become dried and cracked, he finds the corpses of hundreds of cockroaches. (To this unwelcome discovery, however, his stomach has no adverse reaction.) He packs up everything in big black plastic bags and lines them up in his front room. That is a lot of trash, and now everything in his house will feel more mobile. He sits on the sofa looking at everything he has cleared out. And suddenly, he vomits on the floor.

He starts to think back in order to work out why this might have happened. He recalls that his fridge has been having problems recently. It is summer, and his old refrigerator has been moaning with the strain of keeping things cold. He goes to it and opens the door. He sniffs various items: the milk, the butter, a large pot of meat stew. He is convinced there is a slight whiff of decomposition.

'I will buy a freezer,' thinks Gustavo to himself. 'I have made space in the house, and now I will fill it with something useful. That will solve this problem.'

Gustavo clears up the mess on his floor, puts all the sacks of trash outside, and goes to a nearby domestic appliances shop. The man greets him and asks him what he needs. Gustavo looks around and realizes that the shop is empty. He says. 'I am looking for a freezer.'

The man replies, grim-faced,

'I am sorry. No one can afford such expensive items these days. So we do not stock them.'

Gustavo is furious.

'What am I supposed to do with all my food? Throw it out?'

He goes and sits outside the shop. He thinks of all his food losing its shape and spreading out into all the rooms of his house. It is disgusting. Evening comes, and Gustavo has still not thought of another course of action. He begins to return home.

On the way he spots a building he has not seen before. It is called the Ice Hotel.

'That sounds interesting,' he thinks. 'Perhaps they have a freezer I can buy from them. Or at least some ice.'

He goes inside the hotel. There is no one at reception. He rings the bell marked 'Assistance', but there is no response. He rings it again half-heartedly and, with some apprehension, leaves the lobby and wanders into the corridors of the hotel. All the doors are closed and there is no sign of activity. It is one of those grandiose, European-style buildings with high ceilings and ornate plasterwork; it is by now in a state of some disrepair. At the end of the corridor a sign on the wall points down a spiral staircase to the 'Freezer Room'. He walks down the stairs and finds himself in a vast hall. There are gilt-framed mirrors down either side and the ceiling is painted with heroic scenes from Argentinian history: the revolution and the unification struggle. The entire hall is filled with freezers.

He decides to take the smallest one since he will have to carry it up those stairs, which is going to be a very difficult thing to do. He opens it to ensure it is in good working order. To his surprise there is a young woman lying inside, her face covered with a thin layer of ice. She looks like Catherine Deneuve in *Belle de Jour*. He cannot resist the urge to kiss her. She opens her eyes.

'What do you think you are doing? You can't take these freezers,' she says. 'They are not like the freezers you put in your home. They are not meant for food. If you want a freezer, buy your own.'

She sits up.

'My name is Carla. I think I have been in there a long time. Many years. I am grateful to you for rescuing me. Thank you.'

She takes his hand and leads him up the stairs. They walk through the corridors and back into the lobby. Everything is still empty but Gustavo cannot rid himself of the impression that they are being watched. They go out into the street.

Carla looks disconsolately around her.

'Things are different,' she said. 'Things have changed. I wonder where all the people I used to know have gone.'

'It is late. That is why you are scared. Let's go back to my place and sleep. I am not trying to seduce you. I just think you will feel better in the morning.'

They walk to Gustavo's apartment. He is worried about the rotten food but does not know how to tell her. He hopes it will have gone away. As he opens the door he is convinced that the whole apartment has begun to smell very bad. He opens all the windows.

'I'm sorry about the smell. I have a problem with rotten food. That is why I was looking for a freezer. I hope you will not be offended.'

'I can't smell anything,' says Carla.

He makes his bed for her and she climbs into it gratefully. Her hair looks magnificent on his pillow.

'I'll sleep on the sofa.'

He turns out the light, shuts the door, and goes to lie down on the sofa, fully clothed. He sleeps deeply.

2

It is morning and Gustavo is with Carla in his apartment. She is beautiful and it is wonderful to see her in the intimacy of morning undress.

'I'm so hungry,' she says.

Gustavo realizes that he, too, is desperate to eat. He has never been so hungry before. He proposes that they go to a restaurant where they will be able to eat their fill. She says, 'I know one right nearby.'

They leave straightaway and the restaurant she is thinking of is indeed just two minutes' walk away. Its pavement tables are packed with people: there is a joyful ring of cups on saucers and there is morning laughter that floats weightlessly up into the crystal air. They sit down. The man at the next table is hidden behind an outspread copy of *La Nación* whose bizarre headlines – *Frankfurt Overtaken By Monkey Menace* or *Notorious Indian Insane Asylum Collapses: Inmates Escape* – seem like dreams. A baby smears its face and torso contentedly with chocolate ice cream while the adults at the table talk about interior design.

'This is remarkable,' says Gustavo. 'It is as if nothing has happened.'

'What do you mean?' asks Carla.

It seems she is oblivious to the disaster that has hit the country. Gustavo does not want to tell her about it right now. He summarizes evasively.

'Times aren't so good as they used to be. And yet all these people look so prosperous. And content.'

They order food and ask the waiter to bring it quickly. He returns almost immediately with large plates of fruit, meat, and cheese, a basket of every kind of bread, two tall glasses of prune juice, and two steaming espressos. Their gratitude is intense: at that moment Gustavo's feelings towards the waiter approach pure love. They begin to eat. The food is sublime.

As they begin to get to know each other, as Gustavo discovers to his pleasure that they have many things in common, that they share, for instance, both Catalonian *and* Bavarian origins, he begins to feel that the food is not going down in the way it should. Far from descending into his body, in fact, it feels as if it has been caught in the current of a stream that is rising within him. The discomfort grows while Carla continues to talk, and he begins to sweat. But Carla is not so well either, and she is faltering; suddenly, the two of them look at each other with the same expression of alarm, and before they have time to get further than the side of the street they are vomiting violently. Their vomit, both of them, is green and does not seem to be derived from the food they have just eaten.

The people who are cheerfully eating not two metres away turn their heads away in disgust and a waiter appears laden with hastily-snatched bundles of napkins and tries to steer them away from the gaze of other customers. *Everyone* is disgusted, and the magic of the morning moment is broken. The manager comes out to address the embarrassing situation; Gustavo and Carla apologize repeatedly and offer to settle their bill and leave straightaway, but he cannot wait even this long: in an emphatic gesture of eviction he holds out Carla's jacket and handbag that she had left by her chair and tells them not to worry about the money.

They wander off down the street looking back at the waiter, who is trying not to draw attention to himself as he washes away the vomit with a bucket of water. They both feel refreshed from having vomited like this, but cannot explain it.

'No one else seemed to be affected by the food,' observes Carla.

'I know. This is starting to happen a lot with me,' replies Gustavo musingly.

3

Carla and Gustavo are wandering aimlessly in the city. Without really intending it they are drawn onto the Calle Florida where the shops are gleaming and gay, and spirited guitarists and accordionists are playing every few metres. They wander contentedly, discussing items in the windows of the leather shops and designer boutiques, not with any desire to buy but simply for the pleasure of finding out each other's tastes. They draw alongside the dignified solidity of the Harrods department store. There is an amazing display in the window: fifty, no, at least a hundred attractive young people are holding placards saying: 'Death to the Political Classes!' and 'Thieves: Give us our Money!' and 'No more Hunger: Fight for the Government of Workers!'. They march around a number of life-size cardboard cut-outs, all of which represent the same symbolic character: dressed in the garb of the military rulers of the dictatorship, he has 'Argentina' written across his general's cap. They are all dressed in Calvin Klein, Diesel, and Emporio Armani streetwear, and they sway slightly to the fast beat of club music that can also be heard outside in the street through hidden speakers. The leader of the 'protest' is truly beautiful, her blonde hair flowing from under a woollen cap and falling prettily over her breasts. She speaks angrily into a microphone: 'Thirty thousand of our people disappeared during the dictatorship! We have still not finished looking for them. And now our money has disappeared too! This is too much disappearance for us to bear!'

Gustavo is surprised at the boldness of such a window display but does not comment for fear of troubling Carla too much. They content themselves with a few remarks on a particular sort of heavily embroidered jeans, which look very cool on angry young people.

4

Carla slips her hand under Gustavo's arm and he looks straight ahead, enjoying the gesture of affection without seeming to notice it. But her grip is tighter than it should be, and as he looks at her he realizes that her face is deathly pale and that she is holding him to steady herself. She is going to faint and he does not wait for it to happen: he lays her down on the sidewalk so that the blood can flow more easily to her head. The street is crowded, and many people make known their irritation at this blockage in the flow, though some are kinder and stop to offer help. Gustavo assures them that everything is under control:

neither he nor Carla have eaten anything for as long as he can remember, and he realizes that she is fainting simply from lack of food. They are outside a juice bar. He goes in and orders a yoghurt fruit drink that will give her proteins and sugars and sooth her stomach. On an afterthought, he orders one for himself too.

She is still lying down on the concrete slabs and he is alarmed to see her eyeballs rolling freely in their sockets. He kneels behind her and props up her torso, putting the straw in her mouth.

'Drink,' he says. 'You'll feel better.'

She sucks weakly at the straw and swallows a mouthful of the drink. Immediately, she coughs it out again, spitting it out on the sidewalk.

'I – can't,' she gasps. 'I can't eat anything.'

Gustavo is truly alarmed. He stops a passing taxi.

'I need help getting this woman home. We have to go quickly.'

'What's wrong with her? Is it drugs?'

'No. She's sick.'

'If she spoils the cab she pays double.'

Gustavo lifts her up, though he is feeling weak himself, and lays her on the back seat. He takes a look at his drink and realizes that he, too, is unable to stomach anything right now. He leaves it on the sidewalk and climbs into the taxi with her. They set off at high speed.

They arrive home and Gustavo calls a doctor, who comes immediately. He fills the apartment with avuncular smiles, sets down his black leather bag, and hands Gustavo a business card:

CARLOS FERNÁNDEZ, M.D.
PLASTIC SURGEON
Fellow of the American College of Surgeons
Member of the Asociación Médica Argentina
& the Asociación Argentina de Cirugía

'There must be some mistake,' says Gustavo, who is furious with frustration. 'My friend is very sick. She has a stomach complaint. She doesn't need a plastic surgeon!'

'Calm down, sir! Please calm down. Shall we sit? I'm sorry about the card: I haven't bothered to change the wording. And I admit it gives the wrong impression.'

His smile never falters. He becomes confidential.

'It is true that I am one of Buenos Aires' leading plastic surgeons. I have done everything on everyone – politicians, businessmen, singers, porn stars. If you like what you see when you look at the people sitting in the nice restaurants of this city you can bet your bottom dollar that I'm the one to thank! I could tell you some stories . . . But this is really beside the point. The fact is that times have changed, people aren't really taking care of themselves so much – and people like me are branching out into other areas of medicine. That's nothing to worry about – I've done everything in my time, and remember: a body is a body. Doesn't matter who's slicing it up, the same principles apply.'

He clasps Gustavo's hand reassuringly.

'So, let's look at the patient.'

He leans over Carla who moans quietly on the sofa. He feels the pulse in her neck and takes her blood pressure; he looks around in her mouth and massages her stomach gently, occasionally murmuring, 'Interesting'.

At last his examination is over, and he turns to Gustavo.

'Is there a restaurant nearby?' he asks peremptorily.

'Yes.'

'There is no time to waste. Run down and get two plates of steak. Medium rare. Sauce and garnish on the side. As quick as you can. Hurry!'

Gustavo does not know what is happening, but the doctor's urgent tone goads him into action. He runs down to the nearby restaurant and places his order. The steaks are a full twenty minutes coming, and Gustavo goes through agonies of impatience. At last they arrive, and he runs back up to his apartment with two steaming plastic plates.

The spectacle that greets him is distressing. Carla is lying anaesthetized on a sheet on the floor, and the doctor has cut into her stomach so that it is open to the world. Clamps hold the sides of the incision wide apart.

'Give me one of those,' he says, as Gustavo stands dumbstruck in the doorway with the two plates in his hand. Gustavo hands him one of the plates, and he begins to cut the steak up into little pieces with his scalpel. He blows on it to cool it down a bit, and unceremoniously scrapes the whole plate into her gaping stomach. He removes the clamps and sews her up again.

'That should do it,' he says. 'Nothing to worry about. Sometimes we have to resort to extreme measures. Now we just have to watch and wait.'

Gustavo has still not moved. Dr Fernández takes the other plate from him and tucks in greedily to the steak.

'I was very hungry,' he says. 'Do you have any salt?'

Gustavo goes to fetch some from the kitchen. Dr Fernández finishes his meal in no time.

'Delicious,' he observes.

They sit in silence for a while.

'Did you see the news this morning?' offers the doctor. 'Smallpox outbreak in Paris. In this day and age. We think *we* have it bad.'

Gustavo does not answer. The doctor whistles a current pop song, drumming out the beat on the arm of the chair.

Carla begins to stir.

'Ah,' says the doctor. 'Here we go.'

Carla moans and screws up her face; she reaches for her stomach. She feels the bandages and appears confused. Gradually, she begins to focus on what is happening. Dr Fernández presides over all of this with the glow of a father watching his child taking its first steps. Suddenly Carla becomes seized by something inside her: she breaks straight through what remains of her anaesthetic haze and runs to the bathroom where they hear her vomiting repeatedly. The doctor's smile is persistent, though, to Gustavo's concerned examination, more hollow than before.

After a while she emerges, pale and sweaty.

'How do you feel now, my dear?' asks Dr Fernández.

'Slightly better, perhaps,' she replies.

Dr Fernández turns triumphantly to Gustavo.

'There you are! What did I tell you?'

Gustavo is unconvinced. The doctor begins scribbling a prescription for antacid pills.

'Get her to take these. It should clear up in no time. Remarkable case. And here' – he presents Gustavo with another hastily written piece of paper – 'is my bill.'

Gustavo is shocked at the amount of money, which amounts to most of his savings, and which he had not been consulted about before the procedure began. Nevertheless, he writes a cheque, and the doctor departs.

5

Carla has moved into Gustavo's apartment. In other circumstances this would be a joyful scenario for Gustavo, but something is seriously wrong with both of them, and they are unable to live life normally. The fact is, neither of them is able to ingest food. They have tried everything they can think of, but nothing will stay inside their bodies. While at first the situation presented itself as a number of alarming crises, now it has become a chronic situation that leaves them debilitated and morose. The outside world seems to understand nothing of what has affected them, and each of them becomes for the other the sole reassurance that they are not mad, or inhuman. Strangely, though there seem to exist no glimmers of hope for their upended digestive systems, their condition of perpetual hunger and exhaustion seems to have become stable, and death is not an immediate prospect. They lie close together and pool their remaining energy in order to accomplish those activities and bodily processes that are left to them. They do not make love, for that would demand too much exertion, but they occasionally rub each other's backs and genitals in a hollow gesture towards the pleasure of eating. They drift between sleep and wake.

6

Gustavo and Carla are very sick and have become recluses in his apartment, but Gustavo is concerned at what will happen to their minds if they divorce themselves entirely from the world. He proposes that they make an attempt at taking a walk in the park in Palermo. Early one afternoon they put on some clothes to make themselves more presentable and take a bus to their destination. It is a beautiful day, and there are many people walking in the park. They realize how strange they look to everyone else, for the tanned, relaxed crowds in the park make up a scene of quintessential urban health, while they are pale and thin, their eyes have difficulty accepting the light, and they can only move slowly by supporting each other. People avoid coming close to them.

However, as they make their way slowly up a path whose very gradual slope is nonetheless taking a great toll on their energy reserves, someone calls out to them.

'Gustavo!'

Gustavo turns round and sees Señor Ruiz, the psychoanalyst, who is beckoning to them joyfully. He is standing by a large bronze statue that is being pulled down by a municipal truck. They make their way painfully towards him, trying hard to disguise their condition.

'What has happened, Gustavo? You are looking terrible. And your friend. You need help!'

'It's nothing, Señor Ruiz. We are taking good care of each other.' Gustavo forces a smile. 'And you? How are things?'

'These are damn awful days. Terrible. Look – they are even taking my statue down.'

They realize that the statue is a likeness of Señor Ruiz himself, sitting pensively over a notebook next to a couch on which a nondescript figure lies with eyes closed. The inscription reads:

JORGE RUIZ

PSYCHOANALYST

HEALER OF THE ARGENTINE SOUL

'Why are they taking it down?' asks Gustavo.

'I'm not in favour anymore. *Persona non grata*, for Christ's sake. Half of these guys virtually grew up in my consulting room. Now they turn their backs on me. Life, Gustavo. Things turn around. You think the future is just like the present, only more so. It's not true. I'm a psychoanalyst – I don't habitually think much about the future. I think about the past. And it's usually quite easy to see how the present derives from the past. But it's a fallacy to believe on that basis that the future will present no surprises, no nasty turnarounds. God! If I could do it all again I like to think I would have paid more attention to things, been less complacent. But life was just too damn good! There were so many people with so much to forget. I didn't have time to think that things would change.'

As he speaks, the cables on the truck tighten and groan, and the obstinate statue begins to teeter and finally give way, falling to the ground with a loud thump.

'Señor Ruiz, I have something to ask you.'

'What is that?'

'You see, my friend Carla and I are going through some strange things that we cannot explain. I am beginning to think that we might be suffering from some kind of neurosis. It is difficult to understand how we could both share exactly the same symptoms while no one else seems to have been affected, but those are the facts. I wonder if you would mind examining us? Perhaps it is something very simple.'

'I'm sorry, Gustavo. I'd love to, for your father was a great friend of mine, but I'm not in that game anymore. Gave it up. But my new business may be even more help to you than my old.'

'What's that?'

Señor Ruiz becomes guarded and ushers them away from the crowds around the fallen statue. He speaks quietly.

'Now I'm selling visas to Europe. I still have a lot of friends in the government and embassies, the ones who haven't deserted me. We have a whole business going on trying to supply visas to everyone who wants to get out of here. I can cut you a very good deal. For anyone with European grandparents, it's very easy. Get out, Gustavo! There's no future. Even if things get better, the place will have been eviscerated, for everyone who can leave is doing so. The time has come to an end.'

'I'm not leaving, Señor Ruiz. Everything I have is here. I'm sorry.'

'You can't carry on thinking like that, for God's sake. At a certain point you have to abandon things and look for a new future. I can even help you get a job over there. We have a lot of connections. Anyway

– think about it. Meanwhile I can offer you a more short-term cure if you want.'

He reaches in his pocket and takes out a handful of pills.

'What are those?'

'These are dreams. The last ones I have left from my psychoanalysis days. Recycled from some of Buenos Aires' foremost luminaries. Going cheap, these days. I'll give them to you for five pesos each.'

Gustavo and Carla look at each other.

'We'll take one. We're running out of money.'

'Here you are. Guaranteed. How are your parents, by the way?'

'Oh, well. Same as everyone else, I suppose.'

'Give them my best. Your mother never really liked me, did she?'

7

One evening Gustavo and Carla return to his apartment after taking a walk in the park. The landlord is waiting for them. He tells them they are evicted for non-payment of rent.

'It's only been a few days,' says Gustavo.

'I don't see any sign of things changing,' says the landlord. 'Look at you. Look at her. You don't look healthy. You can hardly walk. Don't see anything changing anytime soon.'

'We're sick,' says Gustavo. 'Things are difficult for us right now. Give us some time.'

'I'm sorry,' the landlord says. 'I've already found someone else. I'd like you to leave by tomorrow.'

'How can I move in one day? Where will I go?'

'You'll find somewhere. I'm sure someone will put you up till you find somewhere new. Do it tomorrow, please. The new people are moving in the next morning.'

He does not wait for any more arguments. Gustavo is shattered. It will be tough to move everything out in one day. They look around the apartment and realize that they will be obliged to leave most things. They do not have the strength to start packing things up.

In their condition it takes them the whole of the next day to pack two small suitcases of vital possessions. Gustavo cannot bear to leave behind so much, but he has no choice. He cannot ask his parents to come, for they have problems of their own. They used to have a car; if they still had it . . . Perhaps he will be able to come and collect everything later.

He and Carla leave the apartment and sit in the street on their suitcases to rest for a while.

'What do we do?' he asks.

'I know a place we can go. For a bit.'

They walk with effort, stopping now and then to rest. Carla leads him to a nearby industrial estate where some of the apartments are standing empty. They climb the stairs. It is dark and because there is no lighting they are obliged to feel their way. Many of the apartment doors are broken or ajar but they can see nothing inside and have no idea where they might be bedding down. They climb to the top, imagining that the more effort it is the better it must be, and find the apartment door open. They walk in gingerly, their hands in front of their faces, trying to make out what is around them. Their minds are filling the blackness with knife-wielding hermits and pools of stagnant liquid and rabid cats, but as they calm down they can see by the glow of distant city lights coming through a window that there is nothing untoward in the room. There is even a broken sofa on which the two of them can just fit. They lie down.

Carla is shaking with the effort and her fear. Gustavo offers her the pill he bought from Señor Ruiz, psychoanalyst and family friend. She refuses it, saying that she does not trust Señor Ruiz. She falls asleep. Gustavo takes the pill himself. He has a vivid dream.

8

Carla and Gustavo are squatting in an abandoned building. Many woes have befallen them, and they are both unable to eat. They are weak and listless and can only prop themselves up against the wall during the day. There is little to say, for the future is impossible to think about, while the past is too distant to remember.

So long has it been since they had any nutrition that their bodies have begun to alter mysteriously. Both of them have developed bird beaks and their arms are slowly changing into wings; they already have no hands. Gustavo has even started to grow feathers on the back of his neck.

The realization comes to them that they can eat each other. They love each other very deeply and do not wish to cause each other harm, but the desire to feed themselves is irrepressible and there seems to be nothing else in the world that they can eat. Still, they restrict themselves to more or less superfluous extremities. They peck off each other's ear lobes, nose, and lips with their sharp beaks. The pain is not so bad, compared to the pleasure of eating at last. The worst loss is their eyelids, without which they cannot shut out the light and find it difficult to sleep.

9

Gustavo is having difficulty sleeping after a bad dream and he is awoken by Carla, who is coughing repeatedly. Her breathing is laborious, and her speech is obstructed by something in her throat. Gustavo turns her head towards the window and holds her jaw open so that he can see into her mouth. There is something protruding from the back of her throat. He pulls at it. It is lodged tightly in Carla's oesophagus and he is pulling against a vacuum that sucks it down, but he is able to open a channel of air and to ease it to the front of her mouth. He realizes that it is shit.

He pulls the end out of her mouth, but there is more and more. It is segmented like a tapeworm and bears the imprint of her intestines. Carla is breathing rapidly through her nose, and her eyes are wide with fear. Gustavo continues to ease the shit out through her mouth, and the thick glistening rope of it is coiling up on the floor like a snake. His hands are in the back of her throat, pulling gently to ensure that the length does not break and that he can get it all out; she is salivating heavily and it is running down his arms. At last he feels the end come out.

She falls back on the bed, breathing deeply. The shit smells bad, and he finds an old plastic bag to tie it up in. The whole thing is longer than Carla is.

When he comes back to lie beside her she is already asleep again. She looks relieved, healthier.

10

Gustavo and Carla have spent a night squatting in an old abandoned building. They arrived after dark and had no idea what kind of place it was they were staying in, but in the morning they are awoken by several other people who have been sleeping in the adjacent room. They are greeted with wariness but the people are not unkind. They are concerned to see the condition that the pair of them seem to be in. A former schoolteacher named Pablo asks them how they have been living. Gustavo explains that they have been evicted from their apartment and that they do not know what to do next.

'We all have stories like that,' says Pablo, 'but we're all still getting by. You can do it too. It's just a question of initiative and organization. All of us here earn our money recycling trash. It's tough work, but it does pay. Enough to feed and clothe yourself and leave some over for rebuilding the community.'

Gustavo is feeling dispirited, and he cannot focus on what Pablo is saying. 'I don't know if I'll be much help to you. I feel very weak these days.'

'Don't give into it, my friend! It is only a trick of the mind. Come with us today. We will take care of you.'

Everyone dresses and prepares for the day. They are well organized, with sturdy gloves and shoes and a large number of sacks in which to collect the trash. They troop down the staircase, which, during the day, is a scene of considerable activity: people are sitting on the landings eating breakfast and holding lively meetings. Downstairs there are two ramshackle vans; Gustavo and Carla join Pablo's group in one of them. They drive to upscale La Recoleta where the trash, apparently, is plentiful and of high quality. The van stops and everyone spreads out with their bags. Pablo issues instructions to the newcomers.

'We're only interested in glass, metal, and paper. Keep it clean and compact. Bring as much as you can carry. Be back here in an hour.'

Carla and Gustavo walk together. Carla is slightly recovered today and is markedly stronger than Gustavo. She does all the hard work, for Gustavo is close to collapse. She rummages in the public trash bins and collects beer bottles and newspapers and aluminium cans. She fills three sacks quickly and carries all of them on her back while helping her friend walk back to the van.

They arrive, and Pablo is pleased. 'Good work, Carla,' he says, for it is apparent that Gustavo is doing nothing.

The day continues like this, and Gustavo comes close many times to losing consciousness.

When the evening comes, they load the van for the final time and drive out of town to a trash dump where a recycling company buys what they have collected. There is a huge mound of refuse covered with dogs and crows; its stench is inescapable.

'Look at that,' says Pablo. 'It's magnificent. Imagine the possibilities.'

He and the others go in to have the sacks weighed and to collect the money while Gustavo and Carla stay outside. Carla is fascinated by the rubbish heap that towers against the sky.

'Let's climb up there, Gustavo! Have you ever seen so much waste? It is difficult to believe that a city could produce so much!'

Much against his will she drags him out of the van and they begin to climb the mountain of trash. It is draining, for the surface is uneven and they sink in many times up to their thighs. Everything is there: cans of meat and baked beans, rotting bones, broken sofas and fluorescent tubes, dead pets, used condoms and razors and diapers and tampons, books and magazines on every possible subject, containers of oil and paint and fertilizer, hypodermic needles, broken masonry, stripped-down computers and stereo systems, photograph albums and mouldy carpets, old shoes, bandages, video cassettes and cigarette ends, unwanted table lamps and mutilated children's dolls. They climb to the very top, and gaze far into the distance at the tall buildings of the city that look as if they are nestled in a valley, so high have they come.

While Gustavo sits to regain his breath, Carla looks around at the strange things that have ended up there. She calls out to him, 'Gustavo! Look what I have found!'

He pulls himself up and goes to join her. She has found a freezer. He has a vague memory that at one point he was anxious to find such a thing. She opens it. Unaccountably, it is working, and the inside is covered with frost. Carla stares lengthily at its pristine white interior.

'Gustavo . . .' she says, turning to him guiltily. He waits for her to continue.

'What is it?'

'I think I would like to stay here. I am so sorry. But I have had enough. I want to rest for a while.'

'I don't understand. What does it mean to stay here?'

'I would like to get into this freezer. I just want to forget about everything for a while.'

Gustavo feels pain as he has never felt before.

'How can you leave me, Carla?'

'You don't know how sorry I am. But I can't carry on like this. I need to find some peace.'

'Should I come back for you? In a week? A month?'

'No, Gustavo. I don't think it's a good idea. You should give up on me.'

She climbs into the freezer and lies down, her hands by her sides. She is still wearing his Buenos Aires International Film Festival T-shirt that he had given her long ago and that looked so much better on her than on him.

'Go ahead, Gustavo. Close it.'

He takes one last look at her and cannot resist the urge to plant a final kiss on her lips. She shuts her eyes. Slowly, he closes the freezer.

He sits down on top of the mountain of trash, and, try as he might, is unable to keep himself from weeping tears of self-pity. The sun is setting. As he looks down below he sees Pablo and his team climb into the van, and drive away.

11

Gustavo is walking in the city, looking for a place to spend the night. He has no money and he is almost prostrate with a mysterious sickness. When he has nearly given up hope of finding any shelter and has resigned himself to sleeping on the street, he sees a welcoming sign that gives him renewed optimism:

FREE Board and Lodging
If you give us your dreams

He enters. There are twelve other people staying there, and dinner is being served by an unusually tall chef in army uniform who sings the Hallelujah Chorus from Handel's *Messiah* as he works. Everyone else is seated in a row at a long table but they have kept a place for him in the middle, and he sits down, with six people on either side.

Gustavo has not been able to eat for some time, but in his present situation he finds it imprudent to turn away a free meal, so he begins hesitantly to put the food in his mouth. There is a light soup that tastes surprisingly good, and bread and cold meats. He looks around him. No one is saying anything. He thinks of Carla lying alone in the middle of the night in her lofty freezer and he feels infinitely sad.

Suddenly he feels the familiar surge in his abdomen and runs to the bathroom, where he vomits copiously. He is dazed by the experience, which has used up all his remaining energy. He washes his face and leaves the bathroom to sleep.

To his surprise, all his twelve companions are waiting outside the bathroom. He realizes that they are all afflicted in the same way he is. He goes to bed to the sound of repeated retching. He is completely drained and falls into a deep sleep, only dimly aware of the person who comes to fit electrodes to his head.

12

Gustavo has a dream. In his dream he is hosting a dinner party. It is a special occasion, and he has spared no expense in order to entertain his guests in the most splendid of ways. It is a fancy-dress party; after much experimentation in front of the mirror he has settled on a military uniform that emphasizes his muscular form and makes him look handsome and commanding. He has found musicians from Buenos Aires' great days of tango, and there is a huge banquet with fine wines and costly decorations. He has invited twelve people to the dinner. All of them are simultaneously elated and terrified to be attending a party at his house and he does not want them to think that their terror is without reason: he adopts a carefully rehearsed military tone with each of them when they arrive to ensure they do not feel completely at their ease. The tango musicians start to play passionately, and his guests cannot keep themselves from dancing, but he does not join them. He sits in the seventh of a row of thirteen seats at the dinner table watching sternly, his eyes invisible under the rim of his cap.

The guests become excited under his gaze and their dancing becomes increasingly lascivious. All of the women wish to sleep with him but none of them dare approach; instead they engage in extravagant performances of their sexual willingness with the other men, all of which are intended only for him.

The evening draws on, and still Gustavo serves no food. He wants to ensure everyone is possessed of a superhuman hunger before he will deign to satisfy it. He signals to the tango musicians to play ever more heady music, and watches that wine is never lacking. The guests become more and more aroused and some couples begin to copulate openly on the velvet chairs around the room. Gustavo's expression does not change, but behind his steely face is only disdain for people whose sex comes so easily; only he, it seems, can see past the sensuality of this music to its pain and despair; only he has maintained his integrity while everyone else is tossed from one opportunity for self-gratification to the next.

Like an orchestral conductor he builds the tempo of the evening over time until his guests are at fever pitch and all of them have utterly surrendered to the excesses of the music. His sharpened senses detect the moment when they can go no further and when hunger has taken over all of them, like an obsession. He signals for the music to stop, and the twelve of them take their seats, still perspiring and laughing and clutching at each other. The woman who sits on his right looks like Jeanne Moreau and he finds her very beautiful; she slips her hand into his groin but he ignores the gesture, for he has greater pleasures in mind.

He summons his faithful chef of fifteen years, who has also donned a military uniform in accordance with the *habit de maison*.

'Joseph, I think it is time to serve the delicacy that you have taken from the freezer.'

Joseph bows deeply in assent, and disappears into the kitchen. He returns a moment later carrying a large platter that he places carefully on the table.

To Gustavo's private satisfaction, his guests fall silent and he can see fear on all their faces.

13

Gustavo is rudely awoken in the morning by someone pulling wires from his head.

'Time to get up!'

He opens his eyes, still in the thick of sleep, and wonders if he is still dreaming, for the face that is bent over him is his own. As it appeared in better times.

'Everyone leaves by 9 a.m.,' says the other Gustavo. He is rewinding a tape in a machine by the side of the bed. He begins to play back what is on it, and it is Gustavo's dream of the previous night. The other Gustavo watches it for some time. As it proceeds, his face tightens in disgust.

He looks at Gustavo lying in the bed, and his repugnance is tangible.

'I suggest you leave straightaway. Look at you. Look at the things you dream about while you sleep securely in the warm lap of my charity. You are a sick creature.'

'Do you know who I am?' says Gustavo. 'Don't you recognize me?'

The other Gustavo seems momentarily alarmed. He peers at him anew. But his look remains blank.

'Don't play games with me. Just get out of here.'

Gustavo's television programme, *Los Sueños de los Olvidados*, an extraordinary compilation of thirteen dreams captured from homeless people sleeping in his shelter, catapulted him instantly to fame. After rumours of the fantastic production spread from his local television subscribers to national media executives, Telefe were quick to buy the programme from him (for a rumoured dollar amount running well into the seven digits), and it was broadcast nationally on a Saturday night amid a furore of publicity. The critics fell over each other trying to praise his achievement, and Gustavo's photograph was suddenly everywhere. 'Hilarious', they wrote, and 'Devastatingly funny!' 'A wacky romantic comedy in which absolutely *everything* goes wrong for our lovestruck – and lovable – hero,' opined *La Nación*, while *Clarín* proclaimed: 'A comic masterpiece whose joyful exploration of smut establishes its maker as the Rabelais of our times.'

Gustavo had earned an instant place among the Argentinian media aristocracy, and men and women who were previously just remote celebrities now went to great lengths to ingratiate themselves with him. At another point in his life he might have been happy, even honoured at this turn of events. Instead he felt only boredom in the face of the whole inane stupidity of it all. He refused to read the shimmering reviews, and gave up his subscriptions to every magazine and newspaper that leaped on this idiotic bandwagon. He responded with abuse and sometimes open violence when people approached him in the streets for autographs. He turned down his invitation to the Martín Fierro awards, at which he was the unquestioned favourite to win Best Television Comedy of the Year.

His new-found wealth allowed him to indulge the scorn he now felt for everyone. His mansion was surrounded by security guards who were instructed to treat all visitors with derision. He rarely left its confines, and then, usually, in disguise. He spoke to no one. He devoted his time to his collection of early twentieth-century Argentinian film, which was too beautiful and important for anyone else ever to understand.

At that point, Gustavo woke up. The sun had nearly set, and the last rays on his walls hummed at a frequency that created a disagreeable reverberation in his skull. His mouth was dry, and the insistent sound of the evening crows outside settled on his bloated tongue with an acrid taste. Only the warm blanket was good. As he pulled it more closely around him, spores of light seemed to float dimly across the inner velvet of his closed eyelids.

His stomach ache had not gone, and he could not decide whether he was falling sick or if he was just hungry. It was too tiring to think about, and he turned over and went back to sleep.

DEPARTURES

OUTSIDE THE BUILDING were the first grey whispers of dawn. Throats were heavy, and inactive backs had long ago lost sense and merged with vinyl seats (whose well-calculated rows had been compromised during the night for closer listening). A charcoal glow snaked in surreptitiously around them like a coil of smoke, softening the shadows on tired faces and dulling the nocturnal glare of fluorescent lights; but somehow the long night persisted in the cavities of their bodies: an aftertaste whose comforting blackness shut out, for a brief while, the onset of day.

But through the windows the airport began to respond to time. Small mutant vehicles emerged gingerly from hiding places and scurried smoothly around in the dawn haze; airport workers arrived with untimely energy, clambering around familiarly under the distended steel bellies of aeroplanes like a litter of playful newborns. Far away, over the other side of the concrete and scrub, a gelatinous sun wrestled briefly with the horizon before soaring free, summoning the birds to their first meandering flight of the day, and bathing in orange the township of tarpaulin and corrugated iron that nestled up against the airport's wire fence.

The thirteen passengers squinted uncomfortably in the sun's first rays. A woman took out a compact and lipstick; she held the Dusk Red point poised practisedly over her lower lip as she examined her face closely in the mirror, and then seemed to change her mind, closed the compact and replaced it in her bag. But security guards were throwing open the building, baggage carts were being primed in neat lines for the day's use, and itineraries and Tasks-in-Hand were sidling in among their gathering like brash latecomers at a party. The big black board twitched into life with cascading destinations and to-the-minute timings that made you sit up and take command of yourself, made you realize that the machinery of the world was starting again, it wasn't going to wait for you any longer! The first anxious groups of their fellow passengers began to arrive, prematurely –

(They could have had an hour's more sleep!)

– they were ready to do battle, but there was no one to fight, and they sat down in wary rows, biting nails, monitoring the departures board and watching for signs of resumption. The enormous nocturnal stillness of the hall was thrown out like used sheets from a hotel bed, as more and more of last night's characters arrived, tense and emotional from their early-morning negotiation of barricades and police lines – At this time of day! – they told stories of smashed windows and unpleasant faces in the streets – The place is like a war zone! – cars had been stopped, the police had asked Questions, opened bags – Who do they think they are? – We didn't sleep a wink all night, the hotel was like a railway station, people camping in the lobby and soldiers outside, the kids were terrified! The thirteen storytellers could no longer hear each other speak, and the stories themselves, that had provided their stepping stones through the night, started to fade like dreams. Their group, too, was taken over by the repetition of actions, unzipping and unlocking in order to verify again and again the reassuring presence of passports, tickets, keys, visas, wallets, cameras . . .

A big man spoke:

It was – an honour – to meet you all. An original way to spend a night! Very interesting. Well: I suppose we need to check in soon . . . Don't want to miss it after all that! So . . .

Does anyone have a business card? Email or something. I mean –
after all those stories . . . Maybe . . .

In case you're ever in my neck of the woods . . .

He went from one to the next, handing out business cards. People
stared at the cards confusedly, they had an embossed IBM logo in the
top right-hand corner and an address in Germany, no one really knew
how to respond. One woman reciprocated with her card. He stood
among them and spread his hands –

Well, we still have a flight ahead of us. Still four hours or so. It was
really a nice night. In the end. Who knows – maybe we'll see each other
in Tokyo?

(Walking back from the bathroom, shaking hands dry, someone saw
– it was an astonishing thing – some kind of antediluvian creature
lying dead in a pile of sweepings in a corner. What was it? – some
undiscovered land cousin of the lobster, the crayfish, a long armoured
body, segmented, bristling with hairs and antennae, must be as long
as my forearm! now useless and pale and covered with dust and chocolate wrappers and cigarette ends. It's when you see things like that,
strange things like that, you know you're not at home.)

They all got up together to stand in the check-in queue. People asked
questions: What time will we arrive? – So what are you going to do in
Tokyo? Where are you staying? – It's your first time? Wow. You'll love
it. It's like no other place! – And remind me where you said you were
from? –

Things worked smoothly this morning and they were all ready to
board. Funny how they all still clung together, a big, ungainly group
taking up thirteen seats in the middle of the airport. Efficient voices
announced boarding times and security advisories; the crew for their
flight arrived in tight formation, steered smoothly through every barricade and disappeared onto the plane; other flights came and went. A
queue started to form by their gate.

Friends: I will bid you farewell. (The same Japanese man, his clothes
straightened and tightened for the new day, looking smaller and more
bureaucratic than before.) I don't suppose I shall see any of you again.
I don't travel much, after all – this is very rare for me! – and to be

honest, I'm not a very sociable person. Not that I don't like people but that I really feel much more comfortable with them after I've known them for some time. Five years, ten. A problem for making new friends! Anyway, I just say all this because I don't want you to be offended – this is just my manner – but I think now it's time I left you. Get on the plane and try and get some sleep before the day starts. Yes – it's straight into the office when I get there! No rest for the wicked . . . But let me also thank you for your stories. I shall remember you all – by your stories. So many stories. Makes me think of the leaves that get swept away by the Tokyo Metropolitan Government every autumn! I am getting fanciful . . . But I am glad to have kept these few. Believe me: my wife is going to hear every single one of them. If it takes me another whole night of telling! I remember that man dying in Paris . . . Anyway: time draws on. Farewell to you all.

And with that, he picked up his briefcase, turned his back on them, and went to stand at the back of the queue by Gate 5.

Everyone else was surprised. It was strange of him, after everything they had heard and told. It seemed to put an end to all their conversations – what could you say after that? Somebody started to gather up belongings, there was another call to board their flight, it was probably time to shift anyway, they all stood up together, gathered camera bags and briefcases and rucksacks and went and stood in silent single file behind the suddenly unapproachable Japanese man.

Passports were checked again and a machine sucked up each boarding pass, flashed a name for an instant, and spat back a diminutive stump. They filed through a tunnel, the sounds of the outside reaching them for the first time. Actually, it was good to fly in the morning, the day felt so full of new things and the air was so fresh. The whole ridiculous fiasco – it really hadn't been so bad. A good story to tell, after all.

They shuffled forward; the engines were roaring outside and men were loading their bags from a little truck. The Japanese man reached the entrance, flight attendants smiling more broadly than usual as if to compensate everyone for their troubled night. He nodded shyly as one of them greeted him,

Good morning.

Good morning.

Good morning. 32A? Yes – straight and right.

Good morning.

Good morning.

Good morning.

Good morning.

Good morning. That's in Business Class, madam. Can I – ?

Good morning.

Good morning.

Good morning. 16D is – you know where it is. Well done.

Good morning.

Good morning.

P.S.

Ideas,
interviews
& features...

About the author

About the book

Read on

Global Enchantment

Travis Elborough talks to
Rana Dasgupta

In some of the stories the geographical setting is central to the narrative – in 'The Billionaire's Sleep', for instance, with its international call centres in Delhi, or in 'The Doll', maybe, set in Tokyo. In others it's perhaps less important. I wondered how important location was for this book.
Yes, the two tales you mention are very grounded in their locations, as is 'The Rendezvous in Istanbul'. The question of 'The Changeling' is in some ways the city of Paris itself, and its history in literature and the imagination: the bringing home of the plague, for instance, which Camus exported to the far reaches of the French empire. But there are others like the Warsaw story, or the Lagos story, that could easily have taken place somewhere else. This ambiguity is an important element of the book.

Tokyo Cancelled is about the feeling of globalization. It is therefore more interested in the echoes between life in different locations than in capturing the unique, 'exotic' flavour of a place. It is intended to be a kind of mythology of the twenty-first century city, in which experiences of one place flow into those of another. The idea of the world as being distant and far-flung becomes subordinate to the idea of it being part of the self. And it is a fact that all these places are part of our selves, our imaginations, our everyday reality.

The binding component in the book is, of course, the airport: a neutral territory where

the travellers meet and exchange their stories. There are clearly parallels to the inn in Chaucer's *Canterbury Tales*. Was the idea of the airport there to begin with, or was it something that emerged as the stories themselves came to be formed?

From the very beginning I wanted to have that sense of the medieval cycle. The book is a picture of the world in fragments; and it was essential to have some kind of channel between locations so that the reader is asked to consider not only a series of places but the meaning of an encounter between them. I'd had an experience once of being stuck in Houston airport for a night when trying to get from San Francisco to New York, and talking to the other stranded strangers in a bar by the airport. I found it entertaining: a moment when your day-to-day agenda is forcibly taken away from you, and you find yourself exchanging stories with people you would not normally meet.

The airport is an obvious meeting place for a group of contemporary travellers. But it's also a cold and intimidating space to spend a night in, and it seems to demand of stranded travellers that they fill it with stories in order to make it habitable. The airport can therefore be a place to stage storytelling as the most primordial communication between human beings and the unknown. I like such disjunctions. A lot of the unpromising urban spaces that come into this book turn out to be settings for surprisingly intense experience. ▶

> 6 I like disjunctions. A lot of the unpromising urban spaces that come into this book turn out to be settings for surprisingly intense experience. 9

Global Enchantment *(continued)*

◄ **In its structure, and in its ingenious mix of the mythic and the modern, I couldn't help being reminded of Italo Calvino's *Invisible Cities*. Is he a writer whose work you admire?** I've not actually read that book, although I love his *Italian Folktales*.

One of the problems about writing about our own times is that often the 'stuff' of the contemporary world is felt to be so banal and empty. Highways and shopping malls, consumer baubles, diets, special offers . . . So we often have literature that retreats from the world and seeks out an exquisite interior space in order to preserve the idea that human experience is meaningful. One of the things I was trying to do with this book was to make all this 'stuff' part of a real mythology that would reflect the deep sense we have about it. The artists and thinkers I'm most inspired by are able to do that: to enter these unpromising spaces of modern cities and modern life and find real psychological and philosophical depth there.

Do you not think that many more contemporary writers – Jonathan Franzen in *The Corrections*, for example – are now showing a greater willingness to engage with the issues of business and globalization? Yes, and it's clear that Franzen himself is very interested in all this 'stuff' I'm talking about: antidepressants and package tours and all the rest. But I think that his treatment of the world of business in *The Corrections* follows a pattern you see in a lot of contemporary American writing – I think of writers such as Joyce Carol Oates or E. Annie Proulx – in which it comes into the story as an assault on everything authentic, a machine-like foil to the pure humanity of the characters. That's definitely part of our experience, but there's also another side without which the tragedy of this wouldn't make sense: the euphoria of innovation, the pleasure of products, the drama of growth and profits, the grandeur of global operations. All that is also part of our 'pure humanity' too; there are few people who would like to see it all swept away. That's why our relationship to commerce is so complicated: we see ourselves simultaneously created and destroyed by it. Writing has to capture that complexity – to restore the half of a story that is suppressed and to keep the contradiction alive.

That's one of the things I mean by using the word 'mythic'; for myth is dark and full of the contradictions of our impulses. Sleeping Beauty is a young and beautiful maiden, and the summit of the prince's erotic ambitions; but she is also somewhat over a century old, and is first seen by the prince in the guise of death. With amazing conciseness, this story, which anyone can understand, expresses the beautiful and terrible ambiguities of desire.

You were born and raised in England, but currently live and work in Delhi. How much do you think that city, and being based in India, influenced the book?
The form this book took had a lot to do with the fact it was written in Delhi. A lot of things that are happening in the world today play themselves out in a very graphic way in this city. Competing visions of life translate ▶

❛ With amazing conciseness the story of *Sleeping Beauty*, which anyone can understand, expresses the beautiful and terrible ambiguities of desire. ❜

Global Enchantment *(continued)*

◄ into very visible battles over space and its uses. Shopping malls are built on the site of hastily obliterated older markets, and glass towers spring up in the brush land around the city. Transformations wrought in the name of one class of people result in large numbers of other people losing their homes and their livelihoods, as the settlements they live in are destroyed. Since these transformations are directly linked to global forces, you have a dramatic sense, living in this city, of the personality of those forces, and the extent of their reach and power.

I think this can do one of two things to you, or possibly both. One is that it can make you completely heartless, because you identify so strongly with the vision of efficiency and hygiene that you care nothing for life as a separate principle. On the other hand it can also make you much more compassionate. It can force you to think about human life and happiness in terms of the attempt to survive, in a very real sense: how people accumulate the things around them that they need to live, and how they can get through that process with a certain amount of dignity. Such reflections have been important for a lot of the work I admire most about cities, such as August Sander's photographs of Berlin in the twenties and thirties, or Joseph Roth's journalism, also in Berlin at the same time; and they have been central to my writing, which is why the city of Delhi earned the first acknowledgement in *Tokyo Cancelled*. Living in Europe at the present time, you usually don't confront those things so closely. You are able to export such

6 The decision to narrate the world through a multiplicity of tales in an airport relates to a strong scepticism towards any *single* story of the world. 9

6

things to the far reaches of your mental globe – however falsely – and to create a secure division between yourself and those who need to survive.

The decision to narrate the world through a multiplicity of tales in an airport relates to a strong scepticism towards any *single* story of the world, which I think arises from some of these things. The challenge of what, if anything, can finally be assembled from such multiplicity is the reader's own. In the book, of course, the intensity of the characters' own experiences makes it too difficult for them to incorporate so many other stories into their worldview; and when, in the last story, Gustavo starts to hear about all the things that have been happening in other places it only has the substance of a dream for him.

What about using folk tales to talk about globalization? Can our world really be described in such archaic terms? Does magic really have a place any more?
One of the things this book tries to do is to reject the idea that there is something fundamentally different about the fabric of 'modern people' – different from everyone who went before them, and different from everyone living who is not yet 'modern'. The Enlightenment philosophers talked about human beings 'growing up' from childish superstitions and becoming fundamentally new and different – and we identify with this, partly because we like the sound of it, and partly because we inherit from that period a tradition of science that has delivered things truly unique in the history of the world. ▶

❝ If you really want to know what a world with folk religions, spirits, witchdoctors and magical charms looks like, then just look at our own society. ❞

LIFE AT A GLANCE

Author photo by Monica Narula

BORN
....
Canterbury, 1971

EDUCATED
....
Balliol College, University of Oxford, and University of Wisconsin–Madison

LIVES
....
Delhi

Global Enchantment *(continued)*

◄ But such genuine innovations should not be mistaken for what they are not. The idea that we would cease to be irrational, religious or superstitious – that never happened. My feeling is that if you really want to know what a world with folk religions, spirits, witchdoctors and magical charms looks like, then just look at our own society. We have all these things. We can hardly escape, in fact, from the people who every day offer more enchantments for potency, beauty, supremacy, immortality or legendary wealth. And, like the ordinary human beings we are, we scoff at such fantasies, and still spend our money on them. It's quite obvious that we like to believe lots of things that aren't actually true. So the magic of these stories I feel arises very naturally from the society we live in.

But there are several sides to everything; and there is another sense in which the inadequacy of the language of folk tale to the task of describing our world is the main theme of the book. The folk tales grapple with a vast reality that is not quite their own, and they fall short of it. This opens up the sense of a silence that lies about. That which is beyond expression. The unspeakable. ■

Writing *Tokyo Cancelled*
by Rana Dasgupta

> 'We live in a world ruled by fictions of every kind
> . . . We live inside an enormous novel. It is now less
> and less necessary for the writer to invent the
> fictional content of his novel. The fiction is already
> there. The writer's task is to invent the reality.' –
> J.G. Ballard, Introduction (1995) to *Crash* (1973)

What relationship does such a seemingly perverse statement about reality have to the world in which we live? Surely reality is more ruthlessly self-evident every day? Surely we suffer, in fact, from an excess of it. Are we not weary from how much it demands of us, and are the world's information systems not swamping us with their accounts of it? Moreover, is it not extremely self-serving for a writer to claim that it is on *writers* that the burden of 'inventing' reality must fall? Surely the writer is nothing more than the humble servant of reality. Has the ambition of the novel not always been to learn patiently from it and to fashion it into revealing prose? Has the problem of the novelist in the past century not been, precisely, that there is *too much reality*? We think of Philip Roth, who wrote, in 1961, that

> the American writer in the middle of the 20th
> Century has his hands full in trying to understand,
> and then describe, and then make credible much
> of the American reality. It stupefies, it sickens, it
> infuriates, and finally it is even a kind of
> embarrassment to one's meagre imagination. The
> actuality is continually outdoing our talents . . . ▶

9

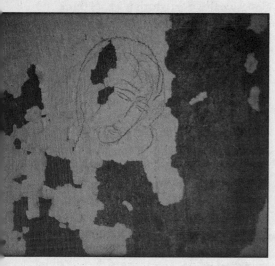

Writing *Tokyo Cancelled* (continued)

◀ But there is another history to be laid alongside this one, which is what I think Ballard is referring to. A growing sense that, as the world becomes more overwhelming, its reality recedes. A sense that hi-tech suburban homes, highway commuting and office jobs are not 'real life'; that the pageant of television, film stars, consumption and PR is all an empty façade; that the reality of the world must lie elsewhere, in some inaccessible, secret place. We can see how entire industries gather to reinvent reality for people troubled by its disappearance, to break the endless circles of illusion with moments of authentic experience. Biographies of people who are exceptionally 'real', drugs to make you feel as you are 'supposed to', package tours to the remaining 'real' places of the earth, various classes of nostalgic politics offering a return to more 'real' times, 'reality' TV, an entire mysticism promising to help you access the 'real' you. All of these things betray themselves by pushing 'reality' further and further away; and Hollywood goes to the logical extreme by staging the *destruction of everything* as the only condition under which reality might re-emerge – even if, as in *The Matrix*, it turns out to be much worse than the illusion.

Perhaps this flight of reality has been most beautifully described in Walter Benjamin's essay, 'The Storyteller' (1936). Sitting in Paris and watching the rush of modernity around him, Benjamin observed that the art of storytelling was coming to an end, that 'more and more often there is embarrassment all around when the wish to hear a story is expressed'. For him the reason for this was quite clear:

> Experience has fallen in value. And it looks as if it is continuing to fall into bottomlessness. Every glance at a newspaper demonstrates that it has reached a new low, that our picture, not only of the external world but of the moral world as well, overnight has undergone changes which were never thought possible. With the [First] World War a process began to become apparent which has not halted since then. Was it not noticeable at the end of the war that men returned from the battlefield grown silent – not richer, but poorer in communicable experience? . . . A generation that had gone to school on a horse-drawn streetcar now stood under the open sky in a countryside in which nothing remained unchanged but the clouds, and beneath these clouds, in a force field of destructive torrents and explosions, was the tiny, fragile human body.

If we are not convinced of the reality of the world it is because of this fundamental discontinuity between the exquisite minutiae of personal experience, on the one hand, and the giant forces of modernity, on the other. *Experience* does not offer us any assistance in attempting to understand a world made up of such forces, and falls in value, as Benjamin says, to the point of utter worthlessness. In order to try to make sense of our world we are forced to leave behind experience, and to take on the perspective of vast systems and never-ending geographies. From such a perspective, the old wisdom of folk tales seems prehistoric, and the rhythms of ▶

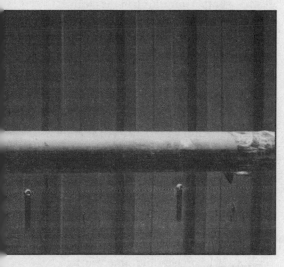

◄ human life – in particular, the reality of death – a bothersome kink in the clean expanse of time. The memory of such things still haunts us, however; and it is their seeming absence from the world we see around us that gives us the impression that it is not truly *real*.

Tokyo Cancelled began as an experiment in how storytelling might respond to this inconsequence of experience. An attempt to inhabit in a new way all those fragments of an immense world that land in our lives, like spam mail, every day. An attempt to flow outwards into that world through a network of contemporary folk tales.

These stories all began with such fragments of reality. Walking around the clothes market in Istanbul, and hearing about its striking relationship to the fall of the Soviet Union. Reading the news of the economic crisis in Argentina, and of all the improvisations people found to survive through it. The newspaper reports of the 'monkey man' who for a time came every night to attack people in certain neighbourhoods of my home city of Delhi. An article in the *New Yorker* about the vats of smallpox virus formerly held by the Soviet Union and now unaccounted for. Seeing the Disney-coloured corporate towers of Shenzhen, and the curious micro-society that has developed around them. The phenomenon of 'outsourcing' that is still shaking up the political and economic landscape in so many countries of the world. These and other slices of 'reality' seemed to gesture outside themselves to great depths of

6 There is a lyricism and an optimism to the idea of strangers all discovering such narrative gifts within themselves. 9

feeling. And yet even an event with such great material and psychological consequences as Argentina's economic crisis was recounted, for the most part, as a mere blip in an abstract system, as if it were impossible to convey anything *felt* or *lived* about it. *Tokyo Cancelled* was an attempt to forge new kinds of mythological connections between ourselves and such a world. To invent, perhaps, the reality that would make such fictions meaningful.

The novel that emerged from this experiment is, I think, quite ambiguous. There is a lyricism and an optimism to the idea of strangers all discovering such narrative gifts within themselves, and yet the situation is also preposterous. The stories contain many of the ancient comforts of fairytales, and yet they emerge into the twenty-first century somewhat mutilated and flat, displaying a wisdom that is either unclear or childishly naïve. There are a number of sensations and images that recur through the stories which help to give a unity to the world, but such a novel-in-fragments would seem to deny the possibility of any easy summary, any singular understanding. For me, such ambiguity is quite appropriate to the simultaneous horror and exhilaration I feel about the world.

Perhaps, however, as the book gently implies, such stories can generate more stories, and readers can take on for themselves the question of what new forms of wisdom we might have to convey to each other. ∎

❛ Ambiguity is quite appropriate to the simultaneous horror and exhilaration I feel about the world. ❜

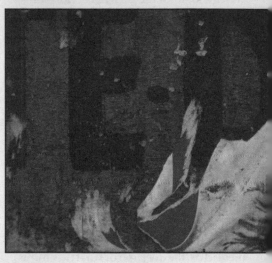

Find Out More

For further musing on the themes of his book Rana Dasgupta suggests . . .

Fish Story *by Allan Sekula*
Photographer and theorist Allan Sekula has created a vast and beautiful essay in images and text that traces the links of the global maritime industry, and all its (often mysterious and remote) ways of life. A truly epic picture of the world, and also an important corrective to an urban imagination that so often forgets its absolute dependence on the sea.

100 Pieces for the Left Hand
by J. Robert Lennon
Lennon's beautifully concise 'short short' stories are written about 'our town', an unspecified small-town location. It is a gesture towards a widely held 'memory' of organic small-town life that is beautiful and melancholy. A brilliant, poetic book.

In What Language? *by Vijay Iyer and Mike Ladd*
This collaboration between jazz musician Iyer and poet Ladd is a very interesting musical reflection on airports and migration.

Naked *and* **Secrets and Lies** *by Mike Leigh*
I find Mike Leigh to be one of the most inspiring film-makers working today. These two films in particular offer a vision of the contemporary world that is rare in its ability to enter the uncanny, unspoken places of life and to find there grand characters and profound social observation.

My writing owes a great debt to the world of contemporary art which, in its cosmopolitan curiosity and its openness to all the disciplines of thought and creativity, is possibly the most dynamic and thoughtful place of contemporary culture. The work of artist groups **Raqs Media Collective**, **The Atlas Group** and **Multiplicity** have been particularly inspiring.

If You Loved This,
You Might Like . . .

Fictions
by Jorge Luis Borges

The Castle
by Franz Kafka

Invisible Cities
by Italo Calvino

Underworld
by Don DeLillo

Everything is Illuminated
by Jonathan Safran Foer

Haroun and the Sea of Stories
by Salman Rushdie

Transmission
by Hari Kunzru

A Question of Bruno
by Alexandar Hemon

Don't Tell Me the Truth About Love
by Dan Rhodes